The Glass Books of the Dream Eaters

"Furiously entertaining . . .
—*Boston Globe*

"Sometimes books, like cakes, can be built upon recipes. In the case of *The Glass Books of the Dream Eaters* by Gordon Dahlquist, that would be one part history, two parts fantasy, three parts deft plotting and skilled narrative, and about 17 heaping cupfuls of suspense . . . and the result is one marvelous confection of a book . . . which serves to keep the reader from doing anything else but, well, read. It makes Dahlquist's tome seem infinitely shorter than it is. I . . . found that it took only three days to finish. The newest Harry Potter took me four. Make of that what you will."
—*Philadelphia Inquirer*

"This is a plump English tea cake of a book: messy, studded with treats, too big and too rich to finish in just one sitting."
—*Entertainment Weekly*

"A combination of science fiction, dark fantasy, thriller and gothic horror, this novel is as flat-out fun, engaging and funny as any tale of mystery and imagination I can recall. . . . The dialogue is wry, the descriptions clever and the complicated plot advances as smoothly as a patrician's pocket watch. . . . At more than 700 pages, this one ends too quickly." —*Cleveland Plain Dealer*

"*The Glass Books of the Dream Eaters* has a clever conceit with a foundation of literature as fantasy. . . . Dahlquist may have created a literary character in Miss Temple, whose resolve to be of one mind between dream and reality also holds the book together."
—*Kansas City Star*

"Carr[ies] the reader on a mind-twisting odyssey... *The Glass Books of the Dream Eaters* is sweeping, highly original and absorbing... well worth the investment." —*Dallas Morning News*

"Fantastic... I was in seventh heaven... somewhere between Dickens, Sherlock Holmes and Rider Haggard."
—Kate Mosse, author of *Labyrinth*

"A kinky, atmospheric look at Victorian England."
—*Washington Post*

"Oh, this guy is goo-ood! The most original thing I've read in years: deftly executed, relentlessly inventive and with a trio of the most unusual and engaging heroes who ever took on a sinister cabal out to rule the world by means of sex and dreams."
—Diana Gabaldon,
author of *Lord John and the Brotherhood of the Blade*

"*The Glass Books of the Dream Eaters* is a big, fat, rich-as-whipped-cream, tart-as-balsamic-vinegar novel that begins like an old-fashioned romance and turns into a wildly imaginative near fantasy with more than a little violence and a climax that will knock your socks off—and promise a sequel, too.... [Dahlquist is] fiction's new golden boy—he really is a richly talented storyteller with a terrific gift for offbeat but recognizable and wonderfully likable characters.... The writing is as chewy and delicious as a nougat, the story gains speed with every page... and the whole reading experience is (as I seem driven to say) as satisfying as a feast." —*Sullivan County Democrat*

"Sometimes sly, other times full-frontally in your face, the author's inventive detail beggars inventory.... A marvelous revival of old-fashioned theatrical melodrama with some contemporary zip... As a storyteller he's awfully good.... The author imparts to the book a tremendous amount of energy.... Builds to a smashing climax... A major confection with serious undertow." —*Locus*

"An immersing and stimulating experience... Set against a backdrop of an unfolding mystery and plenty of action: gun play, sword fights, good old-fashioned brawling. It makes for a fun read.... Make no mistake: *The Glass Books of the Dream Eaters* is a remarkable achievement of imagination and stellar writing. Dahlquist never once breaks from the Victorian-era style, often to great effect, and his descriptions and conversations will delight readers who enjoy charm and subtlety." —*Tampa Tribune*

"Dahlquist introduces so many characters, props and plot twists, near-death experiences and narrow escapes that the novel has the feel of a frantic R-rated classic comic book—if comics were arch."
—*Publishers Weekly*

"Quite an adventure." —*Kirkus Reviews*

"Brimming with atmosphere... *The Glass Books* has the potential to become a cult novel, along the lines of Katherine Neville's brilliant *The Eight*.... *Glass Books* reaches a perfect momentum at the novel's beginning and the surprising, action-packed end."
—*South Florida Sun-Sentinel*

"It's a rare writer who can string so many words together and still be entertaining.... Dahlquist's fine attention to detail, colorful cast of characters and generous spattering of well-written erotica serve to keep the right brain imaginatively excited while the left brain is kept busy tracking cat-and-mouse chase scenes.... It's all very ingenious." —*Richmond Times-Dispatch*

"An engaging work for lovers of over-the-top Victorian suspense and intrigue." —*Library Journal*

"Readers will be eagerly turning the pages to discover just what happens to the intrepid trio (Miss Temple, Cardinal Chang, and Dr. Svenson)—and how those enthralling glass books get their power." —*BookPage*

"The most notable thing about *The Glass Books of the Dream Eaters* is the sheer brio of its erotic inventiveness.... Reading this book—and it is a page-turner—you become immersed, befogged, almost as if you had indeed been looking at one of the glass books.... As stupendous as it is stupefying, *The Glass Books of the Dream Eaters* transcends its flaws."
—*Guardian*

"An erotically charged, rip-roaring adventure for adults with scarcely a dull moment to be had, which defies its great length to keep the reader on the edge of his seat."
—*Daily Mail*

"Bodice-ripping." —*Elle* (UK)

"An outrageously good novel; a gripping gothic roller-coaster of a book...A rip-roaring read. It ends perfectly, poised between cliff-hangers and closure.... *The Glass Books of the Dream Eaters* has the feel of a classic in the making."
—*Scotland on Sunday*

"Extraordinary. An undoubted feat of literary imagination. I cannot recall ever having read a novel comprising so much breaking and entering, spying through keyholes, jumping over walls, hiding in shadows, and listening out for footsteps, nor one with so many miraculous escapes."
—*Daily Telegraph*

"A vivid fantasy, liberally spiced with chases, stakeouts, fights, fetish gear, exotic foreign names and a satisfyingly long trail of bodies."
—*Herald*

"An undoubted feat of literary imagination."
—*Telegraph*

"A Dickens of a plot." —*Evening Standard*

"Churns with adrenaline and leaves us suspended over a gulf of anxiety for the characters' fates."
—*Time Out* (London)

"Think of *The Adventures of Sherlock Holmes:* its lurid plots, its murky pea-soupers. Now, apply the production values of *Buffy the Vampire Slayer,* commission a rewrite by the Marquis de Sade—oh, and lose Sherlock and replace him with Barbarella.... it's literally a ripping yarn."
—*London Paper*

"The three heroes, wonderful. The premise, the glass books—excellent idea! Really fabulous."
—*Books in Bed* (UK)

"Conan Doyle, Jules Verne, Edgar Allan Poe and Alexandre Dumas with shades of Kubrick's *Eyes Wide Shut* thrown in."
—*Irish News*

"From the first few lines, the slick plot has you utterly hooked. What follows is a tumultuous adventure... a vastly enjoyable page-turner of epic proportions."
—*Big Issue*

"Bodice-ripping, adventure-packed." —*Financial Times*

"Wilkie Collins on acid." —*New Statesman*

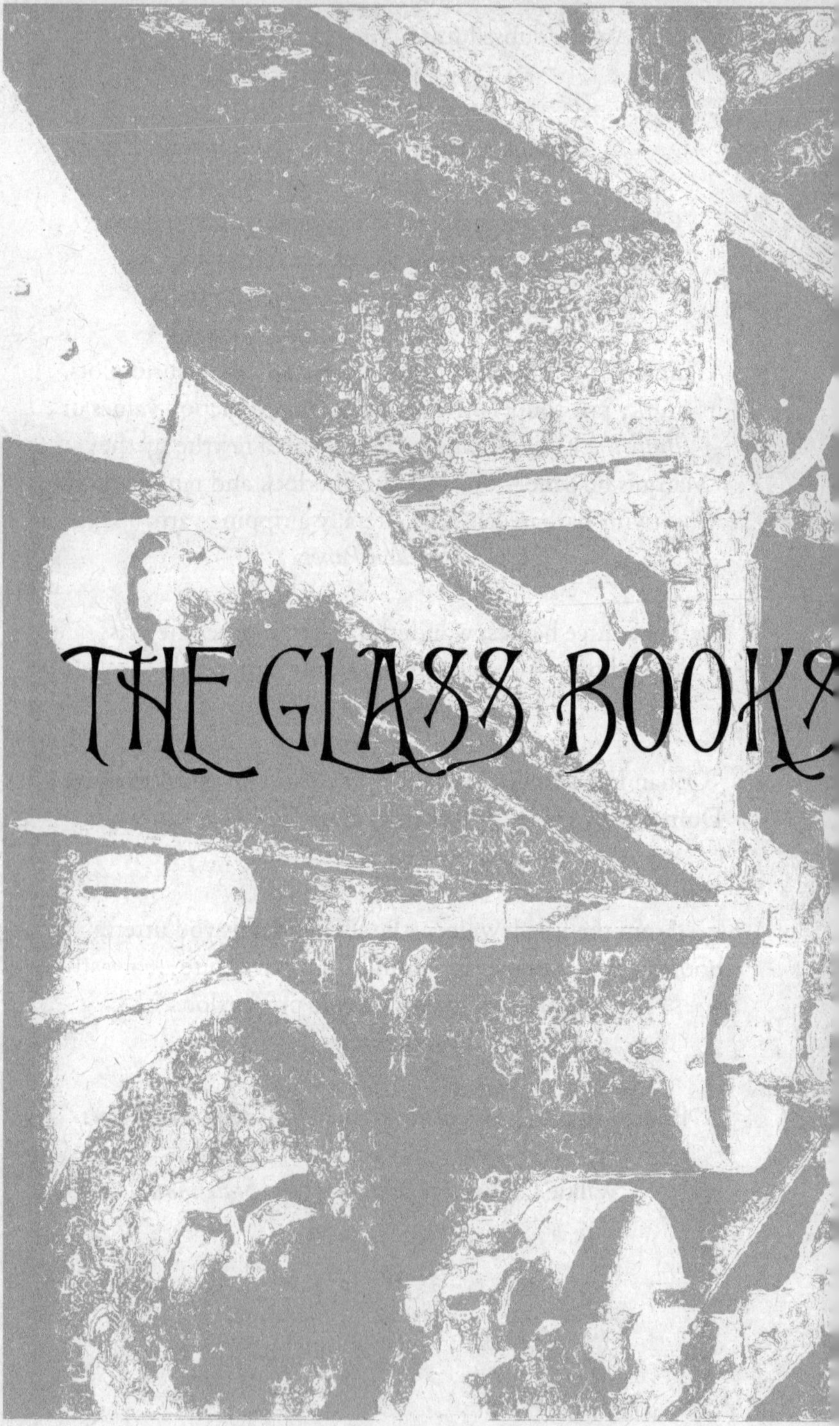

THE GLASS BOOKS

f the DREAM EATERS

VOLUME TWO

Gordon Dahlquist

BANTAM BOOKS

THE GLASS BOOKS OF THE DREAM EATERS, VOLUME TWO
A Bantam Book

PUBLISHING HISTORY
Bantam hardcover edition of Volumes One and Two published September 2006
Bantam trade paperback edition / February 2009

Published by Bantam Dell
A Division of Random House, Inc.
New York, New York

Cover design by Shasti O'Leary Soudant

Book design by Glen M. Edelstein

Library of Congress Catalog Card Number: 2006040740

ISBN 978-0-553-38586-1

Printed in the United States of America
Published simultaneously in Canada

www.bantamdell.com

BVG 10 9 8 7 6 5 4 3 2

Time spent in an imaginary city calls forth a startling array of generosity and patience. To these people, places, and events this book is indebted, and to each I offer my thanks, grateful for the opportunity to do so.

Liz Duffy Adams, Danny Baror, Karen Bornarth, Venetia Butterfield, CiNE, Shannon Dailey, the Dailey family, Bart DeLorenzo, Mindy Elliott, Evidence Room, *Exquisite Realms,* Laura Flanagan, Joseph Goodrich, Allen Hahn, Karen Hartman, David Levine, Beth Lincks, Todd London, the Lower East Oval, Honor Molloy, Bill Massey, John McAdams, E. J. McCarthy, Patricia McLaughlin, *Messalina,* David Millman, Emily Morse, New Dramatists, Octocorp@30th & 9th [RIP], Suki O'Kane, Tim Paulson, Molly Powell, Jim and Jill Pratzon, Kate Wittenberg, Mark Worthington, Margaret Young.

My father, my sister, my cousin Michael.

from [illegible] considerably [illegible] covering areas of [illegible] [illegible] to these people, places, and events. [illegible] book is indebted, and [illegible] my thanks [illegible]

[illegible]

[illegible]

THE GLASS BOOKS of the DREAM EATERS

ONE

Royale

Once she made a decision, Miss Temple considered it an absolutely ridiculous waste of time to examine the choice further—and so from the vantage of her coach she did not debate the merits of her journey to the St. Royale Hotel, instead allowing herself the calming pleasure of watching the shops pass by to either side and the people of the city all about their day. Normally, this was not a thing she cared for—save for a certain morbid curiosity about what flaws could be deduced from a person's dress and posture—but now, as a consequence of her bold separation from the Doctor and Cardinal Chang, she felt empowered to observe without the burden of judgment, committed as she was to action, an arrow in mid-flight. And the fact was, she did feel that merely being in motion had stilled the tempest of feeling that had overtaken her in the Comte's garden and, even worse, in the street. If she was not up to the challenge of braving the St. Royale Hotel, then how could she consider herself any kind of adventurer? Heroines did not pick their own battles—the ones they knew they could win. On the contrary, they managed what they had to manage, and they did not lie to themselves about relying on others for help instead of accomplishing the thing alone. Would she be safer to have waited for Chang and Svenson—however much of the plan was her own devising—so they could have entered the place in force? It was arguable at the very least (stealth, for one) that she alone was best suited for the task. But the larger issue was her own opinion of herself, and her level of loss, relative to her companions. She smiled and imagined meeting them outside the hotel—she chuckled at how long it would take them to find her—

vital information in hand and perhaps the woman in red or the Comte d'Orkancz, now utterly subject, in tow.

Besides, the St. Royale held her destiny. The woman in red, this Contessa Lacquer-Sforza (simply another jot of proof, as if any were needed, of the Italian penchant for ridiculous names) was her primary enemy, the woman who had consigned her to death and worse. Further, Miss Temple could not help wonder at the woman's role in the seduction—there was no other word—of Roger Bascombe. She knew objectively that the primary engine must be Roger's ambition, manipulated with ease by the Deputy Minister, to whose opinions, as a committed climber, Roger would slavishly adhere. Nevertheless, she could not but picture the woman and Roger in a room together... like a cobra facing a puppy. She had seduced him, obviously, but to what actual—which is to say literal, physical—degree? One perfect raised eyebrow and a single purse of her rich scarlet lips would have had him kneeling. And would she have taken Roger for herself or passed him along to one of her minions—one of the other ladies from Harschmort House—that Mrs. Marchmoor—or was it Hooke? There were really too many names. Miss Temple frowned, for thinking of Roger's idiocy made her cross, and thinking of her enemies turning him to their usage with such evident ease made her even crosser.

The coach pulled up outside the hotel and she paid off the driver. Before the man could jump from his box to help her, a uniformed doorman stepped forward to offer his hand. Miss Temple took it with a smile and carefully climbed down to the street. The coach rattled away as she walked to the door, nodding her thanks to a second doorman as he opened it, and into the grand lobby. There was no sign of any person she recognized—all the better. The St. Royale was openly sumptuous, which didn't quite appeal to Miss Temple's sense of *order*. Such places did the work *for* a person, which she recognized was part of the attraction but disapproved of—what was the point of being seen as remarkable when it was not really you being seen at all, but your surroundings? Still, Miss Temple could admire the display. There were scarlet leather banquettes and great gold-rimmed mirrors on the wall, a tinkling fountain with floating lotus flowers, large pots of greenery, and a row of gold and red columns supporting a curving balcony that hung over the lobby, the two colors twisting around the poles like hand-carved ribbons. Above, the ceiling was more glass and gold mirrors, with a crystal chandelier whose dangling end point, a multifaceted ball of glittering glass, was quite as large as Miss Temple's head.

She took all of this in slowly, knowing there was a great deal to see, and that such sights easily dazzled a person, encouraging them to ignore what might be important details: like the row of mirrors against the oddly curving left wall, for example, which were strange in that they seemed placed not so much for people to stand before as to reflect the entirety of the lobby, and even the street beyond it—almost as if they were a row of windows rather than mirrors. Miss Temple immediately thought of the odious comment of the still more odious Mr. Spragg, about the cunning Dutch glass—about her own unintentional display in the Harschmort dressing room. Doing her best to shrug off twin reactions of mortification and thrill, she turned her thoughts more directly to her task. She imagined herself still standing in the lobby, trying to get up her nerve, when Chang and Svenson entered behind her, catching up before she had even done anything—she would feel every bit the helpless fool she was trying not to be.

Miss Temple strode to the desk. The clerk was a tall man with thinning hair brushed forward with a bit too much pomade, so the normally translucent hair tonic had creamed over the skin beneath his hair—the effect being not so much offensive as unnatural and distracting. She smiled with the customary crispness that she brought to most impersonal dealings and informed him she had come to call on the Contessa Lacquer-Sforza. He nodded respectfully and replied that the Contessa was not presently in the hotel, and indicated the door to the restaurant, suggesting that she might desire to take a little tea while she waited. Miss Temple asked if the Contessa would be long in arriving. The man answered that, truthfully, he did not know, but that her normal habit was to meet several ladies for a late tea or early aperitif at this time. He wondered if Miss Temple was acquainted with those ladies, for indeed one or more of them might well be in the restaurant already. She thanked him, and took a step in that direction. He called to her, asking if she wanted to leave her name for the Contessa. Miss Temple told him that it was *her* habit to remain a surprise, and continued into the restaurant.

Before she could even scan the tables for a familiar or dangerous face, a black-coated fellow was standing far too close and asking if she was meeting someone, if she had come for tea or supper or perhaps, his brow twitching in encouragement, an aperitif. Miss Temple snapped—for she did not like to be pestered under any circumstances—that she would prefer tea and two scones and a bit of fruit—fresh fruit, and peeled—and walked past him, looking around the tables. She proceeded to a small table that faced the doorway but was yet some distance into the restaurant, so that she would not be immediately visible from the doorway—or the lobby—and could herself scrutinize anyone who happened to enter. She placed her bag, holding the revolver, onto the next chair, making sure it was beneath the starched tablecloth and unapparent to any passing eye, and sat back to wait for her tea, her mind wandering again to the question of her present solitude. Miss Temple decided that she liked it perfectly well—in fact, it made her feel quite free. To whom was she obliged? Chang and Svenson could take care of themselves, her aunt was packed away—what hold could any enemy now place over her, aside from a threat to her own bodily safety? None at all—and the idea of drawing the revolver and facing down a host of foes right there in the restaurant became increasingly appealing.

* * *

She picked at the weave of the tablecloth—it was of quite a high quality, which pleased her—and found she was equally impressed with the St. Royale's tableware, which, while displaying an elegance of line, did not abjure a certain necessary *weight,* especially important in one's knife, even if all one were to do with that knife was split a scone and slather cream into the steaming crease. Despite Miss Temple having had tea that very morning, she was looking keenly forward to having tea again—indeed, it was her favorite meal. A diet of scones, tea, fruit, and, if she must, some beef consommé before bedtime and she would be a happy young lady. Her tea arrived first, and she was busily occupied with scrutinizing her waiter's handling of the teapot and the hot water pot and the cup and saucer and the silver strainer and the silver dish in which to set the strainer and the little pitcher of milk and the small plate of fresh-cut wedges of lemon. When all had been arranged before her and the man departed with a nod, Miss Temple set about to deliberately re-arrange everything according to her taste and reach—the lemon going to the side (for she did not care for lemon in her tea, but often enjoyed sucking on one or two slices after she had eaten everything else, as a kind of astringent meal-finisher—apart from which, as she had *paid* for the lemon slices, it always seemed she might as well sample them), the strainer near it, the milk to the other side, and the pot and hot water positioned to allow her to easily stand—which was often, due to their weight, the length of her arms, and the leverage involved with her chair (whether or not its height allowed her feet to touch the floor, as hers presently did just with the toes) required of her in order to pour. Finally, she made sure there was ample space left for the soon-to-arrive scones, fruit, jam, and thick cream.

She stood and poured just a touch of tea into her cup to see if it was dark enough. It was. She then poured in a bit of milk and took up the teapot again, tipping it slowly. For the first cup, if one was careful, it was usually possible to forgo the strainer, as most of the leaves would be sodden and at the bottom of the pot. The tea was a perfect pale mahogany color, still hot enough to steam. Miss Temple sat down and took a sip. It was perfect, the kind of hearty, savory brew that she imagined really ought to be somehow cut up with a knife and fork and eaten in bites. Within another two minutes, passed affably with sipping, the rest of her dishes had arrived and she was again pleased to find that the jam was a deeply colored blackberry conserve and that the fruit was, of all things in the world, a lovely orange hothouse mango, arranged on its plate in finger-thick, length-wise slices. She wondered idly how much this tea was going to cost, and then shrugged away her care. Who knew if she would even be alive in the morning? Why begrudge the simple pleasures that might unexpectedly appear?

Though she did make a point, when she remembered, to glance at the restaurant doorway and scrutinize whoever might be entering, Miss Temple spent the next twenty minutes assiduously focused on slicing and preparing the scones with just the right thickness to each half, applying an under-layer of jam, and then on top of that slathering the proper amount of cream. This done, she set these aside and indulged in two strips of mango, one after the other, spearing each with her silver fork on one end and eating her way from the other, bite by bite, down to the tines. After this, she finished her first cup of tea and stood again to pour another, this time using the strainer and also pouring in a nearly equal amount of hot water to dilute the brew that had been steeping all this time. She sampled this, added a bit more milk, and then sat once more and essayed the first half of the first scone, alternating each bite with a sip of tea until it had disappeared. Another slice of mango and she went back to the second half of the first scone, and by the time she had finished that it was also time for another cup of tea, this one requiring just a touch more of the hot water than before. She was down to the final half of her second scone, and the final slice of mango—and trying to decide which of the two to demolish first—

when she became aware that the Comte d'Orkancz stood on the opposite side of her table. It was to Miss Temple's great satisfaction that she was able to smile at him brightly and through her surprise announce, "Ah, it seems you have finally arrived."

It was clearly not what he had expected her to say. "I do not believe we have been introduced," replied the Comte.

"We have not," said Miss Temple. "You are the Comte d'Orkancz. I am Celeste Temple. Will you sit?" She indicated the chair near him—which did not hold her bag. "Would you care for some tea?"

"No thank you," he said, looking down at her with both interest and suspicion. "May I ask why you are here?"

"Is it not rude to so interrogate a lady? If we are to have a *conversation*—I do not know where you are from, they say Paris, but my understanding is even in Paris they are not so rude, or not rude in such an ignorant fashion—it would be much better if you would *sit*." Miss Temple grinned wickedly. "Unless of course you fear I will *shoot* you."

"As you would have it," answered the Comte. "I have no wish to be . . . ill-mannered."

He pulled out the chair and sat, his large body having the odd effect of placing him both near to her and far away at the same time, his hands on the table but his face strangely distant beyond them. He was not wearing his fur coat, but instead an immaculate black evening jacket, his stiff white shirt held with gleaming blue studs. She saw that his fingers, which were disturbingly strong and thick, wore many rings of silver, several of them set with blue stones as well. His beard was heavy but neatly trimmed, mouth arrantly sensual, and his eyes glittering blue. The entire air of the man was strangely powerful and utterly, disturbingly, masculine.

"Would you care for something *other* than tea?" she asked.

"Perhaps a pot of coffee, if you will not object."

"There is no evil in coffee," answered Miss Temple, a bit

primly. She raised her hand for the waiter and gave him the Comte's order when he arrived at the table. She turned to the Comte. "Nothing else?" He shook his head. The waiter darted to the kitchen. Miss Temple took another sip of tea and leaned back, her right hand gently gathered the strap on her bag and pulled it onto her lap. The Comte d'Orkancz studied her, his eyes flicking at her hidden hand with a trace of amusement.

"So . . . you were expecting me, it seems," he offered.

"It did not particularly matter who it was, but I knew one of you would arrive, and when you did, that I would meet you. Perhaps I preferred another—that is, perhaps I have more personal *business* elsewhere—but the substance remains unchanged."

"And what substance is that?"

Miss Temple smiled. "You see, that is the kind of question one might ask a foolish young woman—it is the kind of question an idiot suitor would ask *me* when he is convinced that the path to groping my body on a sofa leads through flatteringly earnest conversation. If we are going to get anywhere, Comte, it will aid us both to be reasonable and clear. Do you not think?"

"I do not think too many men have groped you on a sofa."

"That is correct." She took a bite of her scone—she had been regretting the interruption for some minutes—and then another sip of tea. "Would it be better if I asked questions of you?"

He smiled—perhaps in spite of himself, she could not tell—and nodded. "As you prefer."

But here his coffee arrived and she was forced to hold her tongue as the waiter set down the cup, the pot, the milk, the sugar, and their requisite spoons. When he was gone, she gave the Comte time to sample his drink, and was gratified to see that he consumed it black, minimizing the delay. He set down the cup and nodded to her again.

"The woman—I suppose for you there are so *many* women," she said, "but the woman I refer to was from the brothel, one Angelique. I understand from Doctor Svenson that you might have been genuinely troubled—even surprised—at the unfortunate results of your . . . procedure, with her, at the Royal Institute. I am curious—and it is not an idle curiosity, I promise you, but *professional*—whether you possessed any genuine feeling for the girl, either before or after your work destroyed her."

The Comte took another sip of coffee.

"Would you object if I smoked?" he asked.

"If you must," replied Miss Temple. "It is a filthy habit, and I will have no spitting."

He nodded to her gravely and fished a silver case from an inner pocket. After a moment spent considering its contents, he removed a small, tightly wrapped, nearly black cheroot and snapped the case shut. He stuck the cheroot in his mouth and the case in his pocket and came back with a box of matches. He lit the cheroot, puffing several times until the tip glowed red, and dropped the spent match on his saucer. He exhaled, took another sip of coffee, and looked into Miss Temple's eyes.

"You ask because of Bascombe, of course," he said.

"I do?"

"Certainly. He has dashed your plans. When you ask of Angelique, someone from the lower orders we have taken up to join our work, to whom we have offered *advancement*—social, material, *spiritual*—you also inquire about our feeling for *him,* another, if not from such a dubious social stratum, we have embraced. And equally you speculate, indeed are ferociously hungry to know, what reciprocal feeling our work receives *from* him."

Miss Temple's eyes flashed. "On the contrary, Monsieur le Comte, I ask out of curiosity, as the answer will likely dictate whether your fate is a more perfunctory retribution at the hand of objective justice, or lingering, stinging, relentless *torment* at the hands of vengeance."

"Indeed?" he replied mildly.

"For my own part—well, it matters only that your intrigue fails and you are powerless to further pursue it—which could equally mean the law, a bullet, or fierce persuasion. Roger Bascombe is nothing to me. And yet, as I must feel about your lady friend who has profoundly wronged *me*—this, this *Contessa*—so others feel about *you*—concerning this very Angelique. Because it is rash to assert there are no consequences when a 'mere' woman is at stake."

"I see."

"I do not believe you do."

He did not answer, taking a sip of coffee. He set down the cup and spoke with a certain weariness, as if expanding his opinion even this far involved physical effort. "Miss Temple, you *are* an interesting young lady."

Miss Temple rolled her eyes. "I'm afraid it means very little to me, coming from a murderous cad."

"I have so gathered your opinion. And who is it I have so foully wronged?"

Miss Temple shrugged. The Comte tapped his ash onto the edge of his saucer and took another puff, the cheroot tip glowing red.

"Shall I guess, then? It could well be the Macklenburg Doctor, for indeed through my efforts he was to die, but I do not see him as your sort of wild revenger—he is too much the *raisonneur*—or perhaps this other fellow, whom I have never met, the rogue-for-hire? He is most likely too cynical and grim. Or someone else still? Some distant wrong from my past?" He sighed, almost as if in acceptance of his sinful burden, and then inhaled again—Miss Temple's eyes fixed to the spot of glowing tobacco as it burned—as if to re-embrace the infernal urge that drove him.

"Why exactly have you come to the St. Royale?" he asked her.

She took another bite of scone—quite relishing this serious banter—and another sip of tea to wash it down, and then while she was swallowing shook her head, the chestnut-colored curls to either side of her face tossed into motion. "No, I will not answer your questions. I have been interrogated once, at Harschmort, and that was more than enough. If you want to talk to me, we will do so on my terms. And if not, then please feel free to leave—for you will find out why I am here only exactly when I have planned to show you." She speared the last slice of mango without waiting for his reply and took a bite, licking her lips to catch the juice. She could not help but smile at the exquisite taste of it.

"Do you know," she asked, swallowing just enough of the fruit to speak clearly, "this is quite nearly as delicious as the mangos one can find in the garden of my father's house? The difference—though this is very good—is due, I should think, to the different quality of sunlight, the very positioning of the planet. Do you see? There are great forces at play around us, each day of our lives—and who are we? To what do we pretend? To which of these masters are we in service?"

"I applaud your metaphorical thought," said the Comte dryly.

"But do you have an answer?"

"Perhaps I do. What about . . . art?"

"Art?"

Miss Temple was not sure what he meant, and paused in her chewing, narrowing her eyes with suspicion. Could he have followed her to the art gallery (and if so, when? During her visit with Roger? More recently? Had he been contacted so quickly by the gallery agent, Mr. Shanck?), or did he mean something else . . . but what? To Miss Temple, art was a curiosity, like a carved bone or shrunken head one found at a village market—a vestige of unknown territories it did not occur to her to visit.

"Art," repeated the Comte. "You are acquainted with it . . . with the *idea*?"

"What idea in particular?"

"Of art as alchemy. An act of transformation. Of re-making and rebirth."

Miss Temple held up her hand. "I'm sorry, but do you know . . . this merely prompts me to ask about your relations with a particular painter, a Mr. Oskar Veilandt. I believe he is also from Paris, and most well known for his very large and provocative composition on the theme of the Annunciation. I understand—perhaps it is merely a cruel rumor—that this expressive *masterwork* was cut up into thirteen pieces and scattered across the continent."

The Comte took another drink of coffee.

"I'm afraid I do not know him. He is from Paris, you say?"

"At some point, like so very many people one finds disagreeable."

"Have you seen his work?" he asked.

"O yes."

"What did you think of it? Were you provoked?"

"I was."

He smiled. "*You?* How so?"

"Into thinking you had caused his death. For he *is* dead, and you seem to have stolen a great deal from him—your ceremonies, your Process, and your precious indigo clay. How odd for such things to come from a painter, though I suppose he was also a mystic and an *alchemist*—strange you should just mention *that* too—though I am told it is the usual way of things in that garret-ridden, absinthe-soaked community. You carry yourself so boldly, and yet one wonders, Monsieur, if you have ever had an original thought at all."

The Comte d'Orkancz stood up. With his cigar in his right hand he extended his left to her and as a matter of instinctive response Miss Temple allowed her own hand to be taken—her other groping for purchase on the pistol butt. He raised her hand up to kiss it, an odd moist, brushing whisper across her fingers, released her hand, and stepped back.

"You leave abruptly," she said.

"Think of it as a reprieve."

"For which one of us?"

"For you, Miss Temple. For you will persist . . . and such persistence will consume you."

"Will it indeed?" It was not much of a tart reply as those things go, but the way his eyes glowered it was the best she could do in the moment.

"It will. And that's the thing," he said, placing both hands on the table and leaning close to her face, whispering. "When it comes, you will submit of your own accord. Everyone does. You think you battle monsters—you think you battle us!—but you only struggle with your fear . . . and that fear will shrivel before desire. You think I do not sense your hunger? I see it clearly as the sun. You are already mine, Miss Temple—just waiting for the moment when I choose to take you."

The Comte stood again and stuck the cheroot in his mouth, his tongue flashing wet and pink against the black tobacco. He blew smoke through the side of his mouth and turned without another word, striding easily from the restaurant and Miss Temple's view.

She could not tell if he left the hotel or climbed the great stairs to the upper floors. Perhaps he was going to the Contessa's rooms—perhaps the Contessa had already returned and she had not seen her because of the Comte. But why had he left so abruptly—and after threatening her? She had spoken of the artist, Veilandt. Had that touched a nerve? Did the Comte d'Orkancz *have* nerves? Miss Temple did not know what she ought to do next. Any plan she might have once imagined had vanished in her moment-by-moment desire to frustrate and best the Comte in conversation—yet what had that achieved? She pursed her lips and recalled her first impression of the man, on the train to Orange Canal, his fearsome bulk seemingly doubled by the fur, his harsh, stark penetrating gaze. He had filled her with dread, and after the strange ritualistic presentation in the medical theatre with a darker dread still. But she was quite satisfied with his reaction to the subject of Oskar Veilandt. Despite the Doctor's ruthless tale of the stricken woman and of poison, Miss Temple felt that the Comte d'Orkancz was but another man after all—horrid, arrogant, brutal, powerful to be sure, but with his own architecture of vanity that, once studied, would show the way to bring him down.

* * *

Thus assured, she used the next minutes to call for her bill and finish what remained of her meal, sucking on a lemon wedge as she dug into her bag for the proper amount of coin. She had contemplated signing the cost over to the Contessa's rooms, but decided such a mean trick was beneath her. What was more, she felt a profound disinclination to owe the woman for anything (an attitude evidently not shared by the Comte, who had allowed Miss Temple to buy his coffee). Miss Temple stood, collected her bag, and dropped the husk of lemon onto her plate, wiping her fingers on a crumpled napkin. She walked from the restaurant, which was beginning to fill for the early evening service, with a trace of rising anxiety. Chang and Svenson had not arrived. This was good, in that she had not yet accomplished anything of substance and she did truly want to be free of them to work, and yet, did this mean something had happened to them? Had they attempted some particularly foolish scheme without her? Of course they hadn't—they were merely pursuing their own thoughts, about this Angelique, no doubt, or Doctor Svenson's Prince. Their not showing up was entirely to the good of their larger mutual goals.

She returned to the main desk, where the same clerk informed her the Contessa was still to arrive. Miss Temple cast a sly look about her and leaned closer to him. With her eyes, she indicated the curved wall with the mirrors, and she asked if anyone had engaged the private rooms for the evening. The clerk did not immediately reply. Miss Temple brought her voice nearer to a whisper, while at the same time adopting an idle innocent tone.

"Perhaps you are acquainted with other ladies in the Contessa's party of friends, a Mrs. Marchmoor, for one. Or—I forget the others—"

"Miss Poole?" asked the clerk.

"Miss Poole! Yes! Such a sweet creature." Miss Temple grinned, her eyes conveying to the best of her ability innocence and depravity at the same time. "I wonder if either of them will attend the Contessa, or perhaps the Comte d'Orkancz... in one of your private rooms?"

She went so far as to bite her own lip and blink at the man. The clerk opened a red leather ledger, ran his finger down the page, and then closed it, signaling for one of the men from the restaurant. When the fellow arrived, the clerk indicated Miss Temple. "This lady will be joining the Contessa's party in room *five*."

"There is one other young lady," the waiter said. "Arrived some minutes ago—"

"Ah, well, even better," said the clerk, and turned to Miss Temple. "You will have company. Poul, please show Miss..."

"Miss Hastings," said Miss Temple.

"Miss *Hastings* to room five. If you or the other lady need anything, simply ring for Poul. I will inform the Contessa when she arrives."

"I am most grateful to you," said Miss Temple.

She was led back into the restaurant, where she noticed for the first time a row of doors whose knobs and hinges were cunningly hidden by the patterns in the wallpaper, so they were all but invisible. How had she not seen the previous woman enter—could she have been speaking to the Comte? Could her entry have been what sparked the Comte's exit—could he have done it just to distract her? Miss Temple was intensely curious as to who it might be. There had been three women in the coach with her at Harschmort, two of whom she took to be Marchmoor and Poole—though who knew, there could be any number of so-swayed female minions—but she had no idea as to the third. She then thought of the many people who had been in the audience in the theatre—like the woman with the green-beaded mask in the corridor. The question was whether it could be anyone who would know her by sight. Most of the time at Harschmort she had worn a mask—and those who had seen her without it were either dead or known figures like the Contessa... or so she hoped—but who could say? Who else had been behind the mirror? Miss Temple blanched. Had Roger? She held tightly to her bag, reaching into it for a coin to give the waiter and leaving it open so she could take hold of the revolver.

He opened the door and she saw a figure at the end of the table, wearing a feathered mask that matched the brilliant blue-green of her dress—peacock feathers, sweeping up to frame her gleaming golden hair. Her mouth was small and bright, her face pale but delicately rouged, her throat swanishly long, her small fine hands still wearing her blue gloves. She reminded Miss Temple of one of those closely-bred Russian dogs, thin and fast and perpetually querulous, with the unsettling habit of showing their teeth at anything that set off their uninsulated nerves. She pressed the coin into the waiter's hand as he announced her: "Miss Hastings." The two women nodded to one another. The waiter asked if they required anything. Neither answered—neither *moved*—and after a moment he nodded and withdrew, shutting the door tightly behind him.

"Isobel Hastings," said Miss Temple, and she indicated a chair on the opposite end of the table from the masked blonde woman. "May I?"

The woman indicated that she should sit with a silent gesture and Miss Temple did so, flouncing her dress into a comfortable position without her gaze leaving her companion. On the table between them was a silver tray with several decanters of amber-, gold-, and ruby-colored liquors, and an array of snifters and tumblers (not that Miss Temple knew which glass was for which, much less what the bottles held to begin with). In front of the blonde woman was a small glass, the size of a tulip on a stiff clear stem, filled with the ruby liquid. Through the crystal it gleamed like blood. She met the woman's searching gaze, the shadowed eyes a paler blue than the dress, and tried to infuse her voice with sympathy.

"I am told that the scars fade within a matter of days. Has it been long?"

Her words seemed to startle the woman to life. She picked up her glass and took a sip, swallowed, and just refrained from licking her lips. She set her drink back on the tablecloth, but kept hold of it.

"I'm afraid you are... mistaken." The woman's voice was tutored and precise, and Miss Temple thought a trifle bereft, as if a life of constraint or routine had over time encouraged a certain narrowness of mind.

"I'm sorry, I merely assumed—because of the mask—"

"Yes, of course—that is quite obvious—but no, that is not why—no... I have not—I am here... in secret."

"Are you an intimate of the Contessa?"

"Are you?"

"I should not say so, no," said Miss Temple airily, forging ahead. "I am more an acquaintance of Mrs. Marchmoor. Though I have of course spoken to the Contessa. Did you—if I may speak of it openly—attend the affair at Harschmort House, when the Comte made his great *presentation*?"

"I was there... yes."

"May I ask your opinion of it? Obviously, you are *here*—which is an answer in itself—but beyond that, I am curious—"

The woman interrupted her. "Would you care for something to drink?"

Miss Temple smiled. "What are *you* drinking?"

"Port."

"Ah."

"Do you disapprove?" The woman spoke quickly, an eager peevishness entering her voice.

"Of course not—perhaps a small taste—"

The woman dramatically shoved the silver tray toward her, some several feet down the table, clinking the glasses together and jostling the bottles—though nothing fell or broke. Despite the effect of this strange gesture, Miss Temple still needed to stand to reach the tray and did so, pouring a small amount of the ruby port into an identical glass, replacing the heavy stopper, and sitting. She breathed in the sweet, medicinal odor of the liquor but did not drink, for something about the smell made her throat clench.

"So . . . ," Miss Temple continued, "we were *both* at Harschmort House—"

"What of the Comte d'Orkancz," the woman said, interrupting her *again*. "Do you know *him*?"

"Oh, certainly. We were just speaking," replied Miss Temple.

"Where?"

"Just here in the hotel, of course. Apparently he has other urgent business and cannot join us."

For a moment she thought the woman was going to stand, but she could not tell if her desire was to find the Comte or run away, startled at his being so near. It was the sort of moment where Miss Temple felt the strange injustice of being a young woman of perception and intelligence, for the more deeply her understanding penetrated a given situation, the more possibilities she saw and thus the less she knew what to do—it was the most unfairly frustrating sort of "clarity" one could imagine. She did not know whether to leap up and stop the woman from leaving or launch into a still more nauseating celebration of the Comte's masculine authority. What she wanted was for the woman to do some of the talking instead of her, and to have an easy minute in which to sample the port. The very name of the beverage had always appealed to her, as an islander, and she had never before tasted it, as it was always the province of men and their cigars after a meal. She expected to find it as vile as it smelled—she found most liquors of any kind vile on principle—but nevertheless appreciated that this one's name suggested travel and the sea.

The woman did not stand, but after a poised second or two resettled herself on her seat. She leaned forward and—as if reading Miss Temple's frustrated mind—took up her delicate glass and tipped it to Miss Temple, who then took up her own. They drank, Miss Temple appreciating the ruby sweetness but not at all liking the burn in her mouth and throat, nor the queasy feeling she now felt in her stomach. She set it down and sucked on her tongue with a pinched smile. The masked woman had consumed her entire glass and stood up to reach for more. Miss Temple slid the tray back to her—more elegantly than it had been sent—and watched as her companion pulled the decanter from the tray and poured, drank without replacing the decanter, and then to Miss Temple's frank surprise poured yet again. The woman left the decanter where it was and only then resumed her seat.

Feeling cunning, Miss Temple realized with a sly smile that her disapproval was misplaced, for on the contrary, the drunker and more free-speaking her quarry became the better her inquisition would proceed.

"You have not told me your name," she said sweetly.

"Nor will I," snapped the woman. "I am wearing a mask. Are you a fool? Are all of you people fools?"

"I do beg your pardon," said Miss Temple demurely, repressing the urge to throw her glass at the lady's face. "It sounds as if you have had a rough time of things today—is there another who has caused you annoyance? I do hope there is something I can do to help?"

The woman sighed tremblingly, and Miss Temple was again surprised—even dismayed a little—at the ease with which even a false kindness can pierce the armor of despair.

"I beg your pardon," the woman said, her voice just over a whisper—and it seemed then that her companion was a person who very rarely in her life had need to say those words, and that she only voiced them now out of utter desperation.

"No no, please," insisted Miss Temple, "you must tell me what has happened to make your day so trying, and then together we shall find an answer."

The woman tossed off the rest of her port, choked for a moment, swallowed with difficulty, then poured again. This was getting alarming—it was not even time for supper—but Miss Temple merely wetted her own lips on her glass and said, "It *is* very delicious, isn't it?"

The woman did not seem to hear, but began to speak in a low

sort of mutter, which when combined with her brittle, sharp voice gave the effect of some circus marvel, one of those disquieting carnival automaton dolls that "spoke" through a strange breathy mix of bladders of air and metal plates from a music box. The sound was not exactly the same, but the spectacle was similar in the way the blonde woman's voice was disturbingly at odds with her body. Miss Temple knew this was partially because of the mask—she had done a great deal of thinking about masks—and was oddly stirred by the movement of the woman's coral-pink lips as they opened and shut within a proscenium of vivid feathers... the unsettling spectacle of her pale face, the puffed fleshy lips—though they were thin, they were still quite evidently tender—the glimpse of white teeth and the deeper pink of her gums and tongue. Miss Temple had a sudden impulse to shove two fingers into the woman's mouth, just to feel how warm it was. But she caught her wandering mind and shook away that shocking thought, for the lady *was* finally speaking.

"I am actually most agreeable, even tractable, that is the thing of it—and when one is of such a temperament, one is *known* and thus gets no credit for being so, people take it as assumed and then want more—they always want more, and such is my nature, for I have always strived within the boundaries of polite society to provide what I can to anyone I can, for I have tried not to be proud, for I could be proud, I could be the proudest girl in the land—I have every right to be whatever I want, and it is vexing, for there are times when I feel that I ought to be, that I ought to be another Queen, more than the Queen, for the Queen is old and horrid-looking—and the worst part is that if I just chose to be that way, if I just did start ordering and screaming and demanding, I would get it, I would get exactly that—but now I wonder if that is really true, I wonder if it's all gone on so long that no one would listen, that they would laugh in my face, or at least behind my back, the way they all laugh behind my back—even though I am who I am—and they would simply do what they are doing already, save more openly and without pretense, with disdain which I do not think I could bear, and my father is the worst of them, he has always been the worst and now he does not see me at all, he does not even attempt to care—he has never cared—and I am expected without question to accept a future chosen for me. No one knows the life I lead. None of you care—and this man, this vulgar *man*—I am expected—a foreigner—it is appalling—and my only solace is that I have always known that he—whoever he turned out to be—would prove the utter ruin of my heart."

The woman drank off her fourth glass of port—and who knew how many she'd consumed before Miss Temple's arrival?—grimaced, and reached at once for the decanter. Miss Temple thought of her own father—craggy, full of rage, impossibly distant, only arbitrarily kind. Her only way of understanding her father was to consider him a natural force, like the ocean or the clouds, and to weather sunny days and storms alike without being personally aggrieved. She knew he had fallen ill, that he would most likely not be living once she returned—if she ever did return—to her island home. It was a thought to prick her conscience with sorrow if she let it, but she did not let it, for she did not really know if the sadness was any different from that she felt at missing the tropical sun. Miss Temple believed that change brought sorrow as a matter of course. Was there particular sadness in her father's absence—either on account of distance or death? Was there sorrow in the fact that she could not for certain say? Her mother she had never known—a young woman (younger than Miss Temple was now, which was a strange thought) slain by the birth of her child. So many people in the world were disappointing, who was to say the lack of any one more was a loss? Such was Miss Temple's normal waspish response to the expression of sympathy at her mother's absence, and if there did exist a tiny deeply set wound within her heart, she did not spend time excavating it for the benefit of strangers, or for that matter anyone at all. Nevertheless, for some reason she could not—or chose not to—name, she found her sympathies touched by the masked woman's jumbled ranting.

"If you were to see him," she asked kindly, "what do you guess the Comte d'Orkancz would advise you to do?"

The woman laughed bitterly.

"Then why don't you leave?"

"And where am I to go?"

"I'm sure there are many places—"

"I cannot *leave*! I am *obliged*!"

"Refuse the obligation. Or if you cannot refuse, then turn it to your advantage—you say you ought to be a queen—"

"But no one will *listen*—no one *imagines*—"

Miss Temple was growing annoyed. "If you truly want to—"

The woman snatched up her glass. "You all sound the same, with your prideful *wisdom*—when it only serves to justify your place at my table! 'Be free! Expand your perceptions!' A load of mercenary rubbish!"

"If you are so assailed," replied Miss Temple patiently, "then how have you managed to come here, masked and alone?"

"Why do you think?" The woman nearly spat. "The St. Royale Hotel is the only place I *can* go to! With two coachmen to make sure I am delivered and collected with no other stop in between!"

"That is ridiculously dramatic," said Miss Temple. "If you want to go elsewhere, *go*."

"How can I?"

"I am sure the St. Royale has many exits."

"But then what? Then where?"

"Any place you want—I assume you have money—it is a very large city. One simply—"

The woman scoffed. "You have no *idea*—you cannot know—"

"I know an insufferable child when I see one," said Miss Temple.

The woman looked up at her as if she had been struck, the port dulling her reactions, her expression tinged with both incomprehension and a growing fury, neither of which would do. Miss Temple stood and pointed to the somewhat isolated swathe of red drapery on the left-hand wall.

"Do you know what that is?" she asked sharply.

The woman shook her head. With a huff, Miss Temple walked over to the curtain and yanked it aside—her ingenious plan momentarily crushed by the flat section of wall that was revealed. But before the woman could speak, Miss Temple saw the indented spots in the painted wood—that it *was* painted wood and not plaster—where one could get a grip, and then the deftly inset hinges that told her how it opened. She wedged her small fingers into the holes and pried up the wooden shutters to reveal a darkened window, the reverse of the golden-framed Dutch mirror, offering the two of them an unobstructed view of the lobby of the St. Royale Hotel and the street front beyond.

"Do you see?" she said, herself distracted with the strangeness of the view—she could see people who were only three feet away who could not see her. As she looked, a young woman stepped directly to the window and began to nervously pull at her hair. Miss Temple felt a discomfiting shiver of familiarity.

"But what does it *mean*?" asked the blonde woman in a whisper.

"Only that the world is not measured by your troubles, and that you are not the limit of the intrigue that surrounds you."

"What—what nonsense—it is like looking into a fish tank!"

Then the woman's hand went to her trembling mouth and she looked anxiously for the decanter. Miss Temple stepped to the table and pushed the tray from her reach. The woman looked up at her with pleading eyes.

"Oh, you do not understand! In my house there are mirrors *everywhere*!"

The door behind them opened, causing both to turn toward the waiter Poul as he escorted another lady into their private room.

She was tall, with brown hair and a pretty face marred by the dimming traces of a ruddy looping scar around both eyes. Her dress was beige, set off by a darker brown fringe, and she wore a triple string of pearls tied tightly to her throat. In her hand was a small bag. She saw the women and smiled, slipping a coin to Poul and nodding him from the room as she merrily addressed them.

"You are here! I did not know you would each be free to come—an unhoped-for pleasure, and this way you've had time to get acquainted by yourselves, yes?"

Poul was gone, the door shut behind him, and she sat at the table, in Miss Temple's former spot, moving the port glass to the side as she settled her dress. Miss Temple did not recognize her face, but she remembered the voice—in the coach to Harschmort, the woman who'd told the story of the two men undressing her. The scars on her face were fading—she'd been the one in the medical theatre talking of her changed existence, her newfound missions of power and pleasure... this was Mrs. Marchmoor... Margaret Hooke.

"I wondered if we would meet again," Miss Temple said to her, somewhat icily, intending to alert the blonde woman to the obvious peril this newcomer presented to them both.

"You didn't wonder at all, I am sure," Mrs. Marchmoor replied. "You knew, because you knew you would be hunted down. The Comte tells me you are... of *interest*." She turned to the masked woman in blue, who had drifted back to the table, though she had not resumed her seat. "What do you think, Lydia—from your observation, is Miss Temple a person worth the time? Is she worthy of our investment, or should she be destroyed?"

Lydia? Miss Temple looked at the blonde woman. Could this be the daughter of Robert Vandaariff, the fiancée of the Doctor's drunken Prince, the heiress to the largest fortune imagined? The object of her gaze did not respond, save to search again for the decanter, this time catching it, pulling out the stopper, and pouring another glass.

Mrs. Marchmoor chuckled. Lydia Vandaariff downed the contents—her fifth glass?—and positively bleated, "Shut up. You're late. What are the two of you talking about? Why am I talking to you two when it's Elspeth I'm supposed to see? Or even more—the Contessa! And why are you calling her Temple? She said her name was Hastings."

Miss Vandaariff wheeled to Miss Temple, squinting with suspicion. "Didn't you?" She looked back to Mrs. Marchmoor. "What do you mean, 'hunted down'?"

"She is making a poor joke," said Miss Temple. "I have not been *found*—on the contrary, it is I who have come here. I am glad you spoke to the Comte—it saves me time explaining—"

"But who *are* you?" Lydia Vandaariff was becoming drunker by the minute.

"She is an enemy of your father," answered Mrs. Marchmoor. "She is undoubtedly armed, and intends some mayhem or ransom. She killed two men the night of the ball—that we know of, there may be more—and her confederates have plans to assassinate your Prince."

The blonde woman stared at Miss Temple. *"Her?"*

Miss Temple smiled. "It is ridiculous, is it not?"

"But . . . you *did* say you were at Harschmort!"

"I was," said Miss Temple. "And I have tried to be kind to you—"

"What were you doing at my masked ball?" Miss Vandaariff barked at her.

"She was killing people," said Mrs. Marchmoor tartly.

"That soldier!" whispered Lydia. "Colonel Trapping! They told me—he seemed so fit—but why would anyone—*why would you want him dead*?"

Miss Temple rolled her eyes and exhaled through her teeth. She felt as if she had become marooned in a ridiculous play made up of one rambling conversation after another. Here she had before her a young woman whose father surely sat at the heart of the entire intrigue, and another who was one of its most subtle agents. Why was she wasting time confirming or denying their trivial questions, when it was in her own power to take control? So often in her life Miss Temple was aware of the frustration that built up when she allowed other people their own way of action when she very clearly knew that their intentions were absolutely not her own. It was a pattern followed endlessly with her aunt and servants, and again now as she felt herself a shuttlecock knocked between the two women and their annoyingly at-odds nattering. She thrust her hand into her bag and pulled out the revolver.

"You will be silent, both of you," she announced, "except when answering my questions."

Miss Vandaariff's eyes snapped wide at the sight of the gleaming black pistol, which in Miss Temple's small white hand seemed fearsomely large. Mrs. Marchmoor's reaction was, on the contrary, to adopt an expression of placid calm, though Miss Temple doubted the depths of its serenity.

"And what questions would those be?" Mrs. Marchmoor replied. "Sit *down,* Lydia! And stop drinking! She has a weapon—do try and concentrate!"

Miss Vandaariff sat at once, her hands demurely in her lap. Miss Temple was surprised to see her so responsive to command, and wondered if such discipline had come to be the only kind of attention she recognized and thus, though her entire rambling rant would seem to contradict the idea, what she craved.

"I am looking for the Contessa," she told them. "You will tell me where she is."

"Rosamonde?" Miss Vandaariff began. "Well, she—" She stopped abruptly at a look from the end of the table. Miss Temple glared at Mrs. Marchmoor and then turned back to Lydia, who had placed a hand over her mouth.

"I beg your pardon?" asked Miss Temple.

"Nothing," whispered Miss Vandaariff.

"I should like you to finish your sentence. 'Rosamonde?' "

Miss Temple received no answer. She was particularly annoyed to see a small curl of satisfaction at the corner of Mrs. Marchmoor's mouth. She turned back to the blonde woman with an exasperated snarl.

"Did you not just exclaim to me about the injustice of your position, the predatory nature of those around you, and around your father, the loathsome quality of your intended husband, and the degree to which you—despite your position—are accorded no respect? And here you defer to—to whom? One who has only these weeks shifted her employment from a brothel! One who is an utter minion of the very people you despise! One who quite obviously bears you no good will at all!"

Miss Vandaariff said nothing.

Mrs. Marchmoor's expression devolved into a grim smile. "I believe the girl plays tricks upon us both, Lydia—it is well known she has been thrown over by Roger Bascombe, the prospective Lord Tarr, and no doubt it is some pathetic attempt to regain his affection that brings this person to our door."

"I am not here for Roger Bascombe!" spat Miss Temple, but before she could continue, or wrench the conversation back into her control, the mention of Roger had prompted Miss Vandaariff to carom back to her pose of condescending superiority.

"Can it be any surprise he has dropped her? Just look at her! Pistols in a hotel restaurant—she's a savage! The type that would do well with a whipping!"

"I cannot disagree," replied Mrs. Marchmoor.

Miss Temple shook her head at this scarcely credible idiocy.

"This is nonsense! First you say I am a murderer—an *agent* in league against you—and *now* I am a deluded heartsick girl! Pray make up your mind so I can scoff at you with precision!" Miss Temple confronted Miss Vandaariff directly, her voice rising near to a shout. "Why do you listen to her? She treats you like a servant! She treats you like a child!" She wheeled again to the woman at the end of the table, who was idly twirling a lock of brown hair around a finger. "Why is Miss Vandaariff here? What did you intend for her? Your *Process*? Or merely the thralldom of debauchery? I have seen it, you know—I have seen you—and *him*—in this very room!"

Miss Temple thrust a hand into her green bag. She still had one of the Doctor's glass cards—was it the right one? She took it out, glanced at it and stumbled to her feet—causing Mrs. Marchmoor to menacingly half-rise from the table. Miss Temple recovered her wits—pulling herself out of the blue depths—and brought the revolver to bear, motioning the woman back into her seat. It was the wrong card, with Roger and herself—still the sinister immersion itself might be enough. Miss Temple set the card in front of Miss Vandaariff.

"Have you seen one of these?" she asked.

The querulous blonde looked to Mrs. Marchmoor before answering and then shook her head.

"Pick it up and look into it," said Miss Temple, sharply. "Be prepared for a shock! An unnatural insinuation into the very mind and body of another—where you are helpless, trapped by sensation, subject to their desires!"

"Lydia—do not," hissed Mrs. Marchmoor.

Miss Temple raised the revolver. "Lydia . . . *do.*"

There was something curious, Miss Temple found, in the ease with which one could impose on another an experience that one knew—first hand—to be disquieting, or frightening, or repugnant, and at the grim satisfaction one took in watching the person undergo it. She had no idea of Miss Vandaariff's intimate experience, but assumed, from her childish manner, that she had been generally sheltered, and while she was not thrusting her brusquely into the carnal union of Karl-Horst and Mrs. Marchmoor on the sofa—though she would have been happy to do so—she still felt a little brutal in forcing even this less transgressive card upon her at all. She remembered her own first immersion—the way in which she had naïvely assured Doctor Svenson it was nothing she could not bear (though she had been unable to fully meet his eyes afterwards)—and the shocking sudden delicious troubling rush of sensation she'd felt as the Prince had stepped between his lover's open legs, the lover whose undeniably sweet experience she had herself then shared for that exquisite instant. As a young lady, the value of her virtue had been drilled into her like discipline into a Hessian soldier, yet she could not exactly say where her virtue presently stood—or rather could not separate the knowledge of her body from that of her mind, or the sensations she now knew. If she allowed herself the room to think—a dangerous luxury, to be sure—she must face the truth that her confusion was nothing less than the inability to distinguish her thoughts from the world around her—and that by virtue of this perilous glass her access to ecstasy might be as palpable a thing as her shoes.

Miss Temple had taken out the card as a way to prove to Miss Vandaariff in one stroke the wicked capacity of her enemies and the seductive dangers they might have already offered, to warn her by way of frightening her and so win the heiress to her side, but as she watched the girl gaze into the card—biting her lower lip, quickening breath, left hand twitching on the table top—and then glanced to the end of the table to see Mrs. Marchmoor studying the masked woman with an equally intent expression—she no longer knew if the gesture had been wise. Faced with Lydia's intensity of expression, she even wondered if somehow she had done it to gain perspective on her own experience, as if watching Miss Vandaariff might be watching herself—for she could too readily, despite the need to pay attention, the obvious danger, imagine herself again in the lobby of the Boniface, eyes swimming into the depths of blue glass, hands absently groping her balled-up dress, and all the time Doctor Svenson knowing—even as he turned his back—what was passing with a shudder through her body.

Miss Temple recalled with shock the words of the Comte d'Orkancz—that she would fall prey to her own desire!

Her hand darted forward and she snatched the card away. Before Miss Vandaariff could do anything but sputter in mortified confusion, it had been stuffed back in the green bag.

"Do you see?" Miss Temple cried harshly. "The unnatural science—the feeling of another's experience—"

Miss Vandaariff nodded dumbly, and looked up, her eyes fixed on the bag. "What . . . how could it be possible?"

"They plan to use your place of influence, to seduce you as they have seduced this man, Roger Bascombe—"

Miss Vandaariff shook her head with impatience. "Not them . . . the glass—the *glass*!"

"So, Lydia . . ." chuckled Mrs. Marchmoor from the end of the table, relief and satisfaction in her voice, "you weren't frightened by what you saw?"

Miss Vandaariff sighed, her eyes shining, an exhalation of intoxicated glee. "A little . . . but in truth I don't care about what I saw at all—only for what I *felt* . . ."

"Was it not *astonishing*?" hissed Mrs. Marchmoor, her earlier concern quite forgotten.

"O Lord . . . it *was*! It was the most *exquisite* thing! I was inside his hands, his hunger—groping her—" She turned to Miss Temple. "Groping *you*!"

"But—no, no—" began Miss Temple, her words interrupted by a glance to Mrs. Marchmoor, who was beaming like a lighthouse. "There is another—with *this* woman! And your Prince! Far more intimate—I assure you—"

Miss Vandaariff snapped at Miss Temple hungrily. "Let me see it! Do you have it with you? You must—there must be many, many of them—let me see this one again—*I want to see them all*!"

Miss Temple was forced to step away from Miss Vandaariff's grasping hands.

"Do you not *care*?" she asked. "*That* woman—*there*!—with your *intended*—"

"Why should I care? He is nothing to me!" Miss Vandaariff replied, flapping her hand toward the end of the table. "*She* is nothing to me! But the *sensation*—the submersion into such *experience*—"

The woman was drunk. She was troubled, damaged, spoiled, and now yanking at Miss Temple's arm like a street urchin, trying to get at her bag.

"Control yourself!" she hissed, taking three rapid steps away, raising the pistol—though here she made the realization (and in the back of her mind knew that this was exactly the kind of thing that made a man like Chang a professional, that there *were* things to learn and remember about, for example, threatening people with guns) that whenever one used a gun as a goad to enforce the actions of others, one had best be prepared to use it. If one was not—as, in this moment, Miss Temple recognized she was not prepared to do against Miss Vandaariff—one's power vanished like the flame of a blown-out candle. Miss Vandaariff was too distracted to take in anything save her strangely insistent hunger. Mrs. Marchmoor, however, had seen it all. Miss Temple wheeled, her pistol quite thrust at the woman's smiling face.

"Do not move!"

Mrs. Marchmoor chuckled again. "Will you shoot me? Here in a crowded hotel? You will be taken by the law. You will go to prison and be hanged—we will make sure of it."

"Perhaps—though you shall die before me."

"Poor Miss Temple—for all your boldness, still you comprehend nothing."

Miss Temple scoffed audibly. She had no idea why Mrs. Marchmoor would feel empowered to say such a thing, and thus took refuge in defiant contempt.

"What are you talking about?" whined Lydia. "Where are more of these *things*?"

"Look at that one again," said Mrs. Marchmoor soothingly. "If you practice you can make the card go more slowly, until it is possible to suspend yourself within a single moment as long as you like. Imagine *that,* Lydia—imagine what moments you can drink in again and again and again."

Mrs. Marchmoor raised her eyebrows at Miss Temple and

cocked her head, as if to urge her to give up the card—the implication being that once the heiress was distracted the two of them—the adults in the room—could converse in peace.

Against all her better instincts, perhaps only curious to see if what Mrs. Marchmoor had just said might be true, Miss Temple reached into her bag and withdrew the card, feeling as her fingers touched its slick cool surface the urge to look into it herself. Before she could fully resolve not to, Miss Vandaariff snatched it from her grasp and scuttled away to her seat, eyes fixed on the blue rectangle cupped reverently in her hands. Within moments Lydia's tongue was flicking across her lower lip . . . her mind riveted elsewhere.

"What has it done to her?" Miss Temple asked with dismay.

"She will barely hear us, and we can speak clearly," answered Mrs. Marchmoor.

"She seems not to care about her fiancé."

"Why should she?"

"Do *you* care for him?" she demanded, referring to the explicit interaction held fast within glass. Mrs. Marchmoor laughed and nodded at the blue card.

"So *you* are held within that card . . . and on another *I* am . . . *encaptured* with the Prince?"

"Indeed you are—if you think to deny it—"

"Why should I? I can well imagine the situation, though I confess I don't remember it—it is the price one pays for immortalizing one's experience."

"You do not *remember*?" Miss Temple was astonished at the lady's decadent disregard. "You do not remember—*that*—with the Prince—before *spectators*—"

Mrs. Marchmoor laughed again. "O Miss Temple, it is obvious you would benefit from the clarity of the Process. Such foolish questions should nevermore pass your lips. When you spoke to the Comte, did he ask that you join us?"

"He did not!"

"I am surprised."

"He in fact threatened me—that I should submit to you, being so defeated—"

Mrs. Marchmoor shook her head with impatience. "But that is the same. Listen, you may wave your pistol but you will not stop me—for I am no longer of such a foolish mind to be so occupied with *grievance*—from asking again that you recognize the inevitable and join our work for the future. It is a better life, of freedom and action and satisfied desire. You *will* submit, Miss Temple—I can promise you it is the case."

Miss Temple had nothing to say. She gestured with the revolver. "Get up."

If Mrs. Marchmoor had convinced her of one thing, it was that the private room was too exposed. It had served her purpose to pursue her inquiries but was truly no place to linger—unless she was willing to risk the law. With the revolver and the card both in her bag, she drove the women before her—Mrs. Marchmoor cooperating with a tolerant smile, Miss Vandaariff, still masked, making furtive glances that revealed her flushed face and glassy eyes—up the great staircase and along to the Contessa Lacquer-Sforza's rooms. Mrs. Marchmoor had answered the inquiring look of the desk clerk with a saucy wave and without any further scrutiny they passed into the luxurious interior of the St. Royale.

The rooms were on the third floor, which they reached by a second only slightly less grand staircase, the rods and banisters all polished brass, that continued the curve of the main stair up from the lobby. Miss Temple realized that the winding staircases echoed the red and gold carved ribbons around the hotel's supporting pillars, and found herself gratified by the depth of thought put into the building—that one *could* expend such effort, and that she had been clever enough to note it. Miss Vandaariff glanced back at her again, now with a more anxious expression—almost as if some idea had occurred to her as well.

"Yes?" asked Miss Temple.

"It is nothing."

Mrs. Marchmoor turned to her as they walked. "Say what you are thinking, Lydia."

Miss Temple marveled at the woman's control over the heiress. If Mrs. Marchmoor still bore the scars of the Process, she could only have been an intimate of the Cabal for a short time, before which she was in the brothel. But Lydia Vandaariff deferred to her as to a long-time governess. Miss Temple found it entirely unnatural.

"I am merely worried about the Comte. I do not want him to come."

"But he may come, Lydia," replied Mrs. Marchmoor. "You do well know it."

"I do not like him."

"Do you like me?"

"No. No, I don't," she muttered peevishly.

"Of course not. And yet we are able to get along perfectly well." Mrs. Marchmoor threw a smug smile back to Miss Temple, and indicated a branching hallway. "It is this way."

The Contessa was not in the suite. Mrs. Marchmoor had opened it with her key, and ushered them inside. Miss Temple had removed her revolver in the hallway, once they were off the staircase and out of view, and she followed them carefully, her eyes darting about in fear of possible ambush. She stepped on a shoe in the foyer and stumbled. A shoe? Where were the maids? It was a very good question, for the Contessa's rooms were a ruin. No matter where Miss Temple cast her gaze it fell across uncollected plates and glasses, bottles and ashtrays, and ladies' garments of all kinds, from dresses and shoes to the most intimate of items, petticoats, stockings, and corsets—draped over a divan in the main receiving room!

"Sit down," Mrs. Marchmoor told the others, and they did, next to each other on the divan. Miss Temple looked around her and listened. She heard no sound from any other room, though the gaslight lamps were lit and glowing.

"The Contessa is not here," Mrs. Marchmoor informed her.

"Has the place been pillaged in her absence?" Miss Temple meant it as a serious question, but Mrs. Marchmoor only laughed. "The Lady is not one for particular order, it is true!"

"Does she not have servants?"

"She prefers that they occupy themselves with other tasks."

"But what of the smell? The smoke—the drink—the plates—does she desire *rats*?"

Mrs. Marchmoor shrugged, smiling. Miss Temple scuffed at a corset on the carpet near her foot.

"I'm afraid *that* is mine," whispered Mrs. Marchmoor, with a chuckle.

"Why would you remove your corset in the front parlor of a noble lady?" Miss Temple asked, little short of appalled, but already wondering at the answer, the possibilities disorientingly lurid. She looked away from Mrs. Marchmoor to compose her face and saw herself in the large mirror above her on the wall, a determined figure in green, her chestnut curls, pulled to the back and each side of her head, a darker shade in the warm gaslight, and all around her the tattered litter of decadent riot. But behind her head in the reflection, a flash of vivid blue caught her eye and she turned to see a framed canvas that could only be the work of Oskar Veilandt.

"Another *Annunciation*..." she whispered aloud.

"It is," whispered Mrs. Marchmoor in reply, her voice hesitant and cautious behind her. Hearing it, Miss Temple had the feeling of being watched carefully, like a bird stalked by a slow-moving cat. "You've seen it elsewhere?"

"I have."

"Which fragment? What did it portray?"

She did not want to answer, to acknowledge the woman's

interrogation, but the power of the image drove her to speak. "Her head . . ."

"Of course—at Mr. Shanck's exhibition. The head is beautiful . . . such a heavenly expression of peace and pleasure lives in her face—would you not say? And here . . . see how the fingers hold into her hips . . . you see, in the artist's interpretation, how she has been *mounted* by the Angel . . ."

Behind them, Miss Vandaariff whimpered. Miss Temple wanted to turn to her but could not shift her gaze from the near-seething image. Instead, she walked slowly to it . . . the brush-strokes immaculate and smooth, as if the surface more porcelain than pigment and canvas. The flesh was exquisitely rendered, though the fragment itself—so out of context of the whole, with neither face seen, just their hips and the two blue hands—struck her as at once compelling and somehow dreadful to imagine. She wrenched her eyes away. Both women watched her. Miss Temple forced her voice to a normal tone, away from the sinister intimacy of the painting.

"It is an allegory," she announced. "It tells the story of your intrigue. The Angel stands for your work with the blue glass, the lady for all those you would work upon. It is the Annunciation, for you believe that the birth—what your plans conceive—will—will—"

"Redeem us all," finished Mrs. Marchmoor.

"I've never seen such blasphemy!" Miss Temple announced with confidence.

"You have not seen the *rest* of the painting," said Miss Vandaariff.

"Hush, Lydia."

Miss Vandaariff did not answer, but then suddenly placed both hands over her abdomen and groaned with what seemed to be sincere discomfort . . . then doubled over and groaned again, rocking back and forth, a rising note of fear in her moaning, as if this feeling were something she knew.

"Miss Vandaariff?" cried Miss Temple. "What is wrong?"

"She will be fine," said Mrs. Marchmoor mildly, her hand reaching up to gently pat the stricken woman's rocking back. "Did you perchance drink any of the port?" she asked Miss Temple.

"No."

"I *did* note a second glass . . ."

"A taste to wet my lips, nothing more—"

"That was very prudent."

"What was *in* it?" Miss Temple asked.

Miss Vandaariff groaned again, and Mrs. Marchmoor leaned forward to take her arm. "Come, Lydia, you must come with me—you will feel better—"

Miss Vandaariff groaned more pitifully still.

"Come, Lydia . . ."

"What is wrong with her?" asked Miss Temple.

"Nothing—she has merely consumed too much of the preparatory *philtre*. How many glasses did you see her drink?"

"Six?" answered Miss Temple.

"My goodness, Lydia! It is a good thing I am here to help you void the excess." Mrs. Marchmoor helped Miss Vandaariff to her feet, smiling indulgently. She ushered the young blonde woman in an unsteady shuffle toward an open doorway and paused there to turn back to Miss Temple. "We will return in a moment, do not worry—it is merely to the suite's convenience. It was known she would drink the port—so the preparatory *philtre* was added to it in secret. The mixture is necessary for her—but not to such excess."

"Necessary for what?" asked Miss Temple, her voice rising. "Preparatory for *what*?"

Mrs. Marchmoor did not seem to have heard her and reached up to smooth Miss Vandaariff's hair.

"It will do her good to marry, I daresay, and be past such independent revels. She has no head for them at all."

Miss Vandaariff groaned again, perhaps in protest to this unfair assessment, and Miss Temple watched with annoyance and curiosity as the pair disappeared into the next room—as if she had no revolver and they were no sort of prisoner or hostage! She stood where she was, utterly affronted, listening to the clanging lid of a chamber pot and the determined rustling of petticoats, and then decided it was an excellent opportunity to investigate the other rooms without being watched. There were three doors off of the main parlor she was in—one to the chamber pot, which seemed a maid's room, and two others. Through one open archway she could see a second parlor. In it was set a small card table bearing the half-eaten remains of an uncleared meal, and against the far wall a high sideboard quite crowded with bottles. As she stared in, trying to piece together some sense of the display—how many people had been at the table, how much had they been drinking—as she presumed a real investigating adventurer ought to do, Miss Temple worried she'd had at least one complete mouthful of the port—had it been enough to inflict the insidious purpose of their horrid *philtre* onto her body? What fate was Miss Vandaariff being prepared *for*? Marriage? But it could hardly be that—or not in any normal sense of the word. Miss Temple was reminded of livestock being readied for slaughter and felt a terrible chill.

With a hand against her brow she stepped back into the main room and quickly to the third door, which was ajar, the sounds of groans and scuffling feet still insistent behind her. This was the Contessa's bedroom. Before her was an enormous four-poster bed shrouded in purple curtains, and across the floor was strewn more clothing—but these objects, large and small, seemed to float in a room where the walls were far away and, like the floor, dark with shadow like the surface of a black, dead-placid pool, the discarded garments floating like clumps of leaves. She pulled aside the bed curtains. With a primitive immediacy Miss Temple's nostrils flared... a delicate scent the Contessa's body had left in the bedclothes. Part of it was frangipani perfume, but underneath that flowered sweetness lay something else, steeped gently between the sheets, close to the odor of freshly baked bread, of rosemary, of salted meat, even of lime. The scent rose to Miss Temple and brought to her mind the human quality of the woman, that however fearsome or composed, she was a creature of appetite and frailties after all . . . and Miss Temple had penetrated her lair.

She breathed in again and licked her lips.

Miss Temple quickly wondered if, in such ruinous disorder, the Contessa might have hidden anything of value, some journal or plan or artifact that might explain the Cabal's secret aims. Behind, the complaining groans of Miss Vandaariff persisted. What *had* been done to the woman—it was practically as if she was giving birth! Anxiety gnawed at Miss Temple anew, and she felt a glow of perspiration rise upon her brow and between her shoulder blades. Her truest adversaries—the Contessa and the Comte d'Orkancz—must eventually arrive at these rooms. Was she prepared to meet them? She had brazened out her tea with the Comte well enough, but was much less satisfied by her extended interaction with the two ladies, by any estimation less formidable opponents (if opponent was even the proper word for the distressingly unmoored Miss Vandaariff). Somehow a confrontation that ought to have been taut, antagonistic, and thrilling had become mysterious, distracted, sensual, and lax. Miss Temple resolved to find what she could and leave as quickly as possible.

She first swept her hand beneath the voluminous feather pillows at the head of the bed. Nothing. This was to be expected—a quick lift of the mattress and a look under the bed frame revealed the same result—and it was only with the smallest increase of hope that Miss Temple marched to the Contessa's armoire in search of the drawer containing her intimates. A foolish sort of woman might hide things there, with an idea that somehow the personal nature of the drawer's contents would ward off inquiry. Ever an enemy to the inquisitive, Miss Temple knew the opposite was true—that such silks and stays and hose and whalebone inspired a feral curiosity in almost anyone—who *wouldn't* want to paw through them?—and so the idea of stashing, for example, a tender diary in such a place was tantamount to leaving it in the foyer like a newspaper or, still worse, on the servants' dining table at mealtime. As she expected, no such items of worth were to be found amongst the Contessa's undergarments—though she perhaps dallied a moment running her fingers through the quantities of silk and may have also, with a furtive blush, pressed a luscious delicacy or two to her nose—and she shut the drawer. The best hiding places were the most banal—cunningly in plain sight, or cluttered amongst, say, one's jumbled shoes. But she found nothing save a truly astonishing and expensive range of footwear. Miss Temple turned—did she have time to ransack the entire armoire? Was Miss Vandaariff still groaning?—looking for some ostensibly clever hiding place she could *see.* What she saw was discarded clothing everywhere . . . and Miss Temple smiled. There to the side of the armoire, against the dark wall in shadow, was a pile of blouses and shawls that struck her as quite deliberately set aside from any possible foot traffic. She knelt before it and rapidly sorted apart the layers. In no time at all, its glow nested in a yellow Italian damask wrap like an infant in straw, she had uncovered a large book crafted entirely of blue glass.

It was the size of a middling volume from an encyclopedia—"N" or "F," perhaps—over a foot in height and slightly under that in width, and perhaps three inches thick. The cover was heavy, as if the glass-maker had emulated the embossed Tuscan leather Miss Temple had seen in the market near St. Isobel's, and opaque, for even though it seemed as if she ought to have been able to see clearly into it, the layers were in fact quite dense. Similarly, at first glance the book appeared to be one color, a deep vivid indigo blue, but upon staring Miss Temple perceived it was riven with rippling streaks where the color fluctuated through an enticing palette, from cerulean to cobalt to aquamarine, every twisting shade delivering a disturbingly palpable impact to her inner eye, as if each bore an emotional as well as a visual signature. She could see no words on the cover, nor, when she looked—placing a hand on the book to shift it—on the spine.

At its touch Miss Temple nearly swooned. If the blue card had exerted a seductive enticement upon a person, the book provoked a maelstrom of raw sensation set to swallow her whole. Miss Temple yanked her hand free with a gasp.

She looked to the open door—beyond it the other women were silent. She really ought to return to them—she ought to *leave*—for they would no doubt enter the room after her any second, and on their heels must soon be the Comte or the Contessa. She dug her hand under the damask shawl, so to touch the book with impunity, and prepared to wrap it up and take it with her—for surely here was a prize to amaze the Doctor and Chang. Miss Temple looked down and bit her lip. If she opened the book without touching the glass . . . surely that would protect her . . . surely then she should have even more understanding to share with the others. With another glance behind her—had Miss Vandaariff fallen into a faint?—she carefully lifted up the cover.

The pages—for she could see down through them, each thin layer overlapping the next with its unique formless pattern of swirling blues—seemed as delicate as wasp wings—square wasp wings the size of a dish plate—and were strangely hinged into the spine so that she could indeed turn them like a normal book. She could not tell at once, but there seemed to be hundreds of pages, all of them imbued, like the cover, with a pulsing blue glow that cast the whole of the room in an unnatural spectral light. She was frightened to turn the page for fear of snapping the glass (just as she was frightened to stare at it too closely), but when she gathered her nerves to do so she found the glass was actually quite strong—it felt more like the thick pane of a window than the paper-thin sheet it was. Miss Temple turned one brilliant page and then another. She stared into the book, blinked, and then squeezed her eyes—could the formless swirls be *moving*? The worry in her head had transformed into a heaviness, an urge toward sleep, or if not sleep outright, a relaxation of intention and control. She blinked again. She should close the book at once and leave. The room had become so hot. A drop of sweat fell from her forehead onto the glass, the surface clouding darkly where it landed, then swirling, the dark blot expanding across the page. Miss Temple gazed into it with sudden dread—an indigo knot opening like an orchid or blood blossoming from a wound... it was perhaps the most beautiful thing she had ever seen, though she was filled with fear at what would happen when the dark unfurling had covered the entirety of the page. But then it was done, the last bit of shimmering blue blotted out and she could no longer see through to the lower pages... only into the depths of the indigo stain. Miss Temple heard a gasping sound—dimly aware that it came from her own mouth—and was swallowed.

The images writhed around her mind and then with a rush passed through it, the singular point, both terrifying and delicious, being that *she* did not seem to be present at all, for just as with Mrs. Marchmoor and the card, her awareness was subsumed within the immediacies of whichever sensation had entrapped her. It felt to Miss Temple that she had plunged into the experience of several lifetimes piled up in delirious succession, so wholly persuasive and in such number that they threatened the very idea of Celeste Temple as any stable entity... she was at a masked ball in Venice drinking spiced wine in winter, the smell of the canal water and the dank stone and the hot tallow candles, the hands groping her from behind in the dark and her own delighted poise while she somehow maintained a conversation with the masked churchman in front of her, as if nothing untoward was happening... creeping slowly through a narrow brick passage, lined with tiny alcoves, holding a shuttered lantern, counting the alcoves to either side and then at the seventh on her right stepping to the far wall and slipping aside a small iron disk on a nail and pressing her eye to the hole beneath it, looking into the great bedchamber as two figures strained against each other, a young muscular man, his naked thighs pale as milk, bent over a side table and an older man behind him, face reddened, frothing like a bull... she was riding a horse, her legs gripping the animal with strength and skill, one hand on the reins and another waving a wickedly curved saber, charging across an arid African plain at a flying wedge of horsemen in white turbans, faces dark, she was screaming with fear and pleasure, the red-coated men to either side of her screaming as well, the two lines racing at each other fast as a cracking whip, lowering her body over the neck of her surging mount, saber extended, squeezing the horse between her knees and then one split second of slamming impact—the Arab's blade lancing past her shoulder and her tip digging into his neck, a quick jet of blood and the hideous wrench on her arm as the horses pulled past, the saber yanked free, another Arab in front of her, screaming with exhilaration at the kill... an ecstatic waterfall the size of two cathedrals, she stood among squat red-skinned Indians with their bows and arrows, black hair cut like a medieval king's... mountains of floating ice, the smell of fish and salt, a fur collar tickling her face, behind her voices speaking of skins and ivory and buried metals, in her large gloved hand an unsettling carved figure, squat with a leering mouth and one great eye... a dark marble chamber gleaming with gold, small pots and jars and combs and weapons, all golden, and then the casket itself, little more than the body of the boy-king close-shrouded in a thick hammered sheet of gold and knotted with jewels, then her own hand snapping open a clasp knife and bending down to pry out a singularly fetching emerald... an artist's studio, naked on a divan, reclining shamelessly, looking up into an open skylight, the pearl-grey clouds above her, a man with his skin painted blue between her legs, playfully holding her bare feet in his hands, raising one to his shoulders and then turning, as she also turned, to ask the artist himself about the pose, a figure behind an enormous canvas she could not see as she could not see his face, just his strong hands holding the palette and brush, but before she could hear his answer her attention was drawn pleasantly back to her posing partner who had reached down to luxuriously drag two fingers, just barely making contact, across the length of her shaven labia . . . a stinking sweltering room crowded with dark, slick bodies in clanking chains, striding back and forth, her boots against the planking of a ship, making notes in a ledger . . . a banquet amongst tall, pale, bearded uniformed men and their elegant ladies, dripping with jewels, the great silver trays of tiny glasses rimmed with gold leaf, each one with a clear, fiery, licorice-tinged cordial, tossing down glass after glass, a curtain of violins behind the polite conversation, crystal dishes of black roe in ice, platters of black bread and orange fish, a nod to a functionary wearing a blue sash who casually passed her a black leather volume with one page folded down, she would read it later and smiled, wondering which of the assembled guests it would instruct her to betray . . . crouched before a campfire ringed with stones, the black shadow of a castle dark against the moonlit sky, its high walls rising up from sheer red stone cliffs, feeding piece after piece of parchment to the flames, watching the pages blacken and curl and the red wax seals bubble into nothing . . . a stone courtyard in the hot evening, surrounded by fragrant blooming jasmine and the sounds of birds, on her back on a silken pallet, others around her unconcerned, drinking and speaking and glancing mockingly at the muscled shirtless turbaned guards, her legs apart and her fingers entwined in the long braided hair of the adolescent girl bent over her pelvis, lips and tongue flicking with a measured dreamy insistence, the rise of sensation gathering across her body, an exquisite wave preparing to break, rising, rising, her fingers gripping harder, the knowing chuckle of the girl who chose at that moment to pull back, the tip of her tongue alone slipping across the fervid, yearning flesh and then plunging forward again, the wave that had dipped surging up, higher, fuller, promising to break like the bloom of a thousand blue orchids over and within every inch of her body...

At this very exquisite moment, in the distant reaches of her mind Miss Temple was aware that she had become lost, and with some difficulty located in her memory—or the memories of so many others—a thin voice against the ecstatic roar, the words of Mrs. Marchmoor to Miss Vandaariff about the card, about concentrating on a moment to relive it, to take control of the sensation, of the experience itself. The girl's nimble tongue sparked another spasm of pleasure within her loins and Miss Temple—through the eyes of whoever had given her experience to this book—looked down and with excruciating effort focused her mind on the feeling of the girl's hair between her hands, her fingers pushing against the braids, studded with beads, and then the beads alone, the color... they were blue, of course they were blue... blue glass... she made herself stare into it, deeply, gasping again, thrusting her hips despite herself but somehow pushing her attention past the sweetly searching tongue, driving all other thoughts and sensations from her mind until she saw and felt nothing save the surface of glass and then, in that clear moment, with the force of her entire being, she willed herself elsewhere, pulling free.

Miss Temple gasped again and opened her eyes, surprised to see that her head was against the floor, pressed into the pile of fabric to the side of the book. She felt weak, her skin hot and damp, and pushed herself to her hands and knees, looking behind her. The Contessa's suite of rooms was silent. How long had she been looking at the book? She could not begin to recall all of the stories she had seen—been a part of. Had it taken hours, lifetimes?—or was it like a dream, where hours could transpire within minutes? She rolled back on her heels and felt the unsteadiness of her legs and, to her discomfort, the slickness between them. What had happened to her? What thoughts were now embedded in her mind—what *memories*—of ravaging and being ravaged, of blood and salt, male and female? With a dull irony, Miss Temple wondered if she had become the most thoroughly debauched virgin in all of history.

Forcing her drained body to move, Miss Temple carefully wrapped the damask shawl around the book and tied it. She looked around her for her green bag. She did not see it. Had it not been wrapped around her hand? It had been, she was sure . . . but it was gone.

She stood, taking up the wrapped book, and turned her attention to the still half-open door. As quietly as possible she peered through the gap into the parlor. For a moment she was unsure whether she had truly left the book, so strange was the sight before her, so wholly *composed,* as if she gazed into a Pompeian grotto recreated in the modern world. Mrs. Marchmoor sat reclining on the slope of a divan, her beige dress unbuttoned and pushed to her hips and her corset removed, upper body naked save for the triple row of pearls that tightly spanned her throat. Miss Temple could not help but look at her left breast, heavy and pale, the fingers of the woman's left hand idly teasing the nipple, for her right was quite blocked by Miss Vandaariff's head. Miss Vandaariff, no longer wearing the mask, blonde hair undone down the length of her back, lay fully on the divan next to Mrs. Marchmoor, eyes closed, legs curled, one hand closed in a soft fist in her lap, the other softly supporting the second breast, from which she nursed dreamily, for comfort, like a satiated milk-drunk babe.

Across from them, in an armchair, a cheroot in one hand and his pearl-tipped ebony stick in the other, once more in his fur, sat the Comte d'Orkancz. Behind him, standing in a half-circle, were four men: an older man with his arm in a sling, a short, stout man with a red complexion and livid scars around his eyes, and then two men in uniforms that, from her contact with Doctor Svenson, she knew must be from Macklenburg. One was a severe, hard-looking man with very short hair, a weathered, drawn face, and bloodshot eyes. The other she knew—from the card, she realized, she knew him most intimately—was Karl-Horst von Maasmärck. Her first corporeal impression of the Prince was less than favorable—he was tall, pale, thin, depleted, *and* epicene, lacking a chin, and with eyes reminiscent of uncooked oysters. But past all of these figures her gaze moved quickly to the second divan, upon which sat the Contessa Lacquer-Sforza, her cigarette holder poised perfectly, a thin thread of smoke curling up to the ceiling. The lady wore a tight violet silk jacket with a fringe of small black feathers to frame her pale bosom and throat, and dangling amber earrings. Below the jacket her dress was black and it seemed, as if she were some elemental magic being, to flow down her body and directly into the dark floor . . . where the previous litter of garments had been joined by the wholly savaged contents of Miss Temple's slashed and ruined carpet bag.

With the exception of Miss Vandaariff's, every set of eyes stared at Miss Temple in complete silence.

"Good evening, Celeste," said the Contessa. "You have returned from the book. Quite impressive. Not everyone does, you know."

Miss Temple did not reply.

"I am happy you are here. I am happy you have had the opportunity to exchange views with the Comte, and with my companion Mrs. Marchmoor, and also to acquaint yourself with dear Lydia, with whom you must of course have much in common—two young ladies of property, whose lives must appear to be the very epitome of an endless horizon."

The Comte exhaled a plume of blue smoke. Mrs. Marchmoor smiled into Miss Temple's eyes and slowly turned the ruddy tip of her breast between her thumb and forefinger. The row of men did not move.

"You must understand," the Contessa went on, "that your companion Cardinal Chang is no more. The Macklenburg Doctor has fled the city in fear and abandoned you. You have seen the work of our Process. You have looked into one of our glass books. You know our names and our faces, and the relation of our efforts to Lord Vandaariff and the von Maasmärck family in Macklenburg. You even"—and here she smiled—"must know the facts behind the impending elevation of a certain Lord Tarr. You know all of these things and can, because I'm sure you are as clever as you are persistent, guess at many more."

She raised the lacquered holder to her lips and inhaled, then her hand floated lazily away to again rest on the divan. With a barely audible sigh her lips parted in a wry, wary smile and she blew a stream of smoke from the side of her mouth.

"For all of this, Celeste Temple, it is certain you must die."

Miss Temple did not reply.

"I confess," the Contessa continued, "that I may have misjudged you. The Comte tells me I have, and as I'm sure you know the Comte is rarely wrong. You are a strong, proud, determined girl, and though you have caused me great inconvenience... even—I will admit it—*fury*... it has been suggested that I tender to you an offer... an offer I would normally not make to one I have determined to destroy. Yet it has been suggested... that I allow you to become a willing, valuable part of our great work."

Miss Temple did not reply. Her legs were weak, her heart cold. Chang was dead? The Doctor gone? She could not believe it. She refused to.

As if sensing defiance in her quivering lip, the Comte took the cheroot from his mouth and spoke in his low, rasping, baleful manner.

"It could not be simpler. If you do not agree, your throat will be cut straightaway, in this room. If you do, you will come with us. Be assured that no duplicitous cunning will avail you. Abandon hope, Miss Temple, for it will be expunged... and replaced by *certainty.*"

Miss Temple looked at his stern expression and then to the forbidding beauty of the Contessa Lacquer-Sforza, her perfect smile both warmly tempting and cold as stone. The four men gazed at her blankly, the Prince scratching his nose with a fingernail. Had they all been transformed by the Process, their bestial logic released from moral restraints? She saw the scars on the Prince and on the stout man. It seemed that the older fellow shared their glassy-eyed hunger—perhaps his marks had already faded—only the other soldier bore a normal expression, where certainty and doubt were both at play. On the face of the others was only an inhuman, uncomplicated confidence. She wondered which of them would be the one to kill her. She looked finally to Mrs. Marchmoor, whose blank expression masked what Miss Temple thought was a genuine curiosity... as if she did not know what Miss Temple would do, nor what, once she did submit, might possibly come of it.

"It seems I have no choice," Miss Temple whispered.

"You do not," agreed the Contessa, and she turned to the large man seated next to her and raised her eyebrows, as if to signal her part in the matter was finished.

"You will oblige me, Miss Temple," said the Comte d'Orkancz, "by removing your shoes and stockings."

She had walked in her bare feet—a simple stratagem to prevent her from running away with any speed through the ragged filthy streets—down the stairs and out of the St. Royale Hotel. Mrs. Marchmoor remained behind, but all of the others descended with her—the soldier, the stout scarred fellow, and the older man going ahead to arrange coaches, the Comte and Contessa to her either side, the Prince behind with Miss Vandaariff on his arm. As she walked down the great staircase, Miss Temple saw a new clerk at the desk, who merely bowed with respect at a gracious nod from the Contessa. Miss Temple wondered that such a woman had need of the Process at all, or of magical blue glass—she doubted that anyone possessed the strength or inclination to deny the Contessa whatever she might ask. Miss Temple glanced to the Comte, who gazed ahead without expression, one hand on his pearl-topped stick, the other cradling the wrapped blue book, like an exiled king with plans to regain his throne. She felt the prickling of the carpet fibers between her toes as she walked. As a girl her feet had once been tough and calloused, used to running bare throughout her father's plantation. Now they had become as soft and tender as any milk-bathed lady's, and as much a hindrance to escape as a pair of iron shackles. With a pang of desolating grief she thought of her little green boots, abandoned, kicked beneath the divan. No one else would ever again care for them, she knew, and could not but wonder if anyone would ever again care for her either.

Two coaches waited outside the hotel—one an elegant red brougham and the other a larger black coach with what she assumed was the Macklenburg crest painted on the door. The Prince, Miss Vandaariff, the soldier, and the scarred stout man climbed inside this coach, with the older man swinging up to sit with the driver. A porter from the hotel held open the door of the brougham for the Contessa, and then for Miss Temple, who felt the textured iron step press sharply into her foot as she went in. She settled into a seat opposite the Contessa. A moment later they were joined by the Comte, the entire coach shuddering as it took on his weight. He sat next to the Contessa and the porter shut the door. The Comte rapped his stick on the roof and they set forth. From the time of the Comte's demand for her shoes to the coach moving, they had not spoken a word. Miss Temple cleared her throat and looked at them. Extended silence nearly always strained her self-control.

"I should like to know something," she announced.

After a moment, the Comte rasped a reply. "And what is that?"

Miss Temple turned her gaze to the Contessa, for it was she at whom the question was truly aimed. "I should like to know how Cardinal Chang died."

The Contessa Lacquer-Sforza looked into Miss Temple's eyes with a sharp, searching intensity.

"I killed him," she declared, and in such a way that dared Miss Temple to speak again.

Miss Temple was not yet daunted—indeed, if her captor did not want to discuss this topic, it now constituted a test of Miss Temple's will.

"Did you really?" she asked. "He was a formidable man."

"He was," agreed the Contessa. "I filled his lungs with ground glass blown from our indigo clay. It has many effective qualities, and in such amounts as the Cardinal inhaled is mortal. 'Formidable' of course is a word with many shadings—and physical prowess is often the simplest and most easily overcome."

The ease of speech with which the Contessa described Chang's destruction took Miss Temple completely aback. Though she had only been acquainted with Cardinal Chang for a very short time, so strong an impression had he made upon her that his equally sudden demise was a devastating cruelty.

"Was it a quick death, or a slow one?" Miss Temple asked in as neutral a voice as she could muster.

"I would not call it *quick*. . . ." As the Contessa answered, she reached into a black bag embroidered with hanging jet beads, pulling out in sequence her holder, a cigarette to screw into the tip, and a match to light it. "And yet the death itself is perhaps a generous one, for—as you have seen yourself—the indigo glass carries with it an affinity for dream and for . . . sensual experience. It is often observed that men being hanged will perish in a state of extreme tumescence—" she paused, her eyebrows raised to confirm that Miss Temple was following her, "if not outright spontaneous eruption, which is to say, at least for the males of our world, such an end might be preferable to many others. It is my belief that similar, perhaps even more expansive, transports accompany a death derived from the indigo glass. Or such at least is my hope, for indeed, your Cardinal Chang was a singular opponent . . . truly, I could scarcely wish him ill, apart from wishing him dead."

"Did you confirm your hypothesis by examining his trousers?" huffed the Comte. It was only after a moment that Miss Temple deduced he was laughing.

"There was no time." The Contessa chuckled. "Life is full of regrets. But what are those? Leaves from a passing season—fallen, forgotten, and swept away."

The specter of Chang's death—one that despite the Contessa's lurid suggestion she could not picture as anything but horrid, with bloody effusions from the mouth and nose—had spun Miss Temple's thoughts directly to her own immediate fate.

"Where are we going?" she asked.

"I'm sure you must know," answered the Contessa. "To Harschmort House."

"What will be done to me?"

"Dreading what you cannot change serves no purpose," announced the Comte.

"Apart from the pleasure of watching you writhe," whispered the Contessa.

To this Miss Temple had no response, but after several seconds during which her attempts to glance out of the narrow windows—placed on either side of their seat, not hers, assumedly to make it easier for someone in her position to either remain unseen or, on a more innocent planet, fall asleep—revealed no clear sense of where in the city she might now be, she cleared her throat to speak again.

The Contessa chuckled.

"Have I done something to amuse you?" asked Miss Temple.

"No, but you are about to," replied the Contessa. " 'Determined' does not describe you by half, Celeste."

"Very few people refer to me with such intimacy," said Miss Temple. "In all likelihood, they can be counted on one hand."

"Are we not sufficiently intimate?" asked the Contessa. "I would have thought we were."

"Then what is *your* Christian name?"

The elegant woman chuckled again, and it seemed that even the Comte d'Orkancz curled his lip in a reluctant grimace.

"It is Rosamonde," declared the Contessa. "Rosamonde, Contessa di Lacquer-Sforza."

"Lacquer-Sforza? Is that a *place*?"

"It was. Now I'm afraid it has become an idea."

"I see," said Miss Temple, not seeing at all but willing to appear agreeable.

"Everyone has their own plantation, Celeste, . . . their own island, if only in their heart."

"What a pity for them," declared Miss Temple. "I find an *actual* island to be far more satisfactory."

"At times"—the Contessa's warm tone grew just perceptibly harder—"such is the only way those locations may be visited or maintained."

"By not being *real*, you mean?"

"If that is how you choose to see it."

Miss Temple was silent, knowing that she did not grasp the Contessa's larger point.

"I don't intend to lose mine," she said.

"No one ever does, darling," replied the Contessa.

They rode on in silence, until the Contessa smiled as kindly as before and said, "But you were going to ask a question?"

"I was," replied Miss Temple. "I was going to ask about Oskar Veilandt and his paintings of the Annunciation, for you had another in your rooms. The Comte and I discussed the artist over tea."

"Did you *really*?"

"In fact, I pointed out to the Comte that, as far as I am concerned, he seems to be suspiciously in this fellow's debt."

"Did you indeed?"

"I should say so." Miss Temple did not fool herself that she was capable of angering or flattering either of these two to a point of distraction that might allow her to throw herself from the coach—a gesture more likely than anything to result in her death under the wheels of the coach behind them—and yet, the paintings were a topic that might well produce useful information about the

Process that she might use to prevent her ultimate subversion. She would never understand the science or the alchemy—were science and alchemy the same thing?—for she had always been indifferent to theoretical learning, though she knew the Comte at least was not. What was more, Miss Temple knew he was *sensitive* about the question of the missing painter, and as a rule she was not above being a persistent nuisance.

"And how exactly is that?" asked the Contessa.

"*Because,*" Miss Temple responded, "the *Annunciation* paintings themselves are clearly an allegorical presentation of your Process, indeed of your intrigue as a whole—that the imagery itself is a brazen blasphemy is beside the immediate point, save to convey a scale of arrogance—as you see it, of *advancement* provoked by the effects of your precious blue glass. Of course," she went on with a side glance at the unmoving Comte, "it seems that all of this—for on the back of the paintings are imprudently scrawled the man's alchemical secrets—has been taken by the Comte for his own—taken by all of you—at the expense of the missing Mr. Veilandt's life."

"You said this to the Comte?"

"Of course I did."

"And how did he respond?"

"He left the table."

"It *is* a serious charge."

"On the contrary, it is an obvious one—and what is more, after all the destruction and violence you have put into motion, such an accusation can hardly strike any of you as either unlikely or unprovoked. As the work itself is monstrous, and the murder of its maker even more so, I would not have thought the murderer himself so . . . *tender.*"

For an answer that perhaps too fully fulfilled Miss Temple's hopes of agitation, the Comte d'Orkancz leaned deliberately forward and extended his open right hand until he could place it around

Miss Temple's throat. She uselessly pressed her body back into her seat and tried to convince herself that if he was going to hurt her out of anger he would have seized her more quickly. As the strong fingers tightened against her skin she began to have her doubts, and looked with dismay into the man's cold blue eyes. His grip held her fast but did not choke her. At once she was assailed by hideous memories of Mr. Spragg. She did not move.

"You looked at the paintings—two of them, yes?" His voice was low and unmistakably dangerous. "Tell us . . . what was your *impression*?"

"Of what?" she squeaked.

"Of *anything*. What thoughts were provoked?"

"Well, as I have said, an allegorical—"

He squeezed her throat so hard and so suddenly she thought her neck would snap. The Contessa leaned forward as well, speaking mildly.

"Celeste, the Comte is attempting to get you to *think*."

Miss Temple nodded. The Comte relaxed his grip. She swallowed.

"I suppose I thought the paintings were unnatural. As the woman in them has been given over to the angel—she is given over to—to sensation and pleasure—as if nothing else might exist. Such a thing is impossible. It is dangerous."

"Why is that?" asked the Comte.

"Because nothing would get done! Because—because—there is no border between the world and one's body, one's mind—it would be unbearable!"

"I should have thought it delicious," whispered the Contessa.

"Not for me!" cried Miss Temple.

With a swift rush of fabric the Contessa shifted across the coach next to Miss Temple, her lips pressed close to the young woman's ear.

"Are you sure? For I have seen you, Celeste, . . . I have seen you through the mirror, and I have seen you bent over the book . . . and do you know?"

"Do I know what?"

"That when you were in my room . . . kneeling over so sweetly . . . I could *smell* you . . ."

Miss Temple whimpered but did not know what she could do.

"Think of the book, Celeste," hissed the Contessa. "You remember what you saw! What you did, what was done to you—what you *became*!—through what exquisite realms you traveled!"

At these words Miss Temple felt a burning in her blood—what was happening to her? She sensed her memories of the book like a stranger's footprints in her mind. They were everywhere! She did not want them! But why could she not thrust them aside?

"You are wrong!" Miss Temple shouted. "It is not the same!"

"Neither are you," snarled the Comte d'Orkancz. "You've already taken the first step in your *process* of transformation!"

The coach had become too warm. The Contessa's hand found Miss Temple's leg and then quickly vanished beneath her dress, the knowing fingers climbing up her inner thigh. Miss Temple gasped. These were not the blunt, stabbing, rude fingers of Spragg but—if still invasive—playful, teasing, and insistent. No one had ever touched her this way, in that place. She could not think.

"No—no—" she began.

"What did you see in the book?" The Comte pressed at her with his insistent, terrifying rasp. "Do you know the taste of death and power? Do you know what lovers feel in their blood? You do! You know all of it and more! It has taken root in your being! You feel it as I speak! Will you ever be able to turn away from what you've seen? Will you ever be able to reject these pleasures, having tasted their full intoxicating potency?"

The Contessa's fingers pushed through the slit of her silken pants and slid across her liquid flesh with a practiced skill. Miss Temple shrank from her touch, but the coach seat was so small and the sensation so delicious.

"I don't think you will, Celeste," whispered the Contessa. She softly nuzzled the tips of two fingers, then wetly slipped them deeper while rubbing gently above them with her thumb. Miss

Temple did not know what she was supposed to do, what she was fighting against save the imposition of their will upon her—but she did not want to fight, the pleasure building in her body was heavenly, and yet she also longed to hurl herself away from their openly predatory usage. What did her pleasure matter to them? It was but a goad, a tool, an endless source of thralldom and control. The Contessa's fingers worked slickly back and forth. Miss Temple groaned.

"Your mind is set on fire!" hissed the Comte. "You cannot evade your *mind*—we hold you, you must give in—your body will betray you, your heart will betray you—you are already abandoned, utterly given over—your new memories are rising—surrounding you completely—your life—your *self*—has changed—your once-pure soul has been stained by my glass book's *usage*!"

As he spoke she felt them, doors opening across her spinning mind directly into her fevered body—the masked ball in Venice, the two men through the spy hole, the artist's model on the divan, the heavenly seraglio, and then so many, many more—Miss Temple was panting, the Contessa's fingers deftly plying her most intimate parts, the woman's lips against her ear, encouraging her pleasure with little mocking moans that nevertheless—the very provocative sound of that woman even counterfeiting ecstasy—served as a concrete spur to further delight . . . Miss Temple felt the sweetness gathering in her body, a warm cloud ready to burst . . . but then she shut her eyes and saw herself, in the coach between her enemies, beset, and then Chang dead, his pale face streaked with blood, the Doctor running and in tears, and finally, as if it were the answer she'd been seeking, the hot, clear, open view of barren white sand bordering a blue indifferent sea . . . she pulled herself from the brink—*their* brink she decided, not her own—

And in that exact moment, in such a way that Miss Temple knew they had not perceived her interior victory, the Contessa snatched away her hand and returned in smirking triumph to the other seat. The Comte released her neck and leaned back. She felt the sudden ebb of the pleasure in her body and its instinctive protest against the loss of stimulation—and met their eyes, seeing that they had brought her to the edge only to demonstrate her submission. They looked at her with a condescending disdain that seconds earlier might have been shattering—and before she could say a word, the Contessa's hand—the same hand that had been under her dress—slapped her hard across the face. Miss Temple's head spun to the side, burning. The Contessa slapped her again just as hard, knocking her bodily into the corner of the coach.

"You killed two of my people," she said viciously. "Do not ever believe it is forgotten."

Miss Temple touched her numbed face, shocked and dizzied, and felt the wetness from the Contessa's hand—which was to say from herself. The spike of rage at being struck was dampened by her mortified realization that the close air in the coach was heavy with the smell of her own arousal. She yanked her dress down over her legs and looked up to see the Contessa wiping her fingers methodically on a handkerchief. Their attempt to demonstrate her helplessness had only solidified Miss Temple's defiance. She sniffed again, blinking back tears of pain and further emboldened by the glimpse of her green clutch bag poking out of the side pocket of the Comte d'Orkancz's voluminous fur.

Their coach ride ended at Stropping Station, where once more Miss Temple was made to walk in her bare feet, down the stairs and across the station hall to their train. She was quite certain that her soles would be blackened by the filth of so many travelers and she was not wrong, pausing to scoff at the dirty result with open disgust before she was again pushed forward. Again she was placed between the Comte and the Contessa, the Prince and his fiancée behind them, and the other three men bringing up the rear. Various people they passed gave a polite nod—to the Prince and Miss Vandaariff, she assumed, for they were often recognized—but were nonplussed by the sight of the barefoot young lady who could apparently afford a maid to dress her hair but not even the simplest footwear. Miss Temple gave them no thought at all, even when their questioning looks slipped into open disapproval. Instead, she gazed persistently around her for possible methods of escape but located nothing, dismissing even a pair of uniformed constables—in the company of such elegant nobility, there was no way anyone would credit her account of capture, much less the larger intrigue. She would have to escape from the train itself.

She had just so resolved on this plan when Miss Temple noted with sharp dismay two figures waiting with the conductor on the platform, at the open door of the rearmost car. One, based on the description of Doctor Svenson, she took to be Francis Xonck, sporting a tailcoat worn only on his left arm and buttoned across—the other sleeve hanging free—for his right arm was thickly bandaged. The other, standing tall in a crisp black topcoat, was a man she would no doubt recognize from across the entire station floor until the end of her days. Miss Temple actually stopped walking, only to have her shoulder gently seized by the Comte d'Orkancz and her body carried along for several awkward steps until she had resumed her pace. He released her—never once deigning to look down—and she glanced at the Contessa in time to see her smiling with cruel amusement.

"Ah, look—it is Bascombe and Francis Xonck! Perhaps there will be time on the journey for a lovers' reunion!"

Miss Temple paused again and again the Comte's hand shot out to shove her forward.

Roger's gaze passed over her quite quickly, but she saw, no matter how he hid it behind the fixed face of a government functionary, her presence was no more welcome to him than his to her. When had they spoken last? Nine days ago? Ten? It had still been as engaged lovers. The very word caused Miss Temple to wince—what word could possibly be more changed by the events of her last hours? She knew that they were now separated by a distance she could never have previously imagined, discrepancies of belief and experience that were every bit as vast as the ocean she had crossed to first enter Roger Bascombe's world. She must assume that Roger had given himself over to the Cabal and its Process, to amoral sensation—to one only imagined, if the book were any indicator, what depravities. He must have conspired in the murder of his uncle—how else would he have the title? Had he even stood by—or, who knew, participated?—while murders and worse were enacted, perhaps even that of Cardinal Chang? She did not want to believe it, yet here he was. And what of her own changes? Miss Temple thought back to her night of distress, weeping in her bed over Roger's letter—what was this compared to Spragg's attack, or the Contessa's menace, or the fiendish brutality of the Process? What was this compared to her own discovered reserves of determination and cunning, of authority and choice—or standing as an equal third with the Doctor and the Cardinal, an adventuress of worth? Roger's gaze fell to her dirty feet. She had never allowed herself to be less than immaculate in his presence, and she watched him measure her in that very moment and find her wanting—as he must by necessity find her, something he had cast off. For a moment her heart sank, but then Miss Temple inhaled sharply, flaring her nostrils. It did not matter what Roger Bascombe might think—it would never matter again.

Francis Xonck occupied her interest for a brief glance of estimation and no more. She knew his general tale—the wastrel rakish brother of the mighty Henry Xonck—and saw all she needed of his preening peacock wit and manner in his overly posed, wry expression, noting with satisfaction the apparently grievous and painful injury he had suffered to his arm. She wondered how it had happened, and idly wished she might have witnessed it.

The two men then stepped forward to pay their respects to the Contessa. Xonck first bowed and extended his hand for hers, taking it and raising it to his lips. As if Miss Temple had not been enough abased, she was aghast at the discreet wrinkling of Francis Xonck's nose as he held the Contessa's hand—the same that had been between her legs. With a wicked smile, looking into the

Contessa's eyes—the Contessa who exchanged with him a fully wicked smile of her own—Xonck, instead of kissing the fingers, ran his tongue deliberately along them. He released the hand with a click of his heels and turned to Miss Temple with a knowing leer. She did not extend her hand and he did not reach out to take it, moving on to nod at the Comte with an even wider smile. But Miss Temple paid him no more attention, her gaze fixed despite herself on Roger Bascombe's own kiss of the Contessa's hand. Once more she saw her scent register—though Roger's notice was marked by momentary confusion rather than wicked glee. He avoided looking into the Contessa's laughing eyes, administered a deft brush of his lips, and released her hand.

"I believe you two have met," said the Contessa.

"Indeed," said Roger Bascombe. He nodded curtly. "Miss Temple."

"Mr. Bascombe."

"I see you've lost your shoes," he said, not entirely unkindly, by way of conversation.

"Better my shoes than my soul, Mr. Bascombe," she replied, her words harsh and childish in her ears, "or must I say Lord Tarr?"

Roger met her gaze once, briefly, as if there were something he did want to say but could not, or could not in such company. He then turned, directing his voice to the Comte and Contessa.

"If you will, we ought to be aboard—the train will leave directly."

Miss Temple was installed alone in a compartment in a car the party seemed to claim all for itself. She had expected—or feared—that the Comte or Contessa would use the journey to resume the abuses of her coach ride, but when the Comte had slid open the compartment door and thrust her into it she had turned to find him still in the passageway shutting it again and walking impassively from sight. She had tried to open the door herself. It was not locked, and she had poked her head out to see Francis Xonck standing in conversation some yards away with the Macklenburg officer. They turned at the sound of the door with expressions of such unmitigated and dangerous annoyance that Miss Temple had retreated back into the compartment, half-afraid they were going to follow. They did not, and after some minutes of fretful standing, Miss Temple took a seat and tried to think about what she might do. She was being taken to Harschmort, alone and unarmed and distressingly unshod. What was the first stop on the way to Orange Canal—Crampton Place? Gorsemont? Packington? Could she discreetly open the compartment window and lower herself from the train in the time they might be paused in the station? Could she drop from such a height—it was easily fifteen feet—onto the rail bed of jagged stones without hurting her feet? If she could not run after climbing out she would be taken immediately, she was sure. Miss Temple exhaled and shut her eyes. Did she truly have any choice?

She wondered what time it was. Her trials with the book and in the coach had been extremely taxing and she would have dearly loved a drink of water and even more a chance to shut her eyes in safety. She pulled her legs onto her seat and gathered her dress around them, curling up as best she could, feeling like a transported beast huddling in a corner of its cage. Despite her best intentions Miss Temple's thoughts wandered to Roger, and she marveled again at the distance they had traveled from their former lives. Before, in accounting for his rejection of her, she had merely been one element among many—his family, his moral rectitude—thrown to the side in favor of ambition. But now they were on the same train, only yards away from one another. Nothing stopped him from coming to her compartment (the Contessa was sure to allow it out of pure amusement) and yet he did not. For all that he too must have undergone the Process and was subject to its effects, she found his avoidance demonstrably cruel—had he not held her in his arms? Had he not an ounce remaining of that sympathy or care, even so much as to offer comfort, to ease his own heart at the fate that must befall her? It was clear that he did not, and despite all previous resolve and despite her hidden victories over both the book and her captors—for did these change a thing?—Miss Temple found herself once more alone within her barren landscape of loss.

The door of her compartment was opened by the Macklenburg officer. He held a metal canteen and extended it to her. For all her parched throat she hesitated. He frowned with irritation.

"Water. Take it."

She did, uncorking the top and drinking deeply. She exhaled and drank again. The train was slowing. She wiped her mouth and returned the canteen. He took it, but did not move. The train stopped. They waited in silence. He offered the canteen again. Miss Temple shook her head. He replaced the cork. The train pulled forward. With a sinking heart she saw the sign for Crampton Place pass by her window and recede from sight. When the train had resumed its normal speed, the soldier gave her a clipped nod and left the compartment. Miss Temple tucked her legs beneath her once again and laid her head against her armrest, determined that she would rather sleep than give in again to tears.

She was woken by the officer's reappearance as the train stopped at Packington, and again at Gorsemont, De Conque, and Raaxfall. Each time he brought the steel canteen of water and each time remained otherwise silent until the train resumed its full forward momentum, after which he left her alone. After De Conque Miss Temple was no longer inclined to sleep, partially because it annoyed her to be awoken so relentlessly, but more because the impulse had gone. In its place was a feeling she could not properly name, gnawing and unsettling, which caused her to shift in her seat repeatedly. She did not know where she was—which was to say, she realized with the impact of a bullet, she did not know *who* she was. After having become so accustomed to the dashing tactics of adventure—shooting pistols, escaping by rooftop, digging clues from a stove as if this were the natural evolution of her character (and for a wistful moment Miss Temple occupied herself with a recounting of all the adventurous tasks she had managed in the past few days)—it seemed as if her failure had thrust forward another possibility, that she was merely a naïve and willful young woman without the depth to understand her doom. She thought of Doctor Svenson on the rooftop—the man had been petrified—and yet while she and Chang had leaned over the edge to look into the alley, he had driven himself to walk alone across the top of the Boniface Hotel and the next two buildings—even stepping across the actual (negligible, it was true, but such fear was not born of logic) gaps between structures. She knew what it had cost him, and that the look on his face showed the exact sort of determination recent events had proven she did not possess.

However harsh her judgment, Miss Temple found the clarity helpful, and she began with a clear-eyed grimness—in the irritating absence of a notebook and pencil (oh, how she wished for a pencil!)—to make a mental accounting of her probable fate. There was no telling if she would again be mauled and traduced, just as there was no telling if, despite the Contessa's words, she would finally be slain, before or after torment. Again she shivered, confronting the full extent of her enemies' deadly character, and took a deep breath at a likelihood more dire still—her transformation by the Process. What could be worse than to be changed into what she despised? Death and torment were at least actions taken against *her*. With the Process, that sense of *her* would be destroyed, and Miss Temple decided there in the compartment she could not allow it. Whether it meant throwing herself into a cauldron or inhaling their glass powder like Chang, or simply provoking some guard to snap her neck—she would never give in to their vicious control. She remembered the dead man the Doctor had described—what the broken glass from the book had done to his body . . . if she could just get to the book and smash it, or hold it in her arms and leap headlong to the floor—it must shatter and her life be ended with it. And perhaps the Contessa was right, that death from the indigo glass carried with it a trace of intoxicating dreams.

She began to feel hungry—despite her love for tea, it was not an overly substantial meal—and after an idle five minutes where she was unable to think about anything else, she opened her compartment door and again looked into the passage. The soldier stood where he had before, but instead of Francis Xonck, it was the scarred stout man that stood with him.

"Excuse me," called Miss Temple. "What is your name?"

The soldier frowned, as if her speaking to him was an unseemly breach of etiquette. The scarred man—who it seemed had recovered his sensibilities somewhat, being a bit less glassy about the eyes and more fluid in his limbs—answered her with a voice that was only a little oily.

"He is Major Blach and I am Herr Flaüss, Envoy to the Macklenburg diplomatic mission accompanying the Prince Karl-Horst von Maasmärck."

"*He* is Major Blach?" If the Major was too proud to speak to her, Miss Temple was happy enough to speak about him as if he were a standing lamp. She knew that this was the nemesis of both the Doctor and Chang. "I had no idea," she said, "for of course I have heard a great deal about him—about you both." She really had heard nothing much at all about the Envoy, save that the Doctor did not like him, and even this not in words so much as a dismissive half-distracted shrug—still she expected everyone liked to be talked of, Process or no. The Major, of course, she knew was deadly.

"May we be of service?" asked the Envoy.

"I am hungry," replied Miss Temple. "I should like something to eat—if such a thing exists on the train. I know it is at least another hour until we reach the Orange Locks."

"In truth, I have no idea," said the Envoy, "but I will ask

directly." He nodded to her and padded down the passageway. Miss Temple watched him go and then caught the firm gaze of the Major upon her.

"Get back inside," he snapped.

When the train stopped at St. Triste, the Major entered with a small wrapped parcel of white waxed paper along with his canteen. He gave them both to her without a word. She did not move to open it, preferring to do it alone—there was precious little entertainment else—and so the two of them waited in silence for the train to move. When it did he reached again for the canteen. She did not release it.

"May I not have a drink of water with my meal?"

The Major glared at her. Clearly there was no reason to deny her save meanness, and even that would betray a level of interest that he did not care to admit. He released the canteen and left the compartment.

The contents of the waxed paper parcel were hardly interesting—a thin wedge of white cheese, a slice of rye bread, and two small pickled beets that stained the bread and cheese purple. Nevertheless she ate them as slowly and methodically as she could—alternating carefully small bites of each in succession and chewing each mouthful at least twenty times before swallowing. So passed perhaps fifteen minutes. She drank off the rest of the canteen and re-corked it. She balled up the paper and with the canteen in her hand poked her head back into the passageway. The Major and the Envoy were where they had been before.

"I have finished," she called, "if you would prefer to collect the canteen."

"How kind of you," said Envoy Flaüss, and he nudged the Major, who marched toward her and snatched the canteen from her hand. Miss Temple held up the ball of paper.

"Would you take this as well? I'm sure you do not want me passing notes to the conductor!"

Without a word the Major did. Miss Temple batted her eyelashes at him and then at the watching Envoy down the passageway as the Major turned and walked away. She returned to her seat with a chuckle. She had no idea what had been gained except distraction, but she felt in her mild mischief a certain encouraging return to form.

At St. Porte, Major Blach did not enter her compartment. Miss Temple looked up to the compartment door as the train slowed and no one had appeared. Had she annoyed him so much as to give her a chance to open the window? She stood, still looking at the empty doorway, and then with a fumbling rush began her assault on the window latches. She had not even managed to get one of them open before she heard the clicking of the compartment door behind her. She wheeled, ready to meet the Major's disapproval with a winning smile.

Instead, in the open door stood Roger Bascombe.

"Ah," she said. "Mr. Bascombe."

He nodded to her rather formally. "Miss Temple."

"Will you sit?"

It seemed to her that Roger hesitated, perhaps because she had been found so evidently in the midst of opening the window, but equally perhaps because so much between them lay unresolved. She returned to her seat, tucking her dirty feet as far as possible beneath her hanging dress, and waited for him to stir from the still-open door. When he did not, she spoke to him with a politeness only barely edged with impatience.

"What can a man fear from taking a seat? Nothing—except the display of his own ill-breeding if he remains standing like a tradesman . . . or a marionette Macklenburg soldier."

Chastened and, she could tell from the purse of his lips, pricked to annoyance, Roger took a seat on the opposite side of the compartment. He took a preparatory breath.

"Miss Temple—Celeste—"

"I see your scars have healed," she said encouragingly. "Mrs. Marchmoor's have not, and I confess to finding them quite unpleasant. As for poor Mr. Flaüss—or I suppose it should be *Herr* Flaüss—for *his* appearance he might as well be a tattooed aboriginal from the polar ice!"

With satisfaction, she saw that Roger looked as if a lemon wedge had become lodged beneath his tongue.

"Are you finished?" he asked.

"I don't believe I am, but I will let you speak, if that is what you—"

Roger barked at her sharply. "It is not a surprise to see you so relentlessly fixed on the trivial—it has always been your way—but even *you* should apprehend the gravity of your situation!"

Miss Temple had never seen him so dismissive and forceful, and her voice dropped to a sudden icy whisper.

"I apprehend it very fully . . . I assure you . . . Mr. Bascombe."

He did not reply—he was, she realized with a sizzling annoyance, allowing what he took to be his acknowledged rebuke to fully sink in. Determined not to first break the silence, Miss Temple found herself studying the changes in his face and manner—quite in spite of herself, for she still hoped to meet his every attention with scorn. She understood that Roger Bascombe offered the truest window into the effects of the Process she was likely to find. She had met Mrs. Marchmoor and the Prince—her pragmatic manner and his dispassionate distance—but she had known neither of them intimately beforehand. What she saw on the face of Roger Bascombe pained her, more than anything at the knowledge that such a transformation spoke—and she was sure, in her unhappy heart, that it did—to his honest desire. Roger had always been one for what was ordered and proper, paying scrupulous attention to social niceties while maintaining a fixed notion of who bore what title and which estates—but she had known, and it had been part of her fondness for him, that such painstaking alertness arose from his own lack of a title and his occupation of yet a middling position in government—which is to say from his naturally cautious character. Now, she saw that this was changed, that Roger's ability to juggle in his mind the different interests and ranks of many people was no longer in service to his own defense but, on the contrary, to his own explicit, manipulative advantage. She had no doubt that he watched the other members of the Cabal like an unfailingly deferential hawk, waiting for the slightest misstep (as she was suddenly sure Francis Xonck's bandaged arm had been a secret delight to him). Before when Roger had grimaced at her outbursts or expressions of opinion, it had been at her lack of tact or care for the delicate social fabric of a conversation he had been at effort to maintain—and his reaction had filled her with a mischievous pleasure. Now, despite her attempts to bait or provoke him, all she saw was a pinched, unwillingly burdened *tolerance,* rooted in the disappointment of wasting time with one who could offer him no advantage whatsoever. The difference made Miss Temple sad in a way she had not foreseen.

"I have presumed to briefly join you," he began, "at the suggestion of the Contessa di Lacquer-Sforza—"

"I am sure the Contessa gives you all manner of suggestions," interrupted Miss Temple, "and have no doubt that you follow them eagerly!"

Did she even believe this? The accusation had been too readily at hand not to fling... not that it seemed to find any purchase on its target.

"Since," he continued after a brief pause, "it is intended that you undergo the Process upon our arrival at Harschmort House, it will arise that, although we have been in the last days *sundered,* after your ordeal we shall be reconciled to the same side—as allies."

This was not what she had expected. He watched her, defensively expectant, as if her silence was the prelude to another childish eruption of spite.

"Celeste," he said, "I do urge you to be rational. I am speaking of facts. If it is necessary—if it will clarify your situation—I will again assure you that I am well beyond all feelings of attachment... or equally of resentment."

Miss Temple could not credit what she had heard. Resentment? When it was *she* who had been so blithely overthrown, she who had borne for how many evenings and afternoons in their courtship the near mummifying company of the condescending, starch-minded, middling-fortuned Bascombe family!

"I beg your pardon?" she managed.

He cleared his throat. "What I mean to say—what I have come to say—is that our new alliance—for your loyalties will be changed, and if I know the Contessa, she will insist that the two of us continue to work in concert—"

Miss Temple narrowed her eyes at the idea of what *that* might mean.

"—and it would be best if, as a rational being, you could join me in setting aside your vain affection and pointless bitterness. I assure you—there will be less *pain*."

"And I assure *you,* Roger, I have done just that. Unfortunately, recent days having been so very busy, I've yet had a moment to set aside my virulent *scorn*."

"Celeste, I speak for your good, not mine—truly, it is a generosity—"

"A *generosity*?"

"I do not expect you to see it," he muttered.

"Of course not! I haven't had my mind re-made by a *machine*!"

Roger stared at her in silence and then slowly stood, straightening his coat and, by habit, smoothing back his hair with two fingers, and even then in her heart she found him to be quite lovely. Yet his gaze, quite fixed upon her, conveyed a quality she had never seen in him before—undisguised contempt. He was not angry—indeed, what hurt her most was the exact lack of emotion behind his eyes. It truly made no sense to her—in Miss Temple's body, in her memory, all such moments were rooted in some sort of *feeling,* and Roger Bascombe stood revealed to her as no kind of man she had ever met.

"You will see," he said, his voice cool and low. "The Process will remake you to the ground, and you will see—for the very first time in your life, I am sure—the true nature of your shuttered mind. The Contessa suggests you possess reserves of character I have not seen—to which I can only agree that I have *not* seen them. You were always a pretty enough girl—but there are many such. I look forward to finding—once you've been burned to your bones and then *re-made* by the very 'machine' you cannot comprehend—if any actually remarkable parts exist."

He left the compartment. Miss Temple did not move, her mind ringing with his biting words and a thousand unspoken retorts, her face hot and both of her hands balled tight into fists. She looked out the window and saw her reflection on the glass, thrown up between her and the darkened landscape of salty grassland racing past outside the train. It occurred to her that this dim, transparent, second-hand image was the perfect illustration for her own condition—in the power of others, with her own wishes only peripherally related to her fate, insubstantial and half-present. She let out a trembling sigh. How—after *everything*—could Roger Bascombe still exert any sway over her feelings? How could he make her feel so *desperately* unhappy? Her agitation was not coherent—there was no point from which she could begin to untangle answers—and her heart beat faster and faster until she was forced to sit with a hand over each eye, breathing deeply. Miss Temple looked up. The train was slowing. She pressed her face to the window, blocking the light from the passageway with her hand, and saw through the reflection the station, platform, and white painted sign for Orange Locks. She turned to find Major Blach opening the door for her, his hand inviting her to exit.

Beyond the platform were two waiting coaches, each drawn by a team of four horses. To the first, his fiancée on his arm, went the

Prince, followed as before by his Envoy and the older man with the bandaged arm. The Major escorted Miss Temple to the second coach, opened the door, and assisted her climb into it. He nodded crisply to her and stepped away—undoubtedly to rejoin the Prince—to be replaced by the Comte d'Orkancz, who sat across from her, and then the Contessa, who stepped in to sit next to her opposite the Comte, then Francis Xonck, who sat next to the Comte with a smile, and finally, with no expression in particular on his face, Roger Bascombe, hesitating only an instant when he saw that, due to the size of the Comte and the room accorded Xonck's thickly wrapped arm, the only seat was on the other side of Miss Temple. He climbed into place without comment. Miss Temple was firmly lodged between the Contessa and Roger—their legs pressing closely against hers with a mocking familiarity. The driver shut the door and climbed to his perch. His whip snapped and they clattered on their way to Harschmort.

The ride began in silence, and after a time Miss Temple, who initially assumed this was because of her presence—an interloper spoiling their usual plots and scheming, began to wonder if this was wholly the case. They were wary enough not to say anything revealing, but she began to sense levels of competition and distrust... particularly with the addition of Francis Xonck to the party.

"When can we expect the Duke?" he asked.

"Before midnight, I am sure," replied the Comte.

"Have you spoken to him?"

"Crabbé has spoken to him," said the Contessa. "There is no reason for anyone else to do so. It would only confuse things."

"I know everyone got to the train—the various parties," added Roger. "The Colonel was collecting the Duke personally, and two of our men—"

"Ours?" asked the Comte.

"From the Ministry," clarified Roger.

"Ah."

"They rode ahead to meet him."

"How thoughtful," said the Contessa.

"What of your cousin Pamela?" asked Xonck. "And her disenfranchised brat?"

Roger did not reply. Francis Xonck chuckled wickedly.

"And the little *Princess*?" asked Xonck. *"La Nouvelle Marie?"*

"She will perform admirably," said the Contessa.

"Not that she has any idea of her part," Xonck scoffed. "What of the Prince?"

"Equally in hand," rasped the Comte. "What of his transport?"

"I am assured it sails to position tonight," answered Xonck. Miss Temple wondered why he of all people would be the one with information about ships. "The canal has been closed this last week, and has been prepared."

"And what of the mountains—the Doctor's scientific marvel?"

"Lorenz seems confident there is no problem," observed the Contessa. "Apparently it packs away most tidily."

"What of the . . . ah . . . Lord?" asked Roger.

No one answered at once, exchanging subtle glances.

"Mr. Crabbé was curious—" began Roger.

"The *Lord* is agreeable to everything," said the Contessa.

"What of the *adherents*?" asked the Contessa. "Blenheim sent word that they have arrived throughout the day discreetly," answered Roger, "along with a squadron of Dragoons."

"We do not need more soldiers—they are a mistake," said the Comte.

"I agree," said Xonck. "Yet Crabbé insists—and where government is concerned, we have agreed to follow him."

The Contessa spoke to Roger across Miss Temple. "Has he

any new information about . . . our departed brother-in-law of Dragoons?"

"He has not—that I know of. Of course we have not recently spoken—"

"Blach insists that it's settled," said Xonck.

"The Colonel was poisoned," snapped the Contessa. "It is not the method of the man the Major wishes to blame—aside from the fact that man assured his employer that he did *not* do it, when having done so would have meant cash in hand. Moreover, how would *he* have known when to find his victim in that vulnerable period after undergoing the Process? He would not. That information was known to a select—a *very* select—few." She nodded to Xonck's bandaged arm and scoffed. "Is *that* the work of an elegant schemer?"

Xonck did not respond.

After a pause, Roger Bascombe cleared his throat and wondered aloud mildly, "Perhaps the Major is overdue for the Process himself."

"Do you trust Lorenz to have everything aboard?" asked Xonck, to the Comte. "The deadline was severe—the large quantities—"

"Of course," the Comte replied gruffly.

"As you know," continued Xonck, "the invitations have been sent."

"With the wording we agreed upon?" asked the Contessa.

"Of course. Menacing enough to command attendance . . . but if we do not have the *leverage* from our harvest in the country—"

"I have no doubts." The Contessa chuckled. "If Elspeth Poole is with him, Doctor Lorenz will strive mightily."

"In exchange for her joining *him* in strenuous effort!" Xonck cackled. "I am sure the transaction appeals to his mathematical mind—sines and tangents and bisected spheres, don't you know."

* * *

"And what about our little magpie?" asked Xonck, leaning forward and cocking his head to look into Miss Temple's face. "Is she worthy of the Process? Is she worthy of a *book*? Something else entirely? Or perhaps she cannot be swayed?"

"Anyone can be swayed," said the Comte. Xonck paid no attention, reaching forward to flick one of Miss Temple's curls.

"Perhaps . . . something *else* will happen . . ." He turned to the Comte. "I've read the back of each painting, you know. I know what you're aiming at—what you were trying with your Asiatic whore." The Comte said nothing and Xonck laughed, taking the silence as an acknowledgment of his guess. "That is the trick of banding with clever folk, Monsieur le Comte—so many people are *not* clever, those who *are* sometimes grow into the habit of assuming no one else will ever divine their minds."

"That is enough," said the Contessa. "Celeste has done damage to *me,* and so—by all our agreements—she is indisputably *mine.*" She reached up and touched the tip of Miss Temple's bullet-scar with a finger. "I assure you . . . no one will be disappointed."

The coach clattered onto the cobblestone plaza in front of Harschmort House and Miss Temple heard the calls of the driver to his team, pulling them to a halt. The door was opened and she was handed down to a pair of black-liveried footmen, the cobbles cold and hard beneath her feet. Before Miss Temple had scarcely registered where she was—from the second coach she saw the Prince and his party descending, Miss Vandaariff's expression a shifting series of furtive smiles and frowns—the Comte's iron grasp directed her toward a knot of figures near the great front entrance. Without any ceremony—and without even a glance to see if the others were following—she was conveyed roughly along, doing her best to avoid a stubbed toe on the uneven stones, only coming to a stop when the Comte acknowledged the greetings of a man and woman stepping out from the larger group (a mixture of servants, black-uniformed soldiers of Macklenburg, and red-coated

Dragoons). The man was tall and broad, with grizzled and distressingly thick side whiskers and a balding pate that caught the torchlight and made his entire face seem like a primitive mask. He bowed formally to the Comte. The woman wore a simple dark dress that was nevertheless quite flattering, and her affable face bore the recognizable scars around her eyes. Her hair was brown and plainly curled and gathered behind her head with black ribbon. She nodded at Miss Temple and then smiled up at the Comte.

"Welcome back to Harschmort, Monsieur," she said. "Lord Vandaariff is in his study."

The Comte nodded and turned to the man. "Blenheim?"

"Everything as ordered, Monsieur."

"Attend to the Prince. Mrs. Stearne, please escort Miss Vandaariff to her rooms. Miss Temple here will join you. The Contessa will collect both ladies when it is time."

The man nodded sharply and the woman bobbed into a curtsey. The Comte drew Miss Temple forward and shoved her in the direction of the door. She looked behind her to see the woman—Mrs. Stearne—dipping again before the Contessa and Miss Vandaariff, rising to kiss each of the younger woman's cheeks and then take her hand. The Comte released Miss Temple from his grip—his attention turned to the words passing between Xonck, Blach, and Blenheim—as Mrs. Stearne took up her hand, Lydia Vandaariff stepping into place on the woman's other side. The three of them walked—with four liveried footmen falling in place behind them—into the house.

Miss Temple glanced once at Mrs. Stearne, sure that she had finally located the fourth woman from her first coach ride to Harschmort. This was the pirate, who had undergone the Process in the medical theatre, screaming before the audience dressed in their finery. Mrs. Stearne caught her look and smiled, squeezing Miss Temple's hand.

* * *

Lydia Vandaariff's rooms overlooked a massive formal garden in the rear of the house, what Miss Temple assumed was once the prison's parade ground. The entire idea of living in such a place struck her as morbid, if not ridiculously affected, all the more when the rooms one lived in were so covered in lace as to seem one great over-flounced pillow. Lydia immediately retreated to an inner closet with two of her maids to change clothes, muttering at them crossly and tossing her head. Miss Temple was installed on a wide lace-fringed settee. This had served to expose her filthy feet, prompting Mrs. Stearne to call for another maid with a basin and a cloth. The girl knelt and washed Miss Temple's feet carefully one at a time, drying them on a soft towel. Throughout, Miss Temple remained silent, her thoughts still a-swim at her situation, her heart alternating between anger and despondence. She had committed their path from the front door to Lydia's apartments to memory as best she could, but with only the barest hope of escape for that way was lined with servants and soldiers, as if the entire mansion had become an armed camp. Miss Temple could not but notice that nowhere around her was a single thing—a nail file, a crystal dish for sweets, a letter opener, a candlestick—she might have snatched up for a weapon.

When the girl had finished, collecting her things and nodding first to Miss Temple and then Mrs. Stearne before backing from the room, the two remained for a moment in silence—or near silence, the hectoring comments of Miss Vandaariff to her maids reaching them despite the distance and closed doors.

"You were in the coach," Miss Temple said at last. "The pirate."

"I was."

"I did not know your name. I have since met Mrs. Marchmoor, and heard others speak of Miss Poole—"

"You must call me Caroline," said Mrs. Stearne. "Stearne is my husband's name—my husband is dead and not missed. Of course, I did not know your name either—I knew no one's name, though I think we each assumed the others were old hands.

Perhaps Mrs. Marchmoor was an old hand, but I am sure she was as frightened—and thrilled—as the rest of us."

"I doubt she would admit it," replied Miss Temple.

"So do I." Caroline smiled. "I still do not know how you came to be in our coach—it shows a boldness, to be sure. And what you must have done since . . . I can only guess how hard it was."

Miss Temple shrugged.

"Of course." Caroline nodded. "What choice did you have? Yet, to most people, your path would have been plagued with choice—while to you it seems inexorable—quite like my own. However much our characters may be fixed, they are only revealed to us one test at a time. And so we are here together after all, with perhaps more in common than any of us would care to admit—though only a fool does not admit the truth once it is plain to her."

The woman's dress was simpler than Mrs. Marchmoor's, less ostentatious—less like an actor's idea of how the wealthy dressed, she realized—and she was pained that her heart's impulse was to think of her captor kindly (this being rare enough in Miss Temple's life to be a surprise in itself, captor or no). No doubt the woman had been placed for that very purpose, for a natural sympathy that had somehow survived the Process or could at least be readily counterfeited, to worm Miss Temple's determination that much further from its sticking place.

"I watched you," she said accusingly, "in the theatre . . . you were . . . *shrieking*—"

"I'm sure I was," said Caroline. "And yet, perhaps it is most like having a troubling tooth pulled. The act itself is so distressing as to seem in no way justified . . . and yet, after it is done, the peace of mind . . . the ease of being—and I speak of a former life of no great difficulty, you understand, merely the fraying worries that are part of every day—I cannot now imagine being without this . . . well, it is a kind of bliss."

"Bliss?"

"Perhaps that sounds foolish to you."

"Not at all—I have seen Mrs. Marchmoor—her sort of—of—*spectacle*—and I have seen the book—one of your glass books—I have been inside, the sensation, the debauchery—perhaps 'bliss' *is* an applicable word," said Miss Temple, "though I assure you it is not my choice."

"You mustn't judge Mrs. Marchmoor harshly. She does what she must do for her larger purpose. As we all are guided. Even you, Miss Temple. If you have peered into these extraordinary books then you must know." She gestured toward Miss Vandaariff's dressing closet. "So many are so tender, hungry, so deeply in need. How much of what you read—or indeed, what you remember—was most singularly rooted in painful loneliness? If a person could rid themselves of such a source of anguish . . . can you truly find fault?"

"Anguish and loss are part of life," Miss Temple retorted.

"They are," Caroline agreed. "And yet . . . if they need not be?"

Miss Temple tossed her head and bit her lip. "You present kindness . . . where others . . . well, they are a nest of vipers. My companions have been killed. I am compelled here by force . . . I have been and will be *violated*—as surely as if your finely dressed mob were a gang of Cossacks!"

"I hope that is not the case, truly," said Caroline. "But if the Process has made anything clear to me, it is that what happens here is only the expression of what you yourself have decided—indeed, what you have asked for."

"I beg your pardon?"

"I do not say it to anger you." She held up a hand to forestall Miss Temple's announcement that she was *already* angry. "Do you think I cannot see the bruises on your pretty neck? Do you imagine I enjoy the sight? I am not a woman who dreams of power or fame, though I know there have been deaths—I do not presume to understand their cause—as a result of those dreams. I know there has been murder, around me and within this house. I know that I do *not* know what those above me plan. And yet I also know that these dreams—theirs and mine—bring with them . . . the opposite side of their coin, if you will—a bliss of purpose, of simplicity, and indeed . . . Celeste . . . of surrender."

Miss Temple sniffed sharply and swallowed, determined not to give way. She was not used to hearing her name so freely used and found it unnerving. The woman presented the Cabal's goals in terms of reason and care—indeed, she seemed a higher level of antagonist altogether for not seeming one at all. The room was unbearable—the lace and the perfumes—so many and so thick—were smothering.

"I would prefer it if you referred to me as Miss Temple," she said.

"Of course," said Caroline, with what seemed a gentle, sad sort of smile.

As if by some rotation of the gears of a clock, they no longer spoke, the room settling into silence and subsequently into contemplation. Yet Miss Temple could only think of the oppressive vacuity of the furnishings around her—though she had no doubt they were the heartfelt expression of Miss Vandaariff—and the low ceiling that, despite the luxurious cherry wood, still bespoke confinement. She looked at the walls and decided at least four prison cells had been opened up together for this room alone. Was it inevitable that *this* luxuriously impersonal lodging was her final refuge as a whole-minded person? As if her burdens had become at once too much to bear, Miss Temple's tears broke suddenly forward, quite dissolving her face, her small shoulders shaking with emotion, blinking, her pink cheeks heedlessly streaked, her lips quivering. So often in her life, tears were the consequence of some affront or denial, an expression of frustration and a sense of unfairness—when those with power (her father, her governess) might have acceded to her wishes but out of cruelty did not. Now Miss Temple felt that she wept for a world without any such authority at all . . . and the kind face of Caroline—however much she knew it to represent the interests of her captors—only reinforced how trivial and unanswered her complaints must remain, how insignificant her losses, and how fully removed from love, or if not love, primacy in another's thoughts, she had become.

She wiped her eyes and cursed her weakness. What had happened she had not already known in her heart to expect? What revelations had challenged her pragmatic, grim determination? Had she not hardened herself to this exact situation—and was not that hardness, that firmness of mind, her only source of hope? Still the tears would not cease, and she covered her face in her hands.

No one touched her, or spoke. She remained bent over—who knew how long?—until her sobbing eased, eyes squeezed shut. She was so frightened, in a way even more than in her deathly struggle with Spragg, for that had been sudden and violent and close and this... they had given her time—so much time—to steep in her dread, to roil in the prospect that her soul—or *something,* some fundamental element that made Miss Temple who she was—was about to be savagely, relentlessly changed. She had seen Caroline on the stage, limbs pulling against the leather restraints, heard her animal groans of uncomprehending agony. She recalled her own earlier resolve to jump from a window, or provoke some sudden mortal punishment, but when she looked up and saw Caroline waiting for her with a tender patience, she understood that no such rash gesture would be allowed. Standing next to Caroline were Miss Vandaariff and her maids. The young woman was dressed in two white silk robes, the outer—without sleeves—bordered at the collar and the hem with a line of embroidered green circles. Her feet were bare and she wore a small eye-mask of densely laid white feathers. Her hair had been painstakingly worked into rows of sausage curls to either side of her head and gathered behind—rather like Miss Temple's own. Miss Vandaariff smiled conspiratorially and then put a hand over her mouth to mask an outright giggle.

Caroline turned to the maids. "Miss Temple can change here."

The two maids stepped forward and for the first time Miss Temple saw another set of robes draped over their arms.

Caroline walked between them, black feathered mask across her eyes, holding hands with each, the three followed by another trio of black-coated Macklenburg troopers with echoing black boots. The marble floor of the corridor—the same great corridor of mirrors—was cold against Miss Temple's still bare feet. She'd been stripped to her own silk pants and bodice and, as before, given first the short transparent robe, then the longer robe without sleeves, and finally the white feathered mask—all the time aware of the eyes of Miss Vandaariff and Caroline frankly studying her.

"Green silk," said Lydia approvingly, as Miss Temple's undergarments were revealed.

Caroline's eyes met Miss Temple's with a smile. "I'm sure they must be specially made."

Miss Temple turned her head, feeling her desires—foolish and naïve—on display every bit as much as her body.

The maids had finished tying the string and then stepped away with a deferent bob. Caroline had dismissed them with a request to inform the Contessa that they awaited her word, and smiled at her two women in white.

"You are both so lovely," said Caroline.

"We are indeed." Miss Vandaariff smiled, and then shyly glanced at Miss Temple. "I believe our bosom is the same size, but because Celeste is shorter, hers looks larger. For a moment I was jealous—I wanted to *pinch* them!" She laughed and flexed her fingers wickedly at Miss Temple. "But then again, you know, I am quite happy to be as tall and slender as I am."

"I suppose you prefer Mrs. Marchmoor's bosom above all," said Miss Temple, her voice sounding just a bit raw, attempting to rally her caustic wit. Miss Vandaariff shook her head girlishly.

"No, I don't like her one jot," she said. "She is too coarse. I prefer people around me to be smaller and fine and elegant. Like

Caroline—who pours tea as sweetly as anyone I have ever met, and whose neck is pretty as a swan's."

Before Caroline could speak—a response that surely would have been an answering praise of Miss Vandaariff's features—they heard a discreet tap at the door. A maid opened it to reveal three soldiers. It was time to depart. Miss Temple tried to will herself to run at the window and hurl herself through. But she could not move—and then Caroline was taking her hand.

They were not half-way down the mirrored corridor when behind them erupted a clatter of bootsteps. Miss Temple saw the whiskered man, Blenheim, whom she took to be Lord Vandaariff's chamberlain, racing toward them with a group of red-coated Dragoons in his wake. He carried a carbine, and all of the Dragoons held their saber-sheaths so they would not bounce as they ran.

In a moment his group had passed them by, running ahead to one of the doors on the far right side . . . a room—she had tried to maintain Harschmort's geography in her head as they walked—that bordered the exterior of the house. Caroline pulled on her hand, walking more quickly. Miss Temple could see that they were nearing the very door she had gone through with the Contessa, where she had previously found her robes, the room that led to the medical theatre . . . it seemed a memory from another lifetime. They kept walking. They had reached it—should she try to run?—Caroline did not release her hand but nodded to one of the soldiers to get the door. Just then the door ahead of them—where Blenheim's party had gone—burst open, spewing a cloud of black smoke.

A Dragoon with a soot-smeared face shouted to them, "Water! Water!"

One of the Macklenburg men turned at once and ran back down the hall. The Dragoon disappeared back through the open door, and Miss Temple wondered if she dared dash toward it, but again before she could move, her hand was squeezed by Caroline and she was pulled along. One of the remaining Macklenburg troopers opened the door to the inner room and the other anxiously shepherded them inside away from the smoke. As the door shut behind them Miss Temple was sure she heard an escalation of shouts and the echoing clamor of more bootsteps in the marble hall.

It was once more silent. Caroline nodded to the first soldier and he crossed to the far door, the one cunningly set into the wall, and vanished through it. The remaining man installed himself at the hallway entrance, hands behind his back, and his back square against the door. Caroline looked around, to make certain all was well, and released her grip on their hands.

"There is no need to worry," she said. "We will merely wait until the disturbance is settled."

But Miss Temple could see that Caroline *was* worried.

"What do you think has happened?" she asked.

"Nothing that Mr. Blenheim has not dealt with a thousand times before," Caroline replied.

"Is there really a *fire*?"

"Blenheim is horrid," said Lydia Vandaariff, to no one in particular. "When I have my way he will be *sacked*."

Miss Temple's thoughts began to race. On the far side of the theatre was another waiting room—perhaps that was where the soldier had been forced to go . . . she remembered that her own first visit had revealed the theatre to be empty. What if she were to run to the theatre now? If it was empty again might not she climb into the gallery and then to the spiral staircase, and from there—she knew!—she could retrace the path of Spragg and Farquhar across the grounds and through the servants' passage back to the coaches. And it was only running on floors and carpets and the grassy garden—she could do it with bare feet! All she needed was a momentary distraction. . . .

Miss Temple manufactured a gasp of shock and whispered urgently to Miss Vandaariff. "Lydia! Goodness—do you not see you are most lewdly exposed!"

Immediately Lydia looked down at her robes and plucked at them without finding any flaw, her voice rising in a disquieting whimper. Caroline's attention of course went the same way, as did the Macklenburg trooper's.

Miss Temple darted for the inner door, reaching it and turning the handle before anyone even noticed what she was doing. She had the door open and was already charging through before Caroline called out in surprise . . . and then Miss Temple cried out herself, for she ran headlong into the Comte d'Orkancz. He stood in heavy shadow, fully blocking the doorway with his massive frame, somehow even larger for the thick leather apron over his white shirt, the enormous leather gauntlets sheathing his arms up to each elbow, and the fearsome brass-bound helmet cradled under one arm, crossed with leather straps, great glass lenses like an insect's eyes and strange metal boxes welded over the mouth and ears. She flung herself away from him and back into the room.

The Comte glanced once, disapprovingly, at Caroline, and then down to Miss Temple.

"I have come myself to collect you," he said. "It is long past time you are redeemed."

TWO

Cathedral

Chang made a conscious effort to bend his knees—knowing that a rigid leg could easily mean a shattered joint—and did so just as he collided hard with a curving, hot wall of filthy, slippery metal. The actual time in the air, undoubtedly brief, was enough to allow a momentary awareness of suspension, a rising in his stomach which, due to the total darkness in the shaft, was exceptionally disorienting. His mind made sense of the fall—he'd struck a curve in the pipe, after a drop of perhaps ten or fifteen feet—as his body crumpled and rolled, losing all pretense of balance or control, and then dropped again as the pipe straightened into vertical once more. This time he slammed down even harder, knocking the breath from his lungs on a welded corner—he'd struck a gap where his pipe was joined by another, his upper body striking the seam and his legs continuing past, dragging him downwards. He scrabbled for a grip, couldn't get one on the slick metal—covered with the same slimy deposit caked onto the lattice in the urn—and slid down into the darkness, just keeping hold of his stick as it clattered from under his coat. But the impact had slowed his descent, and he was no longer falling but sliding—this pipe was set at an angle. The air rising up to Chang was more noxious and becoming hotter—it seemed grimly probable that this path would feed him into their furnace. He pressed his legs and his arms to the side of the pipe, grudgingly but surely slowing his descent. By the time he slammed into the next junction he was able to catch hold of the lip and stop himself completely, legs swinging below him in the dark. He pulled himself up with an effort and wedged his torso into the opening, so he was nearly balanced and could relax his arms. Chang caught his breath, wondering how far down he had come, and what in the utter world he had been thinking.

He shut his eyes—he couldn't see anything anyway—and forced himself to focus on what he could hear. From the pipe below came a steady, metallic rattle, in time with regularly spaced gusts of steaming, chemically fouled air. He leaned into the second, joining pipe, which was not as large—large enough to hold him?—and cooler to the touch. He waited, allowing time for a longer cycle, but heard no such rattle from its depths nor felt any such toxic exhalations. He realized absently that his head hurt. The first tendrils of bilious nausea were rising in his stomach. He had to get out. He wrenched himself around in the narrow space and slipped his feet into the narrower pipe. There was just room to fit, and Chang pushed from his mind the prospect of the pipe getting thinner mid-way down—he did not want to think about trying to claw his way back against the slippery interior. He tucked his stick under his coat and pinned it with his left arm, and eased himself down as slowly as he could, pressing his legs against the side of the shaft. There was less of the greasy accretion and Chang found that he could more or less manage his descent, for the pipe went down at a milder angle. The farther he sank from the main shaft, the clearer became the air, and the less he worried about being dropped into a cauldron of molten glass. The pipe continued for some distance—he stopped even trying to guess—and then flattened out, blessedly without narrowing, so that he was on his back (and doing his best to keep his mind from tales of coffins and live burial). The pipe still curved, but now horizontally . . . as if, he thought with a smile, it traveled around the floor of a circular room. He inched along feet first—unable to turn—trying to make as little noise as he could, though he was forced to stop once, preventing by sheer force of will the voiding of his stomach—jaw clenched against the rising bile, huffing like a wounded horse through his scarred nasal passages. He pushed himself on until, so suddenly it took his fogged mind a moment to make sense of what he was seeing—that he was seeing anything at all—the blackness above him was punctuated by a chink of light. He reached up to it carefully and felt the underside of a metal clasp, and then by delicately searching around it sketched out the borders and sweetly welcome hinges of some sort of panel.

Chang turned the clasp to the side, slipping the bolt clear, and then brought both hands beneath the panel and slowly pushed. The hinges gave way with a rusted groan. He stopped, listened, and forced himself to listen more, another whole agonizing minute. A dim light poured into the shaft and he could see with disgust how rusted and filthy it was. He pushed again, and with a longer squeal of protest the panel swung clear. Chang gasped at the cleaner air and sat up. Only his head and the tip of one shoulder fit with ease through the gap. He was in some sort of brick-walled machine room—a secondary one, perhaps, thankfully not in use—with several similarly sized pipes coming through the walls from different directions, all converging at an enormous riveted metal boiler, clotted with dials and smaller hoses. He shifted back inside the pipe and extricated his right arm and once again his head and then, over the course of an awkward, desperate minute, he was able to force his left arm and torso through the gap, gouging his ribs and his shoulder in the process. Feeling like an insect emerging from its sticky cocoon—and just as feeble—Chang inched his way onto the floor and took in the room around him. It was really quite small. Hanging from a row of hooks was a collection of syringes and stoppered glass tubes, a pair of leather gloves and one of the infernal brass and leather helmets. Undoubtedly his escape hatch was employed to test whatever liquid or gaseous concoctions would be steeped in the iron cauldron. Next to the hooks was an inset sconce with the lower third of a fat, guttering tallow candle—the source of the dim light that had wormed through the latched panel. That it was alight told Chang that someone had been in the room recently . . . and would be coming back.

At that moment he did not care about them, the machine, or its purpose. Under the rack of pipes was a dirty leather fire bucket. Chang crawled to it and vomited without any effort at all until his stomach had nothing more to give and his throat was raw. He sat back and dug out a shirt-tail to wipe his mouth, then pulled it out farther to smear the filth of the furnace pipes from his face. Chang forced himself to his feet and looked at his red leather coat with bitter resignation. The pride of his wardrobe was most assuredly ruined. The coal dust could have been cleaned, but as he wiped at the caked chemical deposits he saw the red leather beneath had been discolored and blistered, almost as if the coat itself was burned and bleeding. He scooped away as much of the mess as he could with his fingers and then wiped his hands on his filthy pants, feeling as if he'd just swum through a demonic mire. He took a deep breath. He was still light-headed, pain pounding behind his eyes like a hammer—the kind of pain he knew, barring opium, he would be carrying with him for days. He expected that some sort of pursuit must even now be working its way to these depths of the house, if only to confirm that his bones were cracking and popping in a furnace, or he was choked to death in the pipes above it, stuck like a dead squirrel in a chimney. Chang felt the parch of his throat and the desperate dizziness in his head. He needed water. Without it he would die on the blade of the first Dragoon that found him.

The door was locked, but the lock was old and Chang was able to force it with his skeleton keys. It opened into a narrow, circular corridor of brick lit by a sputtering torch bolted into a metal bracket above the door. He could not see another torch in either direction. He quickly walked into darkness to his right. Just around the curve the way ended at a bricked-in wall whose mortar was noticeably fresher than the side walls or the ceiling. Chang walked back past the boiler room in the other direction, looking up at the oppressive ceiling and the circular path of his corridor. He was sure it corresponded to the side of the larger chamber. It was vital—to give himself some breathing room, and to find Miss Temple—that he find some way to climb.

The next torch was bracketed near an open doorway. Inside was a spiral staircase of stone with a bright iron rail on the inner wall. Chang looked up, but could only see a few yards ahead because of the curving stairs. He listened . . . there was a sound, a low roar, like the wind, or heavy distant rain. He began to climb.

It was twenty steps to another open doorway and another circular corridor. He poked out his head and saw its ceiling was banked as if it were the underside of a stadium. Chang stepped back into the stairwell and shut his eyes. His throat was burning. His chest felt as if it was being squeezed from within—he could just imagine the grains of glass boring into his heaving lungs. He forced himself into the hall, looking for some kind of relief, following the path back to where, on the floor below, his boiler room had been. There was another door in the exact spot, and he forced the lock just as easily. The room was dark. Chang worked the torch from its bracket and thrust it inside: another boiler with another set of metal pipes coming through the walls—perhaps this was the juncture where he'd been unable to hold his grip. His eye saw another leather fire bucket on the floor. He stepped to it and with relief saw that it held water—filthy, brackish, unwholesome, but he did not care. Chang dropped the torch, pulled off his glasses and splashed it onto his face. He rinsed the filthy taste from his mouth and spat, and then drank deeply, gasping, and drank again. He sat back, leaning against the pipe, and looped his glasses back into place. He hawked up another gob of who knew exactly what and let it fly into a dark corner of the room. It was not a night at the Boniface, but it would do.

Chang was back in the hallway, returning to the stairs. He wondered that no one had come down to search for him—either they were sure he was dead . . . or he'd fallen farther than he'd thought . . . or they were concentrating on the most important places he might have landed first . . . all of which made him smile, for it told him his enemies were confident, and that confidence was giving him time. But perhaps they were only making sure he didn't reach a particular room to interrupt some particular event—after which it would not matter if they hunted him down at their leisure. It was possible—and it could only mean Celeste. He was a fool. He ran for the stairway and charged up it two steps at a time. Another door. He stepped out—another narrow, dusty hallway with a banked ceiling—and listened. The dull roar was louder, but he was convinced that these were only service corridors, that he was still below the main access. Would he have to go to the absolute top before he could find a way inside? There had to be another way—the path above was sure to be swarming with soldiers. Chang sprinted down the corridor in each direction, first to the right, where his boiler had been—another door to an empty room whose boiler had either been removed or not yet installed—and another dead end. He turned and jogged to the left. The roar became louder, and when he reached its dead end—no door at all in this part of the corridor—he placed his hand on the brick, and felt a faint vibration in time with the rumbling sound.

He raced up another rotation of the circular stairs—how far *had* he fallen?—and this time came not to an open doorway but a locked metal door. He looked above him, saw no one, and again strained to hear any sort of useful sound. Were those voices? Music? He could not be sure—if so, it told him he was only a few of these levels below the main house itself. He turned his attention to the door. This must be the access he wanted. He nearly laughed out loud. Some idiot had left the key in the lock. Chang took the handle and turned it in the exact instant it was turned from the opposite side. Seizing the opportunity, he kicked at the door with all his strength, driving it into whoever stood on the other side, and charged through, whipping apart his stick. Staggering away from him with a puling cry, clutching his bandaged arm—which had taken the brunt of the door—was the aged Mr. Gray, Rosamonde's creature who had administered the Process to the unfortunate Mr. Flaüss. Chang slashed him across the face with the haft of the stick, spinning him to the floor, and glanced quickly to either side. Gray was alone. This hallway was wider, the ceiling still banked, but lit with gaslight sconces instead of torches, and Chang could see doors—or niches?—lining the inner walls. Before Gray could raise his head and bleat for help—which Chang could see he was about to do—he dropped onto the man's chest, pinning Gray's arms cruelly under his knees, and pressed the haft of his stick hard across his throat. With a venomous hiss that caught Gray's full attention, Chang laid the tip of his dagger on the old man's face, pointing directly at his left eye.

"Where is Miss Temple?" he whispered.

Gray opened his mouth to respond but nothing came out. Chang eased up his pressure on the fellow's windpipe.

"Try again," he hissed.

"I—I do not *know*!" pleaded Mr. Gray.

Chang doubled up his fist holding the dagger and slammed it into Mr. Gray's cheek, knocking his head brutally against the stone.

"Try again," he hissed. Gray began to weep. Chang raised his fist. Gray's eyes widened in desperate fear and his mouth began to move, groping for words.

"I—don't!—I don't—I have not seen her—she's to be taken to the theatre—or the chamber—elsewhere in the house! I do not know! I am only to prepare the works—the great works—"

Chang slammed his fist once more into Mr. Gray's head.

"Who is with her?" he hissed. "How many guards?"

"I cannot *tell* you!" Gray was weeping openly. "There are many Macklenburgers, Dragoons—she is with the Comte—with Miss Vandaariff—they will be processed together—"

"Processed?"

"Redeemed—"

"Redeemed?" Chang felt the natural pleasure of violence blooming directly into fury.

"You are too late! By now it will be started—to interrupt it will kill them both!" Mr. Gray looked up and saw his own reflection in the smoked black lenses over Cardinal Chang's eyes and wailed. "O—they all said you were!—why are you not *dead*?"

His eyes opened even wider, if that were possible, in shock, as Chang drove the dagger into Mr. Gray's heart, which he knew would be quicker and far less bloody than cutting the man's throat. In a matter of seconds Gray's body had relaxed and gone forever still. Chang rolled back onto his knees, still breathing hard, wiped the dagger on Gray's coat, and sheathed it. He spat again, felt the stab of pain in his lungs, and muttered darkly.

"How do you know I am not?"

He dragged the body back to the stairwell and down one full curve before propping it up and tipping it over, doing his best to send the unregretted Mr. Gray all the way to the bottom—wherever it had landed, it was at least out of sight to anyone coming to this door. He pocketed the key Gray had stupidly left in the lock and returned to the corridor, trying to guess what Gray had been doing. Chang sighed. There had been more information to glean from the man, but he was in a hurry, and itching, after being hunted and assailed, to strike some blow in answer. That it was against an aged, wounded man was to Cardinal Chang no matter at all. Every last one of these people was his enemy, and he would not scruple to excuse a single soul.

The niches in the inner wall were old cell doors—heavy metal monstrosities whose handles had been hacked off with a chisel and sealed shut with iron bolts driven into the brick. Chang laced his fingers in the small barred window and strained but could not shift it at all. He peered into the cell. The far wall of bars was draped with canvas. On the other side of the canvas, he knew, was the great chamber, but this was no way for him to reach it. He paced rapidly down the length of the curving hallway. Gray was another fool from the Institute, like Lorenz and the man he'd surprised making the book. As a reader of poetry, Chang believed that learning was dangerous and best suited for private contemplation, not something to put in the service of the highest bidder—as the Institute did, in thrall to the patronage of men with blind dreams of empire. Society was not bettered by such men of "vision"—though, if Chang was honest, was it bettered by anyone? He smiled wolfishly at the thought that it *was* better without the corrupted Mr. Gray, amused at the notion that he himself might be seen as an engine of civic progress.

At the end of the corridor was another door. Gray's key turned sharply in the lock and Chang peered into a room scarcely larger than a closet, with seven large pipes running vertically from the ceiling to disappear through the floor, each one set with an access panel similar to the one he'd emerged through downstairs. The room was stiflingly hot and reeking—even to him—with the acrid, chemical excrescence of indigo clay. To the side was another rack of pegs, dangling another collection of flasks, vials, and unsettlingly large syringes. The roar of the machines echoed in the tiny chamber as if he were near the humming pipes of a massive church organ. Chang noticed a narrow slice of light between two pipes, and then, looking closely, saw similar small gaps elsewhere in the wall they formed . . . and realized that this was literally true—the far wall of the closet *was* the pipes, and beyond them, its brilliant illumination shining through, lay the great chamber. Chang crouched and removed his glasses, pressing his face to the nearest chink of light he could find. The pipes were hot against his skin, and he could only see the smallest view, but what he saw was astonishing: an opposite wall, high as a cliff-face, thick with more pipes flowing the entire height of a gigantic, vaulted chamber, and then, just on the edge of his sight, what looked like the central tower, like the hub of a wheel, whose sheer face of riveted steel was dotted with tiny vents from which the interior of every cell in the old prison could have been viewed. Chang shifted to another gap on his hands and knees, searching for an angle that showed him more. From here he saw a different segment of the opposite wall. Between the banks of pipes lay a tier of exposed cells—actually several tiers—bars still in place, looking for all the world like viewing galleries in a theatre. He sat back and brushed himself off by habit, wincing at how smeared with filth he was. Whatever was going to happen in the chamber, it was designed to have an audience.

He was back in the spiral staircase, climbing quietly, both hands on his stick. The next and final door did not appear until double the usual number of stairs, and when it did, he was surprised to see it was wood, with a new brass doorknob and lock—consistent with the formal decor of Harschmort. Chang had ascended to the—probably lowest—level of the house proper. Gray had said they thought he was dead—but did that mean back at the Ministry or just now in the furnace pipes? Surely he had been recognized in the garden—did it matter? He was more than happy to play the role of avenging ghost. He opened the door a narrow crack and peered, not into the hallway he expected, but a small dark room, blocked by a drawn curtain, under which he saw flickers of light—flickers matching audible footfalls on the curtain's other side. Chang eased through the doorway and crept close to the curtain. He delicately pinched the fabric between two fingers, making a gap just wide enough to peek through.

The curtain merely masked an alcove in a large storeroom, the walls lined with shelves and the bulk of the open floor taken up with freestanding racks stuffed full of bottles and jars and tins and boxes. While he watched, two porters shifted a wooden crate of clinking brown bottles onto a wheeled cart and pushed it from sight, pausing to make conversation with someone Chang couldn't see. After they left, the room was silent . . . save for bootsteps and a metallic knocking Chang had heard too many times before—the jostling of a saber scabbard as a bored guard paced back and forth. But the guard was hidden on the opposite side of the racks. To reach him Chang would have to leave the curtained alcove and only then decide on his angle of attack—while exposed.

Before he could begin he heard approaching steps and a harsh commanding voice he recognized from the garden.

"Where is Mr. Gray?"

"He hasn't returned, Mr. Blenheim," answered the guard—by his accent not one of the Macklenburgers.

"What was he doing?"

"Don't know, Sir. Mr. Gray went downstairs—"

"Damn him to hell! Does he not know the time? The schedule?"

Chang braced himself—they were certain to search. Without the covering noise of the servants there was no way to slip back through the door without them hearing. Perhaps it was better. Mr. Blenheim would pull the curtain aside and Chang would kill him. The guard might sound the alarm before he fell as well—or the guard might kill Chang—either way it was an additional helping of revenge.

But Blenheim did not move.

"Never mind," he snapped irritably. "Mr. Gray can hang himself. Follow me."

Chang listened to their bootsteps march away. Where had they gone—what was so important?

Chang chewed on a handful of bread torn from an expensive fresh white loaf purloined from the storeroom as he walked, recognizing nothing around him from his previous travels through the back passages of Harschmort House. This was a lower story, finely appointed but not opulent. The pipes could have landed him at any point of the house's horseshoe arc. He needed to work his way to the middle—there he would find the entrance to the panopticon tower, to the great chamber—and do it quickly. He could not remember when he'd eaten such delicious bread—he should have stuffed another loaf in his pocket. This caused Chang to glance down at his pocket, where he felt the knocking weight of Miss Temple's green ankle boot. Was he a sentimental fool?

Chang stopped walking. Where *was* he? The truth of his situation penetrated his thoughts as abruptly as a blade: he was in

Robert Vandaariff's mansion, the very heart of wealth and privilege, of a society from which he lived in mutually contemptuous exile. He thought of the very bread he was eating, his very enjoyment of it feeling like a betrayal, a spike of hatred rising at the endless luxury around him, a pervasive ease of life that met him no matter where he turned. In Harschmort House Cardinal Chang suddenly saw himself as he must be seen by its inhabitants, a sort of rabid dog somehow slipped through the door, already doomed. And why had he come? To rescue an unthinking girl from this very same world of wealth? To slaughter as many of his enemies as he could reach? To avenge the death of Angelique? How could any of this scratch the surface of this world, of this inhuman labyrinth? He felt he was dying, and that his death would be as invisible as his life. For a moment Chang shut his eyes, his rage hollowed out by despair. He opened them with a sharp, slicing intake of breath. Despair made their victory easier still. He resumed his pace and took another large bite of bread, wishing he'd found something to drink as well. Chang snorted; that was exactly how he needed to collide with Blenheim, or with Major Blach, or with Francis Xonck—with a bottle of beer in one hand and a wad of food in the other. He stuffed the last of the loaf into his mouth and pulled apart his stick.

As he went he dodged two small parties of Dragoons and one of the black-coated Germans. They all traveled in the same direction and he altered his course to follow them—assuming that whatever event had called Blenheim was calling them as well. But why was no one searching for him? And why did no one look for Mr. Gray? Gray had been doing something with the chemical works, the content of the pipes . . . and none of the soldiers seemed to care. Was Gray doing something for Rosamonde that none of the others knew about—some secret work? Could that mean division within the Cabal? This didn't surprise him—he would have been surprised by its absence—but it explained why no one had come. It also meant that Chang had, without intending it, spoiled Rosamonde's scheme. She would only know that Gray had not returned, but never why, and—he smiled to imagine it—be consumed with doubt and worry. For what if it was the Comte or Xonck who had interrupted her man, men who would know in a moment how she planned to betray them? He smiled to imagine that lady's discomfort.

Chang shifted his thoughts to the great chamber, recalling the tier of cells, where prisoners—or spectators—could see the goings-on below which must, he assumed, be where he would find Celeste. He estimated how far he'd climbed—*that* row of cells might be on this level . . . but how to find it? The curtained alcove had so casually hidden the entrance to the spiral staircase . . . the door to these cells might be hidden in the same offhand manner. Had he already passed it by? He trotted down the hallway, opening every interior-facing door and peering into blind corners, finding nothing and feeling very quickly as if he was wasting time. Shouldn't he follow the soldiers and Blenheim—wouldn't they be guarding the Comte and his ceremony? Couldn't Celeste be with them just as easily? He'd give his search another minute and then run after them. That minute passed, and then five more and still Chang could not pull himself from what he felt was the right path, rushing on through room after room. This entire level of the house seemed deserted. He unheedingly spat on the pale, polished wooden floor and winced at the gob's scarlet color, then turned yet another out-of-the-way corner. Where was he? He looked up.

He sighed. He was an idiot.

Chang was in a sort of workroom, set with many tables and benches, racks of wood, shelves stuffed with jars and bottles, a large mortar and pestle, brushes, buckets, large tables whose surfaces were scarred with burns, candles and lanterns and several large free-standing mirrors—to reflect light?—and everywhere stretched canvases of different dimensions. He was in an artist's studio. He was in the studio of Oskar Veilandt.

There was no mistaking the paintings' author, for they bore the same striking brushwork, lurid colors, and disquieting compositions. Chang walked into the room with the same trepidation as if he were entering a tomb . . . Oskar Veilandt was dead . . . were these his works—more that had been salvaged from Paris? Had Robert Vandaariff made it his business to gather the man's entire *oeuvre*? For all the brushes and bottles, none of the paintings seemed obviously in mid-composition—as if the artist was alive and working. Was someone else restoring or cleaning the canvases to Vandaariff's specifications? On impulse Chang stepped to a small portrait leaning against one of the tables—of a masked woman wearing an iron collar and a glittering crown—and turned it over. The back of the canvas was scrawled, just as Svenson had described, with alchemical symbols and what seemed like mathematical formulae. He tried to locate a signature or a date, but could not. He set the painting down and saw, across the room, a large painting, not leaning but hanging in place, its lowest edge flush with the floor—a life-size portrait of none other than Robert Vandaariff. The great man stood against a dark stone battlement, behind him a strange red mountain and behind that a bright blue sky (these compositional elements reminding Chang of nothing more than a series of flat, painted theatrical backdrops), holding in one hand a wrapped book and in the other a pair of large metal keys. When would it have been painted? Vandaariff had known Veilandt personally—which meant the Lord's involvement went back at least to Veilandt's death.

But standing in the midst of so many of the man's unsettling works, it was hard to believe he was dead at all, so insistent was the air of knowing, insinuating, exultant menace. Chang looked again at the portrait of Vandaariff, like an allegorical emblem of a Medici prince, and realized that it was hung lower than the paintings around it. He crossed and hefted the thing from its hook and set it none-too-gently aside. He shook his head at the obviousness of it. Behind the painting was another narrow alcove and three stone steps leading down to a door.

* * *

It opened inward, the hinges recently greased and silent. Chang entered another low curving hallway, light bleeding in through small chinks on the inner wall, like the interior of an old ship, or—more accurately—like the depths of a prison. The inner wall was lined with cells. Chang stepped to the nearest: here too the handles had been chiseled off and the doors bolted to their frames. He pulled aside the viewing slot and gasped.

The far wall of the cell, though blocked off with bars, revealed the entirety of the great chamber. Chang doubted he'd ever seen a place—so ambitiously a monument to its master's dark purpose—that so filled him with dread, an infernal cathedral of black stone and gleaming metal.

In the center of the room was the massive iron tower, running from the closed ceiling (the chamber's brilliant light came from massive chandeliers of dangling lanterns suspended on chains) all the way to a floor that was tangled and clotted with the bright pipes and cables that flowed down the walls to the base of the tower like a mechanical sea breaking at the foot of a strangely land-bound lighthouse. The slick surface of the tower was pock-marked with tiny spy holes. As a prisoner in the insect-hive of open cells, it would be impossible to know if anyone inside was watching or not. Chang knew that in such circumstances the incarcerated began to act, despite themselves, as if they *were* being watched at all times, steadily amending their behavior, their rebellious spirit inexorably crushed as if by an invisible hand. Chang snorted at the perfect ideological *aptness* of the monstrous structure to its current masters.

He could not see the base of the tower from his vantage point and was about to seek a better view when he heard a metallic clang and spied, in one of the cells opposite him, a flicker of movement . . . legs . . . a man was descending into the cell by way of a ladder. Abruptly he heard another clang much nearer, to his right. Before he could see where it exactly was he heard a third directly above his head, from the very cell he peered into. A hatch in the ceiling had been heaved open and the legs of a man in a blue uniform slithered through, feeling for a metal ladder bolted to the wall that Chang hadn't noticed. All sorts of men and women were climbing into the cells across the chamber, usually a man first who then assisted the ladies, sometimes being handed folding camp chairs, setting up the prison cells as if they were private boxes at the theatre. The air around Chang began to buzz with the excited anticipation of an audience before an unrisen curtain. The man in the blue uniform—a sailor of some sort—called merrily up through the hatch for the next person. Whatever was about to start, Chang wasn't going to do anything about it where he was. However much he'd just discovered, he'd made the wrong decision as far as locating Celeste. Whatever the Comte had arranged for all of the people to watch, Chang was sure she would be part of it—for all he knew she could be descending the central tower that very minute.

As he ran his lungs met each breath with a crest of small sharp pains. Chang spat—more blood this time—and again cursed his stupidity for not killing the Contessa outright when he had the chance. He drove himself forward—looking for a staircase, some way up to the main level, it had to be near—and saw it at the same time as he heard the sound of steps descending straight toward him. He could not get away quickly enough. He pulled apart his stick and waited, breathing deeply, lips flecked with red.

He did not really know whom he expected to see, but it was definitely not Captain Smythe. The officer saw Chang and stopped dead on the stairs. He glanced once above him and then stepped quickly forward.

"Good Lord," he whispered.

"What's happening?" hissed Chang. "Something's happening upstairs—"

"They think you are dead—*I* thought you were dead—but no one could find a body. I took it upon myself to make sure."

Smythe drew his saber and strode forward from the stairs, the blade floating easily in his hand.

Chang called to him. "Captain—the great chamber—"

"I trusted you like a fool and you've killed my man," Smythe snarled, "the very man who saved your treacherous life!"

He lunged forward and Chang leapt away, stumbling into the corridor wall. The Captain slashed at his head—Chang just ducking down and rolling free. The blade bit into the plaster with a pale puff of dust.

Smythe readied his blade for another lunge. In answer—there was no way he could possibly fight him with any hope of survival—Chang stood tall and stepped into the center of the corridor, snapping his arms open wide, cruciform, in open invitation for Smythe to run him through. He hissed at Smythe with fury and frustration.

"If you think that is so—do what you will! But I tell you I did not kill Reeves!"

Smythe paused, the tip of his blade a pace or so from Chang's chest, but within easy range.

"Ask your own damned men! They were there!" snapped Chang. "He was shot with a carbine—he was shot by—by—what's his name—the overseer—*Blenheim*—the chamberlain! Don't be a bloody idiot!"

Captain Smythe was silent. Chang watched him closely. They were close enough that he might conceivably deflect the saber with his stick and get to the Captain with the dagger. If the man persisted in being stupid, there was nothing else for it.

"That was not what I was told..." said Smythe, speaking very slowly. "You used him as a shield."

"And who told you that? Blenheim?"

The Captain was silent, still glaring. Chang scoffed.

"We were speaking—Reeves and I. Blenheim saw us. Did you even look at the body? Reeves was shot in the *back*."

The words landed like a blow, and Chang could see Smythe thinking, restraining his anger by force of will, his thoughts at odds. After another moment the Captain lowered his sword.

"I will go examine the body myself." He looked back at the

stairs and then again to Chang, his expression changing, as if he were seeing him freshly without the intervening veil of rage.

"You're injured," said Smythe, fishing out a handkerchief and tossing it to Chang. Chang snatched it from the air and wiped his mouth and face, seeing the dire nature of his wounds reflected in the officer's concern. Once again the notion that he was truly dying pressed at his resolve to keep on—what was the point, what had ever been the point? He looked at Smythe, a good man, no doubt, bitter himself, but bolstered by his uniform, his admiring men—who knew, a wife and children. Chang wanted to suddenly snarl that he desired none of those things, loathed the very idea of such a prison, loathed the kindness of Smythe himself. Just as he loathed himself for loving Angelique or having come to care for Celeste? He looked quickly away from the Captain's troubled gaze and saw everywhere around him the luxurious, mocking fittings of Harschmort. He was going to die at Harschmort.

"I am, but nothing can be done. I am sorry about Reeves—but you must listen. A woman has been taken—the woman I spoke of, Celeste Temple. They are about to *do* something to her—an infernal ceremony, I have seen it—it is beyond deadly—I assure you she would rather die."

Smythe nodded, but Chang could see that the man was still goggling at his appearance.

"I look worse than I am—I have come through the pipes—the smell cannot be helped," he said. He offered the handkerchief back, saw Smythe's reaction, and then wadded it into his own pocket. "For the last time, I beg you, what is happening above?"

Smythe glanced once up the stairs as if someone might have followed and then spoke quickly. "I'm afraid I barely know—I have just now come in the house. We were outside, for the Colonel's arrival—"

"Aspiche?"

"Yes—it is quite a disaster—they arrived from the country, some sort of accident, the Duke of Stäelmaere—"

"But people are entering the great chamber to watch the ceremony!" said Chang. "There is no time—"

"I cannot speak to that—there are parties of people everywhere and the house is very large," answered the officer. "All of my men are occupied with the Duke's party—after they landed—"

"Landed?"

"I cannot begin to explain. But the whole household has been turned over—"

"Then maybe there's still hope!" said Chang.

"For what?" asked Smythe.

"All I need is to get upstairs and be pointed in the right direction."

He could see that Smythe was torn between helping him and confirming his story. He suspected that the presence of Aspiche had done as much as anything to spur the officer toward mutiny.

"Our transfer to the Palace..." began Smythe quietly as if this were an answer to Chang's request, "was accompanied by a significant rise in pay for all officers... life-saving for men who had spent years abroad and were swimming in debt... it should be no surprise when a reward—the money being now spent—turns out instead to be... an entrapment."

"Go to Reeves," Chang said quietly, "and talk to your men who were there. They will follow you. Wait and stay ready... when the time comes, believe me, you will know what to do."

Smythe looked at him without any confidence whatsoever. Chang laughed—the dry croak of a crow—and clapped the man on the shoulder.

"The house is confusing at first," Smythe whispered to him as they climbed the stairs and crept into the main-floor hallway. "The left wing is dominated by a large ballroom—now quite full of people—and the right by a large hallway of mirrors that leads to private rooms and apartments—again, now quite full of people. Also in the right wing is an inner corridor that takes one to a spiral staircase—I have not climbed it. When I saw it the corridor was lined with Macklenburg guards."

"And the center of the house?" asked Chang.

"The great reception hall, the kitchens, the laundry, staff quarters, the house manager—that's Blenheim—and his men."

"Where is Lord Vandaariff's study?" asked Chang suddenly, his mind working. "At the rear of the house?"

"It is"—Smythe nodded—"and on the main floor. I have not been there. The whole left wing has been restricted to special guests and a very few trusted staff. No Dragoons."

"Speaking of that," said Chang, "what are you doing here? When did you come from the Ministry?"

Smythe smiled bitterly. "The story will amuse you. As my men were relieved from their posts, I received urgent word—from my Colonel I assumed—that we were needed at the St. Royale Hotel. Upon hurrying there—though domestic quarrels are not our usual duty—I was met by an especially presumptuous woman, who *informed* me that I must accompany her at once to this house by train."

"Mrs. Marchmoor, of course."

Smythe nodded. "Apparently she had been agitated by a certain fellow in red—an absolute villain, I understand."

"I believe we took the same train—I was hiding in the coal wagon."

"The possibility occurred to me," said Smythe, "but I could not send a man forward without sending him on the roof—we were forbidden to pass through the iron-bound black railcar."

"What was in it?" asked Chang.

"I cannot say—Mrs. Marchmoor had the key and went in alone. Upon our arrival at Orange Locks we were met by Mr. Blenheim, with carts and a coach. He went into the black car with his men, under Mrs. Marchmoor's eye, and they brought out—"

"What was it?" hissed Chang, suddenly impatient to know, yet fearing to hear the words.

"Again, I cannot say—it was covered with canvas. It could have been another of their boxes, or it could have been a coffin. But as they were loading it I distinctly heard Blenheim order the driver to go slow—so as not to break the *glass*—"

They were interrupted by the sound of approaching bootsteps. Chang pressed himself flat against the wall. Smythe stepped forward and the hallway rang with the unmistakable and imperious voice of Mr. Blenheim.

"Captain! What are you doing apart from your men? What business, Sir, can you have in this portion of the house?"

Chang could no longer see Smythe but heard the tightening of his voice.

"I was sent to look for Mr. Gray," he answered.

"Sent?" snapped Blenheim with open skepticism. "By whom *sent*?"

The man's arrogance was appalling. If Chang were in Smythe's place, knowing the overseer had just murdered one of his men, Blenheim's head would already be rolling on the floor.

"By the Contessa, Mr. Blenheim. Would you care to so interrogate *her*?"

Blenheim ignored this. "Well? And did you *find* Mr. Gray?"

"I did not."

"Then why are you still here?"

"As you can see yourself, I am *leaving*. I understand that you've moved my trooper's body to the stables."

"Of course I have—the last thing the master's guests want to see is a corpse."

"Indeed. Yet I, as his officer, must attend to his effects."

Blenheim snorted with disdain at such petty business. "Then you will *oblige* me by vacating this part of the house, and assuring me that neither you nor your men will return. By the wish of Lord Vandaariff himself, it is for his guests alone."

"Of course. It is Lord Vandaariff's house."

"And I manage that house, Captain," said Blenheim. "If you will come with me."

Chang struck out as best he could for the Lord of the manor's study. His look at the prison plans had not been so detailed as he might like, but it made sense that the warden might have personal access to the central viewing tower. Had Vandaariff simply adopted—and no doubt expanded and layered with mahogany and marble—the previous despot's lair for his own? If Chang's guess was right, Vandaariff's study could then get him to Celeste. It was the thought he kept returning to in his mind, her rescue. He knew there were other tasks—to revenge Angelique, to find the truth about Oskar Veilandt, to discover what falling-out between his enemies had led to Trapping's death—and normally he would have relished the idea of juggling them all together, to carry their evolving solutions in his head as he carried the sifted contents of the Library. But tonight there was no time, no room to fail, no second chances.

He could not risk being seen by anyone, and so was reduced to painful dashes across open corridors, creeping to corners, and scuttling back into cover when guests or servants happened by. With a scoff Chang thought of how nearly everyone in the pyramid of Harschmort's inhabitants was some sort of servant—by occupation, by marriage, by money, by fear, by desire. He thought of Svenson's servitude to duty—duty to *what,* Chang could not understand—and his own doomed notions of obligation and, even if he disdained the word, honor. Now he wanted to spit on them all, just as he was spitting blood on these white marble floors. And what of Celeste—had she been a servant to Bascombe? Her family? Her wealth? Chang realized he did not know. For a moment he saw her, wrestling to reload his pistol at the Boniface . . . a remarkable little beast. He wondered if she had shot someone after all.

* * *

The guests, he saw, were once again masked and in formal dress, and their snatches of conversation all carried a buzzing current of anticipation and mystery.

"Do you know—it is said they will be married—tonight!"

"The man in the cape—with the red lining—it is Lord Carfax, back from the Baltic!"

"Did you notice the servants with the iron-bound chests?"

"They will give us a signal to come forward—I had it myself from Elspeth Poole!"

"I'm sure of it—a shocking vigor—"

"Such dreams—and afterwards such peace of mind—"

"They will come like trusting puppies—"

"Did you see it? In the air? Such a machine!"

"Fades in a matter of days—I have it on the highest authority—"

"I have heard it from one who has been before—a particular *disclosure*—"

"No one has seen him—Henry Xonck himself was refused!"

"I've never heard such screaming—nor right after, witnessed such ecstasy—"

"Such an unsurpassed collection of *quality*!"

"Spoken in front of everyone, 'is not history best written with a whip mark?' The Lady is superb!"

"No one has spoken to him for days—apparently he will reveal all tonight, his secret plans—"

"He's going to speak! The Comte as much as promised it—"

"And then . . . the work will be revealed!"

"Indeed . . . the work will be revealed!"

This last was from a pair of thin rakish men in tailcoats and masks of black satin. Chang had penetrated well into the maze of private apartments and presently stood behind a marble pillar upon which was balanced an ancient and delicate amphora of malachite and gold. The chuckling men walked past—he was in a middling-sized sitting room—toward a sideboard laid with bottles and glasses. The men poured themselves whiskies and sipped them happily, leaning against the furniture and smiling at one another, for all the world like children waiting for permission to unwrap birthday presents.

One of them frowned. He wrinkled his nose.

"What is it?" asked the other.

"That smell," said the first.

"My goodness," agreed the other, sniffing too. "What could it be?"

"I've no idea."

"It's really quite horrid..."

Chang shrank as best he could behind the pillar. If they continued toward him he would have no choice but to attack them both. One of them would surely have a chance to scream. He would be found. The first man had taken an exploratory step in his direction. The other hissed at him.

"Wait!"

"What?"

"Do you think they might be *starting*?"

"I don't understand—"

"The smell! Do you think they're *starting*? The alchemical fires!"

"O my goodness! Is that what they smell like?"

"I don't know—do you?"

"I don't know! We could be late!"

"Hurry—hurry—"

Each tossed back his whisky and slammed down his glass. They rushed unheedingly past Chang, straightening their masks and smoothing their hair.

"What will they make us do?" asked one as they opened the door to leave.

"It does not matter," the other barked urgently, "you must do it!"

"I will!"

"We will be redeemed!" one called with a giddy chuckle as the door closed. "And then *nothing* shall stop us!"

Chang stepped from his spot. With a shake of his head, he wondered if their reaction would have been any different had he not traveled through the furnace pipes, but merely arrived at a Harschmort drawing room bearing the normal odors of his rooming house. *That* smell they would have recognized, he knew—it had been settled into their social understanding. The hideous smells of Harschmort and the Process carried the possibility of advancement, suspending all natural judgment. Similarly, he saw now the Cabal could be as blunt and open as it wished about its aims of power and domination. The beauty was that none of these aspirants—crowding together in their finery, as if they'd managed an invitation to court—saw themselves as people dominated, though their desperate fawning made it obvious that they were. The unreality of the evening—their *induction*—only served to flatter them more, thrilling themselves with the silks and the masks and scheming—enticing trappings that Chang saw were nothing but the distractions of a circus mountebank. Instead of looking up at the Contessa or the Comte with any suspicion, these people were turned gleefully the other way, looking at all the people—from within their new "wisdom"—they might now dominate in turn. He saw the brutal sense of it. Any plan that trusted for success on the human desire to exploit others and deny the truth about one's self was sure to succeed.

Chang cracked open the far doors and looked into the corridor Smythe had described, the whole of its length lined with doors. One of these doors had led him to Arthur Trapping's body. At one end he could see the spiral staircase. He was convinced that Vandaariff's study must lay in the other direction if it held a way down into the great chamber.

But where to start? Smythe had said the house was full of

guests—as he had said the hallway was full of guards . . . but for this moment it was unaccountably empty. Chang could not expect it to stay so while he tried each of what—at a quick glance—seemed to be at least thirty doors. All this time . . . was there any hope that Celeste was alive?

He stepped boldly into the hall, striding away from the staircase. He passed the first doors, one after another, with a rising sense of anticipation. If whatever had happened to Aspiche and the Duke (it was difficult for Chang to think of a more loathsome member of the Royal Family) had indeed served to disrupt the ceremony in the great chamber, then Chang was committed to causing as many additional disturbances as he could. He whipped apart his stick—still no one intruded—he was halfway down the hallway. Could everything have already started in spite of what Smythe had said? Chang stopped. To his left one of the doors was ajar. He crept to it and peered through the crack: a narrow slice of a room with red carpet and red wallpaper and a lacquered stand upon which balanced a Chinese urn. He listened . . . and heard the unmistakable sounds of rustling clothing and heavy breathing. He stepped back, kicked in the door with a crash, and charged forward.

Before him on the carpet was a Macklenburg trooper with his trousers around his knees, desperately trying to pull them up at the same time he hopelessly groped for his saber—the belt and scabbard tangled around his ankles. The man's mouth was opened in fearful protest and there was just time for Chang to register his expression shifting, from shame to incomprehension as he saw who had surprised him, before driving the dagger to the hilt into the trooper's throat, choking off any cry of alarm. He yanked the blade free, stepping clear like a bullfighter of the attending spray of blood, and let the man topple to the side, his pale buttocks uncovered by his dangling shirt-tails.

Was there anything that more signified the helplessness of humanity than the exposed genitals and buttocks of the dead? Chang did not think so. Perhaps a single discarded child's shoe . . . but that was mere sentiment.

Beyond the dead soldier, lying on the carpet with her dress above her waist was a richly clad woman, hair askew, her face aglow with perspiration around a green beaded mask. Her eyes were wild, blinking, and her breathing coarse and drawn . . . but the rest of her body seemed unresponsive, as if she were asleep. The man had clearly been about her rape, but Chang saw that her undergarments were yet only half-lowered—he had been surprised in the midst of his attack. Yet the woman's vacant expression suggested her utter unconcern. He stood for a moment over her, his gaze drawn both to her beauty and by the twitches and spasms that rippled across her frame, as if she lay in the midst of a distended fit. He wondered how long it had taken the soldier to advance from hearing her heavy breathing in the hall, through cautious entry and voyeuristic observation, to outright violation. Chang shut the door behind him—the hall was still empty—and then bent down to restore the woman's dress. He reached up to pull the hair away from her face and revealed, beneath her head like a pillow, what her apparently unseeing eyes so greedily devoured . . . a gleaming blue glass book.

The woman's exhalations rose into a moan, her skin as hot and red as if she had fever. Chang looked at the book and licked his lips. With a decisiveness he did not wholly feel he took hold of the woman beneath her arms and lifted her from it, his eyes flinching from the bright gleam of the uncovered glass. As he pulled her away she whimpered in protest like a drowsing puppy separated from its teat. He set her down and winced—the light from the book stabbed to the center of his head. Chang snapped it closed, his lips stretched back in a grimace, feeling even through his leather gloves a strange pulsing as he touched it and a protesting energetic resistance when he pushed it shut. The woman did not make another sound. Chang watched her, idly wiping his dagger on the carpet—it was already red, what was the harm?—as her breath gradually calmed and her eyes began to clear. He gently pushed aside the hanging mask of beads. He did not recognize her.

She was merely another of the great ladies and gentlemen drawn into the insidious web of Harschmort House.

Chang stood and snatched a pillow from the nearby settee. He ripped open one end with the dagger and he brusquely turned the lining inside out, dumping yellowed clumps of cotton wadding onto the floor. He inserted the book carefully into the pillowcase and stood. The lady could take care of herself as she woke—her fingers fitfully groped against the carpet—and forever wonder about her mysterious delivery... and if she started to scream, it would cause the disturbance he wanted. He stepped back to the door and paused, looking behind him at the room. There was no other door... and yet something caught his eye. The wallpaper was red, with a circular decoration of golden rings that looked vaguely Florentine. Chang crossed the room to a section of wallpaper, perhaps as high as his head. In the middle of one of the golden rings the pattern appeared to be frayed. He pressed at it with his finger and the interior of the ring popped through, leaving a hole. A spy hole. Chang strode past the woman—dreamily shaking her head and struggling to raise herself to one elbow—and out to the corridor.

Once more, Chang's notion that most things are only effectively hidden because no one ever thinks to look for them was confirmed. Once he knew what he sought—a narrow corridor between rooms—it was easy enough to identify what door might lead to it. While it was possible that the other side of the spy hole was in another normal room, Chang felt this went against the entire idea—as he understood it—of Harschmort House, which was the *integrated* nature of the establishment. Why have a spy hole into one room, when one might construct an inner passage that spanned the length of many apartments to either side, so one man with patience and soft shoes could effectively gain the advantage on a whole collection of guests? He chuckled to think that he had here explained Robert Vandaariff's famed success at business negotiation, his uncanny aptitude for knowing what his rivals were planning—a reputation side by side with his renown as a generous host (especially—Chang shook his head at the cunning—to those with whom he most bitterly strove). Not three yards from the one he'd entered Chang found two doors quite closely set together—or more accurately, one door in the space that, elsewhere in the corridor, was only blank wall.

Chang dug out his keys—first Gray's and then his own—and struggled to open the lock. It was actually rather tricky, and differed from others he'd found in the house. He looked around him with growing alarm, trying a second key and then fumbling for a third. He thought he heard a rising noise from the far end, near the staircase... applause? Was there some sort of performance? The key did not work. He felt for the next. With a click that echoed down the length of the corridor, a door was opened in the balcony above the staircase—and then the sound of steps, many people... they would be at the railing any instant. His key caught, the lock turned, and without hesitation Chang slipped the door open and darted through into the bitter dark. He closed it as quickly and silently as he could, with no idea if he'd been seen or heard.

There was nothing for it. He turned the lock behind him and felt his way deeper into the blackness. The walls were narrow—his elbows rubbed the dusty brick on either side as he went—but the floor was smoothly laid stone (as opposed to wood that might warp and in time begin to creak). He felt his way along, hampered by his restored stick in one hand and the wrapped book in the other, and by Miss Temple's boots jostling the walls from his pockets. The spy hole in the woman's room had been at head height, so he placed his hands there as he walked, to feel for any depression in the brick. Surely it had to be near... his impatience nearly caused him to pitch headlong into the dark as his foot struck a step in the blackness below him and he tripped forward—only saved from falling outright, despite a cruel barking on his knee, by another two steps on top of that. He found himself kneeling on what was effectively a small stepladder spanning the width of the passage. Chang carefully set down his stick and the book, and then felt the wall for the hole, finding it by the small half-circle of light caused by his partial dislodging of its plug from the room. He silently pulled the plug free and peered in. The woman had crawled away from the dead soldier, and crouched kneeling on the carpet. Her hands were under her dress—restoring her undergarments or perhaps attempting to see how far along the dead soldier's obvious intentions had proceeded. She still wore her mask, and Chang was curious to see that despite the tears on her cheeks she seemed calm and determined in her manner . . . was this a result of her experience with the book?

He replaced the plug in the wall and wondered that the stair-step should be built across the entire passage . . . was there another spy hole on the opposite wall? Chang shifted his position and felt for it, finding the plug easily. He worked it free as gently as he could and leaned forward to gaze into the second room.

A man sprawled with his head and shoulders on a writing table. Chang knew him despite the black band across his eyes—as he came to know any man he'd followed through the street, identifying him from behind or within a crowd merely by his size and manner of being. It was his former client, the man who had apparently recommended his talents to Rosamonde, the lawyer John Carver. Chang had no doubt the secrets Carver held in his professional possession would open many a door to the Cabal across the city—he wondered how many of the law had been seduced, and shook his head at how simple those seductions must have been. Carver's face was as red as the woman's, and a pearling bead of drool connected his mouth to the table top. The glass book lay flickering under Carver's hand. The upper part of his face lay pressed against it, eyes twitching with an idiot rapture, transfixed by its depths. Chang noted with some curiosity that the lawyer's face and fingertips—the ones touching the glass—had taken on a bluish cast to the skin . . . almost as if they'd been frozen, though his sweat-sheened face belied that explanation. With distaste he noticed Carver's other hand clutched at his groin with a spastic, dislocated urgency. Chang looked around the room for any other occupant, or any other useful sign, but saw nothing. He was not sure what such exposure to the book actually gained the Cabal—apart from this insensibility on the part of the victim. Did it remake them like the Process? Was there something *in* the book they were supposed to learn? He felt the weight of the book tucked under his own arm. He knew—from the glass in his lungs and Svenson's description of that man's shattered glass arms—that the object itself could be deadly, but as a tool, as a *machine* . . . he hadn't even a glimpse into its true destructive power. Chang replaced the plug and felt with his stick for the next set of stairs.

When it came he looked again, prying the plug first from the left, the side where he'd seen the woman. Chang's conscience gnawed at him—should he not ignore the holes and move directly for the office? Yet to do so was to pass up information about the Cabal he would never be afforded again . . . he would go more quickly. He peered into the room and suddenly froze—there were two men in black coats helping an elderly man in red onto a sofa. The churchman's face was obscured—could it be the Bishop of Baax-Saornes? Uncle to the Duke of Stäelmaere and the Queen, he was the most powerful cleric in the land, an advisor to government, a curb to corruption, . . . and here having the spittle wiped from his chin by malevolent lackeys. One of the men wrapped a parcel in cloth—assuredly another book—while the other took the Bishop's pulse. Then both turned to a knock at a door Chang could not see and rapidly walked from the room.

Without a further thought for the ruined Bishop—what could he do for him anyway?—Chang turned to the opposite hole. Another man slumped over a book—how many of these hellish objects had been made?—his red face and twitching eyes pressed down into the glowing surface. It was without question Henry Xonck, his customary aura of power and command quite fully absent... indeed, it seemed to Chang that the man's normal attributes had been drained away... drained *into* the book? The thought was absurd, and yet he recalled the glass cards—the manner in which they became imprinted with memories. If the books managed the same trick on a larger scale... suddenly Chang wondered if the memories were simply imprinted from the victim's mind... or actually removed. How much of Henry Xonck's memories—indeed his very soul—had here been stripped away?

The following spy holes revealed more of the same, and even though Chang didn't recognize every slumped figure, those he did were enough to reveal a naked assault on the powerful figures of the land: the Minister of Finance, the Minister of War, a celebrated actress, a Duchess, an Admiral, a high court judge, the publisher of the *Times*, the president of the Imperial Bank, the widowed Baroness who ran the most important, opinion-setting *salon* in the city, and finally, tempting him to postpone his search even further and intervene, Madelaine Kraft. Each one discovered in the throes of a fitful, nearly narcotic state of possession, utterly absent of mind and unresponsive of body—their only point of attention being the book that had been set before their eyes. In several cases Chang saw masked figures—men and women—monitoring a stricken victim, sometimes collecting the book and starting to wake them, sometimes allowing more time to steep in those blue glowing depths. Chang recognized none of these functionaries. He was certain that but a few days ago their tasks would have been performed by the likes of Mrs. Marchmoor or Roger Bascombe—and a few days before that by the Contessa or Xonck themselves. Now their organization had grown—had absorbed so many new adherents—that they were all freed for more important matters. It was another spur to Chang that something else was happening in the house, perhaps as cover for the subjugation of these particular, spectacularly placed figures, but important enough to draw the Cabal's leaders. He rushed ahead into the dark.

He ignored the remaining spy holes, driving on to the end of the passageway and hoping that when he got there he would find a door. Instead, he found a painting. His stick struck something with a light exploratory touch that was not stone and his hand reached gingerly forward to find the heavy carved frame. It seemed similar in size to the portrait of Robert Vandaariff that had masked the door to the tier of cells, though the passage was so dark that he'd no idea what it actually portrayed. Not that Chang wasted any time on the matter—he was on his knees groping for a catch or lever that might open the hidden door. But why was the painting on the inside? Did that mean the door rotated fully on each usage and someone had already come through? That was unlikely—a simple concealed hinge, opening and closing normally, would be far easier to use and to hide. But then what was on the canvas that it should remain unseen in the dark?

He sat back on his haunches and sighed. Injuries, fatigue, thirst... Chang felt like a ruin. He could keep on fighting—that was instinctive—but actual cleverness felt beyond him. He shut his eyes and took a deep breath, exhaling slowly, thinking about the other side of the door—the catch would be concealed... perhaps it was not *around* the frame, but *part* of it. He ran his fingers along the inside border of the ornately (overly, really) carved frame, concentrating first on the area where a normal doorknob might be... when he found the curved depression, he realized the only trick was the knob being on the left side rather than the right—the kind of silly misdirection that could have easily flummoxed him for another half hour. He dug his fingers around the odd-shaped knob and turned it. The well-oiled lock opened silently and Chang felt the weight of the door shift in his hands. He pushed it open and stepped through.

* * *

He knew it was Vandaariff's study immediately, for the man himself sat before him at an enormous desk, scratching earnestly away at a long page of parchment with an old-fashioned feathered quill. Lord Robert did not look up. Chang took another step, still holding the door open with his shoulder, his eyes darting around at the room. The carpets were red and black and the long room was subdivided into functional areas by the furniture: a long meeting table lined with high-backed chairs, a knot of larger, more upholstered armchairs and sofas, an assistant's desk, a row of tall locked cabinets for papers, and then the great man's desk, as large as the meeting table and covered with documents, rolled-up maps, and a litter of glasses and mugs—all driven to the edge of his present work like flotsam on a beach.

No one else was in the room.

Still, Lord Vandaariff did not acknowledge Chang's presence, his face gravely focused on his writing. Chang remembered his main errand, a secret way to the great chamber. He couldn't see it. On the far wall beyond the table was the main entrance, but it seemed like the only one.

As he stepped forward something caught Chang's attention at the corner of his eye . . . it was the painting behind him—he hadn't looked at it in the light. He glanced again at Vandaariff—who gave Chang no attention at all—and opened the door wide. Another canvas by Oskar Veilandt, but no similar sort of image . . . instead its front was like the back of the *Annunciation* fragments and other paintings—what at first glance seemed mere cross-hatched lines was in truth a densely wrought web of symbols and diagrams. The overall shape of the formulae, Chang saw more with instinct than with understanding, was a horseshoe . . . mathematical equations made in the shape of Harschmort House. It was also, he realized with a certain self-consciousness, wondering if the insight was merely the product of his own low mind, perversely anatomical—the curving U of the house and the peculiarly shaped cylindrical figure, longer than he had imagined, of the great chamber clearly inserted within it . . . whatever else Veilandt's alchemy intended, it was quite clear that its roots lay as much in sexual congress as any elemental transmutation—or was the point that these were the same? Chang did not know what this had to do with the ceremony in the chamber, or with Vandaariff. And yet . . . he tried to remember when Vandaariff had purchased and re-fitted Harschmort Prison—at most a year or two previously. Hadn't the gallery agent told them Veilandt had been dead *five* years? That was impossible—the alchemical painting on the door was definitely the same man's work. Could it be that Veilandt hadn't died at all? Could it be that he was here—perhaps willingly, but given the degree to which Vandaariff and d'Orkancz were exploiting his every discovery it seemed suddenly more likely he was a prisoner, or even worse, fallen victim to his own alchemy, his mind drained into a glass book for others to consume.

And yet—even within his exhaustion and despair Chang could not prevent himself from indulging this tendril of hope—if Veilandt were alive he could be *found*! Where else might they learn how to resist or overturn the effects of the glass? With a stab into his heart Chang realized this was even a chance to save Angelique. At once his heart was torn—his determination to save Celeste, this last prayer to preserve Angelique—it was impossible. Veilandt could be anywhere—shackled in a cage or drooling in a forgotten corner . . . or, if he retained his sanity and his mind, where he could best aid the Cabal . . . with the Comte d'Orkancz at the base of the great tower.

Chang looked again at the painting. It *was* a map of Harschmort . . . as it was equally an alchemical formula of dazzling complexity . . . and also distinctly pornographic. Focusing on the map (for he had no knowledge of alchemy and no time for the lurid), he located to the best of his ability the spot where, within the house, he presently stood. Was there any obvious path depicted to the great chamber and the panopticon column tower within it?

The room itself was signified—he'd had enough Greek to name them—by an alpha and then just above it, as if it were its multiplying power, a tiny omega . . . and from the omega ran one clear scoring line of paint down to the nest of symbols representing the chamber. Chang looked up from the canvas, feeling foolishly literal. If the room was the alpha—where in it might he find the omega? To his best estimate it lay just beyond Vandaariff's desk . . . where the wall was covered by a heavy hanging curtain.

Chang crossed quickly to the spot, watching Vandaariff closely. The man *still* did not stir from his writing—he must have covered half a long page in the time Chang had been there. This was perhaps the most powerful man in the nation—even on the continent—and Chang could not resist his curiosity. He stepped closer to the desk—by all rights his reeking clothes alone should have shattered a saint's concentration—to get a look at Vandaariff's unchangingly impassive face.

It did not seem to Cardinal Chang that Robert Vandaariff's eyes saw anything at all. They were open, but glassy and dull, the thoughts behind them entirely elsewhere, facing down at the desk top but quite to the side of his writing, as if he were instead inscribing thoughts from memory. Chang leaned even closer to study the parchment—he was nearly at Vandaariff's shoulder and still there was no reaction. As near as he could tell, the man was documenting the contents of a financial transaction—in amazingly complicated detail—referring to shipping and to Macklenburg and French banking and to rates and markets and shares and schedules of repayment. He watched Vandaariff finish the page and briskly turn it over—the sudden movement of his arms causing Chang to leap back—continuing mid-phrase at the top of the fresh side. Chang looked on the floor behind the desk and saw page after long page of parchment completely covered with text, as if Robert Vandaariff was emptying his mind of every financial secret he had ever possessed. Chang looked again at the working fingers, chilled by the inhuman insistence of the scratching pen, and noticed that the tips were tinged with blue . . . but it was not cold in the room, and the blue was more lustrous beneath the pale flesh than Chang had ever seen on a living man.

He stepped away from the automaton Lord and felt behind him for the curtain, swept it aside to expose a simple locked door. He fumbled with his ring of keys, sorting out one, and then dropped them all—suddenly full of dread at being in Vandaariff's unfeeling presence, the pen scratching along behind him. Chang scooped up the keys and with an abrupt, anxious impatience simply kicked the wood by the lock as hard as he could. He kicked again and felt it begin to split. He did not care about the noise or any trail of destruction. He kicked once more and cracked the wood around the still-fixed bolt. He hurled himself against it, smashing through, and staggered into a winding stone tunnel whose end sloped downward, out of view.

Apart from his relentless spidery hand, Lord Vandaariff did not move. Chang rubbed his shoulder and broke into a run.

The tunnel was smoothly paved and bright from regularly placed gas-lit globes above his head. The passage curved gently over the course of some hundred paces, at the end of which Chang was forced to reduce his speed. It was just as well, for as he paused to steady his breath—leaning against the wall with one hand and allowing the gob of bloody spit to drop silently from his mouth—he heard the distant sound of many voices raised in song. Ahead the tunnel took a sharp bank to his right, toward the great chamber. Would there be any kind of guard? The singing drowned out any other noise. It came from below . . . from the occupants of the overhanging cells! Chang sank to his knees and cautiously peered around the corner.

The tunnel opened into a narrowed walkway, little more than a catwalk, with railings of chain to either side, extending to a black, malevolent turret of iron that rose into the rock ceiling above him. Through the metal grid of the catwalk rose the sound of singing. Chang peered down but, between the dim light and his squinting eyes, could get no true sense of the chamber below. On the far side of the catwalk was an iron door, massive with a heavy lock and iron bar, that had been left ajar. Chang stopped just to his side of it, waiting, listening, heard no one, and slipped into the dark... and onto another spiral staircase, this one welded together from cast iron plates.

The staircase continued up to the roof of the cavern, toward what must be the main entrance to the tower. But Chang turned downwards, his boots' tapping on steps more sensed than audible over the chorus of voices. He could hear them more clearly, but it was the kind of singing where even if one did know the language the words might well have been those of an Italian (or for all he knew Icelandic) opera, so distended and unnatural was the phrasing imposed by the music. Still, the lyrics he did manage to pick out—"impenetrable blue"... "never-ending sight"... "redemption kind"—only drove him to descend more quickly.

The interior of the tower was lit by regular sconces, but their light was deliberately dim, so as not to show through the open viewing slots. Chang slowed. The step below him was covered by a tangled shape. It was a discarded coat. He picked it up and held it to the nearest sconce... a uniform coat, dark blue at some point but now filthy with dirt and, he saw with interest, blood. The stains were still damp, and soaked the front of the coat quite completely. He did not, however, see any wound or tear *in* the coat—was the blood from the wearer, or from, perhaps, the wearer's enemy? Whoever had worn it might have bled from the head or had their hand cut off and clutched the stump to their chest—anything was possible. It was then that—his mind moving so slowly!—Chang noticed the bars of rank on the coat's stiff collar... he looked again at the cut, the color, the silver braid around each épaulette... he damned himself for a fool.

It was Svenson's coat, without question, and covered in gore.

He quickly searched around him in the stairwell, and on the wall saw the dripping remains of a wide spray of blood. The violence had happened here on the stairs—perhaps only moments ago. Was Svenson dead? How had he possibly reached Harschmort from Tarr Manor? Chang crab-walked another few steps, face close against the iron. There *was* a descending trail of blood, but the trail was smeared... not made by a wounded man walking, but a wounded—or dead—man dragged.

Chang threw the coat aside—if the Doctor had dropped it, he hardly needed to carry it himself—and clattered down as quickly as he could. He knew the distance was roughly what he'd previously climbed—two hundred steps, perhaps? What in the world would he find at the base? Svenson's corpse? What was d'Orkancz possibly doing? And why were there no guards?

Chang's foot slipped on a splash of blood and he clutched at the rail. It would be all too simple for one mistake to land him at the bottom with a broken neck. He forced himself to concentrate—the voices still soared in song, though he had descended past the tiers of viewing cells and the chorus was above him. But when had Svenson arrived? It had to be with Aspiche! Could the Doctor be the cause of Smythe's disturbance? Chang smiled to think of it, even as he winced at the likely retribution the Colonel would have delivered to anyone crossing his path. He did not relish the image of the Doctor standing alone against these men—he was no soldier, nor was he an unflinching killer. That was Chang's place—and he knew he must reach Svenson's side.

And if Svenson *was* dead? Then perhaps Chang's place was to die with him... and with Miss Temple.

He raced down another thirty steps and stopped at a small landing. His lungs were laced with stabbing pains and he knew it was better not to reach the bottom in a state of collapse. One of the viewing slots was near him on the wall and he pulled it aside, grinning with sinister appreciation. The slot was covered with a plate of smoked glass. From the inside, he could see through it, but to any prisoner the glass would mask whether the metal slat had been opened at all. Chang pulled off his spectacles and pressed his face to the glass at the very moment the singing stopped.

Above and opposite him were the viewing cells, full of finely dressed people, all masked, faces pressed to the bars, for all the world like inmates in an asylum. He shifted his gaze down, but could not see the tables. He was still too high.

As he stepped away a voice echoed up from below—unnatural, strangely amplified, deepened, and unquestionably mighty. He did not recognize it immediately... he'd only heard the man speaking a very few words, and those in a rasping whisper to Harald Crabbé, an enormous fur-clad arm enfolding Angelique. But Chang knew... it was the Comte d'Orkancz. Damning his lungs, he began to run, recklessly, his feet flying two and even three steps at a time, hand on the rail with his stick, the other hand holding the wrapped book safely free of collision, his soiled coat flapping behind him, its heavy pockets knocking against his legs. All around him the chamber rang with the Comte's inhuman voice.

"You are here because you believe... in yourselves... in giving yourselves over to a different dream... of the future... of possibility... transformation... revelation... redemption. Perhaps there are those among you who will be deemed worthy... truly worthy and truly willing to sacrifice their illusions... sacrifice the entirety of their world... *which is a world of illusion*... for this final degree of wisdom. Beyond redemption is *designation*... as Mary was made apart from every other woman... as Sarah was made pregnant after a barren lifetime... as Leda was implanted with twin seeds of beauty and destruction... so these vessels before you all have been chosen... *designated* to a higher destiny... a transformation you will witness. You will feel the higher energies... you will taste this greatness... this ethereal ambrosia... before known only to those creatures who were named gods by shepherds... and by the children we all once were..."

Chang toppled off balance into the rail and was forced to stop, clutching with both hands to prevent a fall. He spat against the wall and groped, gasping, for the viewing slat, ripping off his glasses to look. Below him he saw it all, like an iron cathedral from hell laid out for an infernal mass. At the base of the tower was a raised platform—seemingly suspended on a raft of the silver tubing—holding three large surgical tables, each surrounded by racks and trays and brass boxes of machinery. The tables each bore a woman, held with leather straps just as Angelique had been at the Institute, naked, bodies obscured by a sickening nest of slick black hoses. Each woman's face was completely covered by a black mask fitted with smaller hoses—for each ear, each eye, the nose and mouth—and their hair completely wrapped in a dark cloth, so that despite their nudity Chang could not begin to guess who might be on which table. Only the woman nearest to the turret, whom he could barely glimpse from his angle of sight, was distinguished from the others, for the soles of her feet were discolored blue in an identical manner to Robert Vandaariff's hands.

Next to her stood d'Orkancz, with the same leather apron and gauntlets he'd worn at the Institute and the same brass-bound helmet, to which he'd attached another hose, hooking it into the metal box that made the mask's mouth. Into this hose the Comte was speaking, and somehow through its engine his voice was magnified, like a very god's, to crash against every distant corner of the vast chamber. Behind d'Orkancz stood at least four more men, identically dressed, their faces hidden. Men from the Institute, like Gray and Lorenz? Or could one of these be Oskar Veilandt—present either as prisoner or slave? Chang could not see the very base of the tower. Where were the guards? Where was Svenson? Which table held Celeste? None of the women seemed awake—how could he carry her away?

Chang spun at a sound behind him—a clanking from the staircase itself. The stairs wound around an iron pillar—the noise came from within it. He reached across and felt a vibration. The clanking made him think at once of a hotel's dumbwaiter . . . could the pillar be hollow? How else to get things quickly from the top to the bottom? But what was being delivered? This was his chance. When whatever was being sent reached the bottom, someone was going to have to open the tower door to get it—and that would be his moment to break through. He shoved his glasses back into place, set the pillowcase down against the wall and threw himself forward.

The Comte was still speaking. Chang didn't care—it was all the same nonsense—another stage of the circus act to dazzle the customers. Whatever the real effects of this "transformation," he didn't doubt it was but a veil for another unseen web of exploitation and greed. The clanking stopped. As Chang swept around the final curve he saw two men wearing the aprons and gauntlets and helmets bending over the open dumbwaiter, just sliding an iron-bound crate from it and into a wheeled cart. Behind them was the open door to the chamber platform, to either side of it a Macklenburg trooper. Chang ignored the men and the cart and vaulted from the steps at the nearest Macklenburger with a cry, slamming the man across the jaw with his forearm and driving a knee into his ribs, knocking him sprawling. Before the second man could draw his weapon Chang stabbed the stick into his stomach, doubling him over (the man's face falling near enough to Chang that he heard the brusque click of the fellow's teeth). He drove the dagger up under the man's open jaw and just as quickly wrenched it free. He stood—the dead trooper sinking like a timed counterweight—and wheeled back to the first man, planting a deliberate kick to the side of his head. Both troopers were still. The two men in the masks stared at him with the dumb incomprehension of inhabitants from the moon first witnessing the savagery of mankind.

Chang spun to the open door. The Comte had stopped speaking. He was staring at Chang. Before Chang could react he heard a noise behind and without looking threw his body forward out the door—just as the two men in helmets shoved the trolley at his back. The corner clipped him sharply across his right thigh—drawing blood, but not enough to run him down. Chang stumbled onto the platform, the sudden enormity of the cathedral-like void above staggering him with a spasm of vertigo. He groped for his bearings. The platform held four more Macklenburgers—three troopers, who as he watched swept out their sabers in one glittering movement, and Major Blach, calmly drawing his black pistol. Chang glanced wildly around him—absolutely no sign of Svenson or which, if any, of the brass-masked men might be Veilandt—and then up to the dizzying heights and the clustered ring of masked faces peering down in rapt attention. There was no time. Chang's only path away from the soldiers led to the tables and—striding quite directly to cut him off from the women—d'Orkancz.

The troopers rushed forward. Chang in turn charged directly at the Comte before dodging to the left and ducking beneath the first table, swatting through the dangling hoses to reach the other side. The soldiers careened to either side of d'Orkancz. Chang kept going, crouched low, until he was under and past the second table. He emerged on the other side as the Comte shouted to the soldiers not to move.

Chang stood and looked back. The Comte faced him from the far side of the first table, still wearing the mechanical mask, the first woman swathed in hoses before him. At the Comte's side stood Blach, his pistol ready. The troopers waited. Svenson was not here. Nor, as best as he could tell, was Veilandt—or not with his own mind, for the two masked men behind the Comte had not stopped in their working of the brass machinery, looking for all the world like a pair of insect drones. Chang looked at the platform's edge. Below it, on every side, was a steaming sea of metal pipes, hissing with heat and reeking sulphurous fumes. There was no escape.

"Cardinal Chang!"

The Comte d'Orkancz spoke in the same projected, amplified tones that Chang had heard in the tower. Heard this close the words were impossibly harsh, and he winced despite himself.

"You will not move! You have trespassed a place you do not comprehend! I promise you do not *begin* to understand the penalties!"

Without a thought for the Comte, Chang reached out to the woman on the second table and ripped the dark cloth free that held her hair.

"Do not touch them!" screamed the Comte d'Orkancz.

The hair was too dark. It was not Celeste. He scuttled at once to the far side of the third table. The troopers advanced with him, up to the second table. The Comte and Blach remained on the far side of the first, the Major's pistol quite clearly aimed at Chang's head. Chang ducked behind the third woman and pulled the cloth from her hair. Too light and less curled . . . Celeste must be on the first table. He'd charged past her like a fool and left her in the direct control of d'Orkancz.

He stood. Upon seeing him the troopers stepped forward and Chang detected the briefest flicker of movement from Blach. He dropped again as the shot crashed out. The bullet spat past his head and punched into one of the great pipes, spitting out a jet of gas that hung flickering in the air like a blue-white flame. The Comte screamed again.

"Stop!"

The soldiers—nearly at the third table—froze. Chang risked a slow peek over the raft of black hoses—glimpsing between them pale damp flesh—and met the Major's baleful gaze.

The chamber was silent, save for the dull roar of the furnace and the high note of hissing gas behind him. He needed to overcome nine men—counting the two with the cart—and get Celeste from the table. Could he do that without harming her? Was that harm possibly worse than what would happen to her if he didn't? He knew what she would want him to do—as he knew how meaningless any notion of preserving his own life had become. He felt the seething lattice of cuts inside his chest. This exact moment was why he had come so far, this very effort the last defiant, defacing mark he could inflict upon this privileged world. Chang looked up again to the mass of masked faces staring down in suspenseful silence. He felt like a beast in the arena.

The Comte detached the black speaking hose from the mask

and draped it carefully over a nearby pedestal box bristling with levers and stops. He faced Chang and nodded—with the mask on it was the gesture of an inarticulate brute, of a storybook ogre—to the woman nearest Chang, whose hair he had exposed.

"Looking for someone, Cardinal?" he called. His voice was less loud, but issuing from the strange mouth box set into the mask, it still struck Chang as inhuman. "Perhaps I can assist you . . ."

The Comte d'Orkancz reached out and pulled away the cloth that wrapped the final woman's hair. It cascaded out in curls, dark, shining, black. The Comte reached out with his other hand and swept away the hoses hanging across her feet. The flesh was discolored, sickly lustrous, even more so than Vandaariff's hand or John Carver's face when it had lain against the book—pale as polar ice, slick with perspiration, and beneath it, where he had before known a color of golden warmth, was now the cool indifference of white ash. On the third toe of her left foot was a silver ring, but Chang had known from the first glimpse of her hair . . . it was Angelique.

"I believe you are . . . acquainted with the lady," continued d'Orkancz. "Of course you may be acquainted with the others as well—Miss Poole"—he nodded at the woman in the middle—"and Mrs. Marchmoor." The Comte gestured to the woman directly in front of Chang. He looked down, trying to locate Margaret Hooke (last seen on a bed in the St. Royale) in what he saw—the hair, her size, the color of what flesh he could see beneath the black rubber. He felt the urge to be sick.

Chang spat a lozenge of blood onto the platform and called to the Comte, his hoarse voice betraying his fatigue.

"What will you do to them?"

"What I have planned to do. Do you search for Angelique, or for Miss Temple? As you see she is not here."

"Where is she?" cried Chang hoarsely.

"I believe you have a choice," said the Comte in reply. "If you seek to rescue Angelique, there is no human way—for I read the effects of the glass in your face, Cardinal—for you to bear her from this place and *then* do the same for Miss Temple."

Chang said nothing.

"It is, of course, academic. You ought to have died ten times over—is that not correct, Major Blach? You will do so now. But it is perhaps fitting that it take place at the feet—if I am correctly informed—of your own hopeless love."

Staring directly at the Comte, Chang gathered hold of as many of the hoses rising from Mrs. Marchmoor's body as he could and prepared to rip them free.

"If you do that, you kill her, Cardinal! Is that what you desire—to destroy a helpless woman? At this distance I cannot stop you. The forces at work have been committed! None of these may retreat from their destiny—truly their lot is transformation or death!"

"What transformation?" shouted Chang above the rising roar of the pipes, and the hissing gas behind him.

In answer d'Orkancz reached for the speaking hose and jammed it sharply back into the mask. His words echoed through the vaulted heights like thunder.

"The transformation of *angels*! The powers of heaven made flesh!"

The Comte d'Orkancz yanked hard on one of the pedestal's brass levers, and brought his other hand down like a hammer on a metal stop. At once the hoses around Angelique, which had been hanging and lank, stiffened with life as they were flooded with gas and boiling fluid. Her body arched on the table, and the air was filled with a hideous rising whine. Chang could not look away. The Comte pulled a second lever and her fingers and toes began to twitch . . . a third, and to Chang's growing terror their color began to change even more, a deadening, freezing blue. D'Orkancz pushed in two stops at once, and shifted the first lever back. The whine redoubled its intensity, ringing within every pipe and echoing throughout the vaulted cathedral. The crowd above them gasped and Chang heard voices shouting from the cells—cries of excitement and delight, hoots of encouragement—that grew into a second buzzing chorus. Her body arched again and again, rippling the hoses like a dog shaking off the rain, and then within the screams and roars Chang heard another tone that pierced his heart like a spike: the rattle of Angelique's own voice, an insensate moan from the very depths of her lungs, as if the final defenses of her body were expending themselves against the vast mechanical assault. Tears flowed unheeded down the Cardinal's face. Anything he did would kill her—but was she not being destroyed before his eyes? He could not move.

The whining roar snapped at once to nothing, silencing the entire chamber like a gunshot. With a sudden rippling shimmer that Chang could scarce credit he was seeing, a wave of fluid rushed beneath her skin along each limb from her feet and hands, flooding up to her hips and torso and finally enveloping her head.

Angelique's flesh was transformed to a brilliant, shining translucent blue, as if she herself . . . her very body . . . had been before them all transmuted into glass.

The Comte pulled up his stops and pushed in his final lever. He turned up to the throng of spectators and raised his hand in triumph.

"It has been done!"

The crowd erupted into ecstatic cheering and applause. D'Orkancz nodded to them, raised his other hand, and then turned to Blach, for a moment pulling the speaking hose from its place.

"Kill him."

The obscenity of what d'Orkancz had perpetrated on Angelique—was it not a rape of her *essence*?—at once spurred Chang into action and turned his heart to ice. He launched himself around the third table at the two Macklenburg guards at Miss Poole's head, the lessons of a thousand battles pouring into each relentless, bitter blow. Without the slightest pause he swung at them, a feint—their sabers rising to his chest with the unison of German training—and then swept both blades aside with his stick. He slashed his dagger at the nearest man's face, laying it open from the tip of the jaw to the nose—a spray of blood against the silver pipes—the trooper wheeled away. The other riposted, stabbing hard at Chang's body. Chang broke his stick deflecting the thrust past his shoulder, and knew the lunge had brought the trooper too close. He jabbed the dagger beneath the young man's ribs and ripped it free, already—for each second seemed to arrive from a great distance as he watched—dropping to his knees. Above his head, another bullet from Blach flew into the wall of pipes. The third trooper came around from Miss Poole's feet, stepping over his fallen companions. Chang turned and dove forward to Angelique. Blach stepped near Angelique's head to give himself room to shoot. The Comte d'Orkancz stood at Angelique's feet. Chang was boxed in—the trooper was right behind him. Chang wheeled and cut through a handful of hoses. The hideous, reeking gas, spitting out like a polar flame, flew into the trooper's face. Chang wheeled, knocked the saber aside, and drove a fist into the fellow's throat, stunning him where he stood. Before Blach could shoot, he bull-rushed the trooper around the head of the table directly at the Major. A shot crashed out and Chang felt the trooper lurch. Another shot and he felt a burn—the bullet (or was it bone?) blowing through the soldier to graze his shoulder. He shoved the dying man at Blach and immediately dove for the door.

But Blach had done the same thing and they faced each other directly, perhaps two feet apart. Blach swept the gun to bear, firing as Chang slashed at the Major's hand. The shot went wide as the dagger bit into Blach's fingers and the pistol fell to the floor. Blach cried out in a rage and leapt after it. The door was still blocked by the metal cart and the two helmeted men behind. Chang shoved with all his strength, driving them several steps—but they caught themselves and pushed back, stranding him within the chamber. Blach scooped up the pistol with his left hand. The Comte was urgently tying off the steaming hoses with rope. Blach raised the pistol. With a sudden shock Chang saw what the cart held, for the top of the metal casket had become dislodged in the commotion. Without a thought he dropped his dagger, seized the nearest object, and whipped it behind him at the Major, flinging himself into the cart as soon as the thing left his hand.

The glass book lanced toward Blach at the same time he pulled the trigger, shattering it in flight. Half of the shards sprayed back at the tower with the force of the bullet, into the iron walls and through the doorway at the two helmeted men, who threw themselves desperately aside. But half kept flying with the momentum of the book itself. The Comte d'Orkancz was shielded by the table, as Angelique—if in her present state the glass could even have had any effect upon her—was shielded by the hoses, and by the Major himself who stood most directly in the way. His unprotected face and body were instantly savaged by gashes small and large.

Chang raised his head from the cart to see the man shaking with spasms, his mouth open and a hideous hoarse croaking scream rising from his lungs like smoke from a catching fire. Patches of blue began to form around each laceration, spreading, cracking, flaking free. The rattle died in his throat with a puff of pink dust. Major Blach fell to his knees with a snapping crunch and then forward onto his face, the front of which shattered on impact like a plate of lapis-glazed terra cotta.

The great chamber was silent. The Comte rose slowly behind the table. His eyes fell upon Chang, clambering awkwardly free of the cart. The Comte *screamed* with an amplified rage that shook the entire cathedral. He rushed at Chang like a giant rabid bear. Without his dagger (it had fallen somewhere under the iron chest)

Chang hurtled the cart—the two men were on their hands and knees, shaken but not in the Major's straits, their leather aprons having saved them—and shoved the cart behind him into the Comte. Without looking to see its effect he raced to the stairs and began to climb.

Almost immediately, on the seventh step, he slipped on a smear of blood, fell, and looked back, his hand digging into his coat for his razor. The two aproned men were crouched low, still flinching away from the doorway that framed the Comte d'Orkancz, who had snatched up Blach's pistol and was even then aiming it at Chang. Chang knew there was only one bullet left and that with two steps more he would be out of the Comte's line of fire, but behind the Comte, on the table, Cardinal Chang's gaze was fixed on Angelique's glassy blue right arm . . . which had begun to move. Chang screamed. Angelique's hand was flexing, groping. She caught a handful of the hoses and tore them from their seals, shooting blue steam. The Comte turned as she let go and wrenched another handful, pulling at them like weeds in a garden. As d'Orkancz dove for her hand, crying out for his assistants, Chang caught a hideous glimpse, over the large man's shoulder, of Angelique's face, eyes still covered by the partially dislodged mask, twisting with fury, her open mouth, tongue, and lips a glistening dark indigo, her blue-white teeth snapping like an animal. Chang ran up the stairs.

It was another turn before he saw the book he'd set against the wall in the pillowcase. Chang snatched it up as he ran, his right hand finally pulling the razor from his pocket. Below he heard a commotion of voices and a slamming door, and then the lurching clank of the dumbwaiter come again to life. In moments it had reached him—Chang's energy was already beginning to flag—and then sped past. Whoever stood at the upper end would receive warning of his arrival well before Chang could climb. Was it only a matter of moments before he met Blenheim and his men coming down?

Chang doggedly kept on. If he could just reach the gangway to Vandaariff's office...

His thoughts were interrupted by the voice of d'Orkancz, echoing through the chamber to the assembled crowds above.

"Do not be alarmed! As you know yourselves, our enemies are many and desperate—dispatching this assassin to disrupt our work. But that work has not been stopped! Heaven *itself* could not forestall our efforts! Behold what has been done before your eyes! Behold the *transformation*!"

Chang paused on the stairs, despite himself, his mind seared with the image of Angelique's face and arm. He looked behind him down the winding metal depths of the tower and heard outside it, like a rush of wind, a collected gasp of astonishment from the Comte's audience in the cells.

"You see!" the Comte continued. "She lives! She walks! And you see yourselves... her extraordinary *powers*..."

The crowd gasped again—a hissing whisper punctuated by several screams—of fright or joy, he could not say. Another gasp. What was happening? Tears for Angelique were still hot on his face but Chang could not help it. He lurched to a viewing slot and pulled it aside. It was ridiculous to stay—his enemies would be gathering above him any minute—and yet he had to know... was she alive? Was she still *human*?

He could not see her—she must be too close to the base of the tower—but he could see d'Orkancz. The Comte was facing where Angelique must be, and had stepped back to the second table to stand next to another box of levers and stops. Each table had such a box attached to it by way of the black hoses, and Chang was just realizing on a visceral, sickening level that each of the other two women were about to be so transfigured. He looked down at the inert form on the third table and found his heart pricked by the image of Margaret Hooke, savage, wounded, and proud, writhing in agony as her flesh was boiled away to glass. Had she chosen such a fate, or had she merely given herself over to d'Orkancz out of desperate ambition—trusting, because of the first few crumbs of power he had shown her, that his final ends lay in her interest?

The crowd gasped again and Chang felt his knees give, grabbing at the rail to keep balance. His mind spun as sharply as if he'd been kicked in the head, then the moment of nausea passed and he felt himself moving—but it was movement of the mind, a swift restless rushing, as if in a dream, through different scenes—a room, a street, a bed, a crowded square, one after another. Then the momentum of thought eased, settling on one sharp instant: the Comte d'Orkancz in a doorway in his fur, his gloved hand extended and offering a shining rectangle of blue glass. Chang felt his own hand reach out to the Comte, even as he knew it fiercely gripped the iron rail, and saw it touch the glass—the small delicate fingers he knew so well—and felt the sudden rush of erotic power as he—as she—was swept into the memory held within, a rising, impossibly vivid stimulation, irresistible as opium and just as addictive, then quickly, cruelly withdrawn before he could grasp whose sweet memory it had been or even the circumstance. The Comte tucked the card back into his coat and smiled. This had been the villain's introduction to Angelique, Chang knew, and Angelique was now, somehow, projecting her own experience of that intimate moment into the mind and body of every person within a hundred yards.

The image departed from his mind with another spasm of dizziness and he felt himself abruptly empty and cruelly, cruelly alone—her sudden presence in his mind had seemed a harsh intrusion, but once withdrawn there was a part of him that wanted more—for it was her, and he could *feel* it was her, Angelique, with whom he had so long desired this exact sort of impossible intimacy. Chang looked again down the twisting stairs, fighting an impulse to return, to fling himself away to an embrace of love and death. A part of his mind insisted that neither mattered, so long as it came from her.

"You feel the power for yourselves! You experience the truth!"

The Comte's voice broke the spell. Chang shook his head and turned, climbing as quickly as he could. He could not make sense of all he felt—he could not decide what he must do—and so Cardinal Chang retreated, as he often did, into action alone, driving himself on until he found an object for his desolated rage, looking for mayhem to once more clarify his heart.

The rising, grating whine began again, escalating to the heights of the chamber. The Comte d'Orkancz had moved on to the next woman, Miss Poole, pulling the levers to begin her metamorphosis. The sound of screaming machinery was bolstered by cries from the gallery of cells, for now that they knew what they were going to see, the crowd was even more willing to voice encouragement and delight. But Chang was assailed by the image of the woman's arched back, like a twig bent to its limit before snapping, and he ran from their approval as if he ran from hell itself.

He still had no idea where to find Svenson or Miss Temple, but if he was going to help them, he needed to remain free. The screaming of the pipes abruptly ceased, answered after a hanging moment of rapt attention by another eruption from the crowd. Once again the Comte crowed about power and transformation and the truth—each fatuous claim echoed by another bout of applause. Chang's lips curled back with rage. The whining rise in the pipes resumed—d'Orkancz had moved on to Margaret Hooke. There was nothing Chang could do. He ascended two more turns of the stairs and saw the door to the gangway and Lord Vandaariff's office.

Chang stood, breathing hard, and spat. The iron door was closed and did not move—barred from the other side. Chang was to be driven like a breathless stag to the top of the tower. For a final time the roar of the pipes dropped suddenly away and the crowd erupted with delight. All three of the women had undergone the Comte's ferocious alchemy. They would be waiting for him at the top. He had not found Celeste. He had lost Angelique.

He had failed. Chang tucked the razor back into his coat and resumed his climb.

The upper entrance was fashioned from the same steel plates, held together with the heavy rivets of a train car. The massive door swung silently to reveal an elegant bright hallway, the walls white and the floor gleaming pale marble. Some twenty feet away stood a shapely woman in a dark dress, her hair tied back with ribbon and her face obscured by a half-mask of black feathers. She nodded to him, formally. The line of ten red-coated Dragoons behind her, sabers drawn and clearly under command, did not move.

Chang stepped from the turret onto the marble floor, glancing down. The tiles were marked by a wide stain of blood—quite obviously pooled from some violent wound and then smeared by something (the victim, he assumed) dragged through it. The path led straight beneath the woman's feet. He met her eyes. Her expression was open and clear, though she did not smile. Chang was relieved—he had not realized how sick he'd become of his enemies' sneering confidence—but perhaps her demeanor had less to do with him than with the bloody floor.

"Cardinal Chang," she said. "If you will come with me."

Chang pulled the glass book from the pillowcase. He could feel its energy push at him through the tip of each gloved finger, an antagonistic magnetism. He clutched it more firmly and held it out for her to see.

"You know what this is," he said, his voice still hoarse and ragged. "I am not afraid to smash it."

"I'm sure you are not," she said. "I understand you are afraid of very little. But nothing will be settled here. I do not criticize to say you truly do not know all that has happened, or hangs in the balance. I'm sure there are many of whom you want to hear, as I know there are many who would like to see you. Is it not better to avoid what violence we can?"

The bright blood-smeared marble beneath the woman's feet seemed the perfect image for this hateful place, and it was all Chang could do not to snarl at her gracious tone.

"What is your name?" Chang asked.

"I am of no importance, I assure you," she said. "Merely a messenger—"

A harsh catch in Chang's throat stopped her words. His brief sharp vision of Angelique—the unnatural color of her skin, its glassy, gleaming indigo depths and brighter transparent cerulean surface—was seared into Chang's memory but its suddenly overwhelming impact was beyond his ability to translate to sense, to mere words. He swallowed, grimacing with discomfort, and spat again, diving into anger to override his tears. He gestured with his right hand, the fingers clutching with fury at the thought of such an abomination undertaken for the entertainment of so many—so many *respectable*—spectators.

"I have seen this *great work,*" he hissed. "Nothing you can say will sway my purpose."

In answer, the woman stepped aside and indicated with her hand that he might follow along. At her movement the line of Dragoons split and snapped crisply into place to either side, forming a gauntlet for him to pass through. Some ten yards beyond them Chang saw a second line dividing itself with the same clean stamping of boots to frame an open archway leading deeper into the house.

Behind in the turret he heard a muted roar—the crowd in the cells crying out—but before he could even begin to wonder why, Chang's knees buckled with the sudden visceral impact of another vision thrust into his mind. To his everlasting shame, he was presented with *himself,* stick in hand, his appearance fine as he could make it—a threadbare vanity, with an expression of poorly veiled hunger, reaching to take the small hand extended to him—extended, he now knew (and now *felt*), with disinterest and disdain.

He saw himself for one flashing, impossibly sharp moment through the eyes and heart of Angelique, and stood revealed within her mind as a regretted relic of a former life that she had at all times loathed with every fiber of her being.

The vision snapped away from him and he staggered. He looked up to see each of the Dragoons gathering themselves, blinking and regaining their military bearing, just as he saw the woman shake her head. She looked at him with pity, but did not alter her guarded expression. She repeated her gesture for Chang to join her.

"It would be best, Cardinal Chang," she said, "that we move out of *range*."

They had walked in silence, Dragoons in line ahead of them and behind, Chang's pounding heart yet to shake free of the bitter impact of Angelique's vision, his sweetest memories now stained with regret, until he saw the woman glance down at the book in his hand. He said nothing. Chang was caught between fury and despair, physically ruined, his mind drifting deeper into acrid fatalism with each step. He could not look at a soldier, the woman—or at any of the curious well-fed faces from the household that peered at him past the Dragoons as they walked by—without rehearsing in his thoughts the swiftest and most savage angle of attack with his razor.

"May I ask where you acquired that?" the woman asked, still looking at the book.

"In a room," snapped Chang. "It had transfixed the lady it had been given to. When I came upon her she was quite unaware of the soldier in the process of her rape."

He spoke in as sharp a tone as he could. The woman in the black feather mask did not flinch.

"May I ask what you did?"

"Apart from taking the book?" Chang asked. "It's so long ago I can barely recall—you don't mean to say you *care*?"

"Is that so strange?"

Chang stopped, his voice rising to an unaccustomed harshness. "From what I have seen, Madame, it is *impossible*!"

At his tone the Dragoons stopped, their boots stamping in unison on the marble floor, blades ready. The woman raised her hand to them, indicating patience.

"Of course, it must be very upsetting. I understand the Comte's work is difficult—both to imagine and to bear. I have undergone the Process, of course, but that is nothing compared to what . . . what you must have seen . . . in the tower."

Her face was entirely reasonable, even sympathetic—Chang could not bear it. He gestured angrily behind them to the bloodstained floor.

"And what happened there? What *difficult* piece of work? Another execution?"

"Your own hands, Cardinal, are quite covered with blood—are you in any place to speak?"

Chang looked down despite himself—from Mr. Gray to the troopers down below, he was fairly spattered with gore—but met her gaze with harsh defiance. None of them mattered. They were dupes, fools, animals in harness . . . perhaps exactly like himself.

"I cannot tell you what happened here," she went on. "I was elsewhere in the house. But surely it can only reinforce, for us both, how *serious* these matters are."

His lips curled into a sneer.

"If you will continue," she said, "for we are quite delayed . . ."

"Continue where?" asked Chang.

"To where you shall answer your *questions,* of course."

Chang did not move, as if staying would somehow put off the confirmation of the deaths of Miss Temple and the Doctor. The soldiers were staring at him. The woman looked directly into his dark lenses and leaned forward, her nostrils flaring at the indigo stench but her expression unwavering. He saw the clarity in her eyes that spoke to the Process, but none of the pride or the arrogance. As he was closer to the heart of the Cabal, had he here met a more advanced and trusted minion?

"We must go," she whispered. "You are not the center of this business."

Before Chang could respond they were interrupted by a loud shout from the corridor ahead of them, a harsh voice he knew at once.

"Mrs. Stearne! Mrs. Stearne!" shouted Colonel Aspiche. "Where is Mr. Blenheim—he is wanted this instant!"

The woman turned to the voice as the line of Dragoons broke apart to make way for their officer, approaching with another squad of his men behind him. Chang saw that Aspiche was limping. When Aspiche saw him, the Colonel's eyes narrowed and his lips tightened—and he then pointedly fixed his gaze on the woman.

"My dear Colonel—" she began, but he bluntly overrode her.

"Where is Mr. Blenheim? He is wanted some time ago—the delay cannot be borne!"

"I do not know. I was sent to collect—"

"I am well aware of it," snarled Aspiche, cutting her off, as if to expunge his previous employment of Chang he would not even allow the speaking of his name. "But you have taken so long I am asked to collect *you* as well." He turned to the men who had come with him, pointing to side rooms, barking orders. "Three to each wing—quickly as you can—send back at once with any word. He must be found—go!"

The men dashed off. Aspiche avoided looking at Chang and stepped to the woman's other side, offering her his arm—though Chang half-thought this was to help his limp, rather than the lady. He wondered what had happened to the Colonel's leg and felt a little better for doing so.

"Is there a reason he is not in chains, or dead?" asked the

Colonel, as politely as he could through his anger at having to ask at all.

"I was not so instructed," answered Mrs. Stearne—who, Chang realized as he studied her, could not be older than thirty.

"He is uniquely dangerous and unscrupulous."

"So I have been assured. And yet"—and here she turned to Chang with a curiously blank face—"he truly has no choice. The only help for Cardinal Chang—whether it merely be to soothe his soul—is information. We are taking him to it. Besides, I have no wish to lose a book in an unnecessary struggle—and the Cardinal holds one."

"Information, eh?" sneered Aspiche, looking around the woman at Chang. "About what? His whore? About that idiot Svenson? About—"

"Do be *quiet,* Colonel," she hissed, fully out of patience.

Chang was gratified, and not a little surprised, to see Aspiche pull his head back and snort with peevishness. And stop talking.

The ballroom was near. It only made sense to use it for another such gathering—perhaps already the crowds from the great chamber were convening too, along with those from the theatre at the end of the spiral staircase. Chang suddenly wondered with a sinking heart, not having found her in the great chamber, if this theatre was where Miss Temple had been taken. Had he walked right past her, just close enough and in time to hear the applause at her destruction?

With Aspiche in tow, their pace had slowed. The stamping bootsteps of the Dragoons made it difficult to hear any other movement in the house, and he wondered if his own execution or forced conversion was to be the main source of entertainment. He would smash the book over his own head before he allowed that to happen. To all appearances it seemed a quick enough end, and one equally horrible to watch as to experience. It would be something to at least, in his last moments, unsettle his executioners' stomachs.

He realized that Mrs. Stearne was looking at him. He cocked his head in a mocking invitation for her to speak . . . but she was, for the first time, hesitant to do so.

"I would . . . if I may, I would be grateful—for as I say, I was elsewhere occupied—if, with the Comte . . . if you could tell me what you saw . . . down below."

It was all Chang could do not to slap the woman's face.

"What I *saw*?"

"I ask because I do not know. Mrs. Marchmoor and Miss Poole—I knew them—I know that they have undergone—that the Comte's great work—"

"Did they go to him *willingly*?" demanded Chang.

"Oh yes," Mrs. Stearne replied.

"Why not you?"

She hesitated just a moment, looking into his veiled eyes.

"I . . . I must . . . my own responsibilities for the evening—"

She was interrupted by a peremptory snort from Aspiche, a clear admonishment at this topic of conversation—or indeed, conversation with Chang at all.

"Instead of you, it was Angelique."

"Yes."

"Because *she* was willing?"

Mrs. Stearne turned to Aspiche before he could snort again and snapped, "Colonel, do be quiet!" She looked back at Chang. "I *will* go in my turn. But you must know from Doctor Svenson—yes, I know who he is, as I know Celeste Temple—what happened to that woman at the Institute. Indeed, I am led to understand that you yourself were there, even perhaps responsible—I do not mean *intentionally*," she said quickly as Chang opened his mouth to speak, "but only that you well know that her state was grave. In the Comte's mind this was her only chance."

"Chance for *what*? You have not seen what—what—the *thing* she has become!"

"Truly, I have not—"

"Then you should not speak of it," cried Chang.

* * *

Aspiche chuckled.

"Does something amuse you, Colonel?" snarled Chang.

"*You* amuse me, Cardinal. A moment."

Aspiche stopped walking and pulled his arm from Mrs. Stearne. He reached into his scarlet coat and removed one of his thin black cheroots and a box of matches. He bit off the tip of the cheroot and spat. He looked up to Chang with a vicious grin and stuck the cheroot into his mouth, fiddling with the matches for a light.

"You see, I was introduced to you as a man of unfettered depravity—a figure without scruple or conscience, ready to hunt and kill for a fee. And yet, what do I find—in your final hours, with your life boiled down to its essence? A man in shackles to a whore who thinks as little of him as she does yesterday's breakfast, and working in league—the lone wolf of the riverside!—with an idiot surgeon and an even more idiotic girl—or should I say spinster? She is what—twenty and five?—and the only man who'd have her has come to his senses and thrown her aside like a spent nag!"

"They're alive then?" Chang asked.

"Oh . . . I did not say *that.*" Aspiche chuckled, shaking out the match.

The Colonel inhaled through the cheroot's glowing tip and sent a thin stream of smoke out of the side of his mouth. He offered his arm again to Mrs. Stearne, but Chang made no move to continue.

"You will know, Colonel, that I have just come from killing Major Blach and three of his men—or perhaps five, there was no time to be sure. It would give me as much pleasure to do the same to you."

Aspiche scoffed and blew more smoke.

"Do you know, Mrs. Stearne," Chang pitched his voice loud enough that every Dragoon would hear him clearly, "how I was first introduced to the Colonel? I will tell you—"

Aspiche growled and reached for his saber. Chang raised the book high over his head. The two lines of Dragoons all raised their blades in readiness to attack. Mrs. Stearne, her eyes at once quite wide, stepped between them all.

"Colonel—Cardinal—this must not happen—"

Chang ignored her, glaring into Aspiche's hate-filled eyes, hissing with relish. "I met the Colonel-*Adjutant* when he *hired* me—to execute—to *assassinate*—his commanding officer, Colonel Arthur Trapping of the 4th Dragoons."

The words were met with silence, but their impact on the surrounding soldiers was palpable as a slap. Mrs. Stearne's eyes were wide—she had known Trapping as well. She turned to Aspiche, speaking hesitantly.

"Colonel Trapping..."

"Preposterous! What else will you say to divide me from my men?" cried Aspiche, in what, Chang had to admit, was a very credible impression of impugned honor—though Aspiche, being such a blind egotist, had probably already convinced himself that the contract for murder had never occurred. "You are a well-known lying, murdering rogue—"

"Who *did* kill him, Colonel?" taunted Chang. "Have you found that out? How long will you survive before they do it to you? How much time will the sale of your honor purchase? Did they ask you to attend when they sunk his body in the river?"

With a cry, Aspiche drew his saber in a wide scything arc but then, partially unsteadied by his rage, put his weight on his weak leg and just for a moment tottered. Chang shoved Mrs. Stearne to the side and snapped his right fist into Aspiche's throat. The Colonel staggered back, hand at his collar, choking, his face red. Chang immediately stepped away, close to Mrs. Stearne, raising his arms in peace. Mrs. Stearne at once shouted to the Dragoons, who were clearly an instant away from running Chang through.

"Stop! Stop it—*stop it*—all of you!"

The Dragoons hesitated, still poised to attack. She wheeled to Chang and Aspiche.

"Cardinal—you will be silent! Colonel Aspiche—you will behave like a proper escort! We will continue at once. If there is any more nonsense, I will not be responsible for what happens to *any* of you!"

Chang nodded to her and took another careful step away from the Colonel. He had grown so accustomed to Mrs. Stearne's calm manner that her genuine authority had surprised him. It was as if she had somehow *invoked* it from within, like something learned, like a soldier's automatic response from training—only this was emotion, a force of character that allowed a woman who knew nothing of command to assert control over twenty hardened soldiers—and in the direct place of their officer. Once more, the true impact of the Process left Chang amazed and unsettled.

They continued in silence, turning into another back corridor, skirting the kitchens. Chang looked through every open door or archway they passed, searching for any sign of Svenson or Miss Temple, or any hope of escape. The momentary pleasure at baiting Aspiche had gone, and his mind was once more plagued with doubt. If he could smash the book in the direction of one line of soldiers and then dash through the gap it created, he knew he had a chance—but it was useless if he didn't know where he was going. A blind rush was likely to lead straight into another band of soldiers or a malevolent crowd of adherents. He'd be cut to pieces without a qualm.

Chang turned at the sound of running steps behind them. It was one of the Dragoons Aspiche had sent to find Blenheim. The trooper made his way through the rear line of soldiers and saluted the Colonel, reporting that Blenheim was still missing, and that the other groups were fanning out through the interior rooms. Aspiche nodded curtly.

"Where is Captain Smythe?"

The trooper had no answer.

"Find him!" snapped Aspiche, as if he had asked for Smythe in the first place, and the trooper was impossibly stupid. "He should be outside—arranging the sentries—bring him to me at once!"

The Dragoon saluted again and dashed off. Aspiche said nothing more and they continued on.

More than once they were forced to wait while a group of guests crossed their corridor, moving on a different path toward—he assumed—the ballroom. The guests were formally dressed and masked, usually all smiles and eagerness—much like the two men he'd overheard in the drawing room earlier, and they tended to stare at the soldiers and the three in their midst—Chang, Aspiche, and Mrs. Stearne—as if they made some strange allegorical puzzle to be read: the soldier, the lady, the demon. He made a point of leering wickedly at anyone who looked for too long, but with each such meeting Chang felt more his isolation, and saw the extreme degree of his presumption to come to Harschmort at all . . . and the imminence of his doom.

They walked for perhaps another forty yards before they approached a short figure in a heavy cloak and dark spectacles, with an odd sort of bandolier slung across his chest from which hung perhaps two dozen metal flasks. He held up his hand for them to stop. Aspiche shook himself free of Mrs. Stearne and limped forward, speaking low, but not low enough that Chang could not hear.

"Doctor Lorenz!" the Colonel whispered. "Is something amiss?"

Doctor Lorenz did not share the Colonel's need for discretion. He spoke in a needle-sharp tone directed equally to Aspiche and the woman.

"I require some number of your men. Six will do, I am sure. There is not a minute to spare."

"Require?" snapped Aspiche. "Why should you *require* my men?"

"Because something has *happened* to the fellows detailed to help me," barked Lorenz. "Surely that is not too much to grasp!"

Lorenz gestured behind him to an open doorway. Chang

noticed for the first time a bloody handprint on the wooden frame, and a split in the wood clearly ripped by a bullet.

Aspiche turned and with a finger snap detailed six men from the first line, limping with them through the doorway. Lorenz looked after them but did not follow, one hand idly tapping one of the dangling flasks. His attention wandered to Chang and Mrs. Stearne, and then pointedly settled on the book under Chang's arm. Doctor Lorenz licked his lips.

"Do you know which one that *is*?" The question was put to Mrs. Stearne but his gaze did not shift from the glass book.

"I do not. The Cardinal tells me he took it from a lady."

"Ah," replied Lorenz. He thought for a moment. "Beaded mask?"

Chang did not answer. Lorenz licked his lips again, nodded to himself.

"Must have had. Lady Mélantes. And Lord Acton. And Captain Hazelhorst. And I believe, actually, originally Mrs. Marchmoor herself. If I recall correctly. Rather an important volume."

Mrs. Stearne did not reply, which was, Chang knew, her way of saying she was well aware of its importance and not in need of Doctor Lorenz to apprise her.

A moment later Aspiche appeared at the head of his men, all six of them carrying an apparently very heavy stretcher, covered by a sheet of canvas that had been sewn to the frame, sealing in whoever was beneath it.

"Excellent," announced Lorenz. "My thanks to you. This way . . ." He indicated a door on the opposite side of the hall to the stretcher-bearers.

"You're not joining us?" asked Aspiche.

"There is no time," replied Lorenz. "I've lost precious minutes as it is—if the thing's to be done at all it must be done at once—our supply of ice has been exhausted! Please do offer my respects to all. Madame." He nodded to Mrs. Stearne and followed the soldiers out.

* * *

They walked on to the end of the corridor and stopped again, Aspiche sending a man forward to confirm they were clear to continue. As they waited, Chang shifted his grip on the book. The line of Dragoons in front had diminished now from ten to four. An accurate throw of the book could incapacitate them all and open the way . . . but the way to where? He studied the backs of the soldiers walking in front of him and pictured how the book might shatter . . . and then could not but think of Reeves, and of his delicate alliance with Captain Smythe. What had the Dragoons done to him? How could he face Smythe after slaughtering any of his men in such a foul manner? If there was no other way, he would not hesitate . . . but if there was truly no way out, why should he bother with the Dragoons at all? He would keep the book—either as a way to kill what main figures in the Cabal that he could—Rosamonde or the Comte—or use it to bargain, if not for his own life then Svenson's or Celeste's. He had to hope they were alive.

He swallowed with a grimace and saw Mrs. Stearne's eyes on him. Whether it had been intentional or not, their deliberate passage from the turret had taken long enough that the fire of his rage had faded, leaving his body to bear the full weight of exhaustion and sorrow. He felt something on his lip and wiped it with his glove—a smear of bright blood. He looked back at Mrs. Stearne, but her expression betrayed no feeling at all.

"You see I have very little left to lose," he said.

"Everyone always thinks that," commented Colonel Aspiche, "until that little bit is taken away—and feels like the whole of the world."

Chang said nothing, resenting bitterly the slightest glimmer of actual insight coming from the Colonel.

The Dragoon reappeared in the doorway, clicking his heels and saluting Aspiche.

"Begging your pardon, Sir, but they're ready."

Aspiche dropped the cheroot to the floor and ground it with

his heel. He limped forward to enter the ballroom at the head of his men. Mrs. Stearne watched Chang very closely as they followed, and had quite subtly drifted beyond the immediate reach of his arms.

When they entered the ballroom, there were so many people gathered that Chang could not see through the throng as their path was opened by the wedge of Dragoons, spectators retreating like a whispering tide of elegance. They made their way to the center, when at a crisp bark from Aspiche, the Colonel and his Dragoons expanded the open area, marching some six paces in each direction, driving the crowd farther back, before wheeling to face Cardinal Chang and Mrs. Stearne, alone in the open circle.

Mrs. Stearne took a deliberate step forward and curtseyed deeply, dropping her head as if she faced royalty. Before them all, standing like a row of monarchs on a raised dais, were the uncrowned heads of the Cabal: the Contessa di Lacquer-Sforza, Deputy Minister Harald Crabbé, and, his arm satisfyingly swathed with bandages, Francis Xonck. To their side was the Prince, with Herr Flaüss, masked and apparently having regained the power to stand, to his left and to his right, clinging smilingly to his arm, a slim blonde woman in white robes and a white feather mask.

"Very well managed, Caroline," said the Contessa, returning the curtsey with a nod. "You may go on with your duties."

Mrs. Stearne stood again and looked once more at Cardinal Chang before walking quickly away through the crowd. He stood alone before his judges.

"Cardinal Chang—" began the Contessa.

Cardinal Chang cleared his throat and spat, the scarlet mass flying perhaps half the distance to the dais. An outraged whisper ran throughout the crowd. Chang saw the Dragoons nervously glancing at one another as the guests behind them inched forward.

"Contessa," said Chang, returning her greeting, his voice now unpleasantly hoarse. His gaze fell across the rest of the dais. "Minister . . . Mr. Xonck . . . Highness . . ."

"We require that book," stated Crabbé. "Place it on the floor and walk away from it."

"And then what?" sneered Chang.

"Then you will be killed," answered Xonck. "But killed *kindly.*"

"And if I do not?"

"Then what you have already seen," said the Contessa, "will be a trivial prologue to your pain."

Chang looked at the crowd around him, and the Dragoons—still no sign of Smythe, Svenson, or Celeste. He was acutely aware of the luxurious fittings of the ballroom—the crystal fixtures, the gleaming floor, the walls of mirror and glass—and the finery of the masked spectators, all in contrast to his own filthy appearance. He knew that for these people the state of his garments and his body were definitive indicators of his inferior caste. It was also what pained him about Angelique—in this place as much a piece of chattel as he, as much a specimen of livestock. Why else had she been first to undergo the hideous transformation—why had she been taken to the Institute to begin with? Because it did not matter if she died. And yet she could not see their contempt—just as she could not see him (but this was wrong, for of course she did—she merely rejected what she saw), nor beyond her own desperate ambition to the truth of how she had been used. But then Chang recalled the great figures of the city he'd found, one after another, slumped over the glass books in the string of private rooms, and Robert Vandaariff, now a parchment-scratching automaton. The contempt of the Cabal was not limited to those of lower birth or insufficient station.

He had to admit a certain equity of abuse.

Yet Chang sneered at the expressions of disdain and fury that pressed at him through the ring of uncertain Dragoons. Each guest had been offered the chance to lick the Cabal's boots, and now they clamored for the privilege. Who *were* these people to so easily blind so many?

He thought bitterly that half of the Cabal's work was done for it already—the fevered ambition that ran through their adherents had always lurked in the shadows of those lives, hungrily awaiting the chance to come forward. That the chance was only as honest as a baited hook never occurred to anyone—they were too busy congratulating themselves on swallowing it.

He held the gleaming glass book in front of him for all to see. For some reason the act of raising his arm exerted pressure on his seething lungs and Cardinal Chang erupted into a fit of agonized coughing. He spat again and wiped his bloody mouth.

"You *will* make us clean the floor," observed the Contessa.

"I suppose it's inconvenient of me not to have died at the Ministry," Chang hoarsely replied.

"Terribly so, but you've established yourself as quite a worthy opponent, Cardinal." She smiled at Chang. "Would you not agree, Mr. Xonck?" she called, and at least Chang knew she was mocking Xonck's injury.

"Indeed! The Cardinal illustrates the difficult task that is before us all—the determined struggle we must prepare ourselves to undergo," answered Francis Xonck, his voice pitched to reach the far corners of the room. "The vision we embrace will be resisted with all the tenacity of the man you see before you. Do not underestimate him—nor underestimate your own unique qualities of wisdom and courage."

Chang scoffed at this blatant flattery of the crowd, and wondered why it was Crabbé in politics making speeches and not the unctuously eloquent Xonck. He recalled the prostrate form of Henry Xonck—it might not be long before Francis Xonck was more powerful than five Harald Crabbés put together. Crabbé must have sensed this, for he stepped forward, also addressing the whole of the audience.

"Such a man has even this night committed murders—too many to name!—in his quest to destroy our mission. He has killed our soldiers, he has defiled our women—like a savage he has broken into our Ministry and this very house! And why?"

"Because you're a lying, syphilitic—"

"*Because,*" Crabbé shouted down Chang's hoarse voice easily, "we offer a vision that will break the stranglehold this man—*and his hidden masters*—have over you all, to keep you at bay, offering scraps while they profit from your labor and your worth! We say all this must end—and their bloody man has come to kill us! You see it for yourselves!"

The crowd erupted into a chorus of angry cries, and once more Chang felt he had no real understanding of human beings at all. To him, Crabbé's words were every bit as idiotic and servile as Xonck's, every bit as fawning and conjured, patently so. And yet his listeners bayed like hounds for Chang's blood. The Dragoons were losing ground as the crowd pressed nearer. He saw Aspiche, shoved from behind, looking nervously up to the dais—and then to Chang, self-righteously glaring as if this was all *his* fault.

"Dear friends . . . please! Please—a moment!" Xonck was smiling, raising his good hand, calling over the noise. The cries fell away at once. The control was astonishing. Chang doubted that these people had even undergone the Process—how could there have been time? But he could scarce understand such a uniform response from an untrained (or un-German) collection of individuals.

"Dear friends," Xonck said again, "do not worry—this man shall pay . . . and pay directly." He looked at Chang with an eager smile. "We must merely determine the means."

"Put down the book, Cardinal," repeated the Contessa.

"If anyone moves toward me I will smash it across your beautiful face."

"Will you indeed?"

"It would give me *pleasure.*"

"So petty, Cardinal—it makes me think less of you."

"Well then, I do apologize. If it helps at all, I would choose to kill you not because you have surely killed me already with the glass in my lungs, but because you are truly my most deadly foe. The Prince is an idiot, Xonck I've already beaten, and Deputy Minister Crabbé is a coward."

"How very bold you are," she replied, unable to prevent the slightest smile. "What of the Comte d'Orkancz?"

"He works his art, but you determine that art's path—he is finally your creature. You even weave your plots against your fellows—do any of them know the work assigned to Mr. Gray?"

"Mr. . . . who?" The Contessa's smile was suddenly fixed.

"Oh, come now—why be shy? Mr. *Gray*. From the Institute—he was with you in the Ministry—when Herr Flaüss was given the gift of the Process." He nodded to the portly Macklenburger who, despite the doubting look on his face, nodded back. Before the Contessa could reply Chang called out again. "Mr. Gray's work was assigned by you, I assume. Why else would I have found him in the depths of the prison tunnels, tampering with the Comte's furnaces? I have no idea whether he did what you wanted him to do or not. I killed him before we had a chance to exchange our news."

He had to give her credit. The words were not two seconds from his mouth before she turned to Crabbé and Xonck with a deadly serious hiss, barely audible beyond the dais.

"Did you know about this? Did *you* send Gray on some errand?"

"Of course not," whispered Crabbé, "Gray answered to *you*—"

"Was it the Comte?" she hissed again, even more angrily.

"Gray answered to *you*," repeated Xonck, his mind clearly working behind his measured tone.

"Then why was he in the *tunnels*?" asked the Contessa.

"I'm sure he was not," said Xonck. "I'm sure the Cardinal is *lying*."

They turned to him. Before she could open her mouth Chang pulled his hand from his coat pocket.

"I believe this is his key," Chang called out, and he tossed the heavy metal key to clatter on the floor in front of the dais.

Of course, the key could have been anyone's—and he doubted any of them knew Gray's enough to recognize it—but the palpable artifact had the desired effect of seeming to prove his words. He smiled with a grim pleasure, finally feeling a welcoming coldness enter his heart with this final charade of baiting conversation—for Chang knew there was little more dangerous than a man beyond care, and welcomed the chance to sow what dissension he could in these final, doomed moments. The figures on the dais were silent, as was the crowd—though he was sure the crowd lacked the barest idea of what this might mean, seeing only that its leaders were unpleasantly at a loss.

"What *was* he doing there—" began Crabbé.

"Open the doors!" shouted the Contessa, glaring at Chang but raising her voice so it cut like a razor to the rear of the room. Behind him Chang heard the sound of bolts being drawn. At once the crowd began to whisper, looking back and then shifting away. Someone else was entering the ballroom. Chang glanced at the dais—they all seemed as fixed on the new entry as the crowd—and then back, as the whispering became punctuated by gasps and even cries of alarm.

The crowd made way at last, clearing the floor between Cardinal Chang and, walking slowly toward him, the Comte d'Orkancz. In his left hand was a black leather leash, attached by a metal clasp to the leather collar around the neck of the woman who walked behind him. Despite everything, the breath clutched in Chang's throat.

She was naked, her hair still hanging black in lustrous curls, walking pace by deliberate pace behind d'Orkancz, her eyes roving across the room without seeming to fix on any one thing in particular, as if she were seeing it all for the very first time. She moved slowly, but without modesty, as natural as an animal, each footfall carefully placed, feeling the floor deliberately as she looked at their faces. Her body was gleaming blue, shimmering from its indigo depths, its surface slick as water, pliant but still somehow stiff as she walked, giving Chang the impression that each movement required her conscious thought and preparation. She was beautiful and unearthly—Chang could not look away—the weight of her breasts, the perfect proportion of her ribs and her hips, the luscious sweep of her legs. He saw that, apart from her head, there was now no hair on Angelique's face or body—the lack of eyebrows somehow opening the expression on her face like a blankly beatific medieval Madonna's, at the same time her bare sex was both impossibly innocent and lewd.

Only the whites of her eyes were bright. Her eyes settled on Chang.

The Comte flicked her leash and Angelique drifted forward. The ballroom was silent. Chang could hear the click of each footfall on the polished wood. He wrenched his eyes to d'Orkancz and saw cold hatred. He looked to the dais: shock on the faces of Crabbé and Xonck, but the Contessa, however troubled, looking at her companions, as if to gauge the success of this distraction. Chang looked back at Angelique. He could not stop himself. She stepped closer . . . and he heard her speak.

"Car-din-al *Chang*," she said, enunciating each syllable as carefully as ever . . . but her voice was different, smaller, more intense—as if half of what had made it had been boiled away.

Her lips were not moving—*could* they move?—and he realized with a shock that her words were in his head alone.

"Angelique . . ." His voice was a whisper.

"It is finished, Cardinal, . . . you know it is . . . look at me."

He tried to do anything else. He could not. She came nearer and nearer.

"Poor Cardinal . . . you desired me so very much . . . I desired so very much also . . . do you remember?"

The words in his mind expanded, like Chinese paper balls in water, blooming out into bright flowers, until he felt her presence overwhelm him and her projected thoughts take the place of his own senses.

He was no longer in the room.

They stood together at the river bank, gazing into the grey water at twilight. Had they ever done such a thing? They had, he knew, once—once they had by chance met in the street and she allowed him to walk her back to the brothel. He remembered the day vividly even as he experienced it again through her own projected memory. He was speaking to her—the words meaningless—he had wanted to say anything to reach her, relating the history of the houses they passed, of his daring experiences, of the true life of the river bank. She'd barely said a word. At the time he had wondered if it was a matter of language—her accent was still strong—but now, crushingly, with her thoughts in his mind, he knew that she had merely chosen not to speak, and that the entire episode had nothing to do with him at all. She had only agreed to walk with him—had deliberately gone to him in the street—so as to avoid another jealous client who had followed her all the way from Circus Garden. She had barely heard Chang's words, smiling politely and nodding at his foolish stories and wanting solely to be done with it . . . until they had paused for a moment at the quayside, looking down at the water. Chang had fallen silent, and then spoken quietly of the river's passage to an endless sea—observing that even they in their squalid lives, by being in that place, for that time, could truly situate themselves at the border of mystery.

For that image of possible escape, that unintended echo of her own vast imagined life, so far removed . . . she had been surprised. She had remembered that moment, and offered him, here at the end, that much thanks.

* * *

Cardinal Chang blinked. He looked at the floor. He was on his hands and knees, bloody saliva hanging from his mouth. Colonel Aspiche loomed above him, the glass book cradled in his hands. Angelique stood with the Comte d'Orkancz, her gaze wandering with neither curiosity nor interest. The Comte nodded to the dais and Chang forced himself to turn. Near the dais the crowd parted again . . . for Mrs. Stearne. She entered leading by the hand a small woman in a white silk robe. Chang shook his head—he could not think—the woman in white . . . he knew her . . . he blinked again and wiped his mouth, swallowing painfully. The robe was sheer, clinging tightly to her body . . . her feet were bare . . . a mask of white feathers . . . hair the color of chestnuts, in sausage curls to either side of her head. With an effort Chang rose up on his knees.

He opened his mouth to speak as Mrs. Stearne reached behind her and pulled the feathered mask from Miss Temple's face. The scars of the Process were vivid around each grey eye, and burned in a line across the bridge of her nose.

Chang tried to say her name. His mouth would not work.

Colonel Aspiche moved behind him. The force of the blow so spun the room that Chang wondered, in his last moment before darkness, whether his head had been cut off.

THREE

Provocateur

As a surgeon, Doctor Svenson knew that the body did not remember pain, only that an experience had been painful. Extreme fear however was seared into the memory like nothing else in life, and as he pulled himself, hand over agonizing hand, toward the metal gondola, the dark countryside spinning dizzily below him, the freezing winds numbing his face and fingers, the Doctor's grasp on his own sanity was tenuous at best. He tried to think of anything but the sickening drop below his kicking boots, but he could not. The effort denied him the breath to scream or even cry out, but with each wrenching movement he whimpered with open terror. All his life he had shrunk away from heights of any kind—even climbing ladders aboard ship he willed his eyes to look straight ahead and his limbs to move, lest his mind or stomach give way to even that meager height. Despite himself he scoffed—a staccato bark of saliva—at the very notion of *ladders*. His only consolation, feeble in the extreme, was that the noise of the wind and the darkness of the sky had so far hidden him from anyone looking out of a window. Not that he knew for certain he had not been seen. The Doctor's own eyes were tightly shut.

He had climbed perhaps half-way up the rope and his arms felt like burning lead. Already it seemed all he could do to hold on. He opened his eyes for the briefest glimpse, shutting them at once with a yelp at the vertigo caused by the swinging gondola. Where before he'd seen a face at the circular window there was only black glass. Had it truly been Elöise? He had been sure on the ground, but now—now he barely knew his own name. He forced himself upwards—each moment of letting one hand go to stab above him for the rope was a spike of fear in his heart, and yet he made himself do it again and again, feeling his way, his face locked in a shocking rictus of effort.

Another two feet. His mind assailed him—why not stop? Why not let go? Wasn't this the underlying dread behind his fear of heights to begin with—the actual impulse to jump? Why else did he shrink away from balconies and windows, but for the sudden urge to hurl himself into the air? Now it would be so simple. The grassy pastures below would be as good a grave as any sea—and how many times had he contemplated that, since Corinna's death? How many times had he grown cold looking over the iron rail of a Baltic ship, worrying—like a depressive terrier with a well-gnawed stick—the urge to throw himself over the side?

Another two feet, gritting his teeth and kicking his legs, driving himself by pure will and anger. That was a reason to live—his hatred for these people, their condescension, their assumption of privilege, their unconscionable *appetite.* He thought of them in the gondola, away from the freezing cold, no doubt wrapped in furs, soothed by the whispering wind and the whistling buzz of the rotors. Another foot, his arms slack as rope. He opened his hand and snatched for a new grip . . . kicked his boots . . . again . . . again. He forced his mind to think of anything but the drop—the dirigible—he'd never seen anything like it! Obviously full of some gas—hydrogen, he assumed—but was that all? And how was it powered? He didn't know how it could bear the weight of the gondola much less a steam engine . . . could there be some other source? Something with Lorenz and the indigo clay? In the abstract Svenson might have found these questions fascinating, but now he threw himself into them with the mindless fervor of a man reciting multiplication tables to stave off an impending *crise.*

He opened his eyes again and looked up. He was closer than he thought, hanging some ten yards below the long iron cabin. The upper end of the rope was secured to the steel frame of the gasbag itself, just behind the cabin. The rear of the cabin had no window that he could see... but did it have a door? He closed his eyes and climbed, three agonizing feet, and looked up again. Doctor Svenson was suddenly appalled... climbing with his eyes closed he hadn't realized... and for a moment he simply clung where he was. Below and to each side of the cabin were the rear rotors—each perhaps eight feet across—and his path on the rope led right between them. Between the wind and his own exertions, the rope swung back and forth—the blades themselves were turning so fast he couldn't tell how wide the gap really was. The higher he got, the more any exertion might send him too far in either direction—and straight into the blades.

There was nothing he could do except drop, and the longer he delayed out of fear, the less strength was in his arms. He pulled himself up, clamping shut his eyes, and gripped the cable more firmly between his knees to steady the swinging. As he inched higher he could hear the rotors' menacing revolutions more clearly, a relentless chopping of air. He was just beneath them. He could smell the exhaust—the same sharp tang of ozone, sulphur, and scorched rubber that had nearly made him sick in the attic of Tarr Manor—the flying vehicle *was* another emanation of the Cabal's insidious science. He could sense the rotors near to him, invisibly slicing past. He extended a hand up the rope, then another, and then hauled his entire body into range, braced for the savage impact that would shear off a limb. The blades roared around him but he remained somehow unscathed. Svenson inched higher, his entire body shaking with the effort. The gondola was right in front of him—some three feet out of reach. Any attempt to nudge the rope toward it—if he didn't catch hold—would send him straight into the rotors on the backswing. Even worse, there was nothing on the rear of the gondola to grab on to even if he risked the attempt. He looked up. The cable was attached to the metal frame by an iron bolt... it was his only option. Another two yards. His head was above the rotors. He could almost touch the bolt. He inched up another foot, gasping, his body expending itself in a way he could not comprehend. Another six inches. He reached up in agony, felt the bolt, and then above it the riveted steel strut. A spasm of fear shot through him—he was only holding to the rope with one hand and his knees. He swallowed, and fixed his grip on the strut. He was going to have to let go and pull himself up. It should be possible to wrap his legs around the strut and creep over the rotors to the top of the gondola. But he would have to let go of the rope. Suddenly—it was perhaps inevitable—his nerves got the best of him and his rope hand slipped. At once Doctor Svenson thrust both arms toward the metal strut and caught hold, his legs flailing wildly. He looked down to see the rope disappear into the right side rotor, flayed to pieces. He pulled his knees to his chest with a whimpering cry—before the rotors hacked off his feet—and kicked them over the metal bar. He looked up at the canvas gasbag just above his head. Directly below him was death—by dismemberment if not by impact. He slowly slid along the strut, painfully shifting his grip on the freezing metal around the intervening cross-pieces. His hands felt numb—he was gripping as tightly with his forearms as his fingers.

It took him ten minutes to crawl ten feet. The gondola was directly beneath him. As gently as he could he let down his legs and felt the solid metal beneath his feet. His eyes were streaming—whether with tears or the wind, Doctor Svenson hadn't a clue.

The gondola was a smooth metal box of blackened steel, suspended some three feet below the massive gasbag by metal struts bolted to its frame at each corner. The surface of the roof was slick from the cold and the moisture in the foggy coastal air, and Doctor Svenson was both too paralyzed with fear and too numbed by exertion to allow himself so near the edge to cling to one of these corner struts. Instead, he crouched in the center of the roof with his arms wrapped around the same metal brace he'd used to climb forward. His teeth chattered as he forced his staggered mind to examine his circumstances. The gondola was perhaps twelve feet across and forty feet in length. He could see a round hatch set into the rooftop, but going to it would require him to release his hold on the metal brace. He shut his eyes and focused on breathing, shivering despite his greatcoat and his recent exertion—or even because of it, the sweat over his body and in his clothing now viciously chilling his flesh in the bitter wind. He opened his eyes at a sudden lurch, holding on to the metal brace for his life. The dirigible was turning and Svenson felt his grip inexorably weakening as the force of the turn pulled him away. With an insane bark of laughter he saw himself—in a desperate attempt to manage his grip on a swiftly turning airship—in comparison to his lifelong anxiety at climbing *ladders.* He remembered just the day before—was it so recently?—emerging on his hands and knees onto the rooftop of the Macklenburg compound! If he'd only known! Svenson tightened his grip and cackled again—the rooftop! He was clinging to the very answer to the mystery of the Prince's escape—they'd come for him with the dirigible! The rotors would be silent at a lower speed—they could have easily drifted into position and lowered men to liberate the Prince with no one being the wiser. Even the crimped cigarette butt made sense—discarded by the Contessa di Lacquer-Sforza as she watched from a gondola window. What still made no sense however, was *why* the Prince had been stolen without the other Cabal members—Xonck and Crabbé at the least—being aware of it. Like the death of Arthur Trapping, it lay between his enemies without explanation . . . if he could just unravel either mystery . . . he might understand it all.

The dirigible straightened out of the turn. The fog thickened around Svenson, and he moved forward on the strut, careful not to step too heavily—the last thing he wanted was for anyone below to know he was there. He shut his eyes once more and tried to ease his heaving breath to mere gasps and chattering teeth. He would not move until his arms fell off or until the dirigible found its destination, whichever happened first.

When he opened his eyes the dirigible was making another turn, less precipitous than before and—he hadn't realized, but now saw through ragged gaps in the fog—at a lower altitude, some two hundred feet above what looked like a low fennish grassland, with scarcely a single tree in sight. Were they possibly crossing the sea? He saw lights through the gloom, first dim and winking, but as they went on emerging with a growing clarity that allowed him to sketch out the entirety of their destination—for indeed, as he studied it the dirigible continued to descend.

It was an enormous structure, but relatively low to the ground—Svenson's guess was two or three stories—giving out an impression of massive strength. The place as a whole was shaped something like a disconnected jawbone, with the center space taken up by some sort of ornamental garden. As they soared closer he could hear a variation in the sound of the rotors—they were slowing down—as he saw more detail: the large open plaza in front, thronged with coaches and dotted with the ant-like (or as they neared, mouse-like) figures of drivers and grooms. Svenson looked to the other side and saw a pair of waving lanterns on the rooftop and behind the lanterns a group of men—no doubt waiting to wrangle the mooring ropes. They drifted closer... a hundred feet, seventy feet... Svenson was suddenly concerned about being seen, and against all his better wishes dropped down to hang on to the hatch handle, flattening his body over the roof of the gondola. The steel plate was freezing. He had one hand on the handle and the other spread out across the roof for balance, with each boot splayed toward a different corner. They sank lower. He could hear shouts from below, and then the pop of a window being opened and an answering shout from the gondola.

They were landing at Harschmort House.

Doctor Svenson shut his eyes again, now more out of dread at being discovered than at his still-precarious altitude, as all around him he heard the calls and whistles of the craft coming in to land. No one came up through the hatch—apparently the mooring cables were lowered from the front of the gondola. Perhaps once the rotors stopped the cables were re-attached to the bolt where he'd climbed. He had no idea—but it was only a matter of time before he was discovered. He forced his mind to think about his situation, and his immediate odds.

He was unarmed. He was physically spent—as well as his ankle twisted, head battered, and hands raw from the climb. There was on the rooftop a gang of assuredly burly men more than willing to take him in hand, if not fling him to the plaza below. Within the gondola lurked another handful of enemies—Crabbé, Aspiche, Lorenz, Miss Poole . . . and in their power, in who knew what state—or, if he was perfectly honest, with what loyalties—Elöise Dujong. Below him he heard another popping sound and then a loud metallic rattle that ended in a heavy ring of steel striking stone. He suppressed the urge to raise his head and peek. The gondola began to rock slightly as he heard voices—Crabbé calling out and then after him Miss Poole. Someone answered them from below and then the conversation grew to too many voices for him to follow—they were descending from the gondola via some lowered ladder or staircase.

"At long last," this was Crabbé, calling to someone across the rooftop, "is everything ready?"

"A most delightful time," Miss Poole was saying to someone else, "though not without *adventure*—"

"Damnable thing," Crabbé continued. "I've no idea—Lorenz says he can, but that is news to me—yes, twice—the second straight through the heart—"

"Gently! Gently now!" This was Lorenz calling out. "And ice—we're going to need a washtub full at once—yes, all of you—take hold! Quickly now, there is no time!"

Crabbé was listening as someone speaking too low for Svenson to hear briefed him on events elsewhere—could this be Bascombe?

"Yes . . . yes . . . I see . . ." He could picture the Deputy Minister nodding along as he muttered. "And Carfax? Baax-Saornes? Baroness Roote? Mrs. Kraft? Henry Xonck? Excellent—and what of our illustrious host?"

"The Colonel has injured his ankle, yes," Miss Poole chuckled—

was there ever a thing that woman did not find amusing?—"in *battle* against the dread Doctor Svenson. I am afraid the poor Doctor's death was hard—my complexion is quite *ashen* at the prospect!"

Miss Poole—and joining her with a bellowing "haw haw haw" was Colonel Aspiche—erupted in laughter at her pun. In Svenson's spent emotional state, it was something of an abstraction to realize that the object of their sport was his being burnt in an oven.

"This way—this way—yes! I do declare, Miss Poole, the ride does not seem to have suited her!"

"And yet she seemed so recently *tractable,* Colonel—perhaps the lady merely requires more of your kind *attention.*"

They were taking Elöise away—she was alive. What had they done to her? Worse, what did Miss Poole mean by "tractable"? He tormented himself with the image of Elöise on the wooden staircase, the confusion in her eyes... she had come to Tarr Manor for a reason, no matter that it was gone from her memory. Who was Svenson to say who she truly was? Then he remembered the warm press of her lips against his and had no idea what to think at all. Still Svenson's fear at being discovered would not let him look up. The seconds crawled by and he muttered to himself, fervently wishing the pack of them off the rooftop as quickly as possible.

Finally the voices were gone. But what of the men mooring the craft, or guarding it? Doctor Svenson heard a muffled clicking from the hatch beneath him, then felt the handle turning in his hand. He scuttled back as the handle caught the bolt. The hatch rose, and directly after it appeared the grease-smeared face of a man in coveralls. He saw Svenson and opened his mouth in surprise. Svenson drove the heel of his boot into the man's face with all his strength, grimacing at the crunch of impact. The fellow abruptly dropped back through the open hatch, Svenson scrabbling after him. He thrust both legs through the round hole, ignoring the line of iron rungs bolted to the wall, and launched himself down onto the groaning, stunned body sitting at its feet. Svenson landed squarely on the man's shoulders, flattening him hard against the floor with a meaty thud. He stumbled from his unmoving victim and grabbed on to the rungs for balance. Sticking out from a pocket of the man's coveralls was an enormous, greasy wrench. Weighing it in his hand, Svenson recalled both the wrench with which he had doomed Mr. Coates at Tarr Village, and the candlestick with which he had murdered the unfortunate Starck. Had such mayhem become so necessary, so natural a tactic? Was it only the night before when the Comte had brought to mind Svenson's guilt upon poisoning the fellow—the villain, did it matter—in Bremen? Where were those tender scruples now?

He stepped carefully through the gondola, which was divided up into smaller cabins like the cramped yet well-appointed interior of a yacht. Against the wall were leather upholstered benches and small inset tables and what seemed to be a drinks cabinet—the lashed-down bottles visible through the secured glass front. Svenson's numbed fingers fumbled with the leather straps across the cabinet door. His hands were still half-frozen and raw and he could not get them to perform such fine work as unbuckling a simple clasp. He whimpered with impatience and snatched up the wrench. He swung it once against the glass panel and then jammed it through the shattered hole to clear away the jagged fragments from the edge. He carefully extricated a bottle of cognac and pried out the cork with stiff, claw-like fingers. He took a deep swig, coughing once and happy for the warmth, and then took another. He exhaled fiercely, tears at the corner of each eye, and then took another swig. Svenson put the bottle down—he wanted to be warm and revived, not insensible.

On the opposite wall was another, taller wooden cabinet. He stepped to this and tried to pull it open. It was locked. Svenson raised the wrench and with one solid blow smashed in the wood around the lock. He pulled apart cabinet doors to reveal a well-oiled row of five gleaming carbines, five polished cutlasses, and hanging from hooks behind them, three service revolvers. Svenson tossed the wrench onto a leather seat and quickly availed himself of a revolver and a box of cartridges, snapping open the cylinder to load. He looked up, listening as his fingers went about sliding shell after shell into the gun and, after six, snapping the cylinder home. Was someone else outside? He reached for one of the cutlasses. It was a ridiculously vicious weapon, rather like thirty inches of razor-sharp butcher's cleaver, with a shining brass bell hilt that covered his entire hand. He had no idea how to use it, but the thing was so fearsome he was nearly convinced it would kill by itself.

The man in coveralls was not moving. Svenson took a step toward the front, paused, sighed, and then quickly knelt by the man, stuffing the revolver in his pocket. He felt for a pulse at the carotid artery . . . it was there. He sighed again at the man's clearly broken nose, and shifted his position so the blood would drain without choking him. He wiped his hands and stood up, pulling out the revolver. Now that he was sure he retained his humanity, he set forth for revenge.

Doctor Svenson advanced through the next smaller cabin to the doorway—another hatch with a collapsible metal staircase opened out to the surface of the roof some ten feet below. Another staircase led up to the cockpit of the dirigible. He made sure no one at the base of the stairs could see him and listened once more. This center cabin seemed much like the other—benches and tables—when his eye caught an innocuous litter of rope on the floor beneath a metal wall brace. Svenson knelt with dismay. The fragments were cut on one end and bloody . . . Elöise's bonds, her hands, her feet, her mouth. Whoever had confined her had done so without scruple—tight enough to draw blood. Svenson felt a chill at what she had endured, and an answering glimmer of rage in his veins. Did this not demonstrate her virtue? He sighed, for of course it showed nothing other than the Cabal's cruelty and thoroughness. Just as they sacrificed potential adherents at Tarr Manor, so they would hardly scruple to make sure of a new adherent's loyalty—and, of course, any true adherent would undergo every trial without protest. If only he knew what they had said to her, what urgings and temptations, what questions... if only he knew how she had replied.

He pulled the revolver from his pocket. With a deep breath—he was not so transformed that he could descend such a thing, trusting to balance with a weapon in each hand, without some tangle of anxiety—he stepped through the hatch and as swiftly as possible climbed (or careened) down the gangway. He whipped his gaze across the rooftop, looking for any other guard. But as far as he could see he was alone. The craft was moored to the roof by two cables attached to the underside of the gondola, but otherwise unattended. He decided he should not tempt his fate further and strode toward the only way his quarry could have gone—a small stone shed some twenty yards off, its door propped open by a brick.

As Doctor Svenson walked he looked down at his hands—the cutlass in the left, the revolver in the right. Was this the proper arrangement? He was no particular shot at anything but short range, nor had he any experience with the cutlass. For each, using his right hand would make for a more effective weapon—but which would be least hampered in his left? He thought who he might be struggling against—his own Ragnarok troopers or Colonel Aspiche's Dragoons—all of whom would be carrying sabers and savagely trained in their use. With the cutlass in his left hand he hadn't a prayer to parry a single blow. And yet, if the thing was in his right—did he still have any chance—or, more importantly, did he have a better chance than shooting at them? He did not. He kept each weapon where it was.

He opened the door and looked to an empty staircase with smooth white plaster walls and flagstone steps. He heard nothing. Svenson eased the door to its brick stop and stepped back, crossing quickly, swallowing the rising fear in his throat, to the far edge of the rooftop overlooking the garden. This edge was lined, like an ornamental castle, with a low wall of defensive crenellations from which he could both hang on and peer out simultaneously. The fog was still thick, but below him he could see the massive garden as through a veil, with conical tops of formally trimmed fir trees, tips of statuary and decorative urns, and then moving torches all piercing the lurking gloom. The torches seemed to be carried by Dragoons, and he heard cries, but it was difficult to place where they'd come from, as clearly not all the men in the garden had torches. Then the shouts were louder—somewhere near the center? This was followed by a shot and then a strangled cry. Two more shots rang out in direct succession and Svenson could see the torches converging and he scanned ahead of them to find their quarry. The fog was still too thick—yet the fact that they were in motion told him that whoever had been shot was not sufficiently wounded—or not alone.

Suddenly Doctor Svenson saw a movement, nearly below him, as a figure crept from the line of hedges to the grass border of the garden, preparing to dash across the strip of gravel to the house itself. The fog clung to the moist vegetation and dissipated at its border... it was Cardinal Chang. The Dragoons were hunting Chang! Svenson waved his arms like a lunatic, but Chang was looking instead at some window—the fool! Svenson wanted to scream, but what good would that do—aside from getting a squadron of Dragoons running directly to the roof?

Then Chang was gone, darting back into the shadow of the garden—creeping who knew where—a pair of Dragoons arriving at the spot only moments later. Svenson realized with a shudder that if he *had* succeeded in catching Chang's attention, the man would most likely be dead. The Dragoons looked around them with suspicion—and then glanced up, forcing Svenson to duck behind the wall.

What was Chang doing here? And how could none of these running men have noticed the arrival of the airship? Svenson supposed it was the fog and dirigible's dark color and counted himself lucky to have arrived so secretly... if only he could turn it to his advantage.

At the sharp crack of breaking wood in the garden Svenson looked back down and to his surprise found Chang at once, visible from the waist up through the fog—which meant he stood well off the ground—kicking at something inside a massive stone urn. The torches converged around him—there were shouts. With a sudden impulse Svenson leaned over the edge of the roof and flung the cutlass with all his might toward a ground-floor window beneath him. He ducked into cover just as the sound of breaking glass cut through the cries of pursuit. At once there was a confused crossing of shouts and then charging footsteps on the gravel below. At least some men had been diverted to the window, giving Chang that much more time to do whatever it was he was doing... hiding in an urn? Svenson risked one more glimpse but could no longer see him. There was nothing else to do—and the more he stayed in one place, the more vulnerable he was to capture. He dashed back to the staircase door and began his descent into the house. He might attribute some of this energy to the cognac, but the knowledge that—somehow, somewhere—he was not alone, gave his mission a new hope.

The staircase led him ten steps down to the third-floor landing and went no farther, being for roof access alone. Svenson listened at the door and gingerly turned the knob, releasing a breath he had not realized he had been holding when it was not locked. He wondered idly at these people's confidence—but with the exception of three ragged random individuals, who had they not been able to sway? He thought again of Chang—what had brought him? With a jolt—and another snarl of recrimination—he knew it must be Miss Temple. Chang had found her—had traced her to Harschmort. And now Chang was doing his best to survive capture. But Svenson's presence was unknown to them. While they occupied themselves with hunting Cardinal Chang—Svenson could only trust in his comrade's ability to evade them—he himself must supply Miss Temple's rescue.

And what of Elöise? Doctor Svenson sighed in spite of himself. He did not know. Yet, if she was who he hoped—the smell of her hair still sang in his memory—how could he leave her? The house was very large—how could he hope to accomplish both of these goals? Svenson paused and placed a hand over his eyes, balancing in his exhaustion the pull of his heart against that of his mind—for what were these rescues next to his unquestioned larger aim—to reclaim the Prince and the honor of Macklenburg itself? He did not know. He was one man, and for the moment at least, quite alone.

Svenson slipped silently from the staircase onto an open landing. To either side extended corridors to each wing, and before him was the highest point of the splendid main staircase of the house, and a marble balcony that, should he care to look over its edge (which he did not), would allow him to see down to the main entrance two floors below. Both side corridors were empty. If Miss Temple or Elöise had been stashed into a room for safe-keeping, he was certain there would be a guard at the door. He would need to go down another floor.

But what was he looking for? He tried to focus on what he knew—what plans were in motion that might guide his steps? As far as he could tell, the Cabal had used Tarr Manor to gather and refine a massive quantity of the indigo clay—either to make more of the malevolent glass, or to build and house the dirigible, or for something still more sinister... the alchemical genius of Oskar Veilandt as exploited by the Comte d'Orkancz. A second purpose had been to gather—to capture in glass—personal information from the discontented intimates of the highly placed and powerful. So armed, there would be small limit to the Cabal's powers of compulsion and subversion. Who did not have such secret shames? Who would not do what they could to preserve them? This specter of raw power brought to Svenson's mind the fallen Duke of Stäelmaere. The third purpose had been his introduction—in relative isolation—to the Cabal, an attempt to gain his favor and participation. With the Duke dead, at least Crabbé's Palace intrigues had been thrown into disarray.

And what did it mean for Elöise, the author of his death? Perhaps, he thought with a chill, her loyalties did not matter at all—having demonstrated such boldness the Cabal would give her over to the Process and make her theirs forever. As soon as the thought formed he knew it was true. And if his logic was right—and Svenson was dreadfully certain it was—the exact same fate awaited Miss Temple.

The Doctor slipped down the wide oaken staircase, his back against the wall, head craned for the first glimpse of any guard below. He reached the inter-floor landing and looked down. No one. He slid to the far wall and crept on to the second floor proper. He heard voices rising up from the main foyer below, but a quick glance back and forth showed the second-floor corridors empty of guards. Where was everyone from the dirigible? Had they just gone straight to the main floor? How could he follow into the thick of the household?

He had no idea, but crossed the landing to the final staircase leading down—this flight being even wider and more ostentatious than the others, as it was part of a visitor's first impression of the house from the main entrance. Svenson swallowed. Even from his partial perspective he could see a knot of black-coated footmen and a steady passage of elegantly dressed guests coming in from the front. A moment later he heard a clatter of boots and saw a furious-faced balding man with heavy whiskers march through his frame of vision at the head of a line of Dragoons. The footmen snapped to attention at his appearance and saluted like soldiers, calling out his name—Plengham?—all of which the man ignored. Then he was gone and Svenson sighed bitterly—looking down at a mere five or six men he'd have to overcome in the presence of a hundred onlookers.

He whipped his head around at a noise behind him and startled a squeak from each of a pair of girls dressed in black with white aprons and white caps—housemaids. Svenson took in the ingrained deference on their fearful faces and wasted no time in exploiting it—the more time they had to think, the more likely it was they'd scream.

"There you are!" he snarled. "I've just arrived with Minister Crabbé—they directed me here to clean up—I'll need a basin and my coat brushed—just do what you can—quickly now, quickly!"

Their eyes were wide on the revolver in his hand as he thrust it back into his coat pocket and then pulled the coat from his shoulders as he walked, driving the two girls back down the hall where they'd come. He tossed the filthy coat over the arms of one and nodded curtly at the other.

"I'll be speaking with Lord Vandaariff—vital information—extraordinary activity. You've seen the Prince, of course—Prince Karl-Horst? Speak when you're spoken to!"

Both girls bobbed on their knees. "Yes, Sir," they said nearly in unison, one of them—without the coat, dirty brown hair escaping from her cap near her ear, perhaps a bit stouter than her companion—adding, "Miss Lydia's just gone to meet the Prince, I'm sure."

"Excellent," snapped Svenson. "You can tell by my accent, yes—I'm the Prince's man—vital information for your master, but I can hardly meet him like this, can I?"

The girl with the coat darted forward to open a door. The other hissed at her with dismay, and the first hissed back, as if to ask where else they were to take him. The second gave in—all of this happening too rapidly for Svenson to complain at the delay—and they ushered him into a washroom whose trappings dripped with white lace and whose air was a near-suffocating *mélange* of scented candles and dried flowers doused with perfume.

All business, the girls directed Doctor Svenson to the mirror, where it was all he could do not to flinch bodily at what greeted him. As one maid brushed ineffectually at his coat, the other soaked a cloth and began to dab at his face—but he could see the arrant futility of either task. His face was a mask of dirt, sweat, and dried blood—from his own lacerations or his victims', he could not say until the rough surface of the cloth either cleaned it away or caused him to wince. His ice blond hair, normally plastered back in a respectable manner, had broken forward, matted with blood and grime. His intention had been to merely use the maids to get out of sight and find information, but he could not help but take some action at his wretched state. He brushed the fussing hands aside and slapped at his dusty jacket and trousers.

"Attend to my uniform—I'll manage this."

He stepped to the basin and plunged his head directly in it, gasping despite himself at the cold water. He brought up his dripping head, groped for a towel which the girl thrust into his hand, and then stood, vigorously rubbing his hair and face, pressing repeatedly at his re-opened cuts, dappling the towel with tiny red spots. He threw the towel aside, exhaled with some pleasure and smeared his hair back as best he could with his fingers. He caught the maid with his coat watching his face in the mirror.

"Your Miss Lydia," he called to her. "Where is she now—she and the Prince?"

"She went with Mrs. Stearne, Sir."

"Captain," the other corrected her. "He's a Captain, aren't you, Sir?"

"Very observant," answered Svenson, forcing an avuncular smile. He looked again at the basin and licked his lips. "Excuse me..."

Svenson leaned over to the copper pitcher and held it up to his mouth, awkwardly drinking, splashing water on his collar and jacket. He didn't care, any more than he cared what the maids might think—he was suddenly parched. When had he last had a drink—at the little inn at Tarr Village? It seemed half a lifetime past. He set down the pitcher and picked up another towel to wipe his face. He dropped the towel and dug his monocle from his pocket, screwing it into place.

"How is the coat?" he asked.

"Begging your pardon, Captain, but your coat is very unkempt," replied the maid meekly. He snatched it from her hands.

"Unkempt?" he said. "It is *filthy*. You have at least made it recognizable *as* a coat, if not a presentable one—and that is quite an achievement. And you"—he turned to the other—"have turned me into a recognizable *officer,* if not an entirely respectable one—but that fault lies entirely with me. I thank you both." Svenson dug into his trouser pocket and came up with two silver coins, giving one to each girl. Their eyes were wide . . . even suspiciously so. It was too much money—did they think he required some additional unsavory service? Doctor Svenson cleared his throat, his face reddening, for now they were smiling at him coyly. He adjusted his monocle and thrashed his way awkwardly into the greatcoat, his haughty tone giving way to an uncomfortable stammer.

"If you would be kind enough to point me in the direction taken by this M-Mrs. Stearne?"

Doctor Svenson was happily directed by the maids' pointing fingers to a side staircase he never would have seen, reached through a bland-looking door next to a mirror. Still Svenson was unsure as to his responsibility, his best intention. He followed the path of Karl-Horst and his fiancée—yet might it not just as well lead to that of Miss Temple or Elöise? The Cabal would strive to keep the likes of Miss Temple from the sight of its guests—or "adherents" as Miss Poole might arrogantly term them—for as long as possible, as she was sure to give the impression of a prisoner under guard. As they were not on this floor or the one above, this was at least a way for him to descend unseen. But what if he found the Prince before either woman—would that end his search entirely? For an instant he imagined a successful return to Macklenburg, to that life of arid duty, idiot successfully in tow, his heart as ever in its fog of despair. Yet what of the compact he had made on the rooftop of the Boniface, with Chang and Miss Temple? How could he choose between these paths? Svenson left the maids looking after him in the hallway, their heads a-tilt like a pair of curious cats. He fought the urge to wave good-bye and strode on to the staircase.

It was smaller than the main stairs, but only as if to say the Sphinx is smaller than the Pyramids, for it was still magnificent. Every step was intricately inlaid wood of many colors, and the walls were painted with an extremely credible copy, in miniature, of the Byzantine mosaics of Justinian and Theodora at Ravenna. Svenson suppressed an appreciative whistle at the amount Robert Vandaariff must have spent to refinish this one side staircase, and then attempted without success to extrapolate from that imagined sum the cost of fitting out Harschmort Prison into Harschmort House. It was a fortune whose vastness stretched beyond the Doctor's ability with numbers.

At the foot of the steps he had expected to see a door to the first-floor hallway, but there was none. Instead, he found an unlocked door, like a kitchen door on a spring. *Was* he near the kitchens? He frowned for a moment, placing himself in the house. On his previous visit, he had come in the front entrance with the Prince and spent his entire time in the left wing—around the ballroom—and then in the garden, where he'd seen Trapping's body. He was now in unknown territory. He pushed the swinging door gently until there was enough of a gap to peek through.

It was a room of bare wooden tables and a plain stone floor. Around one table were two men and three women—two sitting, and a younger woman pouring beer from a jug into wooden cups—all five in plain, dark woolen work clothes. Between them on the table was an empty platter and a stack of wooden bowls—servants taking a late repast. Svenson threw his shoulders back and marched forward in his best impression of Major Blach, deepening his accent and worsening his diction for maximum haughtiness.

"Excuse me! I am requiring after the Prince Karl-Horst von Maasmärck—he has come this way? Or—excuse me—*this* way he shall be found?"

They stared at him as if he were speaking Chinese. Again Doctor Svenson assumed the natural actions of Major Blach, which was to say he screamed at them.

"The Prince! With your Miss Vandaariff—this way? One of you tells me at once!"

The poor servants shrank back in their chairs, the pleasant end of their evening meal ruined by his insistent, threatening bellow. Three of them pointed with an abject eagerness at the opposite door and one of the women actually stood, nodding with cringing deference, indicating the same door.

"That way, Sir—not these ten minutes—begging your pardon—"

"*Ach,* it is very kind of you I am sure—please and be back to your business!" snapped Svenson, stepping to the door before anyone thought to question who in the world he was and why a man in such a filthy, unkempt state was following the Prince in such a hurry. He could only hope that the demands of the Cabal were as oblique, and the figures just as imperious.

It was not difficult to believe.

Once through the swinging door, Svenson stopped again, reaching behind him to still its movement. He stood at one end of a wider, open drawing room—a sort of servants' corridor with a low overhanging ceiling, designed to allow passage without it being intrusive to the room at large. Above him was a musicians' balcony from which Svenson could hear the delicate plucking of a harp. Directly across the corridor was another swinging door, perhaps ten yards away, but the way across was fully open to the larger room. He threw himself against the small abutment of wall that hid the swinging door and listened to the raised voices of those people directly beyond it.

"They must *choose,* Mr. Bascombe! I cannot suspend the natural order indefinitely! As you know, beyond this immediate matter looms the Comte's transformations, the initiations in the theatre, the many, many important guests identified for collection—to all of which my personal attention is crucial—"

"And as I have told *you,* Doctor Lorenz, I do not know their wishes!"

"One way or the other—it is very simple! He is made use of at once or he is given over to putrefaction and waste!"

"Yes, you have made those choices clear—"

"Not clear enough that they will act!" Lorenz began to sputter with the condescending pedantry of a seasoned academic. "You will see—at the temples, at the nails, at the lips, the discoloration—the seepage—you will no doubt, even *you,* discern the *smell*—"

"Berate me as you please, Doctor, we will wait for the Minister's word."

"I *will* berate you—"

"And I remind you that the fate of the Queen's own brother is not for *you* to decide!"

"I say . . . what was that noise?"

This was another voice. One that Svenson felt he knew but could not place.

More importantly, it referred to the sound of his own entry through the swinging door. The others stopped their argument.

"What noise?" snapped Lorenz.

"I don't know. But I thought I heard something."

"Aside from the harp?" asked Bascombe.

"Yes, that lovely harp," muttered Lorenz waspishly. "Exactly what every slaughtered Royal needs when lying in state in a leaking tub of ice—"

"No, no . . . from over *there* . . ." said the voice, quite clearly turning to the side of the room where Svenson stood, quite minimally concealed.

The voice of Flaüss.

* * *

The Envoy was with them. He would name Svenson and that would be the end of it. Could he run back through the servants? But where after that—up the stairs?

His thoughts were broken by the sound of a large party entering from the far doors, near the others—many footsteps...or more accurately bootsteps. Lorenz called out a greeting in his flat, mocking voice.

"Excellent, how kind of you to finally arrive. You see our burden—I will require two of your fellows to collect a supply of ice, I am told there is an ice *house* somewhere on the premises—"

"Captain," this was Bascombe cutting smoothly through the Doctor's words, "could you make sure we are not troubled by any unwanted visitors from the servants' passage?"

"As soon as you send two men for more ice," insisted Lorenz.

"Indeed," said Bascombe, "two men for ice, four men for the tub, one man to respectfully ask the Minister if there is further word, and one to check the passage. Does that satisfy us all?"

Svenson slipped back to the door and pushed gently against it, straining for silence. It held fast. The door had been bolted from the inner side—the servants making sure he'd not again trespass upon their meal. He shoved again, harder, to no avail. He quickly fished out the pistol—for within the noises of scraping metal and scuffling feet from his enemies across the room came the rapping of deliberate bootsteps advancing directly toward him.

Before he was prepared the man was looking right at him, not two yards away: a tall fellow with hanging lank brown hair, Captain of Dragoons, red coat immaculate, brass helmet under one arm, drawn saber in the other. Svenson met his sharp gaze and tightened his grip on the revolver, but did not fire. The idea of killing a soldier went against the grain—who knew what these fellows had been told, or what they'd been ordered to do, especially by a government figure like Crabbé or even Bascombe? Svenson imagined Chang's lack of hesitation and raised the revolver to fire.

The man's eyes flicked up and down, taking in Svenson's uniform, his rank, his unkempt person. Without any comment he turned to look in the other direction and then casually took a step toward Svenson, ostensibly—for the purpose of anyone watching from the room—to examine the door behind him. Svenson flinched—but still could not pull the trigger. Instead, the Captain leaned near to Svenson, reaching past him to the door and confirming it was locked. Svenson's revolver was nearly pressed against the Captain's chest, but the Captain's saber had been deliberately dropped to his side.

"Doctor Svenson?" he whispered.

Svenson nodded, unprepared to form actual words.

"I have seen Chang. I will take these people to the center of the house—please go in the opposite direction."

Svenson nodded again.

"Captain Smythe?" called Bascombe.

Smythe stepped back. "Nothing unusual, Sir."

"Were you *speaking* to someone?"

Smythe gestured vaguely toward the door as he walked back, out of Svenson's sight.

"There are servants in the next room. They've seen no one—perhaps their movement was what the Envoy heard. The door is now locked."

"Undoubtedly," agreed Lorenz, impatiently. "May we?"

"If you will follow me, gentlemen?" called Smythe. Svenson heard the doors opening, the scuffle and creak of the men lifting the fallen Duke, the *thwop* of water slopping out of the tub, the scuffle of footsteps and finally the closing of the door. He waited. There was no sound. He sighed and stepped around the corner, shoving the revolver back into his coat pocket.

Herr Flaüss stood just inside the far doorway, grinning smugly. Svenson dragged out the revolver. Flaüss snorted.

"What will you do, Doctor, shoot me and announce yourself to every soldier in the house?"

Svenson began to walk deliberately across the wide room

toward the Envoy, his aim never wavering from the man's chest. After all the torments he had passed through, it was bitter to imagine his downfall at the hands of *this* petty and puling creature.

"I knew what I had heard," smiled Flaüss, "just as I knew Captain Smythe was not telling the truth. I've no idea why—and I am indeed curious what power you might have over an officer of Dragoons, especially in your present wholly decrepit state."

"You're a traitor, Flaüss," answered Svenson. "You always have been."

He was within two yards of the Envoy, the main door perhaps a yard beyond that. Flaüss snorted again.

"How can I be a traitor when I do my own Prince's bidding? It is true I did not always understand that—it is true that I have been assisted to my present level of *clarity*—but you are as wrong about me, and the Prince, as you have always been—"

"He's an idiot and a traitor himself," spat Svenson hotly, "betraying his own father, his own nation—"

"My poor Doctor, you are quite behind the times. Much has changed in Macklenburg." Flaüss licked his lips and his eyes gleamed. "Your Baron is dead. Yes, Baron von Hoern—his feeble network of operatives was well known—why else should I attend the every move of an obscure naval *physician*? And of course the Duke himself is also very unwell—your brand of patriotism is *passé*—very soon Prince Karl-Horst will *be* the nation, and perfectly placed to welcome the cooperative financial ventures of Lord Vandaariff and his associates."

Flaüss wore a plain black half-mask across his eyes. With grim recognition Svenson could see the lurid scarring peeking out from the edges.

"Where is Major Blach?" he asked.

"Somewhere about, I am sure—as I am sure he will be most happy at your capture. He and I finally see eye to eye, of course—another blessing! It really is a matter of looking beyond to deeper *truths*. If, as you say, the Prince is not especially gifted in matters of policy, it is all the more important that those who support him are able to make up that lack."

It was Svenson's turn to scoff. He looked behind him. Adding another bizarre touch to his confrontation with the mentally altered Envoy, the concealed harpist continued to play. He turned back to Flaüss.

"If you knew I was there, why didn't you say anything to your *masters,* to Lorenz or Bascombe?" He gestured with the revolver. "Why give me the upper hand?"

"I've done nothing of the kind—as I say, you can't shoot me without dooming yourself. You're no more a fool than you are a brawler—if you want to stay alive, you'll give me your weapon and we shall walk together to the Prince—and I will establish myself as trustworthy in my new role. Especially so, I should say—for to get this far, I imagine you must have avoided a great number of ostensible foes."

The Envoy's smug expression demonstrated for Dr. Svenson the extent and the limit of the Process's transformation. Never before would the man have been so bold as to risk an open confrontation—much less so brazen an admission of his secret plans. Flaüss had always been one for honeyed agreement followed by backhanded plotting, for layered schemes and overlapping patronage. He had despised the blunt arguments of Major Blach and Svenson's own diffident independence as quite equal levels of defiance—and, indeed, personal offense. There was no doubt that the man's *loyalty* had—as he put it—been "clarified" by his alchemical ordeal and his hesitancies weakened, but Svenson saw that his conniving, narcissistic nature remained quite whole.

"Your weapon, Doctor Svenson," repeated Flaüss, his voice pointedly yet somehow comically stern. "I have you boxed with logic. I *do* insist."

Svenson flipped his grip on the revolver, holding on to its barrel and cylinder. Flaüss smiled, as this seemed the first step to politely handing him the butt of the gun. Instead, feeling another uncharacteristic surge of animal capacity, Svenson raised his arm and cracked the pistol butt across the Envoy's head. Flaüss staggered back with a squawk. He looked up at Svenson with an outraged glare of betrayal—as if in flouting the man's "logic" Svenson had broken all natural law—and opened his mouth to scream. Svenson stepped forward, arm raised for another swing. Flaüss darted away, quicker than his portly frame would seem to allow, and Svenson's blow went wide. Flaüss opened his mouth again. Svenson abruptly switched his grip on the revolver and aimed it directly at the Envoy's face.

"If you scream, I *will* shoot you! I'll have no more reason for silence!" he hissed.

Flaüss did not scream. He glared at Svenson with hatred and rubbed the welt above his eye. "You are a *brute*," he insisted. "An outright *savage*!"

Svenson padded quietly down the hallway—now sporting the Envoy's black silk mask, the better to blend in with the locals—following Smythe's directions away from the center of the house, with no idea if this path brought him anywhere near his ostensible targets of rescue. Most likely he was squandering what time he had to save them—he scoffed aloud—like so much else in his life had been squandered. His mind bristled with questions about the Dragoon Captain—he "had seen" Chang (though hadn't Chang been fleeing Dragoons in the garden?), but how had he known *him*? If only there had been time to actually *speak*—it was more than likely the man knew the location of Elöise or Miss Temple. For a moment he'd entertained the idea of interrogating Flaüss, but his skin crawled at the man's physical presence. Leaving him gagged and trussed behind a divan was more than enough time spent with such a toad. Yet he knew Flaüss would be missed—it was frankly odd he'd not been looked for already—and that his period of anonymity inside Harschmort was severely limited. But at the same time, the house was massive, and blundering senselessly through its hallways would only waste his temporary advantage.

The hallway ended at a T junction, with a path to either side. Svenson stood, undecided, like a figure in the forest of a fairy tale, knowing that the wrong choice would lead to the equivalent of a malevolent ogre. One way led to a succession of small parlors, following one to the next like links in a chain. The other opened onto a narrow corridor whose walls were plain, but whose floor was strikingly laid with black marble. Then as he stood, Doctor Svenson quite clearly recognized a woman's scream . . . dimly, as if the cry passed through a substantial intervening wall.

Where had it come from? He listened. It was not repeated. He strode into the black corridor—less comfortable, less wholesome, and altogether more dangerous—for if he chose wrong, the sooner he knew it the better.

The corridor was pocked with small niches for statuary—mostly simple white marble busts on stone pillars with the occasional limb-free torso. The heads were copies (though, given Vandaariff's wealth, who knew?) from antiquity, and the Doctor recognized the varyingly vacant, cruel, or thoughtful heads of Caesars high and low—Augustus, Vespasian, Gaius, Nero, Domitian, Tiberius. As he passed this last, Svenson stopped. Dimly—though louder than the scream—he heard . . . *applause.* He spun to place the source of the noise, and saw, cut into the white wall behind the bust of that pensive, bitter emperor, regular grooves running up to the ceiling . . . *rungs.* Svenson edged behind the pillar and looked up. He looked around him and—taking a breath and shutting his eyes—began to climb.

There was no hatch. The ladder continued into darkness before his hands found a new surface to grasp. The Doctor opened his eyes and blinked, allowing his eyes to adjust to the dark. He was gripping a piece of wooden scaffolding, the end of a low catwalk. He heard distant voices . . . and then again the whisper, like a sudden rustle of leaves, of an audience's applause. Was he backstage at some sort of theatre? The Doctor swallowed, for the dizzying heights from which stagehands operated the lifts and curtains always made him queasy (and his compulsion was to look up again and again, just to torment himself with vertigo). He recalled a performance of Bonrichardt's *Castor und Pollux* where the triumphant finale, the titular pair ascending to heaven—an excruciatingly extended duet as they were raised (the twins operatically portly, the ropes audibly protesting) some hundred feet from view—had him near to heaving with dread into the lap of the unfortunate dowager seated next to him.

Doctor Svenson clambered onto the catwalk and crept along it quietly. Ahead he saw a thin glimmer of light, perhaps a distant door set ajar, allowing a single beam to fall into the darkness. What performance might be hosted in Harschmort on a night like this? The engagement party had been a dual event—a public celebration of the engagement of Karl-Horst and Lydia and a private occasion for the Cabal to transact its private business. Was tonight a similarly double-edged event—and could this performance be the respectable side of whatever other malevolence was at work elsewhere in the house?

Svenson continued forward, wincing at a tightness in his legs and a renewed pain from his twisted ankle. He thought of Flaüss's boasting words—the Baron was dead, the Duke to follow. The Prince was a fool and a rake, eminently subject to manipulation and control. Yet if the Doctor could prise the Prince from the clutches of the Cabal—Process or no—might there not be yet some hope, providing the ministers around him were responsible and sane?

But then with a grim snort he recalled his own brief conversation with Robert Vandaariff over Trapping's corpse. Such was the great man's irresistible influence that any unfortunate or scandalous occurrence—like the Colonel's death—was made to disappear. The grandson of Robert Vandaariff—especially if inheriting as a child and requiring a regent—would be the best return the financier could realize on the investment of his daughter. After the child's birth Karl-Horst would be unnecessary—and, given everything, wholly unregretted at his death.

But what were Svenson's choices? If Karl-Horst were to die *without* issue, the Macklenburg throne would pass to the children of his cousin Hortenze-Caterina, the oldest of whom was but five. Wasn't this a better fate for the Duchy than being swallowed by Vandaariff's empire? Svenson had to face the deeper truth of his mission from the Baron. Knowing what he did of the forces in play, if he could not prevent the marriage, which seemed impossible, he would have to shoot Prince Karl-Horst down—to be a traitor in service to a larger patriotism.

The reasoning left the taste of ash in his mouth, but he could see no other way.

Svenson sighed, but then, like the shift of a mountebank's con-trick, the line of light in front of him—which he had, in the darkness, taken to be a distant door—was revealed for what it was: the thin gap between two curtains, not two feet in front of his face. He gently pushed it aside, both light and sound flooding through the gap, for the fabric was actually quite heavy, as if it had been woven with lead to prevent fire. But now Doctor Svenson could see and hear everything . . . and he was appalled.

It was an *operating* theatre. His catwalk door was perched just to the right of the audience and led across the stage itself at the height of the ceiling—some twenty feet above the raised table and the white-robed, white-masked woman bound to its surface with leather straps. The gallery was steeply raked and full of well-dressed, masked spectators, all gazing with rapt attention at the masked woman who spoke from the stage. Doctor Svenson recognized Miss Poole at once, if only by the woman's irrepressible glow of self-satisfaction.

Behind them all, on a large blackboard, were inscribed the words "AND SO THEY SHALL BE REBORN."

Standing unsteadily next to Miss Poole was another masked woman in white, her blonde hair somewhat disturbed, as if from physical exertion. As she stood Svenson noticed, distracted and disapproving, the very thin and clinging nature of the nearly transparent silk, making plain every contour of her body. To her other side stood a man in a leather apron, ready to support her if she fell. Behind, next to the woman on the table, stood another such man, wearing leather gauntlets and holding under his arm what looked like a brass and leather helmet—just what the Comte d'Orkancz had worn when Svenson had taken the Prince at pistol-point from the Institute. The man by the table set down his helmet and began to remove pieces of machinery from a nest of wooden boxes—the same boxes they'd seen taken from the Institute by Aspiche's Dragoons. The man attached several lengths of twisted copper wire to mechanical elements within the boxes—from his vantage Svenson could only see that they were bright steel with glass dials and brass buttons and knobs—and then to either side of a pair of black rubber goggles, taking a moment to get the wire properly attached. Svenson realized—the electrified rubber mask, the facial scars—that they were about to perform the Process on the woman on the table, as they had no doubt just done to the woman standing with Miss Poole (the cause of the screams!).

The man finished with the wires and raised the hideous mask to the woman's face, pausing quickly to remove one of the white feathers that she presently wore. She shook her head from side to side, a futile bid to avoid his hands—her eyes wide and her mouth—which he saw was blocked with a gag—working. Her eyes were riveting, a cold, glittering grey... Svenson gasped. The man strapped and then brutally tightened the device across her face, his body blocking the Doctor's view. Svenson could not determine her state—was she drugged? Had she been beaten? He knew he had only until Miss Poole was finished with the blonde woman—who was *she,* he wondered?—until their vicious intent was worked irrevocably upon Miss Temple.

* * *

Miss Poole stepped to a small rolling side table—intended, Svenson knew, to hold a tray of medical implements—and took up a glass-stoppered flask. With a knowing smile she uncorked the flask and took a step to the front row of the gallery, holding the open flask up for her spectators to sniff. One after another—and always to Miss Poole's delight—the elegant masked figures recoiled with immediate disgust. After the sixth person, Miss Poole stepped back to the brighter light and her blonde charge.

"A challenge to the most sturdy of sensibilities—as I believe all of you that have smelled this mixture will attest—yet such is the nature of our science and our need that this lovely subject, a veritable arrow in flight toward a target of *destiny,* has been made to consume it not once, but daily, for twenty-eight consecutive days, until her *cycle* is completely prepared. Before this day, such a task could not have been accomplished save by forcibly holding her down, or—as it has actually been managed—hiding tiny amounts of the substance in chocolate or an aperitif. Now, witness the strength of her new-minted will."

Miss Poole turned to the woman and held out the flask.

"My dear," she said, "you understand that you must drink this, as you have in these past weeks."

The blonde woman nodded, and reached out to take the flask from Miss Poole.

"Please smell it," asked Miss Poole.

The woman did. She wrinkled her nose, but showed no other response.

"Please drink it."

The woman put the flask to her lips and tossed off the contents like a sailor quaffing rum. She primly wiped her mouth, held her body still for a moment, as if to better keep the substance down, and then returned the flask.

"Thank you, my dear." Miss Poole smiled. "You've done very well."

The audience erupted into fervent applause, and the young blonde woman shyly beamed.

The Doctor looked ahead of him on the catwalk. Bolted to an iron frame suspended from the ceiling—and in reach, for he realized that the catwalk's sole purpose was to tend them—hung a row of metal-boxed paraffin lamps, as in a theatre. The front of each box was open, to aim the light in one direction, and fixed with a ground-glass lens to focus the light onto a more precise area. For a moment he considered—if he were able to climb out unseen—the possibility of blowing out each lamp and throwing the theatre into darkness . . . but there were at least five lamps over a fifteen-foot length of the iron grid. He could not reach them all before he was seen and most likely shot. But what else could he do? Moving as delicately and as quickly as he could, Doctor Svenson crawled through the curtain and into view of anyone who happened to look up.

Miss Poole whispered in her blonde charge's ear and then led her closer to the audience. The young woman sank into a curtsey, and the audience politely applauded once more. Svenson could swear she was blushing with pleasure. The woman rose again and Miss Poole handed her to one of the Macklenburg soldiers, who offered an arm with a click of his heels. The blonde woman draped her arm in his and with a distinct brightening of her step they disappeared down one of the rampways.

From the same rampway emerged two more Macklenburg soldiers propelling between them a third masked woman in white. Her feet dragged in awkward steps and her head dipped—she was either drugged or injured. Her brown hair unspooled behind her back and around her shoulders, obscuring her features. Again, despite his best intentions, Doctor Svenson found his gaze falling to the lady's body, the white silk clinging across the curve of her hips, her pale arms sticking from the balled-up sleeves.

At their entrance, Miss Poole whipped around in annoyance.

Svenson could not hear what she hissed to the soldiers, nor what they deferentially whispered in return. In the moment of disturbance he looked to Miss Temple, the hideous mask in place across her face, twisting ineffectually against her bonds.

Miss Poole gestured to the new arrival.

"It is a different sort of case I present to you here—perhaps one emblematic of the *dangers* attending our great enterprise, and of the *corrective* power of this work. The woman here before you—you see her ragged appearance and lowly condition—is one who had been invited to participate, and who then took it upon herself, in league with our enemies, to *reject* this invitation. More than this, her rejection took the form . . . of *murder*. The woman before you has killed one of our blameless number!"

The audience whispered and hissed. Svenson swallowed. It was Elöise Dujong. He hadn't recognized her—her hair had been back in a braid and now it wasn't—such a foolish detail, but it nearly caused his heart to crack. All his doubts as to her loyalty fell away before this sudden pang of emotion. Seeing her hair down should have been an intimacy given to him from her, and now she was insensible, vulnerable, the intimacy blithely trammeled. He crawled quickly to the next lamp and dug in his pocket for the revolver.

"And yet," continued Miss Poole, "she has been brought before you to demonstrate the greater wisdom—and the greater *economy*—of our purpose. For despite everything this woman's actions carry with them undenied qualities of resilience and courage. Should these be destroyed simply because she lacks the will or the vision to see her true avenue of advantage? We say it shall not be—and so we will *welcome* this woman into our very bosom!"

She gestured to her attendant. He bent over Miss Temple once more to make sure of his electrical connections and then knelt at the boxes. Svenson looked wildly about him. In a moment it would be too late.

"Both these women—I promise you, more determined villains you could not find outside the *Thuggee* cult!—will join us, one after the next, by way of the clarifying Process. You have seen its effect with a willing subject. Now see it transform a defiant enemy to the fiercest adherent!"

The first shot crashed out from the darkness above the theatre. The man near Miss Temple abruptly stumbled back, and then dropped beneath the blackboard, the blood from his wound pooling in the leather apron. Screams erupted from the gallery. The figures on the stage looked up, but straight into the lamps and could not—at least for another precious moment—see past the glare. The second shot tore through the shoulder of the other aproned man, spinning him away from Elöise and to his knees.

"He is there!" shrieked Miss Poole. "Kill him! *Kill him!*"

She pointed up at Svenson, her face an emblem of fury. The Macklenburg trooper had been pulled off balance by the second man's fall, suddenly taking up the whole of Elöise's weight. He released her—she dropped at once to her hands and knees—and swept out his saber. Svenson ignored him. He was well out of reach of the blade, and knew the Ragnarok troopers did not carry firearms. He aimed the revolver at Miss Poole, but then—what was he thinking! How could he forget her cruelty at the quarry?—hesitated to pull the trigger.

The catwalk behind him lurched. Svenson turned to see two hands grabbing hold of the edge. He shifted on his knees and rapped the gun butt down on each hand one after the other, dropping the man back into the seats. The catwalk lurched again. Now three sets of hands pulled on the edge, tipping the Doctor into the wooden rail. For a moment he looked helplessly down into the outraged crowd—men on each other's shoulders, women shrieking at him as if he were a witch. He shot a foot forward and smashed it down on the nearest hand—but now there were men on either side of him, hefting themselves above the edge. To his left was an athletic young man in a tailcoat, no doubt an ambitious second son of a Lord determined to take an inheritance away from an older brother. Svenson shot him through the upper leg and didn't wait to watch him fall before turning to the second man—a wiry fellow in his shirtsleeves (thoughtful enough to doff an encumbering coat before climbing)—who leapt the rail and crouched like a cat not three feet away. Svenson fired again, but more hands jostled the catwalk. The bullet flew wide and directly into one of the paraffin lanterns, shattering it completely. A shower of hot metal, broken glass, and burning paraffin spattered onto the stage.

The shirtsleeved man launched himself at Svenson, knocking him flat. A woman screamed from the stage—there was smoke—the paraffin—did he smell burning hair? The man was younger, stronger, fresher—an elbow across Svenson's jaw stunned him. He thrust a hand ineffectually at the fellow's eyes, and the catwalk careened as more hands pulled at them and more men climbed aboard—a creak, a popping snap of wood—it could not hold. The woman still screamed. The shirtsleeved man took hold of Svenson's coat with both hands and raised him up—face-to-face with a triumphant leer—as a prelude to flattening the Doctor's nose with his fist.

The catwalk gave way, tipping toward the stage and dumping them both over the rail and into the row of lamps—Svenson hissing with pain at the hot metal against his skin—and then (in one ghastly moment of weightless terror that convulsed Svenson from the top of his spine to his genitals) to the theatre floor.

The impact jarred the Doctor to his teeth and for a moment he merely lay where he was, dimly aware of a great deal of activity around him. He blinked. He was alive. There were screams and shouts from every direction . . . smoke . . . a great deal of smoke . . . and heat—in fact, everything pointed to the theatre being on fire. He tried to move. To his surprise he was not on the floor—he was not on anything *smooth*. He rolled on one shoulder and saw the waxen face of the shirtsleeved man, neck folded unnaturally to the side, tongue blue. Svenson heaved himself to his hands and knees—realizing as it hit the floor with a *clunk* that he still held the revolver.

* * *

The fallen lamps had set a line of flame between the stage and the gallery, effectively blocking one from the other. Through the rising wall of smoke he could see figures and hear their screams and shouts, but he quickly turned away at another scream, much nearer. It was Elöise, terrified but still dulled by the drug, kicking weakly at the flames that licked her smoking silken robe. Svenson stuffed the revolver into his belt and tore off his greatcoat. He lurched forward on his knees and threw it over her legs, patting out any flames, and then quickly pulled her clear of the fire. He turned to the table and felt his way to Miss Temple's hand. Her fingers took hold of his arm—a desperate silent plea—but he was forced to wrench himself away in order to reach the buckle for her leather straps. He fumbled to free her arms and that done was gratified to see her own hands shoot up to the infernal mask around her face. He released her feet and then helped her from the table, once more—for Svenson was never one to become used to the matter—surprised at the meager weight of such an enterprising person. As she tore the wadded gag from her mouth he bent to her ear and shouted above the roar of flame and popping wood.

"This way! Can you walk?"

He pulled her down below the line of smoke and saw her eyes widen at the identity of her rescuer.

"Can you walk?" he repeated.

Miss Temple nodded. He pointed to Elöise, just visible, hunched against the curved wall of the theatre.

"She cannot! We must help her!"

Miss Temple nodded again, and he took her arm—wondering idly if he might not be in the more shattered physical condition. Svenson looked up at a rush of footsteps within the gallery, and then a crashing hiss and a cloud of steam. Men had arrived with buckets. They raised Elöise between them—Miss Temple a good six inches shorter than the woman she supported. Svenson called to her.

"I have seen Chang! There is a flying machine on the roof! The Dragoon officer is a friend! Do not look into the glass books!"

He was babbling—but there seemed so much to say. More water was flung from above—the steam clouds now rivaled the smoke—and more bootsteps. Svenson turned to face them. He raised the revolver and shoved behind him at the ladies, pushing them on.

"Go! Go at once!"

The Macklenburg trooper had returned with a host of others. Svenson aimed the revolver just as more water flew down from the gallery and a plume of ash and steam rose in front of the other rampway. He felt suddenly nauseous at the mix of exhaustion and light-headed recklessness—he'd just shot three men and wrestled a fourth to his death in what seemed like as many seconds. Was this how men like Chang spent their lives? Svenson gagged. He took a step backwards and tripped over the carcass of a shattered lamp, sprawling headlong onto his back with a grunt, smacking the back of his head into the floorboards. Pain exploded across Doctor Svenson's body—all of his injuries from the quarry and Tarr Manor brought back to vivid life. He opened his mouth but could not speak. He would be taken. He moved feebly on his back like a tortoise. The room was nearly dark—only one of the lights remained, its cover dislodged and blocking the beam, sending an eerie orange glow through the murk.

He expected to be swarmed by his enemies, slit like a pig by five sabers at once. Around him were the sounds of flame and water, the shouts of men and, more distant, the cries of women. Had they not seen him? Were they only fighting the fire? Had the flames so cut them off from pursuit? With an effort Svenson rolled over and began to crawl through the glass and metal after the women. He was coughing—how much smoke had he inhaled? He kept going, his right hand still holding the revolver. With a dull apprehension he remembered that the box of cartridges was in the pocket of his greatcoat, which he had given to Elöise. If he did not catch up to her, he was left with just two shells remaining in the gun—against all of the forces of Harschmort.

Svenson reached the ramp and crawled down. The path turned and he felt something in the way—a boot . . . and then a leg. It was the man he'd shot in the shoulder. In this light there was no telling if the man was dead, dying, or merely overcome by smoke. Svenson had no time. He stumbled to his feet and past the fellow and found a door. He pushed his way through and took a heaving lungful of clean air.

The room was empty. Thickly carpeted and lined with wooden cabinets and mirrors, it reminded him of a dressing room for the opera—or, as if there was any real difference, of Karl-Horst's own attiring room at the Macklenburg Palace. The idea that it was connected to a theatre for demonstrations of surgery was perhaps all the more sickening for what it said about Robert Vandaariff. The cabinets were open and in disarray, various garments spilling onto the floor. He took several steps, brushing glass and ash from his uniform, his feet sinking deeply into the luxurious carpet, and stopped. On the floor near the cabinets, in ruins and quite clearly cut from her body, was the dress Elöise had been wearing at Tarr Manor. He looked behind him. Still no sounds of pursuit. Where were the women? His throat was aching. He pushed himself across the room to another door and turned the handle carefully, peering out with one eye through the gap.

He closed it at once. The corridor was full of activity—servants, soldiers, cries for buckets, cries for help. There was no possible way he would not be taken. But could the women have had any better hope? He turned again to the rampway door. His enemies would be coming through it any moment—someone—he had caused too much damage to ignore. Svenson was wracked with regret for the men he had shot, for the injury—flame? falling debris?—that had stricken Miss Poole, despite his hatred for her. But what else could he have done? What else would he yet be forced to do?

There was no time for any of this. Could the women be hiding in the room? Feeling a fool, he whispered aloud.

"Miss Temple? Miss Temple! Elöise?"

There was no reply.

He crossed to the wall of opened cabinets to quickly sort through them, but got no farther than Elöise's dress on the floor. Svenson picked it up, fingering with a distressed intimacy the ripped edges of her bodice and the sliced, dangling bits of lacing. He pressed it to his face and breathed in, and sighed at his own hopeless gesture—the dress smelled of indigo clay—acrid, biting, offensive—and dried sweat. With another sigh he let the dress fall to the floor. He was bound to find the women—of course he must—but—he wanted to cry aloud with distress—what of the Prince? Where was he? What could Svenson possibly do aside from killing him before the wedding? This thought brought the words of Miss Poole back to his mind, in the theatre with the blonde woman and the loathsome potions. She had mentioned the girl's monthly cycle... "until the cycle is prepared"... obviously this was more of the Comte's (or Veilandt's) alchemical evil. Svenson was chilled—Miss Poole had also mentioned the woman's "destiny"—for he was suddenly sure the pliant blonde woman, proven to be the passive instrument of the Cabal, was Lydia Vandaariff. Could Vandaariff be so heartless as to sacrifice his own daughter? Svenson scoffed at the obviousness of the answer. And if the Lord's own flesh meant so little, what would he possibly care for the Prince—or the succession?

He shook his head. His thoughts were too slow. He was wasting time.

Svenson stepped toward the cupboard and felt his boot crunch on broken glass. He looked down—this was not where he'd brushed it from himself—and saw the carpet littered with bright shards... glittering... reflective... he looked up... a mirror? The doors of two nearby cupboards were opened toward each other... the open panels blocking whatever might be behind. He pulled them apart to reveal a large jagged hole in the wall, punched through what had been a full-length mirror with an ornate gold-leaf frame. He stepped carefully over the shards. The glass was slightly odd . . . discolored? He picked up one of the larger pieces and turned it side to side in his hand, then held it up to the light. One side was a standard mirror—but the other side was somehow, granting a slightly darker cast to the image, transparent. It was a spy mirror—and one of the women (it could only be Miss Temple) had known of it and smashed it through. Svenson dropped the shard and stepped through the gap—taking care to pull the cupboards to behind him, to slow any pursuit—and then over a wooden stool that she had evidently used to break the glass, for he could see tiny glittering needles embedded in the wooden seat.

The room on the other side of the mirror confirmed all that Doctor Svenson feared about life in Harschmort House. The walls were painted a bordello red, with a neat square of Turkish carpet that held a chair, a small writing table, and a plush divan. To the side was a cabinet that held both notebooks and inks, but also bottles of whisky, gin, and port. The lamps were painted red as well, so no light would give the game away through the mirror. The experience of standing in the room struck the Doctor as both tawdry and infernal. On one hand, he recognized that there were few things more ridiculous than the trappings of another person's pleasure. On the other, he knew that such an arrangement only served to take cruel advantage of the innocent and unsuspecting.

He knelt quickly on the carpet, feeling for any bloodstains, in case either woman had cut a foot making her way through the glass. There were none. He stood and continued after them—a poor shambling trot. The way was lined with the same red-painted lamps, and twisted and turned without any reason he could see. How long would it take to truly understand the ways of this house? Svenson wondered how often the servants got lost, or for how long—and further what the punishment might be for the wrong servant mistakenly stumbling into an extremely sensitive room, such as this. He half-expected to find a caged skeleton, set up as a sign to warn off all curious maids and footmen.

He stopped—this tunnel just went on—and risked another whisper.

"Miss Temple!" He waited for a reply. Nothing. "*Celeste! Elöise!* Elöise Dujong!"

The corridor was quiet. Svenson turned behind him and listened. He could scarce credit their pursuit had not reached him already. He tried to flex his ankle and winced with pain. It had been twisted again in his fall from the catwalk and soon it would be all he could do to drag it, or lapse again into his absurd hopping. He steadied himself with a hand on the wall. Why hadn't he had more to drink in the airship? Why had he walked right past the bottles in the first red room? By God, he wanted another swallow of brandy. Or a cigarette! The urge fell onto him like a wave of agitated need. How long had it been without a smoke? His case was in the inner pocket of his greatcoat. He wanted to swear out loud. Just a bit of tobacco—hadn't he earned that much? He stuffed a knuckle into his mouth to stifle the urge to scream and bit down, hard as he could bear. It didn't help in the least.

He limped ahead to a crossroads. To his left the corridor went on. Ahead it dead-ended at a ladder going up. To the right was a red cloth curtain. Svenson did not hesitate—he'd had his fill of ladders and his fill of walking. He whipped aside the curtain and extended the revolver. It was a second observation chamber, its far wall another transparent mirror. The red chamber was empty, but the room beyond the mirror was not.

The spectacle before him was like a medieval pageant, a *Danse Macabre* of linked figures from all walks of life being led away by Death and his minions. The line of figures—a red-coated churchman, an admiral, men in the finest topcoats, ladies dripping with jewelry and lace—shambled into the room one after another, assisted by a crew of black-masked functionaries, guiding each to a chaise or chair where they slumped unceremoniously, obviously insensible. If he were a native of the city Svenson was sure he would have known them all—as it was he could pick out Henry Xonck, the Baroness Roote (a *salon* hostess who had invited Karl-Horst once and then never again after he'd spent the entire time drinking—and then sleeping—in his corner chair), and Lord Axewithe, chairman of the Imperial Bank. Such a gathering was simply unheard-of—and a gathering where they had all been so overborne was unthinkable.

In the center of the room was a table, upon which one of each pair of functionaries would—while the other settled their personage—deposit a large brilliant rectangle of blue glass... another glass book... but how many were there? Svenson watched them pile up. Fifteen? Twenty? Standing at the table and watching it all with a smile was Harald Crabbé, hands tucked behind his back, eyes darting with satisfaction between the growing stack of books and the procession of vacant luminaries arranged around the steadily more crowded room. Next to Crabbé, as expected, stood Bascombe, making notes in a ledger. Svenson studied the young man's expression as he worked, sharp nose and thin earnest lips, hair plastered into position, broad shoulders, perfectly schooled posture, and nimble fingers that flipped the ledger pages back and forth and stabbed his pencil in and out of them like an embroidery needle.

Doctor Svenson had seen Bascombe before of course, at Crabbé's side, and had overheard his conversation with Francis Xonck in the Minister's kitchen, yet this was the first time he'd observed the man knowing he had been Celeste Temple's fiancé. It was always curious what particular qualities might bring two people together—a shared taste for gardening, a love of breakfast, snobbery, raw sensual appetite—and Svenson could not help but ask the question about these two, if only for what it revealed about his diminutive ally, to whom he felt a duty to protect (a duty naggingly compromised by the memory of the thin silk robes hanging closely around her body... the suddenly soft weight of her limbs in his arms as he helped her from the table... even the animal spate of effort as she pulled the gag from her stretched lips).

Svenson swallowed and frowned anew at Bascombe, deciding then that he very much disliked the man's proud manner—one could just tell by the way he ticked his notebook. He'd seen enough naked ambition in the Macklenburg Palace to make the man's hunger as plain to his trained eyes as the symptoms of syphilis. More, he could imagine how Bascombe had been served by the Process. What before must have been tempered with doubt or deference had been in that alchemical crucible hardened to steel. Svenson wondered how long it would be before Crabbé felt the knife in his back.

The last functionaries laid the final victim on a divan, next to the uncaring elderly churchman—a handsome woman with vaguely eastern features in a blue silk dress and a fat white pearl dangling from each ear. The last book was set down—the whole pile had to number near thirty!—and Bascombe made his final jabs with the pencil . . . and then frowned. He flipped back through the notebook and repeated his calculations, by his darkening frown coming up with the same unsatisfactory answer. He spoke to the men quickly, sorting through their responses, winnowing their words until he was looking at the somnolent figure of a particularly lovely woman in green, with a mask woven of glass beads that Svenson guessed would be Venetian and extremely expensive. Bascombe called again, as clearly as if Svenson could hear the words, "Where is the book to go with this woman?" There was no answer. He turned to Crabbé and the two of them whispered together. Crabbé shrugged. He pointed to one of the men who then dashed from the room, obviously sending him back to search. The rest of the books were loaded carefully into an iron-bound chest. Svenson noted how all of them wore leather gloves to touch the glass and treated them with deliberate and tender care—their efforts reminding him keenly of sailors nervously stacking rounds of ammunition in an armory.

The clear association of particular books with specific individuals—individuals of obvious rank and stature—had to relate to the Cabal's earlier collection of scandal from the minions of the powerful, at Tarr Manor. Was it merely another level of acquisition? In the country, they had gathered—had stored within those books—the means to manipulate the powerful . . . could the aim have merely been to blackmail those powerful figures into journeying to Harschmort, and then forcing this next step upon them? He shook his head at the boldness of it, for the next step was to seize hold of the knowledge, the memories, the plans, the very dreams of the most mighty in the land. He wondered if the victims retained their memories. Or were they amnesiac husks? What happened when—or was it if?—they awoke to full awareness . . . would they know where they were . . . or who?

Yet there was more to it, if only in simple mechanics. The men wore gloves to touch the glass—indeed to even look within it was perilous, as those who had died at Tarr Manor made clear. But how then did this precious information serve the Cabal—how was it *read*? If a person could not touch a book without risking their life or sanity, what was the point? There must be a way . . . a key . . .

Svenson glanced behind him. Had there been a noise? He listened . . . nothing . . . merely nerves. The men finished loading the chest. Bascombe tucked the notebook under his arm and snapped his fingers, issuing orders: these men to take the chest, these to go with the Minister, these to stay. He walked with Crabbé to the doors—and had the Minister handed something to his assistant? He had . . . but Svenson could not see what it was. And then they were gone.

The two remaining men stood for the barest moment and then, with a palpable relaxation of their manner, stepped one to the sideboard and the other to a wooden cigar box on a side table. They spoke smilingly to one another, nodding at their charges. The one at the sideboard poured two tumblers of whisky and crossed to the other, who was even then spitting out a bitten tip of tobacco. They swapped gifts—tumbler for cigar—and lit up, one after another. Their masters not gone for ninety seconds, they were smacking their lips and puffing away like princes.

Svenson looked around him for ideas. This observation room was less fully appointed than the other—there was no drink and no divan. The two men walked around the room, making a circuit of the furniture and commenting on their charges, and it was only another minute before they were fumbling through the pockets of a tailcoat or a lady's handbag. Svenson narrowed his eyes at the actions of these scavengers, and waited for them to come nearer. Right before him was the divan holding the churchman and the Arabic woman—with her head lolling back (eyes dreamily half-open to the ceiling) the pearl earrings shone brightly against her dark skin . . . they would have to notice them.

As if they had heard his thought, one man looked up, saw the pearls and ignored the five victims in between to hurry directly to them. The other followed, sticking the cigar in his mouth, and soon they were both leaning over the passive woman, their black backs facing Svenson, not two feet away from the glassy barrier.

He placed the barrel flat against the mirror and pulled the trigger. The bullet slammed into the back of the nearest man and then, with an unexpected flourish, out his chest to shatter the tumbler in his hand, sprawling him across the unfortunate cleric. His companion wheeled at the shot and stared without comprehension at the round hole in the mirror. Svenson fired again. The glass starred at this second puncture, a sudden spider's web clouding his vision. He quickly stuffed the revolver into his belt and reached for a small side table of inks and paper, tipping them brusquely to the floor. Three strokes with the table, swinging it like an axe, and the mirror fell away.

He dropped the table and looked behind him. The sound of the shots would have traveled for the most part back through the tunnels, not forward into the house, and he had to trust that they'd been well-insulated for secrecy's sake. *Why* was no one following? On the carpet at his feet the second man was breathing heavily, shot through the chest. Svenson sank to his knees to find the entry-point and quickly concluded the wound was mortal—it would be a matter of a minute. He stood, unable to bear the gaze of the gasping man, and stepped to his fellow, quite dead, rolling him off of the elderly churchman. Svenson shifted the body to the floor, already assailed by feelings of guilt and recrimination. Could he not have wounded them? Shot once and bluffed them into submission, tied with curtain cords like Flaüss? Perhaps . . . but such niceties—had human life become a *nicety*?—left no time to find the women, to secure his Prince, to stop these fellows' masters. Svenson saw that the dead man still held a burning cigar between his fingers. Without a thought he reached down and took it, inhaling deeply and closing his eyes with long-missed pleasure.

The men were unarmed, and with no weapons to pillage Svenson resigned himself to more stealth and theatre, holding the empty revolver as he walked. He'd left the room's other occupants as they were and picked his way through an empty string of parlors, watching for any trace of Bascombe or Crabbé, but hoping it was Bascombe that he found. If what he had guessed of the books from Tarr Manor was true, that they were capable of absorbing—of *recording*—memories, then the chest of books rivaled an unexplored continent for value. He also realized the particular worth of Bascombe's notebook, where the contents of each book—of each mind!—were cataloged and detailed. With those notes as a guide, what question could not be answered from that unnatural library? What advantage not be found?

Doctor Svenson looked around him with annoyance. He'd walked through another sitting room to an airy foyer with a bubbling fountain whose sound obscured any distant footfalls that might point him in the right direction. The Doctor wondered idly if the labyrinth of Harschmort had a Minotaur. He crossed heavily to the fountain and looked into the water—could one ever *not* look into the water?—and laughed aloud, for the Minotaur was before him: his own haggard, soot-smudged, battered visage, cigar in his face, weapon in hand. To the guests of this gala evening, was *he* not their determined, monstrous nemesis? Svenson outright cackled at the idea—and cackled again at the antic hoarseness of his voice, a raven trying to sing after too many cups of gin. He set down his smoke and stuffed the pistol into his belt, and reached into the fountain's pool, scooping water first to drink and then to splash across his face, and to once again smooth back his hair. He shook his hands, the droplets breaking his reflection to rippling pieces, and looked up. Someone was coming. He threw the cigar into the water and pulled out the gun.

It was Crabbé and Bascombe, with two of their functionaries walking behind, and between them, unmistakably, his posture characteristically sharp as a knife-point, Lord Robert Vandaariff. Svenson scrambled to the other side of the fountain and dropped to the floor, for all his fear and fatigue feeling caught out like a character in a comic operetta.

"It is astonishing—first the theatre, and now this!" The Minister was speaking, and with anger. "But the men are now in place?"

"They are," answered Bascombe, "a squad of Macklenburgers."

Crabbé snorted. "That lot has been more trouble than they are worth," he said. "The Prince is an idiot, the Envoy's a grub, the Major's a Teuton boor—and the *Doctor*! Did you hear? He is alive! He is at Harschmort! He must have come with us—but honestly, I cannot imagine how it was accomplished. He can only have been stowed away—hidden by a confederate!"

"But who could that be?" hissed Bascombe. When Crabbé did not reply, Bascombe ventured a hesitant guess. "Aspiche?"

Crabbé's answer was lost, for they had moved through the foyer to the edge of his hearing. Svenson rose to his knees, relieved they had not seen him, and carefully followed. He did not understand it . . . though Vandaariff walked between the two Ministry conspirators, they paid him no attention at all, speaking across his body . . . nor did the Lord take part in the plotting. What was more, what had happened to Bascombe's treasure chest of blue glass books?

"Yes, yes—and it's for the better," Crabbé was saying, "both of them are to take part. Poor Elspeth has lost a quantity of hair, and Margaret—well, she was keen to press ahead. She is *ever* keen, but . . . apparently she had a *confrontation* with this Cardinal at the Royale—she—well, I cannot say—she seems in a *mood* about it—"

"And this is along with the . . . ah . . . other?" Bascombe politely cut in, bringing the conversation back to its subject.

"Yes, yes—*she* is the *test case,* of course. In my own opinion, it all goes too fast—too much effort in too many places—"

"The Contessa *is* concerned about our time-table—"

"As am *I,* Mr. Bascombe," Crabbé replied sharply, "but you will notice for yourself—the confusion, the risk—when we have tried to simultaneously manage *initiations* in the theatre, the Comte's *transformations* in the cathedral, the *collections* in the inner parlors, the *harvest* from Lord Robert"—he gestured casually to the most powerful man in five nations—"and *now* because of that blasted woman, the Duke—"

"Apparently Doctor Lorenz is confident—"

"He is *always* confident! And yet, Bascombe, science is pleased if one experiment out of twenty actually succeeds—the mere *confidence* of Doctor Lorenz is not enough when so much hangs at risk—we need certainty!"

"Of course, Sir."

"Just a moment."

Crabbé stopped, and turned to the two retainers walking behind—prompting Svenson to abruptly crouch behind a molting philodendron.

"Dash ahead to the top of the tower—I don't want any surprises. Make sure it's clear, then one of you return. We will wait."

The men ran off. Svenson peeked through the dusty leaves to see Bascombe in the midst of a deferent protest.

"Sir, do you really think—"

"What I think is that I *prefer* not to be overheard by *anyone.*"

He paused to allow the two men to fully vanish from sight before going on.

"Before anything," began the Deputy Minister, glancing once at the figure of Robert Vandaariff, "what book do we have for Lord Vandaariff, here? We need something as a place-holder, yes?"

"Yes, Sir—though for now it can be the one missing, from Lady Mélantes—"

"Which *must* be recovered—"

"Of course, Sir—but for the moment it may also stand in as the keeper of Lord Vandaariff's secrets—until such time as we have occasion to irreparably *damage* another."

"Excellent," muttered Crabbé. His eyes darted around them and the small man licked his lips, leaning closer to Bascombe. "From the beginning, Roger, I have offered you this opportunity, have I not? Inheritance and title, new prospects for marriage, advancement in government?"

"Yes, Sir, I am well in your debt—and I assure you—"

Crabbé waved away Bascombe's obsequiousness as if he were brushing off flies. "What I have said—about there being too many elements in motion at once—is for your ears alone."

Again, Svenson was astonished to find neither man referring in the slightest to Lord Vandaariff, who stood not two feet away.

"You are intelligent, Roger, and you are cunning as any person in this business—as you have well proven. Keep your eyes open, for both our sakes, for any out of place comment or action . . . from *anyone.* Do you understand? Now is the sticking point, and I find myself brimming with suspicion."

"Do you suggest one of the others—the Contessa, or Mr. Xonck—"

"I suggest nothing. Yet, we have suffered these . . . *disruptions*—"

"But these *provocateurs*—Chang, Svenson—"

"And your Miss Temple," added Crabbé, a tinge of acid in his tone.

"Including her only strengthens the truth, Sir—which they

each have sworn—that they have no master, nor any plan beyond plain antagonism."

Crabbé leaned closer to Bascombe, his voice dropping to an anxious hiss. "Yes, yes—and *yet*! The Doctor arrives by way of the airship! Miss Temple penetrates our plans for Lydia Vandaariff and somehow resists—without assistance, which one can scarcely credit—submersion in a glass book! And Chang—how many has he killed? What havoc has he not set off? Do you flatter these so much that they have done all this without aid? And where else, I ask you, Roger, could that aid have come from, save within our number?"

Crabbé's face was white and his lip shaking with rage—or fear, or both, as if the very idea of being vulnerable set off the Minister's fury. Bascombe did not answer.

"You know Miss Temple, Roger—possibly better than anyone in this world. Do *you* think she could have killed those men? Shrugged off that book? Located Lydia Vandaariff and quite nearly spirited her from our grasp? If it was not for Mrs. Marchmoor's arrival—"

Bascombe shook his head.

"No, Sir . . . the Celeste Temple I know is capable of none of those things. And yet—there *must* be some other explanation."

"Yet do we have it? Is there an explanation for Colonel Trapping's death? All three of our *provocateurs* were in this house that night, yet it is impossible that they would know to kill him without some betrayal from within our ranks!"

They fell silent. Svenson watched them, and with patient slowness reached up to scratch his nose.

"Francis Xonck *was* burned by Cardinal Chang." Bascombe began to speak quickly, sorting out their options. "It is unlikely he would undergo such an injury on purpose."

"Perhaps . . . yet he is extremely cunning, and personally reckless."

"Agreed. The Comte—"

"The Comte d'Orkancz cares for his glass and his transformations—his *vision.* I swear that in his heart he considers all of this but one more canvas—a masterwork, perhaps—but still, his thought is to my taste a bit too..." Crabbé swallowed with some discomfort and brushed his moustache with a finger. "Perhaps it is simply his horrid plans for the girl—not that I even trust those plans have been fully *revealed*..."

Crabbé looked up at the young man, as if he had said too much, but Bascombe's expression had not changed.

"And the Contessa?" Bascombe asked.

"The Contessa," echoed Crabbé. "The Contessa *indeed*..."

They looked up, for one of their men was returning at a jog. They let him arrive without any further conversation. Once he reported the way ahead was clear, Bascombe nodded that the man should rejoin his companion ahead of them. The man crisply turned and the Ministry men again waited for him to disappear before they followed in silence—evidently not finished with their brooding. Svenson crept after them. The possibility of mistrust and dissension within the Cabal was an answer to a prayer he had not dared to utter.

Without the trailing men to block his view, he could see the Minister more clearly—a short determined figure who carried a leather satchel, the sort one might use for official papers. Svenson was sure it was not present when they had collected the books, which meant Crabbé had acquired it since—along with his acquisition of Lord Vandaariff? Did that mean the satchel carried papers *from* Lord Vandaariff? He could still make no sense of the Lord's apparent participation—his unforced accompaniment—at the same time they utterly ignored him. Svenson had assumed Vandaariff to be the plot's prime mover—for not two days before the man had quite deliberately manipulated him away from Trapping's body. However long the Cabal might have planned to spring their trap, whatever control they had established, whatever somnambulism... it had been recently done—for surely they had drawn on the full resources of the Lord's house and name to achieve their ends, which only could have been begun with his full participation and approval. And now he followed along—in his own house—as if he were an affable pet goat. Yet Svenson's first glimpse of the man, as he crouched behind the fountain, had shown his face free of the scars of the Process. How else was he compelled? By way of a glass book? If it were only possible to get Vandaariff to himself for five minutes! Even that much time would afford a quick examination, would give the Doctor some insight into the corporeal effects of this *mind control,* and who could say . . . some insight into its reversal.

For now however, unarmed and outnumbered, he could only follow them deeper into the house. He could hear from the rooms around them a growing buzz of human activity—footsteps, voices, cutlery, wheeled carts. So far their path had skirted any open place or crossroads—undoubtedly to keep Vandaariff from public view. Svenson wondered if the servants of the house knew of their master's mental servitude, and how they might react to the knowledge. He did not imagine Robert Vandaariff to be a kindly employer—perhaps the household *did* know, and happily celebrated his downfall—perhaps the Cabal had dipped into Vandaariff's own riches to purchase his people's loyalty. Either possibility kept Svenson from trusting the servants . . . but he knew his opportunity was quickly slipping away. With each step they traveled closer to the other members of the Cabal.

Svenson took a deep breath. The three men were perhaps ten yards ahead of him, just turning the corner from one long corridor into—he presumed—another. As soon as they disappeared he dashed ahead to make up ground, reached the corner and peeked—five yards away, and onto a thin runner of carpeting! Svenson stepped out, revolver extended, and rapidly advanced, his padded footfalls mixing with theirs—ten feet away, then five, and then he was right behind them. Somehow they sensed his presence, turning just as Svenson reached out and took rough hold of Vandaariff's collar with his left hand, and pressed the revolver barrel against the side of the Lord's temple with his right.

"Do not move!" he hissed. "Do not cry out—or this man will die, and then each of you in turn. I am a crack shot with a pistol, and few things would give me more pleasure!"

They did not cry out, and once again Svenson felt the disquieting capacity for savagery creeping up his spine—though he was no particular shot at all even when his gun was loaded. What he didn't know was the value they placed on Vandaariff. With a sudden chill he wondered if they might actually *want* him killed—something they desired but shrank from doing themselves—especially now that Crabbé had the satchel of vital information.

The satchel. He must have it.

"That satchel!" he barked at the Deputy Minister. "Drop it at once, and step away!"

"I will not!" snapped Crabbé shrilly, his face gone pale.

"You *will*!" snarled Svenson, pulling back the hammer and pressing the barrel hard into Vandaariff's skull.

Crabbé's fingers fidgeted over the leather handle. But he did not throw it down. Svenson whipped the gun away from Vandaariff and extended his arm directly at Crabbé's chest.

"Doctor Svenson!"

This was Bascombe, raising his own hands in a desperate conciliatory gesture that was still for Svenson too much like an attempt to grab his weapon. He turned the barrel toward the younger man, who flinched visibly, then back toward Crabbé who now hugged the satchel to his body, then again to Bascombe, pulling Vandaariff a step away to give himself more room. Why did he not get *better* at this sort of confrontation?

Bascombe swallowed and took a step forward. "Doctor Svenson," he began in a hesitant voice, "this cannot stand—you are inside the hornets' nest, you will be taken—"

"I require my Prince," said Svenson, "and I require that satchel."

"Impossible," piped Crabbé, and to the Doctor's great exasperation the Deputy Minister turned and spun the satchel like a discus down the length of the corridor. It bounced to a stop against the wall some twenty feet beyond them. Svenson's heart sank—God damn the man! If he'd possessed a single bullet he would have put it straight between Harald Crabbé's ears.

"So much for *that,*" Crabbé bleated, babbling fearfully. "How did you survive the quarry? Who helped you? Where were you hidden on the airship? How are you still tormenting my *every plan*?"

The Minister's voice rose to a high-pitched shout. Svenson took another step back, dragging Vandaariff with him. Bascombe—though frightened the man had courage—again stepped forward in response. Svenson put the gun back against Vandaariff's ear.

"Stay where you are! You will answer me—the whereabouts of Karl-Horst—the Prince—I insist..."

His words faltered. From somewhere below them in the house Svenson heard a screaming high-pitched whine, like the brakes of a train slamming down at high speed... and within it, like the silver thread run through a damask coat made for a king, a desperate woman's shriek. What had Crabbé said about the Comte's activity... "the cathedral"? All three stood fixed as the noise rose to an unbearable peak and then just as suddenly cut away. He dragged Vandaariff back another step.

"Release him!" hissed Crabbé. "You only make it worse for yourself!"

"Worse?" Svenson sputtered at the man's arrogance—O for one bullet! He gestured at the floor, at the hideous noise. "What horrors are these? What horrors have I already seen?" He tugged Vandaariff. "You will not have this man!"

"We have him already," sneered Crabbé.

"I know how he is afflicted," stammered Svenson. "I can restore him! His word will be believed and damn you all!"

"You know nothing." Despite his fear, Crabbé was tenacious—no doubt a valuable quality in negotiating treaties, but to Svenson galling as all hell.

"Your infernal Process may be irreversible," announced Svenson, "I have had no leisure to study it—but I know Lord Vandaariff has not undergone that ritual. He bears no scars—he was perfectly lucid and in his own mind but two evenings ago, well before such scars would fade—and what is more, I know from what I have just observed in your theatre that if he *had* been so transformed he would be fighting my grip quite violently. No, gentlemen, I am confident he is under the temporary control of a drug, for which I will locate an antidote—"

"You'll do nothing of the kind," cried Crabbé, and he turned his words to Vandaariff, speaking in a sharp, wheedling tone that one would use to order a dog. "*Robert!* Take his gun—at once!"

To Svenson's dismay, Lord Vandaariff spun and dove for the pistol with both arms. The Doctor stepped away but the Lord's insistent grasping hands would not let go and it was instantly apparent that the automaton Lord was more vigorous than the utterly spent surgeon. The Doctor looked up to see Crabbé's face split with a wicked smile.

It was the last stroke of arrogance that Doctor Svenson could bear. Even as Vandaariff grappled him—a hand across his throat, another stabbing at the weapon—Svenson wrenched the pistol away and thrust it at the Minister's face, drawing back the hammer.

"Call him off or you die!" he shouted.

Instead, Bascombe leapt for Svenson's arm. He slashed the gun at Bascombe as he came, the jagged sight at the end of the barrel digging a raw line across the younger man's cheekbone, knocking him off his feet. At that moment Vandaariff's hand clamped over Svenson's, squeezing. The hammer clicked forward. Svenson desperately looked up and met Bascombe's gaze. They both knew the gun had not fired.

"He has no bullets!" cried Bascombe and he pitched his voice to the far end of the corridor. "Help! Evans! Jones! Help!"

* * *

Svenson turned. The satchel! He threw himself away from Vandaariff and ran for it, though it carried him straight toward the returning escorts. His boots clattered against the slippery polished wood, his ankle spasmed in protest, but he reached the satchel, scooped it up, and began his hobbling run back toward Bascombe and Crabbé. Crabbé screamed to the men who—he had no doubt—were all too close behind him.

"The satchel! Get the satchel! He must not have it!"

Bascombe had regained his feet and came forward, hands out, as if to bar Svenson's way—or at least tackle him until the rest could dash his brains out. There were no side doors, no alcoves, no alternatives but to charge the man. Svenson recalled his days at university, the drunken games played inside the dormitories—sometimes they would even manage horses—but Bascombe was younger and angry, with his own foolish game-playing to draw upon.

"*Stop* him, Roger—*kill* him!" Even enraged, Crabbé managed to sound imperious.

Before Bascombe could tackle him Svenson swung the satchel at his face, an impact more ignominious than painful, but it caused Bascombe to turn his head at the moment of collision. Svenson dropped his shoulder and knocked Bascombe backwards. The man's hands grabbed at his shoulders, but he bulled himself free and Bascombe's grip slipped down his body. Svenson was nearly past, stumbling, when Bascombe caught both hands on his left boot and held fast, pulling him off balance and sending him to the floor. He rolled on his back to see Bascombe sitting in a heap, his face red and blood-smeared. Svenson raised his right boot and kicked it at Bascombe's face. The blow landed on Bascombe's arm—both men crying out at the impact, for this was the Doctor's twisted ankle. Two more hideous kicks and he was free.

But the men in black were there—he had no chance. He scrabbled to his feet—and then in a sudden moment of joy saw that the two men had by instinct and deference stopped to aid both Crabbé and Bascombe. On a sudden urge, Doctor Svenson ran right at them, the satchel in one hand and the revolver in the other. He could hear Crabbé's protests—"No, no! Him! Stop *him*!" and Bascombe's cries of "Satchel! Satchel!"—but he was on them and swinging just as the men looked up. Neither blow—pistol or satchel—landed, but both caused their targets to flinch, and he gained yards of valuable space as he dashed past them down the hall. They were following, but despite his fear and his ankle Doctor Svenson's game-playing spirits were high.

He raced down the corridor, boots slipping, wincing at the impact of each step. Where had Crabbé sent the two men to wait—the "top of the tower"? He frowned—his view from the airship had shown him quite clearly that there was no tower to speak of at Harschmort. What was more, the men had come quite quickly at Bascombe's call for help—that is, they could not have scaled any height. Unless . . . he rounded a corner into a wide marble foyer, the floor a black and white checkerboard, the far wall marked by a strange iron door, wide open onto a dark spiral staircase . . . this place marked the top of a tower leading *down*. Before he could even fully process the thought, Doctor Svenson lost his footing completely and crashed to the floor, sliding all the way across the marble to the far wall. He shook his head and tried to stand. He was dripping with . . . blood! He'd stepped into a wide scarlet pool and with his fall smeared it across the width of the marble, soaking the right side of his body in gore.

He looked up. His two pursuers appeared in the far doorway. Before anyone could move, another piercing mechanical shrieking rose from beyond the open tower door, rising to a head-splitting level of loathsome discomfort. His ears did not deceive him, there was definitely the voice of a woman within the shriek.

Svenson threw the pistol with all his strength at the men, catching one dead on the knee. The man groaned and slumped back against the doorframe, the pistol spinning away across the floor. The second man dove after the gun and snatched it up as Svenson broke for the only other door—a wide hallway leading away from the tower (the last thing he wanted was to go nearer to the screaming). He could hear the clicking of the hammer on empty chambers behind him and then a snarl of anger from the man—as Svenson again stretched his lead.

He rounded a corner into another small foyer, with doors to each side. Quickly and quietly, Doctor Svenson stepped through a swinging door, easing it shut behind him so the door was still, careful not to leave any smear of blood. He had entered some part of the kitchens. The Doctor stepped past barrels and lockers toward an inner door. He had just reached it when the door swung open. He ducked swiftly behind it as it did, hiding him from the rest of the room. A moment later, the far door opened—where he'd come in—and he heard the voice of his pursuer.

"Did anyone come in here?"

"When?" asked a gruff voice not ten inches from where the Doctor presently skulked.

"Just now. Bony fellow, foreigner, covered in blood."

"Not in here. Do you see any blood?"

There was a scuffling pause as both men looked around them. The man nearest him leaned against the door as he looked, causing Svenson to shrink further into the wall.

"Don't know where else he could've run," muttered the man from the hallway.

"Across the way—that goes to the trophy room. Full of guns."

"I'll be damned," hissed his pursuer, and Svenson heard the blessed sound of the door swinging shut. A moment later he heard a locker being opened, the man rooting around in it, and what seemed like the spilling sound of gravel. This done, as quickly as that the man walked back out of the room, pulling the door closed behind him. Svenson breathed a sigh of relief.

He looked at the wall—quite covered in blood from his pressing against it. He sighed—nothing to be done—and wondered if there was anything to drink in one of the lockers. He was hardly safe—enemies but yards away in either direction—but that was becoming a common condition. What was more . . . gravel? Curiosity got the better of him, and Svenson crept to the largest of the lockers—fully large enough to stand in—where he was sure the man had gone. He pulled it open and winced as the frigid air inside flowed over his face. It had not been gravel at all, but ice. A bag of chipped ice poured over the body of the Duke of Stäelmaere, skin blue, reptilian eyes half-open, lying in grisly state in an iron tub.

Why were they keeping him? What did Lorenz think he could do—bring him back to life? That was absurd. Two bullets—the second of which had blown out his heart—had inflicted grievous damage, and now for so many hours, the blood would be cooled and pooling, the limbs stiffened . . . what did they possibly intend? Svenson had a sudden urge to dig out a penknife and do more mischief to the body—open the jugular, perhaps?—to further frustrate Lorenz's unnatural plans, but such actions seemed too unsavory. Without concrete reason, he was not going to stoop to desecrating even this disreputable corpse.

But as he looked down at that corpse, Doctor Svenson felt the nearness of his own despair. He hefted the satchel in his hands—did it bring him any nearer the Prince, any closer to saving the lives of his friends? The corners of his mouth flicked with a wan smile at the word. He did not really remember the last time he'd made what he could call a friend. The Baron was—had been—an employer and gouty mentor to his life in the Palace, but they shared no confidences. Officers he'd served with, in port or shipboard, became companions for that tour of duty, but rarely came to mind once subsequent postings had split them apart. His friends from university were few and mostly dead. His family relations were cast under the shadow of Corinna and quite out of mind. The idea that in these few days he had thrown his lot—not just his life, but whatever that life stood for—with an unlikely pair (or was it now three?) that had he passed them on the street would not have turned his head . . . well, that was not completely true. He would have smiled knowingly at Miss Temple's contained willfulness, shaken his head at Chang's garish advertisement of mystery . . . and contented himself with a tactful appraisal of Eloïse Dujong in her no doubt demure dress. And he would have perilously undersold them all—as their own first impressions of him might not have allowed for his present achievements. Svenson winced at this, glancing down at the sticky blood congealing down the side of his uniform. What had he achieved, at the end? What had he ever achieved at all? His life was a fog since Corinna's death . . . must he fail these others as he had failed her?

He was tired, dangerously so, standing without the first idea of his next step, in the doorway of a meat locker, enemies waiting on the other side of a door whichever way he went. Hanging from a metal pole that went across above his head were a number of wicked metal hooks, set at the end with a small wooden cross-piece for a handle. Intended for handling large cuts of meat, one in each hand would suit him very well indeed. Svenson reached up and selected a pair and smiled. He felt like a pirate.

He looked down at the Duke, for something had caught his eye . . . it did not seem as if anything had changed—the corpse was no more animated and no less blue. He realized that was it . . . the blue was not the normal color of icy dead flesh, of which he had seen more than his share in his Baltic service. No, this was somehow brighter . . . *bluer*. The ice shifted, slipping down as it melted, and Svenson's eye was drawn to the water in the tub . . . the ice and the water . . . the ice was piled at the edge of the tub and over the Duke's lower body, while the water, which must be the center of melting, was pooled over his chest, over his wound. With a sudden curiosity, Svenson stepped behind the Duke and placing his hooks under each of the man's arms lifted him some inches out of the tub, until he could see the actual wound. As the torn flesh broke the surface, he was astonished to see it had been patched—and the wound cavity filled—with indigo clay.

* * *

The door in the room opened and with a start Svenson let go of the body, which slid back into the tub, ice and water spilling loudly onto the floor. He looked up—whoever had entered would have heard the sound as they saw the locker door was open—and quickly freed his two hooks. The satchel! Where was the satchel? He'd put it down when he'd reached up for the hooks. He cursed himself for a fool, dropped one hook into the tub and snatched up the satchel just as the locker door began to move. Svenson threw himself forward, driving his shoulder into the door and, with a satisfying *thud,* the door into whoever stood behind it. Another of the black-coated functionaries tottered backwards, his hands laden with another burlap sack of broken ice, and fell. The sack split and ice slid across the floor in a gleaming sheet. Svenson charged over the man, stepping on him rather than risking a slip on the ice, and burst through the swinging door, leaving a wide red smear on its butter-cream paint as he passed.

This was a kitchen room proper—a wide long table for preparation, an enormous stone hearth, stoves, racks of pots and pans and metal. On the other side of the table stood Doctor Lorenz, black cloak thrown back over his shoulders, thick glasses on the end of his nose, peering at a page of densely written parchment. To the savant's right was spread a cloth roll of metal tools, picks and knives and tiny sharp shears, and to his left was a row of glass vials connected to one another by distilling coils. Svenson saw the bandolier of metal flasks slung over a chair—the Doctor's store of refined indigo clay from the quarry.

On the side of the table nearer to Svenson sat another functionary smoking a cigar. Two others stood by the hearth, tending several metal vessels hanging over the fire, unsettling combinations of a tea kettle and a medieval helmet, vaguely round, banded and bolted with steel, with shiny metal spouts that spat steam. These men wore heavy leather gauntlets. All four men looked up at Svenson in surprise.

* * *

As if he was born to it, fear and fatigue curling in an instant into brutal expedience, Svenson took two steps to the table, swinging with all his strength before the man in the chair could move. The hook landed with a *thwock,* pinning his right hand to the table top. The man screamed. Svenson released the hook and kicked the chair out from under the man, who cried out again as he fell to the floor and drove more weight against his pinioned hand. Svenson dropped the satchel and swung the chair as hard as he could at the nearest man from the fire, already charging at him. The chair struck the man's outstretched arms cruelly and broke his momentum. Stepping aside like a bullfighter—or how he *imagined* a bullfighter might step—Svenson swung again, this time across the fellow's head and shoulders. The chair snapped to pieces and the man went down. The first man was still shrieking. Lorenz was bawling for help. The second man from the fire had charged. Svenson dashed away toward the rack of pans—beyond the rack was a heavy butcher block. Svenson dove to it as he felt the man's hands take hold of his jacket. There was a row of knives but his grasping hand could not reach them. The man pulled him away and spun him around, driving an elbow across his jaw. Svenson was knocked into the butcher block with a grunt, the edge slamming across his arching back with a vicious impact. His hand groped behind him and caught some handle, some tool, and he whipped it forward at the man, just as a fist slammed into his stomach. Svenson doubled over, but his own blow struck hard enough to cause his opponent to stumble back. The Doctor looked up, gasping for breath. He was holding a heavy wooden mallet for tenderizing meat, the flat hammer head cut into sharp wooden spikes for quicker, deeper work. Blood trickled down the staggered fellow's head. Svenson swung again, landing square on the ear, and the man went down.

He looked to Lorenz. The man at the table was still pinned, his face white and drawn. Doctor Lorenz dug furiously at his cloak, glaring at Svenson with hatred. If he could get that bandolier! Svenson heaved himself back toward the table, raising the mallet.

The pinned man saw him coming and dropped to his knees with another scream. Lorenz's face contorted with effort and he finally freed his prize—a small black pistol! The Doctors stared at each other for a brief suspended moment.

"You're as persistent as bed lice!" hissed Lorenz.

"You're all doomed," whispered Svenson. "Every one of you."

"Ridiculous! *Ridiculous!*"

Lorenz extended his arm, taking aim. Svenson threw the hammer into the line of glass vials, smashing them utterly, and flung himself to the floor. Lorenz cried out with dismay—both at the ruined experiment and the broken glass flying up at his face—and the bullet sailed across the room to splinter the far door. Svenson felt the satchel under his hand and once more snatched it up. Lorenz fired again but Svenson had the luck to trip on a pan (screaming himself at yet another searing jolt to his ankle) and so was no longer where Lorenz had aimed. He reached the door and burst through—a third shot splitting the wood near his head—stumbled into the hall, slipped, and sat down hard in a heap. Behind him Lorenz bellowed like a bullock. Svenson lurched across the main hall to another passage, in hopes that he might find Lord Vandaariff's trophy room... before his stuffed head took up a place of honor in it.

He limped blindly down the corridor, seeing no doors, his anxiety rising toward paralysis as he realized what he had just done—the compressed savagery, the calculated mayhem. What had happened to him—potting men from the catwalk as if they were unfeeling targets, murdering the helpless fellows through the mirror, and now this awful slaughter in the kitchens—and he had done it all so easily, so *capably,* as if he were a seasoned killer—as if he were Cardinal Chang. But he was not Chang—he was not a killer—already his hands were shaking and face slick with cold sweat. He stopped, leaning heavily against the wall, his mind suddenly assailed by the image of the poor man's hand, pinned like a pale flipping fish. Doctor Svenson's throat rose and he looked about him for an urn, a pot, a plant, found nothing, and forced his gorge down by strength of will, the taste of bile sharp in his mouth. He could not go on, careening from collision to collision, with no longer the slightest idea of what he sought. He needed to sit, to rest, to weep—any respite, however brief. All around him were the sounds of guests and preparations, music, footsteps—he must be very near the ballroom. With a grateful groan he spied a door, small, plain, unlocked, prayed with all his bankrupt faith that the room was empty, and slipped inside.

He stepped into darkness, closed the door and immediately barked his shin, tripped, and set off an echoing clatter that seemed to take minutes to die. He froze, waiting . . . breathed in the silent dark . . . there were no other noises from within the room . . . and nothing from the hallway. He exhaled slowly. The clatter was wooden, wooden poles . . . mops, brooms . . . he was in a maids' closet.

Doctor Svenson carefully set down the satchel and groped around him to either side. He felt shelves—one of which he'd kicked—and his hands moved cautiously, not wanting to knock anything else to the floor. His fingers sought quickly, moving from shelf to shelf until his right hand slipped over and then into a wooden box, full of slick, tubular objects . . . candles. He plucked one from the box and then continued his search for a box of matches—surely they would be in the same place. In fact, the box was on the next shelf down, and crouching, Svenson carefully struck a match by feel—how often had he done the same in the darkness of a ship at night?—in a stroke transforming his little chamber of mystery into a mundane catalog of house management: soap, towels, brass polish, buckets, mops, brushes, brooms, dusters, pans, smocks, vinegar, wax, candles . . . and, he blessed the thoughtful maid who put it there, a tiny stool. He shifted his body and turned, sitting so he faced the door. A *very* thoughtful maid . . . for stuck into the wall near the door was a small loop of chain on a nail, made to slip around the knob and serve as a lock—but only usable from *within* the closet. Svenson made the chain fast and saw, near the box of matches, a cleared foot of shelf marked with melted wax—the place for occupants to place their candles. He'd ducked into someone's sanctuary, and made it his own. Doctor Svenson shut his eyes and allowed his fatigue to slump his shoulders. If only the maid had left a stash of tobacco.

It would be terribly simple to fall asleep, and he knew it was a real possibility. With a grimace he forced himself to sit up straight, and then—why did it keep slipping his mind?—he remembered the satchel, fetching it onto his lap. He untied the clasp and fished out the contents, a thick sheaf of parchment, densely covered with finely written notes. He leafed through the stack... angling the pages so they caught more candlelight.

He read, quickly, his eyes skimming from line to line, and then from that page to the next, and to the next again. It was a massive narrative of acquisition and subterfuge, and clearly from the pen of Robert Vandaariff. At first Svenson recognized just enough of the names and places to follow the geographical path of finance—money houses in Florence and Venice, goods brokers in Vienna, in Berlin, fur merchants in Stockholm, then diamond traders in Antwerp. But the closer he read—and the more he flipped back and forward between the pages to re-sort out the facts (and which initials stood for institutions—"RLS" being Rosamonde Lacquer-Sforza not, as he'd first suspected, Rotterdam Liability Services, a major insurer of overseas shipping)—the more he understood it was a narrative with two conjoined threads: a steady campaign of leverage and acquisition, and a trail of unlikely individuals, like islands in a stream, determining each in their way how the money flowed. But more than anything what cried out to the Doctor were the many references to his country of Macklenburg.

It was quite clear that Vandaariff had undergone protracted negotiations, both openly and through a host of intermediaries, to purchase an enormous amount of land in the Duchy's mountain district, with an ever-present emphasis on mining rights. This confirmed what Svenson had guessed from the reddish earth at the Tarr Manor quarry, that the Macklenburg hills were even richer in deposits of indigo clay. It also confirmed Vandaariff's knowledge of this mineral as a commodity—its special properties and the insidious uses to which they might be put. Finally, it convinced him again, as he had thought two days ago, that Robert Vandaariff had been very much personally involved in this business.

Bit by bit Doctor Svenson identified the other major figures in the Cabal, noting how each one entered Vandaariff's tale of conquest. The Contessa appeared by way of the Venetian speculation market, and it was through her that Lord Robert became acquainted in Paris with the Comte d'Orkancz as someone who could initially—and discreetly—advise him on the purchase of certain antiquities from a recently discovered underground Byzantine monastery in Thessalonika. But this was a ruse, for the Comte was truly enlisted to study and verify the characteristics of certain mineral samples that Lord Vandaariff had apparently acquired in secret from the same Venetian speculators. Yet he was surprised to see no mention, as far as he could tell, of Oskar Veilandt, from whose alchemical studies so much of the conspiracy's work seemed to spring. Could Vandaariff have known Veilandt (or suborned him) for so long that he saw no need to mention the man? It made no sense, and Svenson flipped ahead to see if the painter was mentioned later, but the narrative quickly branched out to tales of exploration and diplomacy, from scientists and discoverers at the Royal Institute who were also invited to study these samples, the resources of industry given over to certain experiments in fabrication (here Doctor Lorenz and Francis Xonck first appeared), and then to Macklenburg proper, with the subtle interactions between Lord Vandaariff, Harald Crabbé, and their Macklenburg contact—of *course,* Svenson rolled his eyes—the Duke's dyspeptic younger brother, Konrad, Bishop of Warnemünde.

With these agents in motion and his money behind them,

Vandaariff's plans moved ahead seamlessly, using the Institute to locate the deposits, Crabbé to negotiate for the land with Konrad, who acted as an agent for the cash-poor aristocratic property holders. But in a twist he saw there was more to it, for instead of gold, Konrad was selling the land in exchange for contraband munitions supplied by Francis Xonck. The Duke's brother was amassing an arsenal—to assert control of Karl-Horst upon his inheritance. Svenson smiled at the irony. Unbeknownst to Konrad the Cabal had used him, enabling him to essentially import a secret army that, once *they* ruled by proxy through the Prince's soon-to-arrive infant son (and necessarily managed Konrad's death), they could use themselves to defend their investment—whereas bringing in foreign troops would have provoked an uprising. It was exactly the sort of stratagem that made Vandaariff's reputation. And moving between them all were the Comte and the Contessa. For Svenson could see what Vandaariff had not, that as much as the financier imagined himself the architect of this scheme, in fact he was merely its engine. The Doctor had no doubt the Contessa and the Comte had set it all in motion from the start, manipulating the great man. The exact point where they joined forces with the others—whether they had been in league before or after Vandaariff had recruited them—was unclear, but he sensed immediately why they had all agreed to turn on their benefactor. Vandaariff uncontrolled could dictate the profit to them all . . . with him in thrall, the whole of his wealth lay at their disposal.

There was much Svenson didn't understand—still no mention of Veilandt, for one, and how exactly had the Cabal managed to overcome Vandaariff, who was fully his powerful self the night of the engagement party? Could that have been why Trapping had been killed—that he had threatened to tell Vandaariff what was in store for him? But then why did at least some of the Cabal seem ignorant of Trapping's killer? Or did Trapping threaten to tell Vandaariff about the Comte's plans for Lydia, if Lord Robert had not known already? But no, what did Vandaariff's feelings matter if the man was going to be made their slave in any case? Or had

Trapping discovered something else—something that implicated one member of the Cabal against the others? But which one—and what was their secret?

Svenson's head was already swimming with too many names and dates and places and figures. He returned to the pages of tightly scrawled text. So much had happened within Macklenburg itself that he'd never even glimpsed. The roots of the conspiracy had worked their way deeper and deeper, amassing property and influence and, he shook his head to read it, doing whatever they needed to acquire more. There were fires, blackmail, threats, even murder . . . even . . . how long had this been going on? It seemed like *years* . . . he read of experiments—"usefully serving both scientific and practical purposes"—where disease had been introduced into districts where the tenants would not sell.

Doctor Svenson's blood went cold. Before him were the words "blood fever." Corinna . . . could it be that these people had killed her . . . killed *hundreds* . . . infected his cousin . . . in order to drive down the price of *land*?

He heard steps outside his door. Quickly and quietly he stuffed the pages back into the satchel and blew out the light. He listened . . . more steps . . . was that speaking? Music? If only he knew where exactly he was in the house! He scoffed—if only he had a loaded weapon, if only his body was not a painful wreck—he might as well wish for wings! Doctor Svenson covered his eyes with his palm. His hand trembled . . . his own immediate danger . . . the need to find the others . . . the Prince—but it was all thrown to pieces with the idea—no, the *truth*, he had no doubt at all—that this same business, these same people, had—casually, offhandedly, uncaringly—murdered his Corinna. It was as if he could no longer feel his own body, but was somehow suspended above it, commanding his limbs but not inhabiting them. All this time spent wrestling and railing against cruel destiny and a heartless world—and now to find these forces embodied not in the dispassionate course of a disease but in the deliberate handiwork of men. Doctor Svenson put his hand over his mouth to stifle a sob. It had been preventable. It needn't have happened at all.

He wiped his eyes and exhaled with a shuddering whisper. It was too much to bear. Certainly it was too much to bear in a closet. He unlooped the chain from the knob and opened the door, stepping out into the corridor before his nerves got the better of him. All around—visible to either side through open archways—were guests, masked, cloaked. He met the eyes of a cloaked man and woman and smiled, bowing his head. They returned the bow, their expressions a mix of politeness and horror at his appearance. Taking advantage of the moment, the Doctor quickly beckoned them to him with a finger. They paused, the traffic continuing to flow about them, all in the direction of the ballroom. He motioned again, a bit more conspiratorial, with an inviting smile. The man took a step closer, the woman holding his hand. Svenson gestured once more, and the man finally left the woman's grasp and came near.

"I beg your pardon," whispered Svenson. "I am in the service of the Prince of Macklenburg, who you must know is engaged to Miss Vandaariff"—he indicated his uniform—"and there has been an intrigue—indeed, violence—you will see it on my face—"

The man nodded, but it was clear this seemed as much a reason to run from Svenson as to trust him.

"I need to reach the Prince—he will be with Miss Vandaariff and her father—but as you can see, there is no way for me to do this in such a crowd without causing distress and uproar, which I assure you would be dangerous for everyone concerned." He looked either way and dropped his voice even lower. "There may still be confidential agents at large—"

"Indeed!" replied the man, visibly relieved to have something to say. "I am told they have captured one!"

Svenson nodded knowingly. "But there may be others—I must

deliver my news. Is there any way—I am dreadfully hesitant to ask—but is there any way you could see fit to lend me your cloak? I will certainly mention your name to the Prince—and his partners, of course, the Deputy Minister, the Comte, the Contessa—"

"You know the Contessa?" the man hissed, risking a guilty glance back to the woman waiting in the archway.

"O yes." Svenson smiled, leaning closer to the man's ear. "Would you care for an introduction? She is *incomparable.*"

With the black cloak covering his uniform and its stains of blood, smoke, and orange dust, and the black mask he'd taken from Flaüss, the Doctor plunged into the crowd moving toward the ballroom, shouldering through as brusquely as he dared, responding to any complaint in muttered German. He looked up and saw the ballroom ceiling through the next archway, but before he could reach it heard raised voices—and then above them all a sharp, commanding cry.

"Open the doors!"

The Contessa's voice. The bolts were pulled and then a sharp hiss of alarm came from those up front who could see . . . and then an unsettled, *daunted* silence. But who had arrived? What had happened?

He shoved forward with even less care for decorum until he passed the final archway and entered the ballroom. It was thronged with guests who pushed back at him as he came, as if they made room for someone in the center of the chamber. A woman screamed, and then another—each cry quickly smothered. He threaded his way through the palpably disturbed crowd to reach a ring of Dragoons, and then through a gap between red-coated troopers saw the grim face of Colonel Aspiche. Doctor Svenson immediately turned away and found, in the circle itself, the Comte d'Orkancz. He twisted past one more ring of spectators and stopped dead.

* * *

Cardinal Chang crouched on his hands and knees, insensible, drooling. Above him stood a naked woman, for all the world like an animated sculpture of blue glass. The Comte led her by a leather leash linked to a leather collar. Svenson blinked, swallowing. It was the woman from the greenhouse—Angelique!—at any rate it was her body, it was her hair . . . His mind reeled at the mere implications of what d'Orkancz had done—much less *how* he had done it. His eyes went back to Chang with dismay. Was it possible he'd seen greater distress than Svenson himself? The man was a ruin, his flesh slick and pale, spattered with blood, his garish coat slashed and stained and burned. Svenson's gaze darted past Chang to a raised dais . . . all of his enemies in a row: the Contessa, Crabbé (but no Bascombe, that was odd), Xonck, and then his own Karl-Horst, arm in arm with the blonde woman from the theatre—as he had feared, Lydia Vandaariff was as much a tool for the Cabal's cruel usage as her father.

Another rolling whisper, like the hiss of incoming surf, and the crowd parted to allow two more women to enter the circle behind Chang. The first was simply clad in a dark dress, with a black mask and black ribbon in her hair. Behind her was a woman with chestnut hair wearing the white silk robes. It was Miss Temple. Chang saw her and pushed himself up on his knees. The woman in black pulled away Miss Temple's mask. Svenson gasped. She bore the scars of the Process vividly imprinted on her face. She said nothing. Out of the corner of his eye Svenson saw Aspiche, a truncheon in his hand. His arm flashed down and Chang fell flat to the floor. Aspiche motioned to two of the Dragoons and pointed them toward where the women had entered.

Chang was dragged away. Miss Temple did not pay him a single glance.

* * *

His allies were shattered. One overborne physically, the other mentally, and—he had to face it—both beyond hope of rescue or recovery. And if Miss Temple had been taken, what but death or the same servitude could have been dealt to Elöise? If only he hadn't abandoned them—he had failed again—all one disaster after another! The satchel... if he could get the satchel into the hands of some other government—at the least someone else would *know*... but standing in the thick of the crowded ballroom, Doctor Svenson knew this was just one more vain hope. There was scant chance of escaping the house much less of reaching the frontier or a ship... he had no idea what to do. He looked up at the dais, narrowing his eyes at the simpering Prince. If he'd a pistol he would have stepped forth to blaze away—if he could kill the Prince and another one or two of them, it would have been enough... but even that sacrificial gesture was denied.

The voice of the Contessa broke into his thoughts.

"My dear Celeste," she called, "how fine it is that you have... *joined* us. Mrs. Stearne, I am obliged for your timely entrance."

The woman in black sank into a respectful curtsey.

"Mrs. Stearne!" called the rasping voice of the Comte d'Orkancz. "Do you not wish to see your transformed companions?"

The great man gestured behind him and Svenson was jostled as his fellow guests twisted and craned to see two more gleaming blue women, also naked, also wearing collars, step slowly and deliberately into view, their feet clicking against the parquet floor. Each woman's flesh was shining and bright, transparent enough to show darker streaks of murky indigo within its depths. Both women held in their hands a folded-up leash, and as they neared the Comte each extended her hand for him to take... and, once he did, stood gazing over the crowd with clinical dispassion. The woman nearest him... he swallowed... the hair on her head—in fact, as he looked, he realized with an uncomfortable frisson up the back of his neck that this was the only hair on her body—had been burned above her left temple... the operating theatre... the paraffin... he was looking at Miss Poole. Her body was both beautiful and inhuman—the splendid *tension* of its surface, glassy yet somehow soft—Svenson's skin crawled to look at it, yet he could not turn away, and, appalled, felt his lust begin to stir. And the third woman—it was hard to read their features, but it could only be Mrs. Marchmoor.

The Comte tugged lightly on Miss Poole's leash, and she advanced toward the woman in black. Suddenly that woman's head lolled to the side and she staggered, her eyes dulled. What had happened? Miss Poole turned toward Svenson's side of the crowd. He inched away from her strange eyes, for it was as if they could see to his bones. At once his knees trembled and for a terrible moment the entire room fell away. Svenson was on a settee in a darkened parlor . . . his hand—a delicate woman's hand—was stroking Mrs. Stearne's unbound hair as, on that lady's other side, a masked man in a cloak leaned over to kiss her mouth. The gaze of Miss Poole (the vision was from her experience, like the blue glass cards, or like the books . . . she was a *living* book!) turned slightly as, with her other hand, she reached for a glass of wine—her arm in a white robe like Miss Temple's, in fact, *both* women wore the same silk robes of initiation!—but then the parlor snapped away and Svenson was back in the ballroom, fighting the first stirrings of nausea in his throat. All around him, the other guests were shaking their heads, dazed. What violation was this—the effect of the glass cards projected across the audience at large—into every mind!

Doctor Svenson desperately groped to make sense of it—the cards, the Process, the books, and now these women, like three demonic Graces—there was no time! He thought he understood the rest, the Process and the books, for blackmail and influence were standard things, even on such an evil scale, but this—this was alchemy, and he could not comprehend it any more than he could imagine *why* anyone would give themselves over to such—such—abomination!

The Comte was saying something else to Mrs. Stearne—and to the Contessa, and the Contessa was replying—but he could not follow their words, the insistent vision still muddied his brain.

Svenson stumbled into the equally disoriented people behind him, then turned to force his way through the crowd, away from his enemies, away from Miss Temple. He did not get seven steps before his mind reeled with another vision . . . a vision of himself!

He was back at Tarr Manor, facing Miss Poole on the quarry steps, Crabbé scuttling free, the men racing at him, beating aside his feeble blows and snatching him bodily up—and then hurling him over the rail. Again, he was plunged into Miss Poole's experience—of watching his own defeat!—and so immediate that he felt in his nerves the ethereal glide of Miss Poole's amusement at his pathetic efforts.

Svenson gasped aloud, coming back to his senses, on his hands and knees on the parquet floor. People were backing away from him, making room. This is what had happened to Chang. She had sensed him somehow in the crowd. He scrambled wildly to rise, but was rebuffed by the hands around him and propelled against his will toward the center of the room.

He slipped again and fell, flailing with the satchel. It was over. Yet—something . . . he fought to think—ignoring everything—there were shouts, steps . . . but Doctor Svenson shook his head, holding on—to—to what he had just seen! In Miss Poole's first vision—of Mrs. Stearne—the man on the settee had been Arthur Trapping, his face marked with the fresh scars of the Process. The memory was of the evening he had died—the very half hour before his murder . . . and as Miss Poole turned her head to collect her wine, Svenson had seen on the far wall a mirror . . . and in that mirror, watching from the shadow of a half-open doorway . . . the unmistakable figure of Roger Bascombe.

He could not help it. He turned his desperate face to Miss Temple, his heart breaking anew to meet her flat indifferent gaze. Aspiche ripped the satchel from his hand and Dragoons took fierce hold of his arms. The Colonel's truncheon swept savagely down and Doctor Svenson was dragged without ceremony to his doom.

FOUR

Inheritrix

The Comte d'Orkancz had led them all—Miss Temple, Miss Vandaariff, Mrs. Stearne, and the two soldiers—up the darkened rampway into the theatre. It was as desolate of good feeling as Miss Temple had remembered and her gaze fell upon the empty table with its dangling straps and the stack of wooden boxes beneath it, some pried open, spilling sheets of orange felt, with a dread that nearly buckled her knees. The Comte's iron hand had kept hold of Miss Temple's shoulder and he looked behind to confirm they had all arrived before he passed her off with a nod to Mrs. Stearne, who stepped forward between the two white-robed women, taking a hand from each and squeezing. Despite her deeply rooted anger, Miss Temple found herself squeezing back, for she was finally very frightened, though she prevented herself from actually glancing at the woman. The Comte set his monstrous brass helmet onto one of the table's rust-stained cotton pads (or was that dried blood?) and crossed to the giant blackboard. With swift broad strokes he inscribed the words in bold capital letters: "AND SO SHALL BE REBORN." The writing struck Miss Temple as strangely familiar, as if she recognized it from some place other than this same blackboard on her previous visit. She bit her lip, for the matter seemed somehow important, but she could not call up the memory. The Comte dropped the chalk into the tray and turned to face them.

"Miss Vandaariff shall be first," he announced, his voice again sounding crafted of rough minerals, "for she must take her place in the celebration, and to do so must be sufficiently recovered from her *initiation.* I promise you, my dear, it is but the first of many pleasures on your card for this gala evening."

Miss Vandaariff swallowed and did her best to smile. Where a few moments ago her spirits had been gay, the combination of the room and the Comte's dark manner had obviously rekindled her worry. Miss Temple thought they would have kindled worry in the iron statue of a saint.

"I did not know this room was here," Lydia Vandaariff said, her voice quite small. "Of course there are so many rooms, and my father . . . my father . . . is most occupied—"

"I'm sure he did not think you'd an interest in science, Lydia." Mrs. Stearne smiled. "Surely there are storerooms and workrooms you've never seen as well!"

"I suppose there must be." Miss Vandaariff nodded. She looked out beyond the lights to the empty gallery, hiccuped unpleasantly and covered her mouth with one hand. "But will there be people watching?"

"Of course," said the Comte. "You are an example. You have been such all your life, my dear, in the service of your father. Tonight you serve as one for our work and for your future husband, but most importantly, Miss Vandaariff, for your *self.* Do you understand me?"

She shook her head meekly that she did not.

"Then this is still more advantageous," he rasped, "for I do assure you . . . you *will.*"

The Comte reached under his leather apron and removed a silver pocket watch on a chain. He narrowed his eyes and tucked the timepiece away.

"Mrs. Stearne, will you stand away with Miss Vandaariff?"

Miss Temple took a breath for courage as Caroline released her hand and ushered Lydia to the table. The Comte looked past them to nod at the two Macklenburg soldiers.

Before Miss Temple could move the men shot forward and held her fast, raising her up so she stood on the very tips of her toes. The Comte removed his leather gauntlets, tossing them one after the other into the upturned brass helmet. His voice was as deliberate and menacing as the steady strop of a barber's razor.

"As for you, Miss Temple, you will wait until Miss Vandaariff has undergone her trial. You will watch her, and this sight will increase your fear, for you have utterly, utterly lost your very self in this business. Your self will belong to me. And worse than this, and I tell you now so you may contemplate it fully, this *gift,* of your autonomy to my keeping, will be made willingly, happily . . . *gratefully* . . . by you. You will look back with whatever memories you keep at the willful gestures of these last days and they will seem the poor antics of a child—or not even, the actions of a disobedient lap-dog. You will be *ashamed.* Trust this, Miss Temple, you will be reborn in this room, contrite and wise . . . or not at all."

He stared at her. Miss Temple did not—could not—reply.

The Comte snorted, then reached for the pocket watch again and frowned, stuffing it back behind the apron.

"There *was* a disturbance in the outer hallway—" Mrs. Stearne began.

"I am aware of it," rumbled the Comte. "Nevertheless, this . . . *lateness*—the prospective adherents are sure to be waiting already. I begin to think it was a mistake not to send *you*—"

He turned at the sound of an opening door from the opposite rampway and strode to it.

"Have you an *inkling* of the time, Madame?" he roared into the darkness, and marched back to the table, crouching amidst the boxes beneath it. Behind him, stepping up from the darkened rampway, was the figure of a short curvaceous young woman with curling dark brown hair, a round face, and an eager smile. She wore a mask of peacock feathers and a shimmering pale dress the color of thin honey, sporting a silver fringe around her bosom and her sleeves. Her arms were bare, and in her hands she carried several dull, capped metal flasks. Miss Temple was sure she had seen her before—it was an evening for nagging suspicions—and then it came to her: this was Miss Poole, the third woman in the coach to Harschmort, initiated to the Process that night.

"My goodness, Monsieur le Comte," Miss Poole said brightly. "I am perfectly aware of it, and yet I assure you there was no helping the delay. Our business became dangerously protracted—"

She stopped speaking as she saw Miss Temple.

"Who is this?" she asked.

"Celeste Temple—I believe you *have* met," snapped the Comte. "Protracted how?"

"I shall tell you later." Miss Poole let her gaze drift to Miss Temple, indicating none too subtly the reason she preferred not to speak openly of her delay, then turned to wave girlishly at Mrs. Stearne. "Suffice it to say that I simply *had* to change my dress—that orange dust, don't you know—though before you rail at me, it took no more time than Doctor Lorenz took to prepare your precious clay."

Here she handed the flasks to the Comte and once again danced away from the man toward Miss Vandaariff, lighting up with another beaming smile.

"Lydia!" she squeaked, and took the heiress by the hands as Mrs. Stearne looked on with what to Miss Temple seemed a watchful, veiling smile.

"O Elspeth!" cried Miss Vandaariff. "I came to see you at the hotel—"

"I know you did, my dear, and I *am* sorry, but I was called away to the country—"

"But I felt so *ill*—"

"Poor darling! Margaret was there, was she not?"

Miss Vandaariff nodded silently and then sniffed, as if to say that she did not *prefer* to be soothed by Margaret, as Miss Poole was well aware.

"Actually, Miss Temple was there first," observed Mrs. Stearne rather coolly. "She and Lydia had quite some time to converse before Mrs. Marchmoor was able to intervene."

* * *

Miss Poole did not reply, but looked over to Miss Temple, weighing her as an adversary. Returning this condescending gaze, Miss Temple remembered the petty struggle in the coach—for it was Miss Poole's eyes she had poked—and knew that humiliation would remain, despite the Process, in the woman's mind like a whip mark turned to scar. For the rest of it, Miss Poole had just that sort of willfully merry temperament Miss Temple found plain galling to be around, as if one were to consume a full pound of sweet butter at a sitting. Both Mrs. Marchmoor (haughty and dramatic) and Mrs. Stearne (thoughtful and reserved) appeared to be informed by injuries in their lives, where Miss Poole's insistence on gaiety seemed rather a shrill denial. And to Miss Temple's mind all the more repellent, for if she posed as Lydia's true friend, it was only to better ply their awful *philtre*.

"Yes, Lydia and I got on quite well," Miss Temple said. "I have taught her how to poke the eyes of foolish ladies attempting to rise beyond themselves."

Miss Poole's smile became fixed on her face. She glanced back at the Comte—still occupied with the boxes and flasks and lengths of copper wire—and then called to Mrs. Stearne, loud enough for all to hear.

"You did miss so much of interest at Mr. Bascombe's estate—or should I say Lord Tarr? Part of our delay involved the capture and execution of the Prince's physician, Doctor—O what is his name?—a strange fellow, now quite dead, I'm afraid. The other part was one of our subjects; her reaction to the *collection* was averse but not fatal, and she ended up causing, as I say, rather an important problem—though Doctor Lorenz is confident it may be remedied..."

She glanced back to the Comte. He had stopped his work and listened, his face impassive. Miss Poole pretended not to notice and spoke again to Mrs. Stearne, a sly smile gracing the corners of her plump mouth.

"The funny thing, Caroline—and I thought you would be

particularly interested—is that this Elöise Dujong—is tutor to the children of Arthur and Charlotte *Trapping*."

"I see," said Caroline, carefully, as if she did not know what Miss Poole intended with this comment. "And what happened to this woman?"

Miss Poole gestured to the darkened rampway behind her. "Why, she is just in the outer room. It was Mr. Crabbé's suggestion that such spirited defiance be put to use, and so I have brought her here to be initiated."

Miss Temple saw she was now looking at the Comte, pleased to be giving him information he did not have.

"The woman was intimate with the Trappings?" he asked.

"And thus of course the Xoncks," Miss Poole said. "It was through Francis that she was *seduced* to Tarr Manor."

"Did she reveal anything? About the Colonel's death, or—or about—" With an uncharacteristic reticence, the Comte nodded toward Lydia.

"Not that I am aware—though of course it was the Deputy Minister who interrogated her last."

"Where is Mr. Crabbé?" he asked.

"Actually, it is Doctor Lorenz you should be seeking first, Monsieur le Comte, for the *damage* the woman has done—if you will remember who else was attending our business at Tarr Manor—is such that the Doctor would very much appreciate your consultation."

"Would he?" snarled the Comte.

"Most urgently." She smiled. "If only there were two of you, Monsieur, for your expertise is required on so many fronts! I do promise that I will do my best to ferret out any clues from this lady—for indeed it seems that a good many people might have wished the Colonel dead."

"Why do you say that, Elspeth?" asked Caroline.

Miss Poole kept her gaze on the Comte as she replied. "I only echo the Deputy Minister. As someone in *between* so many parties, the Colonel was well-placed to divine . . . secrets."

"But all here are in allegiance," said Caroline.

"And yet the Colonel is dead." Miss Poole turned to Lydia, who listened to their talk with a confused half-smile. "And when it is a matter of *secrets*... who can say what we don't know?"

The Comte abruptly snatched up his helmet and gloves. This caused him to step closer to Miss Poole—who quite despite herself took a small step backwards.

"You will initiate Miss Vandaariff first," he growled, "and then Miss Temple. Then, if there is time—and *only* if there is time—you will initiate this third woman. Your higher purpose here is to inform those in attendance of our work, not to initiate *per se*."

"But the Deputy Minister—" began Miss Poole.

"His wishes are not your concern. Mrs. Stearne, you will come with me."

"Monsieur?"

It was quite clear that Mrs. Stearne had thought to remain in the theatre.

"There are more *important* tasks," he hissed, and turned as two men in leather aprons and helmets came in dragging a slumped woman between them.

"Miss Poole, you will address our spectators, but do not presume to operate the machinery." He called up to the dark upper reaches of the gallery. "Open the doors!"

He wheeled and was at the rampway in two strides and was gone.

Mrs. Stearne looked once at Miss Temple and then to Lydia, her expression tinged with concern, and then met the smiling face of Miss Poole whose dashing figure had just—in her own opinion at least—somehow turned Mrs. Stearne, in her plain severe dark dress, from her place.

"I'm sure we shall speak later," said Miss Poole.

"Indeed," replied Mrs. Stearne, and she swept after the Comte.

When she was gone Miss Poole flicked her hand at the Comte's two men. Above them all the door had opened and people were flowing into the gallery, whispering at the sight below them on the stage.

"Let us get dear Lydia on the table. Gentlemen?"

Throughout Miss Vandaariff's savage ordeal the two soldiers from Macklenburg held Miss Temple quite firmly between them. Miss Poole had stuffed a plug of cotton wadding into Miss Temple's mouth, preventing her from making a sound. Try as she might to shift the foul mass with her tongue, her efforts only served to dislodge moistened clots at the back of her mouth that she then worried she might swallow and choke upon. She wondered if this Dujong woman had been with Doctor Svenson at the end. At the thought of the poor kind man Miss Temple blinked away a tear, doing her best not to weep, for with a sniffling nose she'd have no way to breathe. The Doctor . . . dying at Tarr Manor. She did not understand it—Roger had been on the train to Harschmort, he was not *at* Tarr Manor. What was the point of anyone going there? She thought back to the blue glass card, where Roger and the Deputy Minister had been speaking in the carriage . . . she had assumed Tarr Manor was merely the prize with which Roger had been seduced. Was it possible it was the other way around—that the need for Tarr Manor necessitated their possession of Roger?

But then another nagging thought came to Miss Temple—the last seconds of that card's experience—metal-banded door and the high chamber . . . the broad-shouldered man leaning over the table, on the table a woman . . . that very card had come from Colonel Trapping. The man at the table was the Comte. And the woman . . . Miss Temple could not say.

These thoughts were driven from her head by Lydia's muffled screams, the shrieking machinery, and the truly unbearable smell. Miss Poole stood below the table, describing each step of the Process to her audience as if it were a sumptuous meal—every moment of her smiling enthusiasm belied by the girl's arching back and clutching fingers, her red face and grunts of animal pain. To Miss Temple's lasting disgust, the spectators whispered and applauded at every key moment, treating the entire affair like a circus exhibition. Did they have any idea who lay in sweating torment before them—a beauty to rival any Royal, the darling of the social press, heiress to an empire? All they saw was a woman writhing, and another woman telling them how fine a thing it was. It seemed to her that this was Lydia Vandaariff's whole existence in a nutshell.

Once it was over however, Miss Temple chided herself bitterly. She did not think she actually could have broken from the two soldiers, but she was certain that this period of sparking, ghastly chaos was the only time she might have had a chance. Instead, as soon as the Comte's men unstrapped Lydia and eased her limp form from the table—the unctuous Miss Poole whispering eagerly into the shattered girl's ear—the soldiers stepped forward and hefted Miss Temple into her place. She kicked her legs but these were immediately caught and held firmly down. In a matter of helpless seconds she was on her back, the cotton pads beneath her hot and damp from Lydia's sweat, the belts cinched close across her waist, neck, and bosom and each limb tightly bound. The table was angled so those in the gallery could see the whole of her body, but Miss Temple could only see the glare of the hot paraffin lamps and an indistinct mass of shadowed faces—as uncaring to her condition as those waiting with empty plates are to the frightened beast beneath the knife.

She stared at Lydia as the tottering young woman—sweat-sheened face, hair damp against the back of her neck, eyes dull and mouth slack—was briskly examined by Miss Poole. With a tremor Miss Temple thought of the defiant course of her short life—itself a litany of governesses and aunts, rivals and suitors, Bascombes and Pooles and Marchmoors... she would now join them, edges stripped away, her velocity set to their destinations, her determination yoked like an ox to work in someone else's field.

And what had she wanted instead? Miss Temple was not without insight and she saw how genuinely free the Process had made both Marchmoor and Poole, and—she did not frankly doubt it—how Lydia Vandaariff would now find her will of steel. Even Roger—her breath huffed around the gag with a plangent whine as his visage crossed her inner eye—she knew had been formerly restrained by a decency rooted in fear and timid desire. It did not make them *wise*—she had only to recall the way Roger could not reconcile her present deeds with the fiancée he had known—but it made them fierce. Miss Temple choked again as the cotton wadding nudged the slick softness at the back of her throat. She was *already* fierce. She required none of this nonsense, and if she'd carried a man's strength and her father's horsewhip these villains would as one be on their knees.

But in addition Miss Temple realized—barely listening to Miss Poole's disquisition—that so much of this struggle came down to dreams. Mrs. Marchmoor had been released from the brothel, Mrs. Stearne from fallow widowhood, and Miss Poole from a girlish hope to marry the best man within reach . . . which was all to say that of course she understood. What *they* did not understand—what no one understood, from her raging father to her aunt to Roger to the Comte and the Contessa with their wicked violations—was the particular character of her own desires, her own sunbaked, moist-aired, salt-tinged dreams. In her mind she saw the sinister *Annunciation* fragments of Oskar Veilandt, the expression of astonished sensation on Mary's face and the gleaming blue hands with their cobalt nails pressing into her giving flesh . . . and yet she knew her own desire, however inflamed at the rawness of that physical transaction, was in truth elsewhere configured . . . her colors—the pigments of her need—existed before an artist's interposition—crumbled, primal minerals and untreated salts, feathers and bones, shells oozing purple ink, damp on a table top and still reeking of the sea.

Such was Miss Temple's heart, and with it beating strong within her now she felt no longer fear, but near to spitting rage. She knew she would not die, for their aim was corruption—as if to skip the act of death completely and leap ahead to the slow decomposition of her soul, through worms that they would here place in her mind. She would not have it. She would fight them. She would stay who she was no matter what—no matter what—and she would kill them all! She snapped her head to the side as one of the Comte's attendants loomed over her and replaced her white mask with the glass and metal goggles, pushing them tight so the black rubber seal sucked fast against her skin. She whined against the gag, for the metal edges pressed sharply and were bitter cold. Any moment the copper wires would surge with current. Knowing that agony was but seconds away, Miss Temple could only toss her head again and decide with all the force of her will that Lydia Vandaariff was a weakling, that it would not be difficult at all, that she should thrash and scream only to convince them of their success, not because they made her.

Into the theatre two soldiers brought this Miss Dujong, slumped and unresponsive, and deposited her onto the floor. The unfortunate woman had been bundled into the white robes, but her hair hung over her face and Miss Temple had no clear picture of her age or beauty. She gagged again on the wadding in her mouth and pulled at the restraints.

They did not pull the switch. She cursed them bitterly for toying so. They would *die.* Every one of them would be punished. They had killed Chang. They had killed Svenson. But this would not be the end... Miss Temple was not *prepared* to allow—

The straps around her head were fast, but not so tight that she did not hear the gunshots... then angry shouts from Miss Poole—and then more shots and Miss Poole's voice leapt from outrage to a fearful shriek. But this was shattered by a crash that shook the table itself, another even louder chorus of screams... and then she smelled the smoke and felt the heat of flame—flame!—on her bare feet! She could not speak or move, and the thick goggles afforded only the most opaque view of the darkening ceiling. What had happened to the lights? Had the roof fallen in? Had her "gunshots" actually been exploding joists from an unsound ceiling? The heat was sharper on her feet. Would they abandon her to burn alive? If they did not, if she pretended to be injured they would not hold her tightly—a stout push and she could run the other way . . . but what if her captors had already fled and left her behind to burn?

A hand groped at her arm and she twisted to take hold of whoever it was—she could not turn her head, she could not see through the thickening smoke—and squeeze—they must free her, they must! She curled her toes away from the rising flames, biting back a cry. The hand pulled away and her heart fell—but a moment later hands fumbled at the belt. She was a fool—how could the fellow free her if she held his arm? After another desperately distended moment the strap gave way and her hands were free. Her rescuer's attention dropped to her feet and without a thought Miss Temple's hands flew to her face, ripping at the mask. She found the release screw—for she had felt the point from which the thing was tightened—and scraped her finger tearing it loose. The goggles fell away and Miss Temple caught a handful of copper wire and sat up, dangling the contraption behind her like a medieval morning star, ready to bring it down on the head of whatever conscience-stricken functionary had thought to save her.

He'd managed the other straps and she felt the man's arms snake under her legs and behind her back to scoop her from the table and set her feet down on the floor. Miss Temple snorted at the presumption—the silk robes might as well have been her shift, a shocking intimacy no matter the circumstance—and raised her hand to swing the heavy goggles (which bore all sorts of jagged metal bolts that might find vicious purchase), while with her other hand she pried the sopping gag from her mouth. The smoke was thick—across the table the flames flickered into view, an orange line dividing gallery from stage and blocking off the far rampway, where she could hear shouts and see figures looming in the murk.

She took a lungful of foul air and coughed. Her rescuer had his hand around her waist, his shoulder leaning close. She took aim at the back of his head.

"This way! Can you walk?"

Miss Temple stopped her swing—the voice—she hesitated—and then he pulled her down below the line of smoke. Her eyes snapped open, both in unlooked-for delight at the man she found before her, and at the desperately stricken image that man presented, as if he had indeed crawled up through hell to find her.

"Can you walk?" Doctor Svenson shouted again.

Miss Temple nodded, her fingers releasing the goggles. She wanted to throw her arms around his shoulders and would have done that very thing had he not then pulled her arm and pointed to the other woman—Dujong?—who had come from Tarr Manor and was now hunched against the curved wall of the theatre with the Doctor's coat thrown across her legs.

"She cannot!" he shouted above the roaring flames. "We must help her!"

The woman looked up to them as the Doctor took her arm and duty-bound Miss Temple took her other side. They lifted her with an awkward stumble—in the back of her mind Miss Temple was entirely unsure—in fact, annoyed—about the choice to adopt this new companion, though at least now the woman was able to move and mutter whatever she was muttering to Doctor Svenson. Hadn't Miss Poole described her as "seduced by Francis Xonck"? Wasn't she some sort of adherent possessing privileged information? The last thing Miss Temple desired was the company of such a person, any more than she appreciated the Doctor's earnest frown of concern as he brushed the hair from the woman's sweat-smeared face. Behind them she heard steps and a piercing wave of sharp hissing—buckets emptied into the fire—and then coughed at the roiling smoky steam that billowed into their faces. The Doctor leaned across the Dujong woman to call to her.

"—Chang! There is a—machine—the Dragoon—do not—glass books!"

Miss Temple nodded but even apart from the noise the information was too thick to make sensible in her mind—too many other sensations crowded for her attention—hot metal and broken wood beneath her bare feet, with one hand under the woman's arm and the other out before her, feeling in the gloom. What had happened to the lights? From the once-blazing array she saw but one distracted orange glow, like a weak winter sun unable to reach through fog—what *had* happened to Miss Poole? Doctor Svenson turned—there was motion behind them—and thrust his half of the woman wholly onto Miss Temple, who stumbled forward. His hand was shoving at her, driving her on. In the shadows she saw Doctor Svenson extend a revolver toward their pursuers and heard him shout.

"Go! Go at once!"

Never one to misunderstand her own immediate needs, Miss Temple dipped her knees, threw the burdensome woman's arm over her shoulder and then stood straight with a grunt, Miss Temple's other hand around her waist, doing her best to carry what weight she could, rolling on her tiptoes away from the wall to stumble down the rampway, hoping the slope would create enough momentum to keep Miss Dujong propelled. They slammed into the far wall at the curve, both of them crying out (the bulk of the impact absorbed by the taller woman's shoulder), careened backwards and wavered, nearly toppling, until Miss Temple managed to angle them along the next part of the pitch-black passage. Her feet caught on something soft and both women went down in a heap, their fall broken by the inert body that had tripped them. Miss Temple's groping hand fell onto leather—the apron—this was one of the Comte's attendants—and then into a sticky trail on the floor that must be his blood. She wiped her hand on the apron and got her feet beneath her and her hands under the arms of Miss Dujong, heaving her over the body. She heaved her again—Miss Temple huffed with the knowledge that she simply was not meant for this sort of work—and felt in front of her for the door. It was not locked, nor did the fallen man block its opening. With another gasp she pulled Miss Dujong through its bright archway, into light and cool sweet air.

She dragged the woman as far as she could onto the carpet with one sustained burst of effort, until her legs caught beneath her and she tripped, sitting down. On her hands and knees Miss Temple crawled back to the open door and looked for any sign of Doctor Svenson. Smoke seeped into the room. She did not see him, and slammed the door, leaning against it to catch her breath.

The attiring room was empty. She could hear the commotion in the theatre behind her, and racing footsteps in the mirrored hall on the other side. She looked down to her charge, presently attempting to rise to her hands and knees, and saw the blacked soles of the woman's bare feet and the singed, discolored silk at the hem of her robes.

"Can you understand me?" Miss Temple hissed impatiently. "Miss Dujong? *Miss Dujong.*"

The woman turned to her voice, hair across her face, doing her best to move in the awkward robe that, with Doctor Svenson's greatcoat, was tangling her legs. Miss Temple sighed and crouched in front of the woman, doing her best to give an impression of kindness and care, knowing well there was precious little time—or, to be honest, feeling—for either.

"My name is Celeste Temple. I am a friend of Doctor Svenson. He is behind us—he will catch up, I am sure—but if we do not escape his efforts will be wasted. Do you understand me? We are at Harschmort House. They are keen to murder us both."

The woman blinked like a rock lizard. Miss Temple took hold of her jaw.

"Do you *understand*?"

The woman nodded. "I'm sorry... they..." Her hand fluttered in a vague and indefinite gesture. "I cannot think..."

Miss Temple snorted and then, still gripping her jaw, sorted the woman's hair from her face with brisk darts of her fingers, tucking away the wisps like a bird stabbing together its nest. She was older than Miss Temple—in her presently haggard condition it was unfair to guess by how many years—and as she allowed herself to be held and groomed, there emerged in her features a delicate *wholeness* with which Miss Temple grudgingly found a certain reluctant sympathy.

"Not thinking is perfectly all right." Miss Temple smiled, only a little tightly. "I can think for the pair of us—in point of fact I should prefer it. I cannot however *walk* for the pair of us. If we are to live—to *live,* Miss Dujong—you must be able to move."

"Elöise," she whispered.

"I beg your pardon?"

"My name is Elöise."

"Excellent. That will make everything much easier."

Miss Temple did not even risk opening the far door, for she knew the corridor beyond would be full of servants and soldiers—though why they did not come at the fire through this room she had no idea. Could the prohibition against entering such a secret room—one that so obviously loomed in the Cabal's deepest designs—carry over in the staff to even this time of crisis? She turned back to Elöise, who was still on her knees, holding in her arms a savaged garment—no doubt the dress she had arrived in.

"They have destroyed it," Miss Temple told her, crossing past to the open cabinets. "It is their way. I suggest you turn your head..."

"Are you changing clothes?" asked Elöise, doing her best to stand.

Miss Temple pushed aside the open cabinet doors and saw the wicked mirror behind. She looked about her and found a wooden stool.

"O no," she replied, "I am breaking glass."

Miss Temple shut her eyes at the impact and flinched away, but all the same the destruction was enormously satisfying. With each blow she thought of another enemy—Spragg, Farquhar, the Contessa, Miss Poole—and at every jolting of her arms her face glowed the more with healthy pleasure. Once the hole was made, but not yet wide enough to pass through, she looked back at Miss Dujong with a conspiratorial grin.

"There is a secret room," she whispered, and at Miss Dujong's hesitant nod wheeled round to swing again. It was the sort of activity that could easily have occupied another thirty minutes of her time, chipping away at this part and at that, knocking free each hanging shard. As it was, Miss Temple called herself to business, dropped the stool, and carefully stepped back to Elöise's tattered dress. Between them they spread it across their path to absorb at least what fallen glass it could, and made their way through the mirror. Once in, Miss Temple gathered the dress and, balling it in her hands, threw it back across the room. She looked a last time at the inner door, her worry grown at the Doctor's non-arrival, and reached for the cabinet doors on either side, pulling them to conceal the open mirror. She turned to Elöise, who clutched the poor man's coat close to her body.

"He will find us," Miss Temple told her. "Why don't you take my arm?"

They did not speak as they padded along the dim carpeted passageway, their pale, smoke-smeared faces and their silken robes made red in the lurid gaslight. Miss Temple wanted to put as much distance as she could between themselves and the fire, and only then address escape and disguise . . . and yet at each turn she looked back and listened, hoping for some sign of the Doctor. Could he have effected their rescue only to sacrifice himself—and what was more, maroon her with a companion she neither knew nor had reason to trust? She felt the weight of Elöise on her arm and heard again his urgent words to go, go at once . . . and hurried forward.

Their narrow path came to a crossroads. To the left it went on, the dead-end wall ahead of them was fitted with a ladder rising into a darkened shaft, while to the right was a heavy red curtain. Miss Temple cautiously reached out with one finger and edged the curtain aside. It was another observation chamber, looking into a rather large, empty parlor. If she truly wanted to evade pursuit, the last thing she needed to do was leave a second broken mirror in her trail. She stepped back from the curtain. Elöise could not climb the ladder. They kept walking to the left.

"How do you feel?" Miss Temple asked, putting as much hearty confidence as she could into a stealthy whisper.

"Palpably better," answered Elöise. "Thank you for helping me."

"Not at all," said Miss Temple. "You know the Doctor. We are old comrades."

"Comrades?" Miss Dujong looked at her, and Miss Temple saw disbelief in the woman's eyes—her size, her strength, the foolish robes—and felt a fresh spike of annoyance.

"Indeed." She nodded. "It would perhaps be better if you understood that the Doctor, myself, and a man named Cardinal Chang have joined forces against a Cabal of sinister figures with sinister intent. I do not know which of these you know—the Comte d'Orkancz, the Contessa di Lacquer-Sforza, Francis *Xonck*"—this name offered rather pointedly with a rise of Miss Temple's eyebrows—"Harald Crabbé, the Deputy Foreign Minister, and Lord Robert Vandaariff. There are many lesser villains in their party—Mrs. Marchmoor, Miss Poole—whom I believe you know—Caroline Stearne, Roger Bascombe, far too many Germans—it's all quite difficult to summarize, of course, but there is apparently something about the Prince of Macklenburg and there is a *great* deal to do with a queer blue glass that can be made into books, books that hold—or consume—actual memories, actual experiences—it's really quite extraordinary—"

"Yes, I have seen them," whispered Elöise.

"You have?" Miss Temple's voice was tinged with disappointment, for she found herself suddenly eager to describe her own astonishing experience to someone else.

"They exposed each of us to such a book—"

"Who 'they'?" asked Miss Temple.

"Miss Poole, and Doctor... Doctor Lorenz." Elöise swallowed. "Some of the women could not bear it... they were killed."

"Because they would not look?"

"No, no—because they did look. Killed by the book itself."

"*Killed?* By looking in the books?"

"I do believe it."

"I was not killed."

"Perhaps you are very strong," answered Elöise.

Miss Temple sniffed. She rarely discredited flattery, even when she knew the point of the moment lay elsewhere (as when Roger had praised her delicacy and humor at the same time that his hand around her waist sought to wander exploratively southward), but Miss Temple *had* pulled herself from the book, by her own power—an achievement even the forever condescending Contessa had remarked upon. The idea that the opposite was possible—that she could have been swallowed utterly, that she could have *perished*—sent a brittle shiver down her back. It would have been absolutely effortless, true—the contents of the book had been so seductive. But she had not perished—and what was more, Miss Temple felt fully confident that should she look into another of these books its hold would be even weaker, for as she had pulled free once, she would know she could do so again. She turned back to Elöise, still unconvinced of the woman's true character.

"But you must be strong as well, of course, as a person our enemies sought to add to their ranks—just as you were brought to Tarr Manor to begin with. For this is why we wear these robes, you know—to initiate our minds into their insidious mysteries, a Process to bend our wills to their own."

She stopped and looked down at herself, plucking at the robes with both hands.

"At the same time, though I would not call it *practical,* the feel of silk against one's body is nevertheless... *well*... so..."

Elöise smiled, or at least made the attempt, but Miss Temple saw the woman's lower lip hesitantly quiver.

"It is just...you see, I do not *remember*...I know I went to Tarr Manor for a reason, but for my life I cannot call it to mind!"

"It is best we keep on our way," Miss Temple said, glancing to see if the quivering lip had been followed by tears, and breathing with relief that it had not. "And you can tell me what you do remember of Tarr Manor. Miss Poole mentioned Francis Xonck, and of course Colonel Trapping—"

"I am tutor to the Colonel's children," said Elöise, "and known to Mr. Xonck—indeed, he has been most attentive ever since the Colonel disappeared." She sighed. "You see, I am a confidante of Mr. Xonck's sister, the Colonel's wife—I was even present here, at Harschmort House, the night the Colonel disappeared—"

"You were?" asked Miss Temple, a bit abruptly.

"I have asked myself if I inadvertently witnessed some clue, or overheard some secret—anything to entice Mr. Xonck to curiosity, or that he might use against his siblings, or even to conceal his own part in the Colonel's death—"

"Is it possible you knew who had killed him or why?" asked Miss Temple.

"I have no idea!" cried Elöise.

"But if those memories are gone, then it follows they must have been worth taking," observed Miss Temple.

"Yes, but because I learned something I should not have? Or because I was—there is no other word—seduced to even take part?"

Elöise stopped, her hand over her mouth, tears gleaming in each eye. The woman's despair struck Miss Temple as real, and she knew as well as anyone—after her experience of the book—how temptation might sway the sternest soul. If she could not remember what she'd done, if she was here stricken with regret, did the truth of it really matter? Miss Temple had no idea—no more than she might parse the relative state of her own bodily innocence. For the first time she allowed a gentle nudge of pity to enter her voice.

"But they did not enlist you," she said. "Miss Poole told the Comte and Caroline that you were quite a nuisance."

Elöise exhaled heavily and shrugged Miss Temple's words away. "The Doctor rescued me from an attic, and then was taken. I followed, with his gun, and tried to rescue him in turn. In the process—I'm sorry, it is difficult to speak of it—I shot a man. I shot him dead."

"But that is excellent, I'm sure," replied Miss Temple. "I have not shot anyone, but I have killed one man outright and another by way of a cooperative coach wheel." Elöise did not reply, so Miss Temple helpfully went on. "I actually spoke of it—well, as much as one speaks of anything—with Cardinal Chang, who you must understand is a man of few words—indeed, a man of *mystery*—the very first time I laid eyes upon him I knew it was so—granted, this was because he was wearing all red in a train car in the very early morning holding a razor and reading poetry—and wearing dark spectacles, for he has suffered injury to his eyes—and though I did not know him I did remark him, in my mind, and when I saw him again—when we became comrades with the Doctor—I knew who he was at once. The Doctor said something about him—about Chang—just now, I mean to say, in the theatre—I didn't make sense of any of it for that abominable shouting and the smoke and the fire—and do you know, it is a queer thing, but I have noticed it, how at times the extremity of, well, *information,* assaulting one of our senses overwhelms another. For example, the *smell* and the *sight* of the smoke and flames absolutely inhibited my ability to *hear.* It is exactly the sort of thing I find fascinating to think on."

They walked for a moment before Miss Temple recalled the original drift of her thought.

"But—*yes*—the reason I spoke to Cardinal Chang—well, you see, I must explain that Cardinal Chang is a *dangerous* man, a very deadly fellow—who has probably killed a man more often than I have purchased shoes—and I spoke to him about the men I had killed, and—well, honestly it was very difficult to talk about, and what he ended up telling me was exactly how someone like myself ought to use a pistol—which was to grind the barrel as tightly into the body of your target as you can. Do you see my point? He was telling me what to *do* as a way of helping me sort out how to *feel*. Because at the time, I had no idea how to talk of anything. Yet these things that have happened—they tell us what kind of world we are in, and what sort of actions we must be prepared to take. If you had not shot this fellow, would either yourself or the Doctor be still alive? And without the Doctor to take me off that table, would I?"

Elöise did not answer. Miss Temple saw her wrestling with her doubts and knew from experience that to overcome those doubts and accept what had occurred was to become a significantly less innocent person.

"But this was the Duke of Stäelmaere," Elöise whispered. "It is assassination. You do not understand—I will assuredly hang!"

Miss Temple shook her head.

"The men *I* killed were villains," she said. "And I am sure this Duke was the same—most Dukes are simply *horrid*—"

"Yes, but no one will care—"

"Nonsense, for I care, as you care, as I am sure Doctor Svenson cared—it is the exact heart of the matter. What I do *not* give a brass farthing for is the opinion of our enemies."

"But—the *law*—their word will be believed—"

Miss Temple gave her opinion of the law with a dismissive shrug.

"You may well have to leave—perhaps the Doctor can take you back to Macklenburg, or you can escort my aunt on a tour of Alsatian restaurants—but there is always a remedy. For example—look how foolish we are, waltzing along who knows where without a second's thought!"

Elöise looked behind them, gesturing vaguely. "But—I thought—"

"Yes, of course." Miss Temple nodded. "We will surely be pursued, but have either of us had the presence of mind to look through the Doctor's pockets? He is a resourceful man—one never knows—my father's overseer would not step foot from his door, as a rule, without a knife, a bottle, dried meat, and a twist of tobacco that could fill his pipe for a week." She smiled slyly. "And who can say—in the process it may afford a glimpse into the secret life of Doctor Svenson..."

Elöise spoke quickly. "But—but I am sure there is no such thing—"

"O come, every person has some secrets."

"I do not, I assure you—or at least nothing indecent—"

Miss Temple scoffed. "*Decent?* What are you wearing? Look at you—I can see your legs—your bare legs! What use is decency when we have been thrust into this peril—treading about without even a corset! Are we to be judged? Do not be silly—here."

She reached out and took the Doctor's coat, but then wrinkled her nose at its condition. The ruddy light might hide its stains but she could smell earth and oil and sweat, as well as the strongly unpleasant odor of indigo clay. She batted at it ineffectually, launching little puffs of dust, and gave up. Miss Temple dug into the Doctor's side pocket and removed a cardboard box of cartridges for his revolver. She handed it to Elöise.

"There—we now know he is a man to carry bullets."

Elöise nodded impatiently, as if this were against her wishes. Miss Temple met her gaze and narrowed her eyes.

"Miss Dujong—"

"Mrs."

"Beg pardon?"

"Mrs. Mrs. Dujong. I am a widow."

"My condolences."

Elöise shrugged. "I am well accustomed to it."

"Excellent. The thing is, Mrs. Dujong," Miss Temple's tone was still crisp and determined, "in case you had not noticed, Harschmort is a house of masks and mirrors and lies, of unscrupulous, brutal advantage. We cannot afford illusion—about ourselves least of all, for this is what our enemies exploit *most* of all. I have seen notorious things, I promise you, and notorious things have been done to me. I too have undergone—" She lost her way and could not speak, taken unawares by her own emotion, gesturing instead with the coat, shaking it. "*This* is nothing. Searching someone's *coat*? Doctor Svenson may have given his *life* to save us—do you think he would scruple the contents of his pockets if they might help us further—or help us to save him? It is no time to be a foolish woman."

Mrs. Dujong did not answer, avoiding Miss Temple's gaze, but then nodded and held out her hands, cupping them to take whatever else might come from the coat pockets. Working quickly—despite the pleasure it gave her, Miss Temple was not one to continue with criticism once her point was made—she located the Doctor's cigarette case, matches, the other blue card, an extremely filthy handkerchief, and a mixed handful of coins. They gazed at the collection and with a sigh Miss Temple began to restore them to their places in the coat—for that seemed the simplest way to carry them.

"After all of that, it appears you are right—I do not think we have learned a thing." She looked up to see Elöise studying the silver cigarette case. It was simple and unadorned save for, engraved in a simple, elegant script, the words "*Zum Kapitänchirurgen Abelard Svenson, vom C. S.*"

"Perhaps it commemorates his promotion to Captain-Surgeon," whispered Elöise.

Miss Temple nodded. She put the case back in its pocket, knowing they were both wondering at who had given it to him—a fellow officer, a secret love? Miss Temple draped the coat over her arm and shrugged—if the last initial was "S" it needn't be interesting at all, most likely a dutiful token from some dull sibling or cousin.

* * *

They continued down the narrow red-lit passage, Miss Temple dispirited that the Doctor had not caught up, and a bit curious that no one else had pursued them either. She did her best not to sigh with impatience when she felt the other woman's hand on her arm, and upon turning tried to present a tolerant visage.

"I am sorry," Elöise began.

Miss Temple opened her mouth—the last thing she appreciated after berating a person was that they should *then* waste her time with apology. But Elöise touched her arm again and kept on speaking.

"I have not been thinking . . . and there are things that I must say—"

"Must you?"

"I was taken aboard the airship. They asked me questions. I do not know what I could have told them—in truth I know nothing that they cannot already know from Francis Xonck—but I do remember what they asked."

"Who was it asking?"

"Doctor Lorenz gave me the drug, and bound my arms, and then he and Miss Poole made certain I was under their influence by the most impertinent demands . . . I was powerless to refuse . . . though I am ashamed to think of it . . ."

The woman's voice dipped deeper in her throat. Miss Temple thought of her own experience at the mercy of the Comte and Contessa, and her heart went out—yet she could not help speculating on the exact details of what had happened. She patted the woman's silk-covered arm. Elöise sniffed.

"And then Minister Crabbé interrogated me. About the Doctor. And about you. And about this Chang. And then about my killing the Duke—he would not believe I had not been put up to it by another party."

Miss Temple audibly scoffed.

"But *then* he asked me—and in a voice that I do not think was heard by the others—about Francis Xonck. At first I thought he meant my employment by Mr. Xonck's sister, but he wanted to know about Mr. Xonck's plans *now*. Was I in service to him *now*. When I replied that I was not—or at least did not *know*—he asked about the Comte and the Contessa—especially about the Contessa—"

"It seems a long list," replied Miss Temple, who was already impatient. "What about them *exactly*?"

"If they had killed Colonel Trapping. He was particularly suspicious of the Contessa, for I gather she does not always tell the others what she plans to do, or does things without caring how it may ruin their plans."

"And what did you tell Deputy Minister Crabbé?" Miss Temple asked.

"Why, nothing at all—I *knew* nothing."

"And his response?"

"Well, I do not know the man, of course—"

"If you were to hazard a *guess*?"

"That is just it . . . I should say he was frightened."

Miss Temple frowned. "I do not mean to insult your former employer," she said, "but from all accounts . . . well, it seems the Colonel is not exactly *missed* for his good qualities. Yet as you describe Deputy Minister Crabbé's curiosity, so I heard the Comte d'Orkancz pressing Miss Poole for the same information—and indeed the Contessa and Xonck asking as well, in a coach from the station. Why should all of them care so much for such a, well . . . such a *wastrel*?"

"I cannot think they would," said Elöise.

Whoever killed the Colonel defied the rest of the Cabal in doing so . . . or was it that they had *already* defied the Cabal—already planned to betray them? Somehow Trapping knew and was killed before he told the others! The Colonel still breathed when Miss Temple had left him: either he had just been poisoned or was poisoned directly afterwards. She had been on her way to the theatre . . . by the time she got there, the Comte was *in* the theatre . . . as was Roger—she'd watched Roger climb the spiral staircase before her. She had not seen Crabbé or Xonck—she'd no idea then who Xonck *was*—nor any of the Macklenburgers. But behind her—behind everyone and alone in the corridor... had been the Contessa.

Their passage came to an end. To one side was a third curtained alcove, and to the other was a door. They peeked around the curtain. This viewing chamber was dominated by a larger chaise draped with silken quilts and furs. In addition to the drinks cabinet and writing desk they had seen before, this room was fitted with a brass speaking tube and a metal grille that must allow for instructions to be relayed between each side of the mirror. It was not a room for observation alone, but for interrogation... or a more closely directed private performance.

The room that lay beyond the wall of glass was like no other Miss Temple had seen at Harschmort, but it might have disturbed her even more than the operating theatre. It was a pale room with a simple floor of unvarnished planking, lit by a plain hanging lamp that threw a circle of yellow light onto the single piece of furniture, a chaise identical to the one before them, distinguished by both an absence of silks and furs and the metal shackles bolted to its wooden frame.

But it was not for the chaise that upon looking through the mirror Miss Temple's breath stopped fast, for in the open doorway of the room, looking down at its single piece of furniture, stood the Contessa di Lacquer-Sforza, red jewel-teared mask over her face and a smoking cigarette holder at her lips. She exhaled, tapped her ash to the floor and snapped her fingers at the open door behind her, stepping aside to allow two men in brown cloaks to carry in between them one of the long wooden boxes. She waited for them to pry open the box top with a metal tool and leave the room, before snapping her fingers again. The man who entered, his manner an awkward mix of deference and amused condescension, wore a dark uniform and a gold-painted mask over the upper half of his face. His pale hair was thin and his chin was weak, and when he smiled she saw his teeth were bad as well. On his finger however was a large gold ring... Miss Temple looked again at the uniform... the ring was a signet... this was Doctor Svenson's Prince! She had seen him in the suite at the Royale—and had not recognized him at once in a more formal uniform and different mask. He sat on the chaise and called back to the Contessa.

They could not hear. Moving quietly to the brass grille, Miss Temple saw a small brass knob fitted to it. The knob did not pull, so she tried to turn it, moving ever so slowly if it should squeak. Its movement was silent, but suddenly they could hear the Prince.

"—gratified of course, most enthusiastically, though not surprised, you must know, for as the mighty among animals will recognize one another across an expanse of forest, so those in society matched by a natural superiority will similarly gravitate, it being only fitting that spirits united in an *essential* sympathy be followed by a sympathy of a more *corporeal* nature—"

The Prince was in the midst of unbuttoning the collar of his tunic. The Contessa had not moved. Miss Temple could not readily credit that such a man could be so shamelessly describing to such a woman the destined aspect of their imminent assignation—though she knew one could scarcely underestimate the arrogance of princes. Still, she pursed her lips with dismay at his droning prattle, as he all the while dug at the double row of silver buttons with a pale hooked finger. Miss Temple looked to Mrs. Dujong, whose expression was equally unsteady, and leaned her lips quite close against her ear.

"That is the Doctor's Prince," she whispered, "and the Contessa—"

Before she could say more the Contessa took another step into the room and closed the door behind her. At the sound the Prince paused, interrupting his words with an unhealthily gratified leer that revealed a bicuspid gone grey. He dropped a hand to his belt buckle.

"Truly, Madame, I have longed for this since the moment I first kissed your hand—"

The Contessa's voice was loud and sharp, her words spoken clearly and without regard for sense.

"Blue Joseph blue Palace ice consumption."

The Prince went silent, his jaw hanging open, his fingers still. The Contessa stepped closer to him, inhaled thoughtfully from her lacquered holder and let the smoke pour from her mouth as she spoke, as if upon exercising her hidden power she had become that much more demonic.

"Your Highness, you will believe you have had your way with me in this room. Though it would very much give you pleasure, you will be unable to convey this information to anyone else under any circumstances. Do you understand?"

The Prince nodded.

"Our *engagement* will have occupied your time for the next thirty minutes, so it will be impossible that I have in this time seen either Lydia Vandaariff or her father. During our encounter I have also confessed to you that the Comte d'Orkancz prefers the erotic companionship of boys. You will be unable to convey this information to anyone else either, though because of it you will not begrudge any request the Comte might have for unaccompanied visits to your bride. Do you understand?"

The Prince nodded.

"Finally, despite our encounter this evening, you will believe that upon this night you have taken the virginity of Miss Vandaariff, before you are married, so rapacious is your sexual appetite, and so little can she resist you. In the event she conceives, it is therefore entirely as a result of your own impulsive efforts. Do you understand?"

The Prince nodded. The Contessa turned, for at the door behind her came a gentle knock. She opened it a crack, and then, seeing who it was, wide enough for that person to enter.

Miss Temple put her hand over her mouth. It was Roger Bascombe.

* * *

"Yes?" asked the Contessa, speaking quietly.

"You wanted to know—I am off to collect the books from this night's *harvest,* and meet the Deputy Minister—"

"And deliver the books to the Comte?"

"Of course."

"You know which one I need."

"Lord Vandaariff's, yes."

"Make sure it is in place. And watch Mr. Xonck."

"For what?"

"I'm sure I do not know, Mr. Bascombe—thus the need to watch him closely."

Roger nodded. His eyes glanced past the Contessa to the man on the chaise, who followed their words with an ignorant curiosity, like a cat captivated by a beam of light thrown from a prism. The Contessa followed Roger's gaze and smirked.

"Tell the Comte this much is done. The Prince and I are in the midst of a torrid assignation, do you see?"

She permitted herself a throaty chuckle at the ridiculousness of that prospect and then sighed with contemplative pleasure, as if she were in the midst of a thought.

"It is a terrible thing when one is unable to resist one's impulses . . ." She smiled to Bascombe and then called to the Prince. "My dear Karl-Horst, you are having your way with my body even now—your mind is writhing with sensation—you have never felt such ecstasy and you never will again. Instead you will always measure your future pleasure against this moment . . . and find it lacking."

She laughed again. The Prince's face was pink, his hips twitching awkwardly on the chaise, his nails scratching feebly at the upholstery. The Contessa glanced at Roger with a wry smile that to Miss Temple was confirmation that her ex-fiancé was just as much subject to this woman's power as the Prince. The Contessa turned back to the man on the chaise.

"You . . . may . . . *finish,*" she said, teasing him as if he were a dog awaiting a treat.

At her words the Prince went still, breathing air in gulps, whimpering, both hands clutching the chaise. After what seemed to Miss Temple a very brief time, he exhaled deeply, his shoulders sagged from his effort, and the unpleasant smile returned to his face. He absently plucked at his darkening trousers and licked his lips. Miss Temple scoffed with abhorrence at the entire spectacle.

Her eyes snapped to the Contessa and her hand flew up to cover her mouth. The Contessa glared directly into the mirror. The speaking tube—the knob had been turned. Miss Temple's scoff had been heard.

The Contessa barked harshly at Roger. "Someone is there! Get Blenheim! Around the other side—*immediately*!"

Miss Temple and Eloïse stumbled back to their curtain as Roger dashed from sight and the Contessa strode toward them, her expression dark with rage. As she passed, the Prince attempted to stand and take her into his arms.

"My darling—"

Without a pause she struck him across the face, knocking him straight to his knees. She reached the mirror and screamed as if she could see their startled faces.

"Whoever you are—whatever you are doing—you will die!"

Miss Temple dragged Eloïse by the hand through the curtain and to the nearby door. It did not matter where it went, they had to get out of the passage at once. Even wearing a half-mask the fury on the Contessa's face had been that of a Gorgon, and as her hand tore at the doorknob Miss Temple felt her entire body trembling with fear. They barreled through the door and slammed it behind—and then both squealed with alarm at the brooding figure that loomed suddenly over them. It was only the back side of the door, covered by a striking, somber portrait in oils of a man in black with searching eyes and a cold thin mouth—Lord

Vandaariff, for behind the figure rose the specter of Harschmort House. And yet, even as she continued to run, her heart in her mouth, Miss Temple recognized the painting as the work of Oskar Veilandt. But—was he not dead? And Vandaariff only in residence at Harschmort for two years? She groaned at the annoyance of not being able to pause and think!

As one she and Elöise cut through a strange ante-room of paintings and sculpture, its floor inlaid with mosaic. They could already hear approaching footsteps and dashed heedlessly in the other direction, careening around one corner and then another, until they reached a foyer whose flooring was slick black and white marble. Miss Temple heard a cry. They had been seen. Elöise ran to the left, but Miss Temple caught her arm and pulled her to the right, to a formidable dark metal door she thought they might close behind them to seal themselves off from pursuit. They rushed through, bare feet pattering across the marble and onto a landing of cold iron. Miss Temple thrust the coat at Elöise and shoved the woman toward a descending spiral staircase of welded steel while she tried to close the door. It did not move. She heaved again without success. She dropped to her knees, pried out the wooden wedge that had held it and then thrust the heavy door shut just as she heard footsteps echoing off the marble. The latch caught and she quickly dropped to her knees again and with both hands drove the wedge back under the door. She leapt after Mrs. Dujong, her pale feet soft and moist against the metal steps.

Being a spiral staircase, as the steps reached the iron column in the center they became quite narrow, and so because she was smaller Miss Temple felt it only fair she take the inside going down, half a step behind Elöise but holding on to her arm—as Elöise with her other hand held on to the rail. The metal staircase was very cold, especially so on their feet. Miss Temple felt as if she were scampering around the scaffolds and catwalks of an abandoned factory in her nightdress—which was to say it felt very like one of those strange dreams that always seemed to end up in unsettling situations involving people she but barely knew. Racing down the stairs, still genuinely amazed at this dark metal tower's very existence—*under* the *ground*—Miss Temple wondered what new peril she had launched them into, for the pitiless tower struck her as the most unlikely wrinkle yet.

Was there someone behind—a noise? She pulled Elöise to a stop, patting her arm to indicate urgency and silence, and looked back up the stairs. What they heard was not footsteps from within the tower, but what seemed very much like footsteps—and scuffles and snippets of talk—*outside* of it. For the first time Miss Temple looked at the tower walls—also welded steel—and saw the queer little sliding slats, like the ones sometimes seen between a coach and driver. Elöise slid the nearest open. Instead of an open window, it revealed an inset rectangle of smoked glass through which they could see . . . and what they saw quite took their breath away.

They looked out and down from the top of an enormous open chamber, like an infernal beehive, walls ringed with tier upon tier of walled prison cells, into which they could gaze unimpeded.

"Smoked glass!" she whispered to Elöise. "The prisoners cannot see when they are spied upon!"

"And look," her companion answered, "are these the new prisoners?"

Before their eyes, the upper tier of cells was filling up like theatre boxes with the elegantly dressed and masked guests of the Harschmort gala, climbing down through hatches in the cell roofs, setting out folding chairs, opening bottles, waving handkerchiefs to one another across the open expanse through fearsome metal bars—the whole as unlikely, and to Miss Temple's mind inappropriate, as spectators perched in the vault of a cathedral.

So high were they that even pressing their faces angled down against the glass did not allow them to see the floor below. How many cells were there? Miss Temple could not begin to count how many prisoners the place might hold. As for the spectators, there seemed to be at least a hundred—or who knew, numbers not being her strongest suit, perhaps it was three—their mass emitting a growing buzz of anticipation like an engine accelerating to speed.

The only clue to the purpose of the gathering, or indeed the cathedral itself, was the bright metal tubing that ran the height of the chamber, lashed together in bunches, emerging from the walls like creeping vines the width of a tree trunk. While Miss Temple was sure that the layers of cells covered the whole of the chamber, she could not see the lower tiers for all the metal pipes—which told her sensible mind that the pipes, not the cells, had become the main concern. But where were the pipes going and whatever substance did they hold?

Miss Temple's head spun back, where a grating shove echoed down to them like a whip crack—someone was opening the wedged door. At once Miss Temple took Elöise's arm and leapt ahead.

"But where are we going?" hissed Elöise.

"I do not know," whispered Miss Temple, "take care we do not get tangled in that coat!"

"But"—Elöise, annoyed but obliging, shifted the coat higher in her arms—"the Doctor cannot find us—we are cut off! There will be people below—we are marching directly to them!"

Miss Temple simply snorted in reply, for about no part of this could anything be done.

"Mind your feet," she muttered. "It is slippery."

As they continued their descent, the noise above them grew, both from the spectators in their cells and then, with another sharp scraping exclamation of the door being forced, from their pursuers at the top of the tower. Soon there were hobnails clattering against the steel steps. Without a word to each other the women increased their speed, racing around several more turns of the tower—how far down could it extend?—until Miss Temple abruptly stopped, turning to Elöise, both of them out of breath.

"The coat," she panted, "give it to me."

"I am doing my best to carry it safely—"

"No no, the bullets, the Doctor's bullets—quickly!"

Elöise shifted the coat in her arms, trying to find the right pocket, Miss Temple feeling with both hands for the bulky box, and then desperately digging it out and prying up the cardboard lid.

"Get behind me," hissed Miss Temple, "keep going down!"

"But we have no weapon," whispered Elöise.

"Exactly so! It is dark—and perhaps we can use the coat as a distraction—quickly, remove whatever else—the cigarette case and the glass card!"

She pushed past Elöise, and working as quickly as she could began to scatter the bullets across the metal steps, emptying the box and covering perhaps four steps with the metal cartridges. The bootsteps above them were audibly nearer. She turned to Elöise, impatiently motioning her to *go on—quickly!*—and snatched away the coat, spreading it out some three steps lower than her bullets, plumping and plucking at the sleeves to make as intriguing a shape as possible. She looked up—they could only be a turn above—and leapt down, lifting up her robes, legs flashing pale, darting away from view.

She had just caught up to Elöise when they heard a shout—someone had seen the coat—and then the first crash, and then another, the cries, and the echoing clamor of scattered bullets, flailing blades, and screaming men. They stopped to look above them, and Miss Temple had just an instant to apprehend a swift metallic slithering and see the merest flash of reflected light. With a squeak she flung herself at Elöise with all her strength, lifting their bodies just enough that they each sat on the handrail, buttocks poorly balanced but feet clear of the disembodied saber that scythed at them, as if the steps were made of ice, then bounced past to ring and spark its way to the bottom of the steps. The women tumbled off the rail, amazed at their own sudden escape, and continued down, the rage of confusion and gruesome injury clamorous above them.

* * *

The saber was a problem, Miss Temple thought with a groan, for its arrival below would surely alert whoever was there that something was wrong. Or perhaps not—perhaps it would run them through! She snorted at her own unquenchable optimism. She had no more clever ideas. They came round the final turn of the spiral and faced a landing as cluttered with boxes as a holiday foyer. To the right, leading out to the base of the great chamber, was an open door. To the left, another man with a brass helmet and leather apron crouched near an open hatchway, perhaps the size of a large coal furnace, set directly into the steel column that rose through the center of the staircase. The man carefully examined a wooden tray of bottles and lead-capped flasks that he had obviously pulled from the hatch and set down on the floor. Next to the hatch, affixed into the column, was a brass plate of buttons and knobs. The column was a dumbwaiter.

In the middle of the floor, its blade imbedded—presumably in silence, given the man's inattention—in a discarded heap of packing straw, was the saber.

From the doorway marched a second helmeted man, walking directly past the pile of straw, to gather two wax-capped bottles, one bright blue, the other vibrant orange, and rush back through the door without another word. The women stood still, unconvinced they had yet to be seen—could the helmets so impede the men's peripheral vision and muffle their hearing? Through the open door Miss Temple heard urgent commands, the sounds of work, and—she was quite certain—the voices of more than one woman.

From above them came the deliberate pinging of a kicked bouncing bullet, striking the steps and the wall in turn. The men above had resumed their descent. The bullet flew past them and bounced off of the stack of crates on the far wall, coming to rest on the floor near the man's feet. He cocked his head and registered its unlikely presence. They were ruined.

Outside the door a man's voice erupted into speech at such a volume that Miss Temple was bodily startled. She had never before heard such a human noise, not even from the roaring sailors when she'd crossed the sea, but this voice was not loud because of any extremity of effort—its normal tone was mysteriously, astonishingly, and disturbingly exaggerated. The voice belonged to the Comte d'Orkancz.

"Welcome to you *all*," the Comte intoned.

The man in the helmet looked up. He saw Miss Temple. Miss Temple leapt down the final steps, dodging past.

"It is time to begin," cried the Comte, "as you have been instructed!" From the cells above them—incongruously, fully the last thing Miss Temple would have ever expected—the gathered crowd began to sing.

She could not help it, but looked through the open door.

The tableau, for it was framed as such by the door in front and the silver curtain of bright shining pipes behind, was the operating theatre writ large, the demonic interests of the Comte d'Orkancz given full free rein—*three* examination tables. At the foot of each rose a gearbox of brass and wood, into which, as if one might slide a bullet into the chamber of a gun, one of the helmeted men inserted a gleaming blue glass book. The man with the two bottles stood at the head of the first table, pouring the blue liquid into the funneled valve of a black rubber hose. Black hoses coiled around the table like a colony of snakes, slick and loathsome, yet more loathsome still was the shape that lurked beneath, like a pallid larva in an unnatural cocoon. Miss Temple looked past to the second table and saw Miss Poole's face disappear as an attendant strapped a ghoulish black rubber mask in place... and then to the final table, where a third man attached hoses to the naked flesh of Mrs. Marchmoor. Looking up at the cells was a final figure, mighty and tall, the mouth of his great mask dangling a thick, slick black tube, like some demonic tongue—the Comte himself. Perhaps one second had passed. Miss Temple reached out and slammed the door between them.

And just as suddenly she knew, this echoing vision provoking her memory of the final instant of Arthur Trapping's blue glass card . . . the woman on its table had been Lydia Vandaariff.

Behind her Elöise screamed. The helmeted man's arms took crushing hold around Miss Temple's shoulders and slammed her into the newly shut door, then threw her to the ground.

She looked up to see the man holding the saber. Elöise seized one of the bottles of orange liquid from the tray and hefted her arm back, ready to hurl it at him. To the immediate shock of each woman, instead of running her through, the man stumbled back and then sprinted up the stairs as fast as the awkward helmet and apron would allow. All he needed was a set of bat's wings, Miss Temple thought, to make a perfect shambling imp of hell.

The women looked at each other, baffled at their near escape. The platform door was shaken again from the outside, and the stairwell above them echoed with shouts from the running man—shouts that were answered as he met their initial pursuers. There was no time. Miss Temple took Elöise brusquely by the arm and shoved her toward the open hatch.

"You must get in!" she hissed. *"Get in!"*

She did not know if it had room for two, or even if the lift would carry their weight if there was, but nevertheless leapt to the brass plate of controls, forcing her tired mind—for her day had been more than full, and she had not eaten or drunk tea in the longest time—to make sense of its buttons . . . one green, one red, one blue, and a solid brass knob. Elöise folded her legs into the hatch, her mouth a drawn grim line, one hand a tight fist and the other still holding the orange bottle. The shouting above had turned and someone pounded on the outside door. At the green button the dumbwaiter lurched up. At the red, it went down. The blue did not seem to do a thing. She tried the green again. Nothing happened. She tried red, and it went down—perhaps a single inch, but all the way to the end.

The door to the platform shook on its hinges.

She had it. The blue button meant the dumbwaiter must continue its course—it was used to prevent needless wear on the engines caused by changing directions mid-passage. Miss Temple stabbed the blue button, then the green, and dove for the hatch, Elöise's arms around her waist, gathering her quickly in, Miss Temple's wriggling feet just barely slipping through the narrowing hatchway before they rose into the pitch-black shaft, their last view the black boots of Macklenburg soldiers limping down the final steps.

The fit was incredibly awkward and, after the initial relief that first they were indeed climbing and second the men had not stopped their way and third that she had not been sheared of any limbs, Miss Temple attempted to shift herself to a more comfortable position only to find that the effort ground her knees into her companion's side, and Elöise's elbow sharp against her ear. She turned her face the other way and found her ear pressed flat on the other woman's chest, Elöise's body warm and damp with perspiration, her flesh soft and the cushioned thrum of her heartbeat reaching Miss Temple despite the dumbwaiter's clanking chains, like a precious secret risked by whisper in a crowded parlor. Miss Temple realized that her torso was curled between the other woman's legs, legs drawn tightly up to Elöise's chin, while her own legs were cruelly bent beneath them both. There had not been time to shut the hatch, and Miss Temple held her feet tucked with one arm—the other close around Elöise—so they did not, with the jarring of the dumbwaiter, accidentally pop out into the shaft. They did not speak, but after a moment she felt the other woman tug free an arm and then Miss Temple, already grateful despite herself for the comfort afforded by the unintended and therefore unacknowledged close contact with her companion's body, felt the other woman's hand smoothing her hair with soft and gentle strokes.

"At the top, they will try to reverse it before we can get out," she whispered.

"They will," agreed Elöise quietly. "You must get out first. I will push you."

"And then I shall pull your feet."

"That will be fine, I am sure."

"What if there are more men?"

"It's very possible."

"We will surprise them," observed Miss Temple quietly.

Elöise did not answer, but held the younger woman's head to her bosom with an exhalation of breath that to Miss Temple was equal parts sweetness and sorrow, a mixture she did not completely understand. Such physical intimacy with another woman was unusual for Miss Temple, much less any emotional intimacy—but she knew that their adventures had already hastened a connection to each other, as a telescope eliminated the distance between a ship and the shore. It was the same with Chang and Svenson, men who she in truth knew not at all yet felt were the only souls in the world she could rely on or even—and this surprised her, for to form the thought was to place the events of the recent days within the context of her whole life—care about. She had never known her mother. Miss Temple wondered—self-conscious and rapidly becoming less sure of herself, as this was no time to drift into reckless contemplation or indulgent feeling—if her present sensations of warm flesh, of life, of contact, and, for the space of their isolated climb at least, unquestioned care resembled what having a mother might be like. Her cheeks flushing at the exposure of her frailty and her desire, Miss Temple burrowed her face into the crook between the woman's arm and bosom and let out a sigh that by its end left her entire body shuddering.

They rose in the darkness until the car lurched to a stop without warning. The door slid open and Miss Temple saw the astonished faces of two men in the black servants' livery of Harschmort, one having slid open the door and the other holding another wooden tray of flasks and bottles. Before they could close the door and before the men below could call the car back down, she kicked both feet—the soles of which she knew were filthy as any urchin's—vigorously in their faces, driving them back out of disgust if not fear. With Elöise shoving her from behind, Miss Temple shot out the door, screaming at the men like a mad thing, hair wild, face smeared with soot and sweat and then, her eyes desperately looking for it, lunged to the brass control panel, stabbing the green button that kept the car in place.

The men looked at her with their mouths open and expressions darkening, but their response was cut short as their gaze was pulled to Elöise clambering out, feet first, silk robes rising up to the very tops of her pale thighs as she scooted forward and revealing her own pair of small silk pants, the split seam gaping for one dark, flashing instant that rooted both men to the spot before she slid her upper body free and landed awkwardly on her knees. In her hand was the bottle of bright orange fluid. At the sight of it the men took another step back, their expressions shifting in a trice from curious lust to supplication.

The moment Elöise was clear Miss Temple released the button and stepped directly to the man without the tray and shoved him with both of her hands and all of her strength back into the man who held it. Both servants retreated tottering through the metal door and onto the slick black and white marble, their attention focused solely on not dropping any of their precious breakables. Miss Temple helped Elöise to her feet and took the orange bottle from her. Behind them the dumbwaiter clanked into life, disappearing downward. They dashed into the foyer, but the servants, recovered somewhat, would not let them past.

"What do you think you're *doing*?" shouted the one with the tray, nodding urgently at the bottle in Miss Temple's hand. "How did you get that? We—we could—we *all* could have—"

The other simply hissed at her. *"Put that down!"*

"*You* put it down," Miss Temple snapped. "Put down the tray and leave! Both of you!"

"We will do no such thing!" snapped the man with the tray,

narrowing his eyes viciously. "Who are you to give orders? If you think—just because you're one of the master's *whores*—"

"Get out of the way!" the other man hissed again. "We have work to do! We will be whipped! And you've made us wait *again* for the dumbwaiter!"

He tried to edge around them toward the tower door, but the man with the tray did not move, glaring with a rage that Miss Temple knew arose from injured pride and petty stakes.

"They will not! They're not going anywhere! They need to explain themselves—and they'll do it to me or to Mr. Blenheim!"

"We don't need Blenheim!" his partner hissed. "The *last* thing—for God's sake—"

"*Look* at them," said the man with the tray, his expression growing by the moment more ugly. "They're not *at* any of the ceremonies—they're running *away*—why else was she screaming?"

This thought penetrated the other man, and in a pause both studied the two less-than-demurely-clad women.

"If we stop them I wager we'll be rewarded."

"If we don't get this work done we'll be sacked."

"We have to wait for it to come back up anyway."

"We do . . . do you reckon they've stolen those robes?"

Throughout this fatiguing dialog, Miss Temple debated her course, edging farther from the door, half-step by half-step, as the two men hesitated and bickered—but she could see that they were about to be ridiculous and manly, and so she must act. In her hand was the orange bottle, which evidently held some appallingly violent chemical. If she broke it over one of their heads, it was probable that both men would be incapacitated and they could run. At the same time, the way everyone flinched from it, like schoolgirls from a spider, she could not depend that once shattered it might not—by fumes, perhaps—afflict herself and Elöise. Further, the bottle was an excellent weapon to keep for a future crisis or negotiation, and anything of value Miss Temple much preferred to possess rather than spend. But whatever she did must be decisive enough to forestall these fellows' pursuit, for she was deeply annoyed at all this seemingly endless *running*.

With a dramatic gesture Miss Temple drew back the bottle and with a cry brought her arm forward, as if to break it over the head of the man who held the tray and who—because of the tray—could not raise his own hands to ward off the blow. But such was the threat of the bottle that he could not stop his hands from trying and as Miss Temple's arm swept down he lost his grip on the tray, which dropped to the marble floor with a crash, its contents of bottles and flasks smashing and bursting against each other with an especially satisfying clamor.

The men looked up at her, both hunched at the shoulders against the impact of her blow, their faces gaping at the fact that Miss Temple had never released—had never intended to release—the orange bottle. At once the gazes of all four dropped to the tray, whose surface erupted with hissing and steaming and a telltale odor that made Miss Temple gag. This odor was not, as she would have anticipated, the noxious indigo clay, but one that brought her back to the coach at night as she struggled free of Spragg's heavy spurting body—the concentrated smell of human blood. Three of the broken flasks had pooled together and in their mixture transformed—there was no other way to say it—into a shining bright arterial pool that spilled from the tray onto the floor in a quantity larger than the original fluids—as if the combination of chemicals not only made blood, but made *more* of it, gushing like an invisible wound across the marble tile.

"What is this *nonsense*?"

All four looked up at the flatly disapproving voice that came from the doorway behind the two men, where a tall fellow with grizzled whiskers and wire spectacles stood holding in his arms an army carbine. He wore a long dark coat, whose elegance served to make his balding head appear more round and his thin-lipped mouth more cruel. The servants immediately bowed their heads and babbled explanations.

"Mr. Blenheim, Sir—these women—"

"We were—the dumbwaiter—"

"They attacked us—"

"Fugitives—"

Mr. Blenheim cut them off with the finality of a butcher's cleaver. "Return this tray, replace its contents, and deliver them at once. Send a maid to clean this floor. Report to my quarters when you are finished. You were told of the importance of your task. I cannot answer for your continued employment."

Without another word the men snatched up the dripping tray and trotted past their master, hanging their heads obsequiously. Blenheim sniffed once at the smell, his eyes flitting over the bloody pool and then back to the women. His gaze paused once at the orange bottle in Miss Temple's hand, but betrayed no feeling about it either way. He gestured with the carbine.

"You two will come with me."

They walked in front of him, directed at each turn by blunt monosyllabic commands, until they stood at an aggressively carved wooden door. Their captor looked about him quickly and unlocked it, ushering them through. He followed them in, showing a surprising swiftness for a man of his size, and once more locked the door, tucking the key—one of many on a silver chain, Miss Temple saw—back into a waistcoat pocket.

"It will be better to speak in isolation," he announced, looking at them with a cold gaze that in its flat and bland nature belied a capacity for pragmatic cruelty. He shifted the carbine in his hand with dangerous ease.

"You will put that bottle on the table next to you."

"Would you like that?" asked Miss Temple, her face all blank politeness.

"You will do it at once," he answered.

Miss Temple looked about the room. Its ceilings were high and painted with scenes of nature—jungles and waterfalls and expansively dramatic skies—that she assumed must represent someone's idea of Africa or India or America. On each wall were display cases of weapons and artifacts and animal trophies—stuffed heads, skins, teeth, and claws. The floors were thickly carpeted and the furniture heavily upholstered in comfortable leather. The room smelled of cigars and dust, and Miss Temple saw behind Mr. Blenheim an enormous sideboard bearing more bottles than she thought were made in the civilized world, and reasoned that, given the exploratory nature of the decor, there must among them be many liquors and potions from the dark depths of primitive cultures. Mr. Blenheim cleared his throat pointedly, and with a deferent nod she placed her bottle where he had indicated. She glanced to Elöise and met the woman's questioning expression. Miss Temple merely reached out and took hold of Elöise's hand—the hand that held the blue glass card—effectively covering it with her own.

"So, you're Mr. Blenheim?" she asked, not having the slightest idea what this sentence might imply.

"I am," the man answered gravely, an unpleasant tang of self-importance clinging to his tone.

"I had wondered"—nodded Miss Temple—"having heard your name so many times."

He did not reply, looking at her closely.

"*So* many times," added Elöise, striving to push her voice above a whisper.

"I am the manager of this household. You are causing trouble in it. You were in the master's passage just now, spying on what you shouldn't have been like the sneaks you are—do not bother to deny it. And now I'll wager you've disrupted things in the tower—as well as having made a mess of my floor!"

Unfortunately for Mr. Blenheim, his litanies—for he was clearly a man whose authority depended on the ability to catalog transgression—were only damning to those who felt any of this was a source of guilt. Miss Temple nodded to at least acknowledge the man's concerns.

"In terms of management, I should expect a house this size is rather an involving job. Do you have a large staff? I myself have at various times given much thought to the proper size of a staff in relation to the size of a house—or the ambition of the house, as often a person's social aim outstrips their physical resources—"

"You were *spying*. You broke into the master's inner passage!"

"And a wicked inner passage it is," she replied. "If you ask me, it is your *master* you should call a sneak—"

"What were you doing there? What did you hear? What have you stolen? Who has paid you to do this?"

Each of Mr. Blenheim's questions was more vehement than the one before, and by the last his face was red, quite accentuating the amount of white hair in his grizzled whiskers, making him appear to Miss Temple even more worth mocking.

"My goodness, Sir—your complexion! Perhaps if you drank less gin?"

"We were merely lost," Elöise intervened smoothly. "There was a fire—"

"I am aware of it!"

"You can see our faces—my dress—" and here Elöise helpfully drew his eyes to the blackened silk that fell about her shapely calves.

Blenheim licked his lips. "That means nothing," he muttered.

But to Miss Temple it meant a great deal, for the fact that the man had not by this time delivered them to his master told her that Mr. Blenheim had ideas of his own. She indicated the animal heads and the display cases of weapons with a vague wave and a conspiratorial smile.

"What a curious room this is," she said.

"It is not curious at all. It is the trophy room."

"I'm sure it must be, but that is to say it is a room of men."

"And what of that?"

"We are women."

"Is that of consequence?"

"*That,* Mr. Blenheim"—here she batted her eyes without shame—"is surely our question to you."

"What are your names?" he asked, his mouth a tightly drawn line, his eyes flicking quickly as he stared. "What do you know?"

"That depends on who you serve."

"You will answer me directly!"

Miss Temple nodded sympathetically at his outburst, as if his anger were at the uncooperative weather rather than herself. "We do not want to be difficult," she explained. "But neither do we want to offend. If you are, for example, deeply attached to Miss Lydia Vandaariff—"

Blenheim waved her past the topic with a violently brusque stab of his hand. Miss Temple nodded.

"Or you had particular allegiances with Lord Vandaariff, or the Contessa, or the Comte d'Orkancz, or Mr. Francis Xonck, or Deputy Minister Crabbé, or—"

"You will tell me what you know no matter what my allegiance."

"Of course. But first, you must be aware that the house has been penetrated by *agents.*"

"The man in red—" Blenheim nodded with impatience.

"And the other," added Elöise, "from the quarry, with the airship—"

Again Blenheim waved them to another topic. "These are in hand," he hissed. "But why are two adherents in white gowns running through the house and defying their masters?"

"Once more, Sir, which masters do you mean?" asked Miss Temple.

"But..." he stopped, and nodded vigorously, as if his own thoughts were confirmed. "Already, then... they plot against each other..."

"We knew you were not a fool." Elöise sighed, hopelessly.

Mr. Blenheim did not at once reply, and Miss Temple, though she did not risk a glance at Elöise, took the moment to squeeze her hand.

"While the Comte is down in the prison chamber," she said, speaking with bland speculation, "and the Contessa is in a private room with the Prince . . . where is Mr. Xonck? Or Deputy Minister Crabbé?"

"Or where are they *thought* to be?" asked Elöise.

"Where is your own Lord Vandaariff?"

"He is—" Blenheim stopped himself.

"Do you know where to find your own master?" asked Elöise.

Blenheim shook his head. "You still have not—"

"What do you *think* we were doing?" Miss Temple allowed her exasperation to show. "We escaped from the theatre—escaped from Miss Poole—"

"Who came with Minister Crabbé in the airship," added Elöise.

"And then made our way to overhear the actions of the Contessa in your secret room," resumed Miss Temple, "and from there have done our best to intrude upon the Comte in his laboratory."

Blenheim frowned at her.

"Who have we *not* troubled?" Miss Temple asked him patiently.

"Francis Xonck," whispered Mr. Blenheim.

"You have said it, Sir, not I."

He chewed his lip. Miss Temple went on. "Do you see . . . *we* have not divulged a thing . . . you have seen these things for yourself and merely deduced the facts. Though . . . if we were to help you . . . Sir . . . might it go easier with us?"

"Perhaps it would. It is impossible to say, unless I know what sort of *help* you mean."

Miss Temple glanced to Elöise, and then leaned toward Blenheim, as if to share a secret.

"Do you know where Mr. Xonck is . . . at this very moment?"

"Everyone is to gather in the ballroom . . . ," Blenheim muttered, ". . . but I have not seen him."

"Is that *so*?" replied Miss Temple, as if this were extremely significant. "And if I can show you what he is doing?"

"Where?"

"Not where, Mr. Blenheim—indeed, not *where* . . . but *how*?"

Miss Temple smiled and, slipping it from Eloïse's grasp, held up the blue glass card.

Mr. Blenheim snatched at it hungrily, but Miss Temple pulled it from his reach.

"Do you know what this—" she began, but before another word could be uttered Blenheim surged forward and took hard hold of her arm with one hand and wrenched the card free from her grip with the other. He stepped back, and licked his lips again, glancing back and forth between the card and the women.

"You must be careful," said Miss Temple. "The blue glass is very dangerous. It is disorienting—if you have not looked into it before—"

"I know what it is!" snarled Blenheim, and he took two steps away from them, toward the door, blocking it with his body. He looked up at the women a last time, then down into the glass.

Blenheim's eyes dulled as he entered the world of the glass card. Miss Temple knew this card showed the Prince and Mrs. Marchmoor, no doubt more entrancing to Mr. Blenheim than Roger ogling her own limbs on the sofa, and she reached out slowly, not making a sound, to the nearest display case to take up a sharp short dagger with a blade that curved narrowly back and forth like a silver snake. Mr. Blenheim's breath caught in his throat and his body seemed to waver—the cycle of the card had finished—but a moment later he had not moved, giving himself over to its seductive repetition. Taking care to position her feet as firmly as she could and recalling Chang's advice for practical action, Miss Temple stepped to the side of Mr. Blenheim and drove the dagger into the side of his body to the hilt.

He gasped, eyes popping wide and up from the card. Miss Temple pulled the dagger free with both hands, the force of which caused him to stagger in her direction. He looked down at the bloody blade, and then up to her face. She stabbed again, this time into the center of his body, shoving the blade up under his ribs. Mr. Blenheim dropped the card onto the carpet and wrestled the dagger from Miss Temple's grasp, tottering backwards. With a grunt he dropped to his knees, blood pouring from his abdomen. He could not draw breath nor—happily for the women—make noise. He toppled onto his side and lay still. Miss Temple, gratified to see that the carpet bore a reddish pattern, knelt quickly to wipe her hands.

She looked up to Elöise, who had not moved, fixed on the fading breaths of the fallen overseer.

"Elöise?" she whispered.

Elöise turned to her quickly, the spell broken, eyes wide.

"Are you all right, Elöise?"

"O yes. I am sorry—I—I don't know—I suppose I thought we would creep past—"

"He would have followed."

"Of course. Of course! No—yes, my goodness—"

"He was our deadly enemy!" Miss Temple's poise was suddenly quite fragile.

"Of course—it is merely—perhaps the quantity of blood—"

Despite herself, the prick of criticism had punctured Miss Temple's grim resolve, for after all it was not as if murder came to her naturally or blithely, and though she knew she *had* been clever, she also knew what she had done—that it *was* murder—not even strictly a *fight*—and once more she felt it all had moved so quickly, too fast for her to keep her hold on what she believed and what her actions made of her. Tears burned the corners of each eye. Elöise suddenly leaned close to her and squeezed her shoulders.

"Do not listen to me, Celeste—I am a fool—truly! Well done!"

Miss Temple sniffed. "It would be best if we dragged him from the door."

"Absolutely."

They had each taken an arm, but the effort of transporting the substantial corpse—for he had finally expired—behind a short bookcase left them both gasping for breath, Elöise propped against a leather armchair, Miss Temple holding the dagger, wiping its blood on Mr. Blenheim's sleeve. With another sigh at the burdens one accepted along with a pragmatic mind, she set the dagger down and began to search his pockets, piling all of what she found in a heap: banknotes, coins, handkerchiefs, matches, two whole cigars and the stub of another, pencils, scraps of blank paper, bullets for the carbine, and a ring of so many keys she was sure they would answer for every door in the whole of Harschmort. In his breast pocket however was another key . . . fashioned entirely of blue glass. Miss Temple's eyes went wide and she looked up to her companion.

Elöise was not looking at her. She sat slumped in the chair, one leg drawn up, her face open, eyes dull, both hands holding the blue card in front of her face. Miss Temple stood with the glass key in her hand, wondering how long her work had taken . . . and how many times her companion had traveled through the sensations of Mrs. Marchmoor on the sofa. A little gasp escaped Elöise's parted lips, and Miss Temple began to feel awkward. The more she considered what she had experienced by way of the blue glass—the hunger, the knowledge, the delicious submersion, and of course her rudely skewed sense of self—the less she knew how she ought to feel. The attacks upon her person (that seemed to occur whenever she set foot in a coach) she *had* sorted out—they filled her with rage. But these *mental* incursions had transfigured her notions of propriety, of desire, and of experience itself, and left her usual certainty of mind utterly tumbled.

Elöise was a widow, who with her marriage must have found a balance with these physical matters, yet instead of reason and perspective Miss Temple was troubled to see a faint pearling of perspiration on the woman's upper lip, and felt a certain restless shifting at her thighs at being in the presence of someone else's unmediated desire (a thing she had never before faced, unless one could count her kisses with Roger and Roger's own attempts to grope her body, which now—by force of absolute will—she refused to do). Miss Temple could not, for she was both curious and proud, but wonder if this was how she had looked as well.

The widow's cheeks were flushed, her lower lip absently plucked between her teeth, her fingers white with pressure as they squeezed the glass, her breath shot through with sighs, the silk robe sliding as she moved, soft and thin enough to show the stiffened tips of each breast, the barely perceptible rocking of her hips, one long leg stretched out to the carpet, its toes flexing against some hidden force, and on top of all of this, to Miss Temple's discomforting attraction, was the fact that Elöise still wore her feathered mask—that, to some degree, Miss Temple felt she was not gazing at Elöise at all, but simply a Woman of Mystery, as she had made of herself in the Contessa's Dutch mirror. She continued to stare as Elöise repeated the cycle of the card, Miss Temple now able to locate, at the same slight inhalation of breath, the moment of Mrs. Marchmoor pulling the Prince's body into hers, hooking her legs around his hips and pressing him tight... and she wondered that she herself had been able to remove her attention from the card without difficulty—or without difficulty beyond her own embarrassment—where Elöise seemed quite trapped within its charms. What had she said about the book—about people being killed, about her own swooning? With a resolve that, as perhaps too often in her life, cut short her fascination, Miss Temple reached out and snatched the card from her companion's hands.

Elöise looked up, quite unaware of what had happened and where she was, mouth open and her eyes unclear.

"Are you all right?" Miss Temple asked. "You had quite lost yourself within this card." She held it up for Elöise to see. The widow licked her lips and blinked.

"My heavens . . . I do apologize . . ."

"You are quite flushed," observed Miss Temple.

"I'm sure I am," muttered Elöise. "I was not prepared—"

"It is the same experience as the book—quite as *involving*, if not as *deep*—for as there is not as much glass, there is not as much *incident*. You did say the book did not agree with you."

"No, it did not."

"The card seems to have agreed with you perhaps too well."

"Perhaps . . . and yet, I believe I have discovered something of use—"

"I blush at what it must be."

Elöise frowned, for despite her weakness she was not ready to accept the mockery of a younger woman so easily, but then Miss Temple smiled shyly and patted the woman's knee.

"I thought you looked very pretty," Miss Temple said, and then adopted a wicked grin. "Do you think Doctor Svenson would have found you even prettier?"

"I'm sure I don't know what you mean," muttered Elöise, blushing again.

"I'm sure he doesn't either," answered Miss Temple. "But what have you discovered?"

Elöise took a breath. "Is that door locked?"

"It is."

"Then you had best sit down, for we must *reason*."

"As you know," Elöise began, "my position is—or at least was—tutor to the children of Arthur and Charlotte Trapping, Mrs. Trapping being the sister of Henry and Francis Xonck. It is generally held that Colonel Trapping's rapid advancement was due to the machinations of Mr. Henry Xonck, though I see now that in fact Mr. Francis Xonck manipulated it all to engineer—by way of his new allies—a way to wrest the family business from his brother, and all of it arranged—because the Colonel became privy to all sorts of useful government secrets—with that same brother's blessing. The unwitting key to this had been Colonel Trapping, who would report faithfully back to Henry—passing on both the information and *mis*-information that Francis could supply. Further, it was Francis who persuaded *me* to visit Tarr Manor with whatever secrets I might supply—again, designed to give him the leverage of blackmail over his siblings. But *this* was made suddenly necessary exactly because the Colonel had been killed—do you see? He was killed despite the fact that, either willingly or in ignorance, he was *serving* the Cabal."

Miss Temple nodded vaguely, perched on the arm of the chair, feet dangling, hoping that a larger point would soon emerge.

Elöise went on. "One wonders why precisely because the Colonel was so very unremarkable."

"The Doctor did find the second blue card on the Colonel's person," replied Miss Temple, "the one drawn from the experience of Roger Bascombe. It was evidently sewn into the lining of his uniform. But you said you discovered—"

But Elöise was still thinking. "Was there anything within it that seemed particularly . . . secret? That would justify concealing it—protecting it—so?"

"I should say not, save for the part containing *me*—except—well, except the very final moment, where I am sure one can glimpse Lydia Vandaariff on an examination table with the Comte d'Orkancz—well, you know, *examining* her."

"What?"

"Yes," said Miss Temple. "I only realized it now—when I saw the tables, and then of course I remembered seeing Lydia—and at the time I saw the card I did not know who Lydia was—"

"But, Celeste"—Miss Temple frowned, as she was not entirely sure of her companion even now, and certainly not comfortable with being so familiar—"that the card remained sewn into the Colonel's coat meant that no one had found it! It means that what he knew—what the card proved—died with him!"

"But it did not die at all. The Doctor has the card, and we the secret."

"Exactly!"

"Exactly what?"

Elöise nodded seriously. "So what I've found may be even more important—"

Miss Temple could only bear this for so long, for she was not one who stinted from absolutely shredding the wrapping paper around a present.

"Yes, but you have not said what it *is*."

Elöise pointed to the blue card on Miss Temple's lap. "At the end of the cycle," she said, "you will recall that the woman—"

"Mrs. Marchmoor."

"Her head turns, and one sees *spectators*. Among them I have recognized Francis Xonck, Miss Poole, Doctor Lorenz—others I do not know, though I'm sure you might. Yet beyond these people... is a *window*—"

"But it is *not* a window," said Miss Temple, eagerly, inching forward. "It is a *mirror*! The St. Royale's private rooms are fitted with Dutch glass mirrors that serve as windows on the lobby. Indeed, it was recognizing the outer doors of the hotel through this mirror that sent the Doctor to the St. Royale in the first place—"

Elöise nodded impatiently, for she had finally reached her news.

"But did he note who was *in* the lobby? Someone who had quite obviously stepped out of the private room for a chance to speak apart from those remaining in it, distracted by the, ah, *spectacle*?"

Miss Temple shook her head.

"Colonel Arthur Trapping," whispered Elöise, "speaking most earnestly... with Lord Robert Vandaariff!"

*   *   *

Miss Temple placed a hand over her mouth.

"It *is* the Comte!" she exclaimed. "The Comte plans to use Lydia—use the marriage, I can't say exactly how—in another part of Oskar Veilandt's alchemical scheme—"

Elöise frowned. "Who is—"

"A painter—a mystic—the discoverer of the blue glass! We were told he was dead—killed for his secrets—but now I wonder if he lives, if he might even be a prisoner—"

"Or his memories drained into a book!"

"O yes! But the point is—do the *others* know what the Comte truly intends for Lydia? More importantly, did her *father* know? What if Trapping found Roger's card and recognized Lydia and the Comte? Is it possible that the Colonel did not understand the truth of his associates' villainy and threatened them with exposure?"

"I am afraid you never met Colonel Trapping," said Elöise.

"Not to actually exchange words, no."

"It is more likely he understood exactly what the card meant and went to the one person with even deeper pockets than his brother-in-law."

"And we have not *seen* Lord Vandaariff—perhaps even now he weaves his own revenge against the Comte? Or does he even know—if Trapping promised him information but was killed before he could reveal it?"

"Blenheim had not seen Lord Robert," said Elöise.

"And the Comte's plan for Lydia remains in motion," said Miss Temple. "I have seen her drinking his poisons. If Trapping was killed to keep her father in ignorance—"

"He must have been killed by the Comte!" said Elöise.

Miss Temple frowned. "And yet . . . I am certain the Comte was as curious as anyone as to the Colonel's fate."

"Lord Robert must at least be warned by his secret agent's demise," reasoned Elöise. "No wonder he is in hiding. Perhaps it is he who now holds this missing painter—seeking some sort of exchange? Perhaps he now weaves his own plot against them all!"

"Speaking of *that,*" said Miss Temple, casting her eyes down to the heavy shoes of Mr. Blenheim, just visible behind a red leather ottoman, "what do we make of Mr. Blenheim's possession . . . of *this*?"

She held the key of blue glass to the light and studied its gleam.

"It is the same glass as the books," said Elöise.

"What do you think it opens?"

"It would have to be extremely delicate . . . something *else* made of the glass?"

"My exact conclusion." Miss Temple smiled. "Which leads me to a second point—that Mr. Blenheim had no business carrying this key at all. Can you imagine any of the Cabal trusting such a thing—which must be priceless—to someone not of their direct number? He is the overseer of the house, he can only figure in *their* plots as much as these Dragoons or Macklenburg stooges. Who would trust him?"

"Only one person," said Elöise.

Miss Temple nodded. "Lord Robert Vandaariff."

"I believe *I* have an idea," Miss Temple announced, and hopped off the armchair. Taking care to step over the darkened smear on the carpet—it had been difficult enough to shift the body, they agreed not to concern themselves with stains—she made her way to the cluttered sideboard. Working with a certain pleasurable industry, she found an unopened bottle of a decent age and a small sharp knife to dig past the wax seal and into the crumbling cork beneath, at least enough to pour through—for she did not mind if the cork dust crept into the liquid, for it was not the liquid that she cared for. Selecting a largely empty decanter, Miss Temple began, tongue poking from her mouth in concentration, to pour out the deep ruby port, doing her best to empty the bottle. When at last she saw the first bits of muddy sediment, she left off the decanter and reached for a wineglass, emptying the rest of the port bottle, sediment and all, into this. She then took another wineglass and, using the little knife as a dam, poured off the liquid until all that remained in her first glass were the ruddy, softened dregs. She looked up with a smile at Elöise, whose expression was tolerant but baffled.

"We cannot proceed with our investigations trapped within this room, nor can we rejoin the Doctor, nor can we escape, nor can we gain revenge—for even carrying sacrificial daggers we must be taken captive or killed once we attempt to leave."

Elöise nodded, and Miss Temple smiled at her own cunning.

"Unless, of course, we are clever in our disguise. The fire in the operating theatre was a site of great confusion and, I am willing to wager, one that prevented any clear account of exactly what occurred—too much smoke, too many shots and screams, too little light. My point being"—and here she waved her hand across the maroon dregs in the wineglass—"no one quite knows whether we underwent the Process or not."

They walked down the corridor in their bare feet, backs straight, unhurried, doing their level best to appear placid of character while paying attention to the growing turmoil around them. Miss Temple held the serpentine dagger in her hand. Elöise held the bottle of orange fluid and had tucked the cigarette case, the blue glass card and the glass key into her shift, as it had thoughtfully been made with pockets. They had pulled their masks around their necks to give everything a bit more time to dry, for meticulously applied and patted and smeared and dabbed around their eyes and across their noses, in as exact an imitation of the looping scars of the Process as they could manage, were the reddish-ruddy dregs of port. Miss Temple had been quite satisfied looking into the sideboard mirror, and only hoped that no one leaned so near as to smell the vintage.

During their time in the trophy room the traffic of guests and servants had increased dramatically. At once they found themselves amongst men and women in cloaks and topcoats and formal gowns, masked and gloved, all nodding to the white-robed pair with the calculated deference one might show to a tomahawk-bearing red Indian. They answered these greetings not at all, imitating the post-Process stupor that Miss Temple had seen in the theatre. The fact that they were armed only served to make room around them, and she realized the guests accorded them a higher status—acolytes of the inner circle, so to speak. It was all she could do not to shake the dagger in each obsequious set of faces and growl.

The traffic drove them toward the ballroom, but Miss Temple was not convinced it was where they ought to go. It seemed more likely that what they really needed—clothing, shoes, their comrades—would be found elsewhere, in some back room like the one where she'd met Farquhar and Spragg, the furniture covered with white sheets, the table littered with bottles and food. She reached for Elöise's hand and had just found it when a noise behind caused them both to turn and break the grip. Marching toward them, driving the hurrying guests to either side of the corridor, an action marooning Miss Temple even more obviously in its middle, was a double line of red-jacketed Dragoons in tall black boots, a scowling officer at their head. She nodded Elöise urgently into the crowd but was herself jostled back into the soldiers' path, ridiculously in their way. The officer did his best to stare her down, and she looked again to Elöise—vanished behind a pair of waspish gentlemen in oyster grey riding cloaks. The guests around them stopped to watch the impending collision. The officer snapped his hand up and his men immediately stamped themselves to a concise, orderly halt. The corridor was suddenly silent . . . a silence that allowed Miss Temple to hear what would have been a previously inaudible chuckle, somewhere behind her. She slowly turned to see Francis Xonck, smoking a cheroot, head cocked in an utterly contemptuous bow.

* * *

"What pearls are found," he drawled, "unexpected and unlooked-for, in the wilds of Harschmort House..."

He stopped speaking as he took in the markings on her face. Miss Temple did not reply, merely inclining her head to acknowledge his authority.

"Miss Temple?" he asked, curious and warily skeptical. She dropped into a simple, bobbing curtsey, and rose again.

He glanced once at the officer, and reached out to take hold of her jaw. She passively allowed him to move her head around however he liked, never making a sound. He stepped away, staring at her evenly.

"Where have you come from?" he said. "You will answer me."

"The theatre," she said, as thickly as she could. "There was a fire—"

He did not let her finish, sticking the cheroot into his mouth and reaching forward with his one unbandaged hand to fondle her breast. The crowd around them gasped at the cold determination of his face as much as his brazen action. With the sternest resolve Miss Temple's voice did not shift in the slightest, nor did she pause as he continued to forcefully grope across her body.

"—from the lamps, there was smoke, and shooting... it was Doctor Svenson. I did not see him... I was on the table. Miss Poole—"

Francis Xonck slapped Miss Temple hard across the face.

"—disappeared. The soldiers took me off the table."

As she spoke, just as she had seen in the theatre, and with pleasure, her hand shot out toward Francis Xonck, doing her level best to stab him in the face with the serpentine dagger. Unfortunately, he had seen the blow coming. He parried the blow with his arm against her wrist, then took hold of her wrist and squeezed. As it would give her away to struggle, Miss Temple released the dagger, which hit the floor with a clang. Francis Xonck lowered her hand to her side, and stepped away. She did not move. He looked past her at the officer, flared his nostrils in a sneer—which she was sure meant the officer had shown his disapproval of what he'd just witnessed—and picked up the dagger. He stuck it in his belt and turned on his heels, calling airily over his shoulder.

"Bring the lady with you, Captain Smythe—and quickly. You're *late.*"

Miss Temple could only risk the barest glance for Elöise as she walked away, but Elöise was gone. Captain Smythe had taken her by the arm, not roughly but with insistence, enforcing her compliance with their speed. She allowed herself a look at the officer, masking herself with an expression of bovine disinterest, and saw a face that reminded her of Cardinal Chang, or of the Cardinal beset with the burdens of command, hated superiors, fatigue, self-disgust, and of course without the disfigurement of his eyes. The Captain's eyes were dark and warmer than the bitter lines around them seemed to merit. He glanced down at her with brisk suspicion and she returned her attention to the receding, well-tailored back of Francis Xonck, parting the crowds ahead of them with the imperious ease of a surgeon's scalpel.

He led them through the thickest knots of the gathering crowd, their passage a spectacle for whispers and gawking—Xonck reaching to either side for handshakes and hearty back-slaps to particular men and brief kisses to similarly high-placed or beautiful women—and then beyond them, skirting the ballroom proper to an open space at the meeting of several corridors. Xonck gave Miss Temple one more searching stare, crossed to a pair of wooden doors, opened them, and leaned his head from view, whispering. In a moment he had pulled his head back and shut the door, ambling again to Miss Temple. He pulled the cheroot from his mouth and looked at it with distaste, for he was nearing the stub. He dropped it to the marble floor and ground it beneath his shoe.

"Captain, you will position your men along this corridor in either direction, specifically guarding access to these"—he pointed to two doors farther down the hall away from the ballroom—"inner rooms. Colonel Aspiche will provide further instructions upon his arrival. For now, your task is one of waiting, and making sure of this woman's continued presence."

The Captain nodded crisply and turned to his men, detailing them along the length of the corridor and at each inner door. The Captain himself remained within saber's reach of Miss Temple, and, for that matter, Francis Xonck. Once he had spoken however, Xonck paid the officer no further mind, his voice dropping to a whisper as coiled with menace as the hiss of a snake preparing to strike.

"You will answer me quickly, Celeste Temple, and I will know if you lie—and if you *do* lie, *do* know it means your head."

Miss Temple nodded blankly, as if this meant nothing to her either way.

"What did Bascombe tell you on the train?"

This was not what she'd expected. "That we should be allies," she replied. "That the Contessa desired it."

"And what did the Contessa say?"

"I did not speak to her aboard the train—"

"Before that—*before*! At the hotel—in the *coach*!"

"She said I must pay for the deaths of her men. And she put her hands upon me, quite indecently—"

"Yes, yes," snapped Xonck, impatiently waving her on, "about *Bascombe*—what did she say about *him*?"

"That he would be Lord Tarr."

Xonck was muttering to himself, glancing over his shoulder at the wooden doors. "Too many others must have been there... what else, what else—"

Miss Temple tried to recall what the Contessa *had* said to her, or anything provocative that might inflame Xonck's obvious suspicions...

"The Comte was there too—"

"I am aware of that—"

"Because she did ask *him* a question."

"What question?"

"I do not think I was supposed to hear it—for I'm sure it made no sense to me—"

"Tell me what she said!"

"The Contessa asked the Comte d'Orkancz how he thought Lord Robert Vandaariff had discovered their plan to alchemically impregnate his daughter—that is, who did he think had betrayed them?"

Francis Xonck did not reply, his eyes boring into hers with a palpably dangerous intent, doing his best to measure the true degree of her compliance. Miss Temple somehow kept the fear from her face, concentrating upon the patterns of shadow on the ceiling beyond his shoulder, but she could tell that Xonck was so provoked by these last words that he was about to slap her again, or launch into an even more debasing physical assault—when behind them, topping his rising agitation as an erupting whistle announces the boiling of a kettle, the wooden doors opened and the Macklenburg Envoy's freshly scarred and deferential face poked through.

"They are ready, Mr. Xonck," the man whispered.

Xonck snarled and stepped away from Miss Temple, his fingers tapping the handle of the dagger in his belt. With one more searching stare at her face he spun on his heels to follow the Envoy into the ballroom.

It was perhaps the length of two minutes before Miss Temple concluded, with the rise of different voices piercing murkily through the doors, that the members of the Cabal were holding forth to their assembled guests. She was aware of the silent Captain Smythe behind her and the general presence of his soldiers, within direct call however distant their posts might be. She took a deep breath and let it out slowly. She could only hope that eagerness for information had blinded Xonck to her disguise—which was more designed to fool ignorant guests in the hall than seasoned members of the Cabal. With a sudden urge toward self-preservation, Miss Temple restored her feathered mask into position. She sighed again. She could not go anywhere . . . but perhaps she could measure the strength of her cage. She turned to Captain Smythe and smiled.

"Captain, . . . as you have seen *me* interrogated . . . may I ask *you* a question?"

"Miss?"

"You seem unhappy."

"Miss?"

"Everyone *else* at Harschmort House seems . . . well, eminently *pleased* with themselves."

Captain Smythe did not answer, his eyes flicking back and forth between his nearest men. Accordingly, Miss Temple dropped her voice to a demure whisper.

"One merely wonders *why*."

The Captain studied her closely. When he spoke it was near to a whisper.

"Did I hear Mr. Xonck correctly . . . that your name is . . . *Temple*?"

"That is so."

He licked his lips and nodded to her robes, the slight gaping around her bosom that allowed a glimpse of her own silk bodice showing through the layers of translucent white.

"I was informed . . . you did favor the color green . . ."

Before Miss Temple could respond to this truly astonishing comment, the doors behind her opened again. She turned, composing her face to a suitable blandness, and met the equally distracted Caroline Stearne, so preoccupied and so surprised to see Miss Temple in the first place as to pay no attention whatsoever to the officer behind her.

"Celeste," she whispered quickly, "you must come with me at once."

Miss Temple was led by the hand through a silent crowd that parted for them impatiently, each person begrudging the distraction from what held their attention in the center of the room. She steeled herself to be calm, expecting that at the words of Francis Xonck she must now submit to public examination by the entire Cabal in front of hundreds of masked strangers, and it was only this preparation that forestalled her gasp of shock at the sight, as she was pulled so briskly onto the open floor by Caroline Stearne, of Cardinal Chang, on his knees, spitting blood, his every inch the image of a man who had passed through the pits of hell. He looked up at her, and with his gaze, his face pale and bloodied, his movements slow, his eyes blessedly veiled behind smoked glass, came the gazes of those other figures before her—Caroline, Colonel Aspiche, and the Comte d'Orkancz, who stood in his great fur holding a leash that went to the neck of a small figure—a lady of perhaps Miss Temple's own height and shape—distinguished first by her nakedness and second, and more singularly, by the fact that she seemed to be completely fabricated of blue glass. It was when this statue turned *its* head to look at Miss Temple, its expression unreadable and its eyes as depthless as a Roman statue's, slick, gleaming, and swirled indigo marbles, that Miss Temple understood the woman—or creature—was *alive.* She was fully rooted to the ground with amazement, and could not have cried out to Chang if she had wanted.

Caroline Stearne pulled Miss Temple's white mask down around her neck. She waited through agonizing seconds of silence, sure that someone would denounce her . . . but no one spoke.

Chang's mouth opened haltingly, as if he could not form words or gather breath to speak.

Then, as if everything was happening too quickly to see, Colonel Aspiche was swinging his arm and whatever he held in it smashed down onto Cardinal Chang's head, knocking him flat in a stroke. With a brusque nod from their Colonel, two Dragoons detached themselves from the ring of men keeping back the crowd and took hold of Chang's arms. They dragged him past her, his body utterly lifeless. She did not turn to follow his passage, but made herself look up, despite her racing heart and the pressing nearness of her tears, into the intelligent, searching face of Caroline Stearne.

Behind, the voice of the Contessa snapped through the air like the crack of a particularly exultant whip.

"My dear Celeste," she called, "how fine it is that you have... *joined* us. Mrs. Stearne, I am obliged for your timely entrance."

Caroline, who was already facing the Contessa, sank into a respectful curtsey.

"Mrs. Stearne!" called the rasping voice of the Comte d'Orkancz. "Do you not wish to see your transformed companions?"

Caroline turned along with everyone else in the ballroom, for the Comte's gesture was one of grand showmanship, to see two more glass women stalking into the open circle with their deliberate, clicking gait, arms strangely floating, their uncovered bodies an arrogant assertion of ripe, ghastly, unsettling allure. It took Miss Temple a moment—what had the Comte said to Caroline, "companions"?—to recognize with shock Mrs. Marchmoor and, some new disfiguring scorch across her head, Miss Poole. What did it mean that her enemies had—*willingly?*—been transformed, *transfigured,* into such... such *things*?

The Comte gathered up Miss Poole's leash and flicked her toward Mrs. Stearne. Miss Poole's lips parted ever so slightly with a chilling smile and then Caroline staggered where she stood, her head lolling to the side. An instant later, as the effect spread to the first rank of the crowd like a rippling pool, Miss Temple felt herself swallowed up and thrust into a scene so enticingly real that she could scarcely remember the ballroom at all.

* * *

She was on a plush settee in a dark, candlelit parlor and her hand was occupied with stroking Caroline Stearne's lovely, soft unbound hair. Mrs. Stearne wore—as Miss Temple saw that she (that is, Miss Poole) wore as well—the white robes of initiation. On the other side of Mrs. Stearne sat a man in a black cloak and a tight mask of red leather, leaning over to kiss her mouth, a kiss to which Mrs. Stearne responded with a passionate moan. It was like Mrs. Marchmoor's story of the two men in the coach, only here it was a man and two women. Mrs. Stearne's hunger caused Miss Poole to condescendingly chuckle as she turned to reach for a glass of wine... and with this action her shifting gaze took in an open door and a lurking figure half-visible in the light beyond... a figure whose shape Miss Temple knew at once as that of Roger Bascombe.

The vision was withdrawn from Miss Temple's mind, like a blindfold whipped from her eyes, and she was back in the ballroom, where every person she could see was blinking with confusion, save for the Comte d'Orkancz, who smiled with a smug superior pleasure. He called again to Caroline—some vulgar jest about sisterhood and opportunities for taking the veil—but Miss Temple did not mark their conversation, so provoked were her thoughts by what she'd just beheld....

Miss Poole and Caroline Stearne had been wearing their white robes, and the man with them on the settee—she had seen him, she had taken that very cloak for her own!—was none other than Colonel Trapping. Miss Temple groped to make sense of it, as if she were in a hurry to open a door and could not get the right key in the hole... it had been that same night at Harschmort... and just before the Colonel's murder, for the women had changed into their white robes but not yet undergone the Process. This meant it had been while she was creeping through the hall of mirrors and past the queer man with the boxes—only minutes before she herself had entered Trapping's room. She had already worked out that

Roger and the Contessa were the Cabal members nearest to the Colonel at his death . . . could these women have killed him instead—on instructions of the Comte? If the Colonel had been in secret agreement with Lord Vandaariff . . . but why, she suddenly wondered, had Miss Poole chosen to share *this* memory—one that must obviously stir up questions about the murdered Colonel—with Caroline Stearne? There had been a rivalry between them in the theatre—was it merely to mock Caroline's affections for a dead man, and what was more a dead traitor to the Cabal? In front of *everyone*?

She was startled—was she an idiot? She must pay attention—by a hoarse cry and then the total immersion without warning into another vision: a tall wooden staircase, lit by orange torchlight under a blackened sky, a sudden rush of men, a scuttling figure in a black topcoat—Minister Crabbé!—and then the mob converging upon and raising up a kicking figure in a steel-blue greatcoat, a flash of his drawn face and ice-pale hair confirming him as Doctor Svenson an instant before, with a heaving surge, the crowd of men launched him without ceremony over the rail.

Miss Temple looked up—just piecing together that this must be an image from the quarry at Tarr Manor—back in the ballroom again, to see a disturbance in the crowd, an undulating progress toward the center that with a lurch deposited the haggard figure of Doctor Svenson, breathless and battered, onto his hands and knees—exactly where Chang had been. Svenson looked up, his wild eyes searching for some escape but instead finding her face, the sight of which stopped him cold. Colonel Aspiche stepped forward, ripping a leather satchel from the Doctor's grasp with one hand, and then bringing his truncheon down pitilessly with the other. It was a matter of seconds. Like Chang before him, Doctor Svenson was dragged past Miss Temple from the room.

* * *

Unable to watch him go without giving herself away, Miss Temple instead found her gaze rooted to the gleaming glass women. As disturbing as they were—and the sight of Miss Poole, if this unconscionably animated statue could still so be named, licking her lips with the slick, livid tip of a cerulean tongue caused Miss Temple to shiver with an unnameable dismay—it nevertheless put off the moment when she must face the Contessa's piercing violet eyes. But then Caroline took her hand, spinning her to the raised dais where the members of the Cabal stood—the Contessa, Xonck, Crabbé, and then the Prince and Lydia Vandaariff, still in her mask and white robes, and behind this pair, like a furtive eavesdropping child, lurked the Envoy, Herr Flaüss. Against all reason Miss Temple's eyes went straight to the Contessa, who met her glance with an implacably cold stare. It was to her great relief when it was Harald Crabbé, and not the Contessa, who stepped forward to speak.

"Assembled *guests*... devoted *friends*... faithful *adherents*... now is the time when all our plans are ripe... hanging like fruit to be plucked. It is our present labor to *harvest* that fruit, and prevent it from falling fallow and uncared-for to the insensate *ground*. You all understand the gravity of this night—that we in truth usher in a new epoch—who could doubt it, when we see the evidence before us like angels from another age? Yet tonight all rests in the balance—the Prince and Miss Vandaariff will depart for their Macklenburg wedding... the Duke of Stäelmaere is appointed head of the Queen's Privy Council... the most mighty figures of this land have in this house given over their power... and all of *you*—perhaps most importantly of all!—all of *you* will execute your own assignments—achieve your own destinies! Thus shall we here construct our common dream."

Crabbé paused and met the eyes of first Colonel Aspiche—who rapped out a sharp command that cut through the buttery flattering tone of the Deputy Minister's speech, at which point every door to the ballroom was slammed shut with a crash—and next of the Comte d'Orkancz, who flicked his leashes like an infernal circus master, sending each glass creature stalking toward a different portion of the crowd. The impression was very much of lions in an arena sizing up an impressive number of martyrs, and Miss Temple was no less unsettled to find it was the third woman—the one of her own size and shape—the Comte had sent toward her. The creature advanced to the end of its leash and having pulled it taut stood flexing its fingers with impatience, the people nearest inching away with discomfort. Miss Temple felt a pressing on her *thoughts*—thoughts clouded now with sensations of ice-blue cold...

"You will all accept," continued Crabbé, "that there is no room for risk, no place for second thoughts. We must have *certainty*—every bit as much as all of you, having pledged yourselves, must have it of each man and woman in this ballroom! No one in this room has not undergone the Process, or submitted their interests to one of our *volumes,* or otherwise demonstrated total allegiance... or such is our assumption. As I say... you will understand if we make *sure.*"

The Comte tugged the leash of Mrs. Marchmoor, who arched her back and swept her gaze across the crowd. The men and women before her were staggered and stunned, they went silent, they whimpered or cried, they lost their balance and fell—all as their minds were scoured for any deception. Miss Temple saw that the Comte had his eyes shut as well in concentration... could Mrs. Marchmoor be sharing with him what she saw? Then the Comte abruptly opened his eyes. One of the two men in the oyster grey riding cloaks had dropped to his knees. The Comte d'Orkancz gestured to Colonel Aspiche and two Dragoons dragged the fallen man, now sobbing with fear, without mercy from the room. The Comte shut his eyes again and Mrs. Marchmoor continued her silent inquisition.

After Mrs. Marchmoor came Miss Poole, moving just as remorselessly through her portion of the crowd, isolating two more men and a woman who were given swift cause to regret their decision to attend. For a moment Miss Temple wondered if these could be people like herself—desperate enemies of the Cabal's villainy—but as soon as they were pulled from their places by the soldiers it was clear the exact opposite was the case. These were social climbers who had managed to forge an invitation or bluff their way into what they hoped was an especially exclusive *soirée* for the bright lights of society. As much as she was rattled by their pleas, she did not spare their fates another thought . . . for Miss Poole had finished, and the Comte had snapped the third woman's leash.

The invisible wave of the woman's scrutiny inched toward her like a fire, or like a burning fuse whose end must mean her death. Closer and closer; Miss Temple did not know what to do. She must be found out completely. Should she run? Should she try to push the woman over in hopes that she might shatter? Miss Temple's exposure was but seconds away. She took a breath for courage and tensed herself as if for a blow. Caroline stood straight, also waiting, and glanced once quickly at Miss Temple, her face more pale—Miss Temple realized suddenly that Caroline was terrified. But then the woman's gaze went past Miss Temple's shoulder. There was a noise—the door?—and then the sudden sharp voice of Deputy Minister Crabbé.

"If you please, Monsieur le Comte, that is enough!"

Quite directly behind Miss Temple an astonishing party had entered the room. All around, people in the crowd lowered their heads with respect for the tall man, deathly pale with long iron-grey hair, with medals on his coat and a bright blue sash across his chest. He walked with great stiffness—he walked rather like the glass women, actually—with one hand clutching a black stick and the other the arm of a small, sharp-faced man with greasy hair and glasses who did not strike her as any kind of normal companion for a royal personage. Given the Deputy Minister's speech she knew it must be the Duke of Stäelmaere, a man who, if the rumors were true, only employed impoverished aristocrats as his servants, so much did he abhor the presence of common folk. What was such a man doing at so large—and so common—a gathering? Yet this was but the half of it, for walking directly next to the Duke—almost as if they were a bride and groom—was Lord Robert Vandaariff. Behind him, and supporting Lord Robert's near arm, walked Roger Bascombe.

"I do not believe we had quite finished with the examinations," said Francis Xonck, "which as you have said, Minister, are most *crucial*."

"Indeed, Mr. Xonck." Harald Crabbé nodded, and spoke loud enough for the crowd to hear him. "But this business cannot stay! We have before us the two most eminent figures in the land—perhaps the continent!—one of them our very host. It strikes me as prudent, as well as polite, to allow their urgent needs to trump our own."

Miss Temple saw Francis Xonck glance once her way, and knew that he had been watching very closely for the results of her inquisition. She turned toward the new arrivals—as much as she did not want to see Roger she wanted to see Xonck and the Contessa even less—and realized, with the dull deliberate *clonk* of a brick hitting the floor, that Crabbé's halt of the examinations had nothing to do with her at all, but *these* figures, for the glass woman's scrutiny must have swept them up as well, revealing their inner minds to the waiting Comte d'Orkancz. But who was Harald Crabbé protecting? The Duke? Vandaariff? Or his own aide Bascombe—and the secret plans they'd hatched between them? And why had Caroline been so frightened? She wanted to stamp her foot with frustration at all she did not know—was Vandaariff the leader of the Cabal or not? Was he locked in a struggle with the Comte to save his daughter? Did Crabbé's action—and Roger's presence—indicate an allegiance with Vandaariff? But then what did she make of Roger being in the doorway just before Trapping must have been killed? Suddenly Miss Temple remembered her fiancé's appearance in the secret room, where the Contessa had tormented the Prince—could Roger have a secret allegiance of his own? If Roger *had* killed Trapping (her mind could scarcely accept it—*Roger*?) was it to serve the Contessa?

The Duke of Stäelmaere began to speak, his voice halting and dry as a mouthful of cold cinders.

"Tomorrow I become head of the Queen's Privy Council . . . the nation is in crisis . . . the Queen is unwell . . . the Crown Prince is without heir and without merit . . . and so he has this night been given the gift of his dreams, a gift which must ensnare his weakened soul . . . a *glass book of wonders* in which he will drown."

Miss Temple frowned. This did not sound like any Duke she'd ever heard. She glanced carefully behind her and saw the glass woman's attention fully fixed on the Duke, and behind her, his bearded lips moving ever so slightly with each word that issued from the Duke of Stäelmaere's mouth, the Comte d'Orkancz.

"The Privy Council will govern . . . our *vision,* my allies, . . . will find expression . . . will be written on the world. Such is my promise . . . before you all."

The Duke then turned to the man next to him with a glacial nod.

"My Lord . . ."

While Robert Vandaariff's voice was not so openly sepulchral as the Duke's, it nevertheless served to further chill Miss Temple's blood, for before he spoke a single word he turned to Roger and accepted a folded piece of paper, passed with all the deference of a clerk . . . yet the Lord had only turned at a squeeze from Roger on his arm. Vandaariff unfolded the paper and at another squeeze—she was watching for it—began to read, in a hearty voice that rang as hollow to her ear as footfalls in an empty room.

"It is not my way to make speeches and so I ask forgiveness that I rely upon this paper—yet tonight I send my only child, my Princess, Lydia, to be married to a man I have taken to my heart like a son."

At a third subtle squeeze from Roger—whose face, she saw, was directed at the floor—Lord Robert nodded to the Prince and his daughter on the dais. Miss Temple wondered what emotions about her father remained beneath the girl's mask . . . how the Process had rarefied her depthless need and her rage at being abandoned, and what effect these vacant formal words could have. Lydia bobbed in a curtsey and then curled her lips in a grin. Did she know her father was Roger Bascombe's puppet? Could that be why she smiled?

Lord Robert turned back to the assembled guests, and located his place on the page. "Tomorrow it must be as if this night had never been. None of you will return to Harschmort House. None of you will acknowledge you have been here, any more than you will acknowledge each other, or news from the Duchy of Macklenburg as anything other than unimportant gossip. But the efforts here of my colleague the Duke will be mirrored in that land, and from that nation to nations beyond. Some of you will be placed among my agents, traveling where necessary, but before you leave tonight, all will be given instructions, in the form of a printed cipher book, from my chamberlain, . . . Mr. *Blenheim.*"

Vandaariff looked up, instructed here to point out Blenheim from the crowd . . . but Blenheim was not there. The pause drifted toward confusion as faces glanced back and forth, and there were frowns on the dais and sharp glances in the direction of Colonel Aspiche, who answered them with haughty shrugs of his own. With a deft—and therefore to Miss Temple equally galling and impressive—display of initiative, Roger Bascombe cleared his throat and stepped forward.

"In Mr. Blenheim's absence, your instructive volumes can be collected from *me* in the chamberlain's offices, directly after this gathering adjourns."

He glanced quickly to the dais, and then whispered into Lord Robert's ear. Roger returned to his place. Lord Robert resumed his speech.

"I am *gratified* to be able to aid this enterprise, as I am *thankful* to those who have most imagined its success. I beg you all to enjoy the hospitality of my home."

Roger gently took the paper from his hands. The crowd erupted into applause for the two great men, who stood without any particular expression whatsoever, as if it were the rain and they insensible statues.

Miss Temple was astonished. There was no struggle between Vandaariff and the Comte at all—Lord Robert had been utterly overcome. Trapping's news had never reached him, and Lydia's fate—whatever hideous design had been in motion—was sealed. It did not matter if Oskar Veilandt was prisoner in the house, just as it no longer mattered who had killed Trapping—but then Miss Temple frowned. If Vandaariff was their creature, then why had Crabbé stopped the examinations? If the members of the Cabal themselves did not know Trapping's killer, could things be so settled? Could the struggle for Lydia's fate be just one fissure between her enemies? Could there be others?

At the same time, Miss Temple wondered who this performance by the Duke and Lord Robert was expected to fool—she had heard more elevating and persuasive words from half-drunken fishwives on the pier. Taking her cue from Caroline Stearne, she lowered her head as the two luminaries and their assistants—or should she say puppet-masters?—advanced across the ballroom. As they passed she looked up and met the eyes of Roger Bascombe, who frowned with a typically veiled curiosity at the scars across her face. As they reached the far side she was surprised to see the Comte hand Mrs. Marchmoor's leash to Roger and that of Miss Poole to the shorter sharp-faced man. As the doors were opened by the Dragoons—for she could only with difficulty shift her eyes from Roger for any length of time—she saw her fiancé step close to Colonel Aspiche and snatch—there was no gentler word for it—a leather satchel from the Colonel's grasp. A satchel, she realized, that had arrived in the possession of Doctor Svenson . . .

Behind her, the Contessa called out to the crowd, just before either Xonck or Crabbé could do the same, for each man's mouth was poised for speech, their expressions giving out just a flicker of frustration before they were agreeably nodding along with her words.

"Ladies and gentlemen, you have heard the words of our host. You know the preparations you must make. Once these duties are satisfied you are released. The pleasures of Harschmort House this night are yours, and after this . . . for every night . . . the pleasures of the world. I give you all good night . . . I give you all our victory."

The Contessa stepped forward and, beaming at her listeners, began to applaud them all. She was joined by every person on the dais, and then by the entirety of the crowd, each person eager to register delight at the Contessa's favor and to bestow—from that enhanced position—their own approval upon each other. Miss Temple clapped along, feeling like a trained monkey, watching the Contessa speak quietly to Xonck and Crabbé. At some silent agreement, the members of the Cabal swept off the dais and toward the doors. Before Miss Temple could react Caroline Stearne's voice was in her ear.

"We are to follow," she whispered. "Something is wrong."

As they walked toward the open doors, attracting inquisitive glances from the guests who were all gaily exiting in the opposite direction in the wake of Vandaariff and the Duke, Miss Temple felt someone behind her aside from Caroline. Though she dared not look—curiosity of that sort did not become the staid confidence born of the Process—the sound of clicking steps told her it was the Comte and the last remaining of the three glass Graces, the woman she did not know. This was some blessing at least—a fresh slate was better than the knowing sneers and penetrating disbelief she could expect from Marchmoor and Poole—but in her heart she knew it did not matter which of them ransacked her mind, her pose would be revealed. Her only hope was that the same instinct that had led Crabbé to prevent the examination of the Duke or Lord Vandaariff would prevent them from risking the woman's talents in such close quarters—for surely the rest of the Cabal would not choose to deliver their open minds to the Comte . . . at least not if they were betraying one another . . .

She entered the open foyer where she had waited with Captain

Smythe, who had withdrawn some yards away so as not to intrude on the deliberations of his betters, betters who in turn waited in impatient silence for the last of their number to arrive, at which point the doors in every direction were closed, shielding their words from the tender ears of any passing *adherent.* As the latches caught and bolts were shot, Miss Temple wondered wistfully what had happened to Elöise, and whether Chang or Svenson might be alive, thoughts brusquely smothered by the figure of the Contessa di Lacquer-Sforza lighting a cigarette in her shining black holder, puffing on the thing three times in succession before she spoke, as if each ascending inhalation stoked the fires of her rage. Perhaps even more disturbingly, not one of the powerful men around her presumed to interrupt this openly menacing ritual.

"What was that?" she finally snarled, fixing her gaze on Harald Crabbé.

"I do beg your pardon, Contessa—"

"Why did you interfere with the examinations? You saw yourself how at least five interlopers were revealed—any one of whom might have undone our plans while we are in Macklenburg. You know this—you know this work is not *finished.*"

"My dear, if you felt so strongly—"

"I did not say anything because Mr. Xonck *did* say something, only to be overruled—in front of *everyone*—by you. For any of us to disagree further would have presented the exact lack of unity we have—with some *great effort,* Deputy Minister—managed to avoid."

"I see."

"I don't believe you *do.*"

She spat out another mouthful of smoke, her eyes burning into the man like a basilisk. Crabbé did his best to clear his throat and start fresh, but before he spoke a single word she'd cut him off.

"We are not fools, Harald. You stopped the examinations so certain people would not be revealed to the Comte."

Crabbé made a feeble gesture toward Miss Temple, but again whatever words he might have said were halted by the Contessa's condescending scoff.

"Do not insult me—we'll get to Miss Temple in time—I am speaking of the Duke and Lord Vandaariff. Both of whom should have presented no difficulty at all, unless of course, we are misled as to their true status. Enough of us have seen the Duke's corpse that I am willing to say that Doctor Lorenz has done his work fairly—work that perforce was done in cooperation with the Comte. This leaves us with Lord Robert, whose transformation I believe was your *own* responsibility."

"He is absolutely under our control," protested Crabbé, "you saw yourself—"

"I saw no proof at all! It would have been simple to counterfeit!"

"Ask Bascombe—"

"Excellent—of course, we shall rely on the word of your own trusted assistant—now I shall sleep soundly!"

"Do not take anyone's word," snapped Crabbé, growing angry in his turn. "Call Lord Robert back—go see him yourself, do whatever you like, you'll see he is our slave! Exactly as planned!"

"Then *why*," said Francis Xonck in a calm dangerous tone, "did you interrupt the examination?"

Crabbé stammered, gesturing vaguely with his hands. "Not for the precise reason I stated at the time—I admit that—but so as not to compromise the apparent authority of the Duke and Lord Robert by publicly degrading them with scrutiny! Much rests on our remaining invisible behind these figureheads—including them in the examinations would have revealed them for what they are, our servants! So much is in turmoil already—Blenheim was to escort his master to begin with, to maintain appearances—if it were not for Roger's quick thinking to step forward—"

"Where *is* Blenheim?" snapped the Contessa.

"He seems to have vanished, Madame," answered Caroline. "I have questioned the guests as you asked, but no one has seen him."

The Contessa snorted and looked past Miss Temple to the door, where Colonel Aspiche stood, having entered last of all.

"I do not know," he protested. "My men searched the house—"

"Interesting, as Blenheim would be loyal to Lord Robert," observed Xonck.

"Lord Robert is under our control!" insisted Crabbé.

"The control of your man Bascombe, at least," said Xonck. "And what were those papers?"

This was to Aspiche, who did not understand the question.

"A satchel of papers!" cried Xonck. "You took them from Doctor Svenson! Bascombe took them from you!"

"I have no idea," said the Colonel.

"You're as bad as Blach!" scoffed Xonck. "Where is he anyway?"

The Comte d'Orkancz sighed heavily. "Major Blach is dead. Cardinal Chang."

Xonck took this in, rolled his eyes, then shrugged. He turned back to Colonel Aspiche.

"Where is Bascombe now?"

"With Lord Robert," said Caroline. "After Mr. Blenheim—"

"Where else *ought* he to be?" cried Crabbé, growing exasperated, "Where else? Distributing the message books—someone had to do it in Blenheim's absence!"

"How fortunate he thought to step in," said the Contessa icily.

"Mrs. Marchmoor is with him—surely you trust her as much as I trust Bascombe!" sputtered Crabbé. "Surely they have *both* proven their loyalty to us *all*!"

The Contessa turned to Smythe. "Captain, send two of your men to collect Mr. Bascombe as soon as he is finished. Bring him here, along with Lord Robert, if necessary."

Smythe gestured immediately to his men, and the Dragoons clattered off.

"Where is Lydia?" asked Xonck.

"With the Prince," answered Caroline, "saying good-bye to the guests."

"Thank you, Caroline," said the Contessa, "at least *someone* is paying attention." She called to Smythe. "Have your men collect them as well."

"Bring them to me," rasped the Comte d'Orkancz. "Their part of our business is not finished."

The Comte's words hung balefully in the air, but the others remained silent, as if to speak at all would restart a now-settled disagreement. The Captain detailed two more Dragoons and returned to his place on the far wall, looking at his boots as if he could not hear a word.

"All this can be settled with ease," announced the Deputy Minister, turning to the Comte d'Orkancz, "if we consult the book wherein Lord Robert's thoughts have been stored. That book will make it perfectly clear that I have done what we agreed. It should contain a detailed account of the Lord's participation in this entire affair—facts that only he could know."

"At least one book was destroyed," rasped the Comte.

"Destroyed *how*?" asked the Contessa.

"Chang."

"Damn his bloody soul!" she snarled. "That really is the *limit.* Do you know which book it was?"

"I cannot know until I compare those remaining against the ledger," said the Comte.

"Then let us do so," said Crabbé waspishly. "I would be *exonerated* as soon as possible."

"The books are in transit to the rooftop," said the Comte. "As for the ledger, as you well know it remains in the possession of your assistant."

"My goodness!" cried Xonck. "It seems Bascombe's become a powerfully valuable fellow!"

"He will bring it with him!" protested Crabbé. "It will be settled. All of this is a ridiculous waste of our time—it has divided our efforts and created dangerous delays—and the most likely explanation for all these questions stands before us." He thrust his chin toward Miss Temple. "She and her comrades have caused no end of trouble! Who is to say it was not *they* who have killed Blenheim!"

"Just as Cardinal Chang slew Mr. Gray . . . ," observed Xonck quietly, turning his gaze to the Contessa. Crabbé took in his words, blinked and then, heartened by the shift of inquiry, nodded with agreement.

"Ah! Yes! Yes! I had forgotten it—it had been quite blown from my mind! Contessa?"

"What? As Chang is a murderer and Mr. Gray gone missing, I have no doubt the man was killed. I know not where—my instructions for Mr. Gray were to assist Doctor Lorenz with the Duke."

"Yet Chang says they met underground—near the pipes!" cried Crabbé.

"I had not heard this . . . ," rasped the Comte d'Orkancz.

The Contessa looked up at him and pulled her spent cigarette from the holder, dropping it to the floor and stepping on the smoking butt while she screwed a new one in its place.

"You were occupied with your *ladies,*" she replied. Miss Temple perceived just a whisper of discomfort cross the Contessa's face as she took in the small glass woman, standing placidly as a tamed leopard, careless of their bickering, her brilliant indigo color more striking for her proximity to the Comte's dark fur. "Chang claimed Mr. Gray had been tampering with your works—at my instruction. The clearest evidence of this, of course, would be if something had gone wrong with your efforts—however, as far as I can tell, you have produced three successful transformations. As this is a process I quite freely admit I do not understand *in the slightest,* I offer your results as evidence that Cardinal Chang is a liar."

"Unless he killed Gray *before* he could do his damage," said Crabbé.

"Which is idle, baseless speculation," growled the Contessa.

"Which does not mean it is not true—"

The Contessa swept to the Deputy Minister and her hand—apparently occupied with replacing her cigarette case in her bag—was now wrapped with the bright band. Its glittering spike was hard against Crabbé's throat, digging at a visibly throbbing vein.

Crabbé swallowed.

"Rosamonde . . . ," began the Comte.

"Say it again, you bothersome little man," hissed the Contessa, "and I will rip you open like a poorly sewn sleeve."

Crabbé did not move.

"Rosamonde . . . ," said the Comte again. Her attention did not shift from Crabbé.

"Yes?"

"Might I suggest . . . the young lady?"

The Contessa moved two quick steps away from Crabbé—clear of any counter-stroke from a weapon of his own—and wheeled to Miss Temple. The woman's face was flushed—with open pleasure, it seemed—and her eyes flared with excitement. Miss Temple doubted she had ever been in such peril.

"You underwent the Process in the theatre?" The Contessa smiled. "Is that it? Yes, directly after Lydia Vandaariff?"

Miss Temple nodded quickly.

"What a shame Miss Poole cannot confirm it. But *here* we are not helpless . . . let me see . . . orange for Harschmort . . . attendant whore . . . hotel, I suppose . . . and of course, doomed . . ."

The Contessa leaned forward and hissed into Miss Temple's ear.

"Orange Magdalene orange Royale ice consumption!"

Miss Temple was taken by surprise, stammering for a response, then recalling—too late—the Prince in the secret room—

The Contessa took hold of Miss Temple's jaw, wrenching her head so the women stared at each other. With a cold deliberate sneer the Contessa's tongue snaked from her mouth and smeared its way across each of Miss Temple's eyes. Miss Temple whimpered as the Contessa licked again, pressing her tongue flat over her nose and cheek, digging its narrow tip along her lashes. With a triumphant scoff the Contessa shoved Miss Temple stumbling into the waiting arms of Colonel Aspiche.

Miss Temple looked up to see the elegant lady wiping her mouth with her hand and mockingly smacking her lips.

"'Thirty-seven Harker-Bornarth, I should say... excellent vintage... shame to waste it on a savage. Get her out of here."

She was dragged without ceremony down a nearby hallway and thrown, there was no other word for it, like a sack of goods into a dimly lit room guarded by two black-coated soldiers of Macklenburg. She sprawled to her knees and wheeled back to the open door, hair hanging in her eyes, in time to see Aspiche abruptly slam it shut. A moment later it was locked, and his boot-steps retreated into silence. Miss Temple sank back on her haunches and sighed. She dabbed at her face, still sticky with saliva and port, with the sleeve of her robe, and looked around her.

It was, as she had speculated earlier, the exact sort of dusty, disused parlor where she had met Spragg and Farquhar, but with a cry Miss Temple saw that she was not alone. She leapt to her feet and lunged at the two figures sprawled facedown on the floor. They were warm—both warm and—she whimpered with joy—they breathed! She had been reunited at last with her comrades! With all her available strength, she did her best to turn them over.

Miss Temple's face was wet with tears, but she smiled as Doctor Svenson erupted into a fearsome spate of coughing, and she did her best to wedge her knees under his shoulders and help him to sit up. In the dim light she could not see if there was blood, but she could smell the pungent odors of the indigo clay infused throughout his clothing and his hair. She shoved again and swiveled his body so he could lean back against a nearby settee. He coughed again and recovered so far as to cover his mouth with a hand. Miss Temple brushed the hair from his eyes, beaming.

"Doctor Svenson—" she whispered.

"My dear Celeste—are we dead?"

"We are not, Doctor—"

"Excellent—is Chang?"

"No, Doctor—he is right here—"

"Are we still at Harschmort?"

"Yes, locked in a room."

"And your mind remains your own?"

"Oh yes."

"Capital . . . I am with you in a moment . . . beg pardon."

He turned away from her and spat, took a deep breath, groaned, and heaved himself to a full sitting position, his eyes screwed tightly shut.

"My suffering Christ . . . ," he muttered.

"I have just been with our enemies!" she said. "Absolutely everything is going on."

"Imagine it must be . . . pray forgive my momentary lapse . . ."

Miss Temple had scuttled to the other side of Cardinal Chang, doing her best not to cry at the spectacle he presented. If anything, the noxious smell was even more intense, and the dried crusts of blood around his nose and mouth and his collar, and the deathly paleness of his face, made clear the extremity of his health. She began to wipe his face with her robe, her other hand holding his head, when she realized that his dark glasses had come off as she'd rolled him over. She stared at the truly vicious scars across each eye and bit her lip at the poor man's torment. Chang's breath rattled in his chest like a shaken box of jumbled nails. Was he dying? Miss Temple pulled his head to her bosom and cradled it, whispering gently.

"Cardinal Chang, . . . you must come back to us . . . it is Celeste . . . I am with the Doctor . . . we cannot survive without you . . ."

Svenson heaved himself from his place and took hold of Chang's wrist, placing his other hand upon the man's forehead. A moment later his fingers were probing Chang's throat and then Svenson had placed his ear against Chang's chest, to gauge his ragged breath. He raised himself, sighed, and gently disengaged Miss Temple and searched with deliberate fingers along the back of Chang's skull, where he'd been struck by the Colonel's truncheon.

She stared helplessly at his probing fingers, stalking pale through Chang's black hair.

"I thought you'd undergone their Process," he observed mildly.

"No. I was able to counterfeit the scars," she said. "I'm sorry if—well, I did not mean to disappoint you—"

"Hush, it sounds an excellent plan."

"The Contessa found me out nevertheless."

"That is no shame, I'm sure... I am happy to find you whole. May I ask—I am almost afraid to say it—"

"Elöise and I became separated. She bore the same false scars—I do not think she has been taken, but do not know where she is. Of course I am not entirely sure I know *who* she is."

The Doctor smiled at her, rather lost and wan, his eyes achingly clear. "Nor am I... that is the strangest part of it." He looked pointedly at Miss Temple with the same troubling open gaze. "Of course, when does one ever know?"

He pulled his eyes from hers and cleared his throat.

"Indeed," sniffed Miss Temple, moved by this unexpected glimpse into the Doctor's heart, "still, I am terribly sorry to have lost her."

"We have each done our best... that we are alive is a marvel... these things are equal between us."

She nodded, wanting to say more but having no idea what those words might be. The Doctor sighed, thinking, and then with an impulsive gesture reached out to pinch tight Chang's nose with one hand and cover his mouth with the other. Miss Temple gasped.

"But what—"

"A moment..."

A moment was all it took. Like a man brought back to life Chang's eyes snapped open and his shoulders tensed, his arms groped at Svenson and the rattle in his lungs redoubled in strength. The Doctor removed his hands with a flourish and the Cardinal erupted with his own fit of coughing, dauntingly moist and accompanied by sprays of bloody saliva. Svenson and Miss Temple each took one of the Cardinal's arms and raised him to his knees where he could more easily vent his body's distress and its attendant discharge.

Chang wiped his mouth with his fingers and smeared them on the floor—there was no point in wiping them on his coat or trousers, Miss Temple saw. He turned to them, blinked, and then groped quickly at his face. Miss Temple held out his glasses with a smile.

"It is so very good to see you both," she whispered.

They sat for a moment, giving each other time to gather their strength and wits, and in Miss Temple's case to wipe away her tears and regain control over her tremulous voice. There was so much to say and so many things to do, she scoffed at her own indulgence, even if the scoff was half-heartedly blown through a sniffling nose.

"You have the advantage, Celeste," muttered Chang hoarsely. "From the blood in the Doctor's hair, I assume we both lack any knowledge of where we are, who guards us . . . even the damned time of day."

"How long since we were taken?" asked Svenson.

Miss Temple sniffed again.

"Not long at all. But so much has happened since we spoke, since I left you—I am so sorry—I was childish and a fool—"

Svenson waved away her concerns.

"Celeste, I doubt there is time—nor does it matter—"

"It matters to me."

"Celeste—" This was Chang, struggling to rise.

"Be quiet, the both of you," she said, and stood up so she was taller than either of them. "I will be brief, but I must first apologize for leaving you at Plum Court. It *was* a foolish thing to do and one that nearly ended my life—and nearly finished both of yours as well." She held up a hand to stop Doctor Svenson from speaking. "There are two Macklenburg soldiers outside the door, and down the corridor at least ten Dragoons with their officer and their Colonel. The door is locked, and—as you both can see—our room is without windows. I assume we have no weapons."

Chang and Svenson patted their pockets somewhat absently, not finding a thing.

"We will acquire them, it does not signify," she said quickly, not wanting to lose her place.

"If we get out the door," said Svenson.

"Yes, of course—the important thing is stopping our enemies' plan."

"And what exact plan is that?" asked Chang.

"That is the issue—I only know a portion of it. But I trust you've each seen a portion of your own."

Keeping her promise to be brief, Miss Temple breathlessly launched into her tale: the St. Royale, Miss Vandaariff's potion, the painting in the Contessa's room, her battle with the book, her battle—in a strictly abbreviated version—with the Comte and Contessa in the coach, her train ride to Harschmort, and her journey to the theatre. Both Chang and Svenson opened their mouths to add details but she hushed them and went on—the secret room, the Contessa and the Prince, the killing of Blenheim, Elöise's discovery in the blue card, Trapping, Vandaariff, Lydia, Veilandt, the ballroom, and, finally, the vicious argument between the Contessa and her allies not ten minutes before. The entire narrative took perhaps two hurriedly whispered minutes.

When she was finished, Miss Temple took a deep breath, hoping she hadn't forgotten anything vital, though of course she had—simply too much had *happened*.

"So . . ." The Doctor pushed himself up from the floor onto the settee. "They have taken control of this government with the Duke—who I promise you was *killed*—and are on their way to taking over that of Macklenburg—"

"If it is not offensive to you, Doctor," said Miss Temple, "I do not understand the *to-do* about one amongst so many German kingdoms."

"Duchy, but yes—it is because our mountains hold more of this indigo clay than a hundred Tarr Manors put together. They have been acquiring the land for years..." His voice caught and again he shook his head. "In any case—if they journey tonight to Macklenburg—"

"We will need to travel—" muttered Chang. His words were followed by another wracking cough he did his best to ignore, digging into each side pocket of his coat. "I have carried these quite a way, for this exact moment..."

Miss Temple squeaked with happy surprise, blinking again at a new tickling of tears in each eye. Her green boots! She sat down on the floor without the slightest hesitation or thought of modesty and snatched them up, working her lost treasures joyfully onto each foot. She looked up at Chang, who was smiling—though still coughing—and set to tightening the laces.

"I cannot tell you what this means," she said, "you will laugh at me—you're laughing now—I know they are only shoes, and I have many shoes, and to be honest I should not have given a pin for these four days before, but now I would not lose them for the world."

"Of course not," said Svenson quietly.

"O!" Miss Temple said. "But there are things of yours—from your greatcoat, which we lost, but as I said, we took the card, and there was also a silver case, for your cigarettes! Well, now that I say it, I do not have it—Elöise does, but once we find her, you shall have it back."

"Indeed... I... that is excellent—"

"It seemed as if it might be precious to you."

The Doctor nodded, but then looked away, frowning, as if he did not want to say more. Chang coughed again, congestion echoing wetly in his chest.

"We must do something for you," said Svenson, but Chang shook his head.

"It is my lungs—"

"Powdered glass," said Miss Temple. "The Contessa explained how she'd killed you."

"I am sorry to disappoint the Lady . . ." He smiled.

Svenson looked at Chang quite soberly. "The glass alone would be harmful to your lungs—that it bears such toxic properties as well, it is a marvel you have not succumbed to hypnotic visions."

"I should prefer them to this coughing, I assure you."

"Is there any way to get it out?" asked Miss Temple.

The Doctor frowned in thought. The Cardinal spat again, and began to speak.

"My story is simple. When we did not know where you went, we split up, the Doctor to Tarr Manor and I to the Ministry, neither of us guessing correctly. I met Bascombe and the Contessa, witnessed the Process in action, fought Xonck, nearly died, then tracked you—too late—to the St. Royale—thus the boots—and made the train for Harschmort. Once here I have seen the most powerful figures overborne, their minds drained into these books, and Robert Vandaariff, mindless as an ape, filling page after page with a narrative of his secrets. I was unable to prevent the transformation of the three women . . ." Chang paused for a moment—Miss Temple was becoming steadily aware of the degree to which each man had pressed the limit of not only his strength but also his heart, and her own went out to them utterly—and then cleared his throat. "Though I did kill your Major Blach. But the rest was capture and failure—except I also managed to kill the Contessa's man, Mr. Gray—"

"O! They were arguing about it fiercely!" exclaimed Miss Temple.

"He was on some errand—secret from the others, I am sure. I do not know what it was." He looked up at Miss Temple. "Did you say our guards were Dragoons?"

"Not directly outside the door, no—but in the corridor, yes—perhaps a dozen men with their officer, Captain Smythe, and their Colonel—"

"Smythe, you say!" Chang's face visibly brightened.

"I met him," said Svenson. "He saved my life!"

"He knows me too, somehow," said Miss Temple. "It was actually rather unsettling . . ."

"If we can get rid of Aspiche then Smythe will come to our cause, I am sure of it," said Chang.

Miss Temple glanced back at the door. "Well, if *that* is all we require, then we will soon be on our way. Doctor?"

"I can speak as we go—save to say that there is an airship on the roof—it is how we came from Tarr Manor. They may use it to reach a ship at the canal, or farther up the coast—"

"Or go all the way to Macklenburg," said Chang. "These machines I have seen are prodigiously powerful."

Svenson nodded. "You are right—it is ridiculous to undervalue their capacity in any way—but this too can wait. We must stop the marriage. We must stop the Duke."

"And we must find Elöise," exclaimed Miss Temple, "especially as she has the glass key!"

"What glass key?" rasped Chang.

"Did I not mention it? I believe it is the way to safely read the books. We got it from Blenheim's pocket."

"How did *he* have it?" asked Chang.

"Exactly!" Miss Temple beamed. "Now, both of you—back on the floor—or, all right, I'm sure it is fine if you are on a settee—but you must shut your eyes and remain inert."

"Celeste, what are you doing?" asked Svenson.

"Managing our escape, naturally."

She knocked on the door and called out as sweetly as she could to the guards on the other side. They did not answer, but Miss Temple kept knocking and although she was forced to switch several times from one hand to the other as her knuckles became tender, at last the lock was turned and the door cracked open a single suspicious inch, through which Miss Temple glimpsed the pale, cautious face of a young soldier from Macklenburg—younger than herself, she saw, which only increased the sweetness of her smile.

"I do beg your pardon, but it's very important that I see the Colonel. I have information for the Contessa—the *Contessa,* you understand—that she will be most anxious to have."

The trooper did not move. Did he even *understand* her? Miss Temple's smile hardened as she leaned forward and spoke more loudly, with a sharp, unmistakable intent.

"I must see the Colonel! At once! Or *you* will be *punished*!"

The trooper looked to his comrade, out of view, clearly unsure of what he should do. Miss Temple barked past him at the top of her lungs.

"*Colonel Aspiche!* I have vital news for you! If the Contessa does not get it, *she will cut off your ears*!"

At her scream the guard slammed the door and fumbled for the lock, but Miss Temple could already hear the angry stride of heavy boots. In a moment the door was flung wide by Aspiche, face crimson with rage, cheroot in one hand and the other on the hilt of his saber, glaring down at her like a red-coated schoolmaster ready to deal out a whipping.

"Thank you so much," said Miss Temple.

"What information are you screeching about?" he snarled. "Your manners are quite unbecoming—even more so if I find this is a *lie.*"

"Nonsense," said Miss Temple, shivering for the Colonel's benefit and slipping a theatrical quaver into her voice. "And you do not need to *scare* me so—the state of my allies and the Contessa's power have left me helpless. I am only trying to save my own life." She wiped her nose on her sleeve.

"What information?" repeated Aspiche.

Miss Temple glanced behind him at the guards, who were staring with undisguised curiosity, and then leaned forward with a whisper.

"It is actually rather *sensitive*…"

Aspiche leaned forward in turn with a tight, put-upon expression. Miss Temple brushed his ear with her lips.

"Blue . . . Caesar . . . blue . . . Regiment . . . ice . . . consumption . . ."

She looked up and saw the Colonel's eyes did not move, gazing at a point just beyond her shoulder.

"Perhaps we ought to be alone," she whispered.

Aspiche wheeled on the guards with fury.

"Leave me with the prisoners!" he barked. The guards stumbled back, as Aspiche reached out with both hands and slammed the door. He turned back to Miss Temple, his face without any expression at all.

"Cardinal, . . . Doctor, . . . you may rise . . ."

She kept to her whisper, not wanting the guards to hear. Chang and Svenson stood slowly, staring at the Colonel with morbid curiosity.

"Everyone who undergoes the Process is instilled with some sort of control phrase," Miss Temple explained. "I overheard the Contessa use one on the Prince, and again when she attempted to use one on me—to prove I had *not* been converted. I wasn't able to work it all out—it was a guess—"

"You risked this on a guess?" asked Svenson.

"As it was a *good* guess, yes. The phrase has several parts—the first is a color, and I deduced that the color was about where the Process was administered. You remember that the different boxes had different colors of felt packing—"

"Orange at Harschmort," said Chang. "Blue at the Institute."

"And seeing as he was converted *before* they moved the boxes from the Institute, the color for the Colonel was blue."

"What was the rest of the phrase?" asked Svenson.

"The second word is about their *role,* using a Biblical metaphor—I'm sure it is all part of the Comte's ostentation. For the Prince it was Joseph—for he will be the father to someone else's child, as poor Lydia must be Mary—for me it would have been Magdalene, as for all of the white-robed initiates—and for the Colonel, as the representative of the state, I guessed correctly it would be 'Caesar'... the rest follows the same way—'Regiment' instead of 'Palace' or 'Royale'—"

"Is he understanding this?" asked Svenson.

"I think so, but he is also waiting for instructions."

"Suppose he should cut his own throat?" suggested Chang, with a moist chuckle.

"Suppose he tells us if they've captured Elöise," said Svenson, and he spoke slowly and clearly to Colonel Aspiche. "Do you know the whereabouts of Mrs. Dujong?"

"Shut your filthy hole before I shut it for you!" Aspiche roared.

Svenson darted back a step, his eyes wide with surprise.

"Ah," Miss Temple said, "perhaps only the person who speaks the phrase can command." She cleared her throat. "Colonel, do you know where we can find Mrs. Dujong?"

"Of course I don't," snapped Aspiche, sullenly.

"All right... when did you last see her?"

The Colonel's lips curled into an unabashed and wicked smile. "Aboard the airship. Doctor Lorenz asked her questions, and when she did not answer Miss Poole and I took turns—"

Doctor Svenson's fist landed like a hammer on the Colonel's jaw, knocking him back into the door. Miss Temple turned to Svenson—hissing with pain and flexing his hand—and then to Aspiche, sputtering with rage and struggling to rise. Before he could, Chang's arm shot forth and snatched the Colonel's saber from its sheath, a wheeling bright scythe that had Miss Temple scampering clear with a squeak. When she looked back, the Cardinal had the blade hovering dangerously in front of the man's chest. Aspiche did not move.

"Doctor?" she asked quietly.

"My apologies—"

"Not at all, the Colonel is a horrid beast. Your hand?"

"It will do fine."

She stepped closer to Aspiche, her face harder than before. She had known Elöise endured her own set of trials, but Miss Temple thought back to her own irritation at how the woman, drugged and stumbling, had slowed their progress in escaping the theatre. She was more than happy to expend the sting of her guilt and regret on the villain before her.

"Colonel, you will open this door and take us into the hall. You will order both of these guards into this room and then lock the door behind them. If they protest, you will do your level best to kill them. Do you understand?"

Aspiche nodded, his eyes wavering between her own and the floating tip of the saber.

"Then do it. We are wasting time."

The Germans gave them no trouble, so inured were they to following orders. It was only a matter of moments before they stood again in the open foyer where the members of the Cabal had argued with one another. The Dragoons lining the corridor were gone, along with their officer.

"Where's Captain Smythe?" she asked Aspiche.

"Assisting Mr. Xonck and the Deputy Minister."

Miss Temple frowned. "Then what were *you* doing here? Did you not have orders?"

"Of course—to execute the three of you."

"But why were you waiting in the corridor?"

"I was finishing my cigar!" snapped Colonel Aspiche.

Chang scoffed behind her.

"Every man reveals his soul eventually," he muttered.

Miss Temple crept to the ballroom doors. The enormous space was empty. She called back to her prisoner.

"Where is everyone?" He opened his mouth to answer but she cut him off. "Where are each of our enemies—the Contessa, the Comte, Deputy Minister Crabbé, Francis Xonck, the Prince and his bride, Lord Vandaariff, the Duke of Stäelmaere, Mrs. Stearne—"

"And Roger Bascombe," said Doctor Svenson. She turned to him, and to Chang, and nodded sadly.

"And Roger Bascombe." She sighed. "In an orderly manner, if you please."

The Colonel had informed them—sullen twitches around his mouth evidence of a useless struggle against Miss Temple's control—that their enemies had split into two groups. The first occupied themselves with a sweeping progress through the great house, gathering up their guests and collecting the stupefied luminaries whose minds had been drained into the glass books on the way, to send off the Duke of Stäelmaere with ceremony suitable to his imminent *coup d'état.* Accompanying the Duke's progress would be the Contessa, the Deputy Minister, and Francis Xonck, as well as Lord Vandaariff, Bascombe, Mrs. Stearne, and the two glass women, Marchmoor and Poole. The second group, about which Aspiche could provide no information as to their errand, consisted of the Comte d'Orkancz, Prince Karl-Horst von Maasmärck, Lydia Vandaariff, Herr Flaüss, and the third glass woman.

"I did not recognize her," said Miss Temple. "By all rights the third subject ought to have been Caroline."

"It is *Angelique,* the Cardinal's acquaintance," replied Doctor Svenson, speaking delicately. "The woman we searched for in the greenhouse. You were right—she did not perish there."

"Instead, the Comte kept her alive to use as a test subject," rasped Chang. "If his transformation failed, then he need not sacrifice the others—if it worked and made moot the issue of her damaged body, then all the better. All in all you see, it is an admirable expression of *economy.*"

Neither Miss Temple nor the Doctor spoke, letting Chang's bitterness and anger have their sway. Chang rubbed his eyes beneath his glasses and sighed.

"The question is what they are doing, and which group we ought to follow. If we agree that stopping the Duke and the Prince's marriage are both vital, it is of course possible that we split up—"

"I should prefer not to," said Miss Temple quickly. "In either place we shall find enemies *en masse*—it seems there is strength in numbers."

"I agree," said the Doctor, "and my vote is to go after the Duke. The rest of the Cabal journeys to Macklenburg—the Duke and Lord Vandaariff are their keys to maintaining power here. If we can disrupt that, it may upset the balance of their entire plot."

"You mean to kill them?" asked Chang.

"Kill them *again,* in the case of the Duke," muttered the Doctor, "but yes, I am for assassinations all round." He sighed bitterly. "It is exactly my plan for Karl-Horst, should his neck ever come within reach of my two hands."

"But he is your charge," said Miss Temple, a little shocked by Svenson's tone.

"My charge has become their creature," he answered. "He is no more than a rabid dog or a horse with a broken fetlock—he must be put down, preferably *before* he has a chance to sire an heir."

Miss Temple put her hand over her mouth. "Of course! The Comte is using his alchemy to impregnate Lydia—it is the height of *his* part of this plan—it is Oskar Veilandt's alchemical *Annunciation* made flesh! And they are doing it tonight—even now!"

Doctor Svenson sucked on his teeth, wincing, looking back and forth between Miss Temple and Chang.

"I still say we stop the Duke. If we do not—"

"If we do not, mine and Miss Temple's lives in this city are ruined," said Chang.

"And after that," asked Miss Temple, "the Prince and Lydia?"

Svenson nodded, and then sighed. "I'm afraid they are already doomed . . ."

Chang abruptly cackled, a sound as pleasant as a gargling crow. "Are we so different, Doctor? Save some of your pity for us!"

At Miss Temple's command Aspiche led them toward the main entrance of the house, but it became quickly clear they could not go far that way, so thronged had it become with the many, many guests gathered for the Duke's departure. With a sudden inspiration, Miss Temple recalled her own path with Spragg and Farquhar through the gardener's passage between the wings of the house and around to the carriages. Within two minutes—Aspiche huffing as sullenly as his conditioning allowed—they had arrived, their breath clouding in the chilly air, just in time to watch a procession flow down the main stairs toward the Duke's imperious, massive black coach.

The Duke himself moved slowly and with care, like a particularly delicate, funereal stick insect, guided on one side by the small greasy-haired man—"Doctor Lorenz," whispered Svenson—and on the other by Mrs. Marchmoor, no longer with a leash around her neck, her gleaming body now covered in a thick black cloak. Behind in a line came the Contessa, Xonck, and Deputy Minister Crabbé, and behind them, stopping at the steps and waving the Duke on his way, stood the similarly aligned knot of Robert Vandaariff, Roger Bascombe, and Mrs. Poole, also leashless and cloaked.

The Duke was installed in his coach and joined a moment later by Mrs. Marchmoor. Miss Temple looked to her companions—now was clearly the time to dash for the coach if they were going to do so—but before she could speak she saw with dismay, boisterously shouting to the Duke and to each other as they sought their own amongst the many coaches, the rest of the guests all preparing to leave. Any attack on the Duke's coach was all but impossible.

"What can we do?" she whispered. "We are too late!"

Chang hefted the saber in his hand. "I can go—one of us alone, I can move more quickly—I can track them to the Palace—"

"Not in your condition," observed Svenson. "You would be caught and killed—and you know it. Look at the soldiers! They have a full escort!"

As he pointed Miss Temple now saw that it was true—a double rank of mounted Dragoons, perhaps forty men, moving their horses into position ahead and behind the coach. The Duke was completely beyond their reach.

"He will convene the Privy Council," rasped Chang hollowly. "He will make whatever they want into law."

"With the Duke's power, and Vandaariff's money, the Macklenburg throne, and an inexhaustible supply of indigo clay . . . they'll be unstoppable . . . ." whispered Svenson.

Miss Temple frowned. Perhaps it was a futile gesture, but she would make it.

"On the contrary. Cardinal Chang, if you would please return the Colonel's saber—I do insist."

Chang looked at her quizzically, but carefully passed the weapon to Aspiche. Before the man could do a thing with it, Miss Temple spoke to him quite firmly.

"Colonel Aspiche, listen to me. Your men protect the Duke—this is excellent. No one else—no one, mind—is to come within reach of the Duke during his journey back to the Palace. You will go now, collect a horse, and join his train—immediately, do not speak to anyone, do not return to the house, take the mount of one of your men if you must. Once you reach the Palace, being very particular to avoid the scrutiny of Mrs. Marchmoor, you will find time—the appropriate time, for you must *succeed*—but nevertheless *before* the Privy Council can meet—to hack the Duke of Stäelmaere's head clean from his body. Do you understand me?"

Colonel Aspiche nodded.

"Excellent. Do not breathe a word of this to anyone. Off you go!"

She smiled, watching the man stride into the crowded plaza, possessed by his mission, toward the nearest stand of horses, pretending not to see the astonished expressions of Svenson and Chang to her either side.

"Let's see them stick it back on with library paste," she said. "Shall we find the Prince?"

The Colonel had not known exactly where the Comte and his party had gone, merely that it was somewhere below the ballroom.

From his own journeys through Harschmort House, Cardinal Chang was convinced he could find the way, and so Miss Temple and Doctor Svenson followed him back through the gardener's passage and then indoors. As they walked, Miss Temple looked up at Chang, daunting despite his injuries, and wished for just a moment that she might see inside his thoughts like one of the glass women. They were on their way to rescue—or destroy, but the goal was the same—the Prince and Lydia, but the Cardinal's lost woman, Angelique, would be there as well. Did he hope to reclaim her? To force the Comte to reverse her transformation? Or to put her out of her misery? She felt the weight of her own sadness, the regret and pain of Roger's rejection, of her own habitual isolation—were these feelings, feelings that because they were hers felt somehow small, however keenly they plagued her, anything like the burdens haunting a man like Chang? How could they be? How could there not be an impassable wall between them?

"The two wings mirror each other," he said hoarsely, "and I have been up and down the lower floors on the opposite side. If I am right, the stairway down should be right . . . about . . . *here* . . ."

He smiled—and Miss Temple was struck anew, perhaps by his especially battered condition, of what a provocative mix of the bodily compelling and morally fearsome Cardinal Chang's smile actually was—and indicated a bland-looking alcove covered with a velvet curtain. He whisked it aside and revealed a metal door that had boldly been left ajar.

"Such *confidence*"—he chuckled, pulling it open—"to leave an open door . . . you'd think they might have learned."

He spun to look behind them, his face abruptly stern, at the sound of approaching footsteps.

"Or *we* would have . . . ," muttered Doctor Svenson, and Chang hurriedly motioned them through the door. He closed it behind them, letting the lock catch. "It will delay them," he whispered. "Quickly!"

They heard the door being pulled repeatedly above them as they followed the spiral staircase for two turns, reaching another door, also ajar, where Chang eased past Miss Temple and Svenson to peek through first.

"Might I suggest we acquire *weapons*?" whispered the Doctor.

Miss Temple nodded her agreement, but instead of answering Chang had slipped through the door, his footfalls silent as a cat's, leaving them to follow as best they could. They entered a strange curving corridor, like an opera house or a Roman theatre, with a row of doors on the inner side, as if they led to box seats, or toward the arena.

"It is like the Institute," Svenson whispered to Chang, who nodded, still focused on the corridor ahead. They had advanced, walking close to the inner wall, just so the staircase door was no longer visible behind them, when a scuffling noise beyond the next curve caused Chang to freeze. He held his open palm to indicate that they should stay, then carefully moved forward alone, pressed flat against the wall.

Chang stopped. He glanced back at them and smiled, then darted forward in a sudden rush. Miss Temple heard one brief squawk of surprise and then three meaty thuds in rapid succession. Chang reappeared and motioned them on with a quick toss of his head.

On the ground by another open door, his breathing labored, blood flowing freely from his nose, lay the Macklenburg Envoy, Herr Flaüss. Near his feebly twitching hand lay a revolver, which Chang snatched up, breaking it open to check the cylinder and then slamming it home. While Doctor Svenson knelt by the gasping man, Chang extended the weapon for Miss Temple to take. She shook her head.

"Surely you or the Doctor," she whispered.

"The Doctor, then," replied Chang. "I am more useful with a blade or my fists." He looked down to watch Svenson briskly ransack the Envoy's pockets, each search answered by an ineffectual gesture of protest from the injured man's hands. Svenson looked up, behind them toward the staircase—footsteps. He stood, abandoning the Envoy. Chang pressed the pistol into Svenson's hands and took hold of the Doctor's sleeve and Miss Temple's arm, pulling them both farther down the corridor until they could no longer see the Envoy. Svenson whispered his protest.

"But, Cardinal, they are surely *inside*—"

Chang tugged them both into an alcove and pressed a hand over his mouth to stifle a cough. Down the corridor Miss Temple heard rushing steps... that suddenly fell silent. She felt Chang's body tense, and saw the Doctor's thumb moving slowly to the hammer of the pistol. Someone was walking toward them, slowly... the footsteps stopped... and then retreated. She strained her ears... and heard a woman's haughty, angry hiss.

"*Leave* the idiot..."

Chang waited... and then leaned close to them both.

"Without getting rid of the body, we could not enter in secret—at this moment they are searching the room, assuming we have entered. This alone will halt whatever is happening inside. If we enter *now,* there is a chance to take their rearmost by surprise."

Miss Temple took a deep breath, feeling as if she had somehow in the last five minutes become a soldier. Before she could make sense of—or more importantly, protest against—this wrong-headed state of affairs Chang was gone and Doctor Svenson, taking her hand in his, was pulling her in tow.

The Envoy remained in the doorway, raised to a sitting position but still incapacitated and insensible. They stepped past with no reaction from Herr Flaüss save a snuffle of his bleeding nose, into a dim stone entryway with narrow staircases to either side to balconies that wrapped around the room. Chang swiftly ducked to the left, with Svenson and Miss Temple directly behind him, crowding as quietly as possible out of sight. Miss Temple wrinkled her nose with distaste at the harsh reek of indigo clay. Ahead of them, through the foyer, they heard the Contessa.

"He has been attacked—you heard nothing?"

"I did not," answered the dry, rumbling voice of the Comte. "I am *busy*, and my business makes noise. Attacked by *whom*?"

"I'm sure I do not know," replied the Contessa. "Colonel Aspiche has cut the throats of each *likely* candidate . . . thus my *curiosity*."

"The Duke is away?"

"Exactly as planned, followed by those selected for book-harvest. As agreed, their distraction and loss of memory have been blamed on a virulent outbreak of blood fever—stories of which will be spread by our own adherents—a tale with the added benefit of justifying a quarantine of Harschmort, sequestering Lord Robert for as long as necessary. But that is not our present difficulty."

"I see," grunted the Comte. "As I am in the midst of a very delicate procedure, I would appreciate it if you explained what in the depths of hell you are all doing here."

Miss Temple did her best to follow the others up the narrow stairs in silence. As her head cleared the balcony floor, she saw a domed stone ceiling above, lit by several wicked-looking iron chandeliers that bristled with spikes. Miss Temple could never see a chandelier under the best of circumstances without imagining the destructive impact of its sudden drop to the floor (especially if she was passing beneath), and these instinctive thoughts, and these fixtures, just made the Comte's laboratory that much more a chamber of dread. The balcony was stacked with books and papers and boxes, all covered by a heavy layer of dust. Svenson indicated with a jab of his finger that she could inch forward to peek through the bars of the railing.

Miss Temple had not been to the Institute, but she had managed a powerful glimpse of the hellish platform at the base of the iron tower. This room (as the walls were lined with bookshelves it seemed to have once been some sort of library) was a strange mix of that same industry (for there were tables cluttered with steaming pots and boiling vials and parchment and wickedly shaped metal tools) and a sleeping chamber, for in the center of the room, cleared by pushing aside and stacking any number of tables and chairs, was a very large bed. Miss Temple nearly gagged, covering her mouth with her hand, but she could not look away. On the bed, her bare legs dangling over the side, lay Lydia Vandaariff, her white robes around her thighs, each arm outstretched and restrained by a white silk cord. Her face shone with exertion, and each of her hands tightly gripped its cord, as if the restraint were more a source of comfort than punishment. The bedding between Lydia's legs was wet, as was the stone floor beneath her feet, a pooling of watered blue fluid streaked with curling crimson lines. The embroidered hem of Lydia's robe had been flipped down in a meager gesture toward modesty, but there was no ignoring the flecks of blue and red on her white thighs. She looked up at the ceiling, blinking.

Slumped in a nearby chair, a half-full glass in his hand and an open bottle of brandy on the floor between his legs, sat Karl-Horst von Maasmärck. The Comte wore his leather apron, his black fur slung over a pile of chairs behind him, and cradled a bizarre metal object, a metal tube with handles and valves and a pointed snout that he wiped clean with a rag.

On the walls behind them, hung on nails hammered carelessly into the bookcases, were thirteen distinct squares of canvas. Miss Temple turned to Chang and pointed. He had seen them as well, and made a deliberate gesture to flatten his hand and then turn it over, as to turn a page. At the St. Royale, Lydia had muttered something about the *rest* of the *Annunciation* fragments—indicating that she had seen them collected. Miss Temple knew the squares of canvas represented the entire reconstituted work, but she had not expected the Comte to hang each painting face to the wall, for what she saw was not the complete blasphemous image (which she was frankly by now more than a little curious to see), but its canvas backing—Oskar Veilandt's alchemical formulae as they traveled across every piece, for which the painting was but a decorative veil, a detailed recipe for his own Annunciation, the unspeakable impregnation of Lydia Vandaariff by way of his twisted science. Around each canvas were pasted scores of additional notes and diagrams—no doubt the Comte's own attempts to understand Veilandt's blasphemous instructions. Miss Temple looked down at the girl on the bed and bit her knuckle to keep silent...

She heard an impatient sigh below her and the flicking catch of a match. Miss Temple scooted forward on her belly and gained a wider view of the room. With a tremor of fear she saw, almost directly beneath, the Contessa's large party. How had they not heard them in the corridor? Next to the Contessa—smoking a fresh cigarette in her holder—stood Francis Xonck and Crabbé, and behind them at least six figures in black coats, carrying cudgels. She glanced again to Chang and Svenson and saw Chang's attention focused elsewhere, underneath the opposite balcony. Glittering in the shadows, as the orange flames from the Comte's crucibles reflected off her skin, stood the third glass woman, Angelique, silently waiting. Miss Temple stared at her, and was just beginning to examine the woman's body with the new understanding that it was the object of Chang's ardent affection—and in fact, its consummation, for the woman *was* a whore—which meant... Miss Temple's face became flushed, suddenly jumbling her memories from the book with thoughts of Chang and Angelique—when she shook her head and forced her attention to the rather agitated conversation below.

"We would not have bothered you," began Xonck, his eyes drawn with some distaste to the spectacle before them, "save we are unaccountably unable to locate a workable *key*."

"Where is Lorenz?" asked the Comte.

"Readying the airship," replied Crabbé, "and surrounded by a host of soldiers. I would prefer to leave him be."

"What of Bascombe?"

"He accompanies Lord Robert," snorted the Contessa. "We

will meet him with the trunk of books and his ledger—but he does not have a key either, and for any number of reasons I would prefer not to involve him."

Crabbé rolled his eyes. "Mr. Bascombe is absolutely loyal to us all—"

"Where is *your* key?" the Comte asked, glaring pointedly at the Deputy Minister.

"It is not *my* key at all," replied Crabbé somewhat hotly. "I do not believe I am even the last to have it—as the Contessa says, we were collecting the books, not *exploring* them—"

"Who *was* the last to have it?" cried the Comte, openly impatient. He shifted his grip on the repulsive metal device in his hand.

"We do not *know*," snapped the Contessa. "I believe it was Mr. Crabbé. He believes it was Mr. Xonck. *He* believes it was Blenheim—"

"Blenheim?" scoffed the Comte.

"Not Blenheim directly," said Xonck. "*Trapping*. I believe Trapping took it to look at one of the books—perhaps idly, perhaps not—"

"*Which* book?"

"We do not *know*," said the Contessa. "We were *indulging* him—I am still not satisfied as to his death. Blenheim either took it from Trapping's pocket when the body was moved, or he was given it by Lord Robert."

"I take it Blenheim is still missing?"

The Contessa nodded.

"The question is whether he is dead," said Crabbé, "or *independent*?"

"Perhaps we can *query* Lord Robert," said the Comte.

"We could if he retained his memory," observed Xonck. "But as you know it has been put into a book—a book we cannot find. If we did find it, we could not safely read it without a key! It is ridiculous!"

"I see . . ." said the Comte, his brooding face dark with thought. "And *what* has happened to Herr Flaüss?"

"We do not *know*!" cried Crabbé.

"But don't you think we should?" asked the Comte, reasonably. He turned to Angelique and clapped his hands. At once she stepped into the light like a tamed tiger, drawing the wary attention of every other person in the room.

"If there is someone hiding here," the Comte said to her, looking up to the balconies, "*find* them."

Miss Temple spun to Chang and Svenson, her eyes wide. What could they do? She searched around them—there was no other place to hide, to shield themselves! Doctor Svenson silently rolled back on his heels and pulled out the gun, his eyes measuring the distance to Angelique. Chang put a hand on the Doctor's arm. The Doctor shrugged it off and eased back the hammer. Miss Temple felt the strange blue coldness approaching her mind. Any moment they would be found.

Instead, the pregnant silence in the room was broken by a crash from the opposite balcony, directly above Angelique. In an instant Xonck had the serpentine dagger in his hand and was sprinting to the narrow stairs. Miss Temple heard a scuffle and then a woman's gasping protests as Xonck dragged her twisting body brusquely down the staircase and thrust her to her knees before the others. It was Elöise.

Miss Temple looked to Svenson and saw his frozen expression. Before he could do a thing she reached for his hand that held the pistol, gripping it tightly. This was no time for reckless impulse.

Xonck backed away from Elöise, indeed as did they all, for at a nod from the Comte Angelique stepped forward, her feet clicking against the stone floor like a new-shod pony's. Elöise shook her head and looked up, utterly bewildered by the splendid, naked creature, and screamed. She screamed again—Miss Temple squeezing the Doctor's arm as tightly as she could—but it died in her throat, as the expression of terror on her face faded to a quivering passivity. The glass woman had savagely penetrated her mind and was rummaging through its contents with pitiless efficiency. Again, Miss Temple saw the Comte d'Orkancz had closed his eyes, his face a mask of concentration. Elöise did not speak, her mouth open, rocking back and forth on her knees, staring helplessly into the cold blue eyes of her inquisitor.

Then it was done. Elöise dropped in a heap. The Comte came forward to stand over her, looking down.

"It is Mrs. Dujong," whispered Crabbé. "From the quarry. She shot the Duke."

"Indeed. She escaped from the theatre with Miss Temple," said the Comte. "Miss Temple killed Blenheim—his body is in the trophy room. Blenheim *did* have the key—she herself wondered why. It is tucked in Mrs. Dujong's shift, along with a silver cigarette case and a blue glass demonstration card. Both were acquired by way of Doctor Svenson."

"A glass card?" asked the Contessa. Her gaze darted judiciously across the room. "What does it happen to *show*?"

Elöise was panting with exertion, groping to rise to her hands and knees. The Comte shoved his hand roughly into her shift, feeling for the objects he'd described. He stood again, peering at the cigarette case, all the time not answering the Contessa's question. Xonck cleared his throat. The Comte looked up and tossed the silver case to him, which Xonck awkwardly managed to catch.

"Also Svenson's," he said, and glanced over at the Prince, who was still in his chair, watching it all through a veil of drunken bemusement. "The card is imprinted with an experience of Mrs. Marchmoor, within a room at the St. Royale... an *encounter* with the Prince. Apparently it made quite an *impression* on Mrs. Dujong."

"Is that... all?" asked the Contessa, again rather carefully.

"No." The Comte sighed heavily. "It is not."

He nodded again to Angelique.

To the immediate dismay of the other members of the Cabal, the glass woman turned toward them. They shrank back, as Angelique began to walk forward.

"W-what are you *doing*?" sputtered Crabbé.

"I am getting to the bottom of this *mystery,*" rasped the Comte.

"You cannot finish this without our help," hissed Xonck. He waved a hand at the girl on the bed. "Haven't we done enough for you—haven't we all accommodated your *visions*?"

"Visions at the core of your *profit,* Francis."

"I have never denied it! But if you think to turn me into a husk like Vandaariff—"

"I think nothing of the kind," answered the Comte. "What I am doing is in our larger interest."

"Before you treat us like animals, Oskar, . . . and make me your *enemy,*" said the Contessa, raising her voice and speaking quite fiercely, "perhaps you could explain what you intend."

Miss Temple clapped a hand over her mouth, feeling like a fool. Oskar! Was it so stupidly obvious? The Comte had not stolen the works of Oskar Veilandt, the painter was no prisoner or mindless drone . . . the two men were one and the same! What had Aunt Agathe told her—that the Comte was born in the Balkans, raised in Paris, an unlikely inheritance? How was that incompatible with what Mr. Shanck had said of Veilandt—school in Vienna, studio in Montmartre, mysteriously disappeared—into respectability and wealth, she now knew! She looked over to Chang and Svenson, and saw Chang shaking his head bitterly. Svenson had eyes for nothing but Elöise's slumped figure, glaring down at the poor woman with helpless agitation.

The Comte cleared his throat and held up the glass card.

"The *encounter* is attended by spectators—including you, Rosamonde, and you, Francis. But the clever Mrs. Dujong has perceived, through the viewing mirror, a *second* encounter, in the lobby . . . that of Colonel Trapping speaking most earnestly with Robert Vandaariff."

This revelation was met with silence.

"What does that *mean*?" asked Crabbé.

"That is not *all*," intoned the Comte.

"If you would simply tell us, Monsieur!" protested Crabbé. "There is no great amount of time—"

"Mrs. Dujong's memory tells of a *second* card—one the Doctor cut from the lining of Arthur Trapping's uniform. Evidently his body was not fully *searched*. Among other things this card conveys an image of myself performing a preparatory examination on Lydia."

"Arthur intended to give it to Vandaariff," said Xonck. "The greedy fool would not have been able to resist . . ."

Crabbé stepped forward, narrowing his eyes.

"Is this your way of informing us that *you* killed him?" he hissed at the Comte. "Without telling anyone? Risking everything? Pushing forward our entire time-table? No wonder Lord Robert was so agitated—no wonder we were forced to—"

"But that is the point, Harald," rumbled the Comte. "I am telling you *all* this exactly because *I* did not harm a hair on Arthur Trapping's head."

"But—but why else—" began Crabbé, but he then fell silent . . . as every member of the Cabal studied one another.

"You said she had this from Svenson?" the Contessa asked. "Where did *he* get it?"

"She does not know."

"From me, of course," drawled a sluggish voice from the other side of the room. Karl-Horst was attempting to pour himself more brandy. "He must have found it in my room. I never even noticed Trapping, I must say—more interested in *Margaret*! It was the first bit of glass I'd ever seen—a present to entice my participation."

"A present from whom?" asked Francis Xonck.

"Lord knows—is that important?"

"It is perhaps crucial, Your Highness," said the Contessa.

The Prince frowned. "Well . . . in *that* case . . ."

It seemed to Miss Temple that each member of the Cabal

watched the Prince with the barest restraint, every one of them wishing they could slap his face until he spat out what he knew, but none daring to show the slightest impatience or worry in front of the others...and so they waited as he pursed his lips and scratched his ear and sucked on his teeth, all the time enjoying their undivided attention. She was beginning to get worried herself. What if Angelique were to continue her search? Who was to say the glass woman could not somehow smell the presence of their minds? Miss Temple's leg tingled from being crouched so long, and the dusty air was tickling her nose. She glanced at Chang, his lips pressed shut, and realized he had controlled his cough this entire time. She'd not given it a second thought, but suddenly the possibility—the inevitability!—of him exposing their presence terrified her. They must take some action—but what? What possibly?

"I suppose it must have been Doctor Lorenz, or—what was his name?—Mr. Crooner, from the Institute, the one who died so badly. They were the ones working the machines. Gave it to me as a sort of *keepsake*—don't know how that villain Svenson found it unless he had help—I stashed it most brilliantly—"

The Contessa cut him off. "Excellent, Your Highness, that's very helpful."

She crossed to the Comte and relieved him of the items he'd taken from Elöise, speaking with a barely veiled anger.

"This gets us nowhere. We have what we came for—the key. Let us at once return to the books, to find what we can from Lord Robert's *testimony*. Perhaps we will finally learn why the Colonel was killed."

"You don't believe it was Chang?" asked Crabbé.

"Do you?" scoffed the Contessa. "I would be happy to hear it—my life would be simpler. But no—we all remember the delicacy and risk involved in our final *swaying* of Robert Vandaariff, who up to that point quite believed the entire campaign was his own conception. We know the Colonel was brokering secrets—who can say how many secrets he knew?" She shrugged. "Chang's a killer—this is *politics.* We will leave you, Monsieur, to your work."

The Comte nodded to Lydia. "It is done . . . save for the settling."

"Already?" The Contessa looked down at Miss Vandaariff's spent body. "Well, I don't suppose she would have taken pleasure in drawing things out."

"The pleasure is in the final outcome, Rosamonde," the Comte rasped.

"Of course it is," she replied, her gaze drifting to the spattered bedding. "We have intruded enough. We will see you at the airship."

She turned to leave but stopped as Xonck stepped forward and nodded at Elöise.

"What will you do with *her*?"

"Is it up to me?" asked the Comte.

"Not if you'd prefer it otherwise." Xonck smiled. "I was being polite . . ."

"I would prefer to get on with my work," snarled the Comte d'Orkancz.

"I am happy to oblige you," said Xonck. He pulled Elöise to her feet with his good hand, and dragged her from the room. A moment later the Contessa, Crabbé, and their retinue followed.

Miss Temple looked to her companions and saw that Chang's hand was clapped across Svenson's mouth. The Doctor was in torment—yet if they made any noise at all, Angelique would sense their presence and overcome them as easily as she had Elöise. Miss Temple leaned forward again, peeking down into the laboratory. The Comte had watched the others depart, and then returned to his table. He glanced over to Lydia and to Angelique, ignored the Prince, and unscrewed a small valve that stuck out from the metal implement's side. With more delicacy than she would have credited a man of his size, Miss Temple watched the Comte pour steaming liquid from one of the heated flasks into the valve, never spilling a drop, and then screw the valve closed.

He lifted the metal implement and walked back to the bed, setting it down next to Lydia's leg.

"Are you awake, Lydia?"

Lydia nodded. It was the first time Miss Temple had seen the girl move.

"Are you in pain?"

Lydia grimaced, but shook her head. She turned, distracted by movement. It was the Prince, pouring more brandy.

"Your fiancé will not remember any of this, Lydia," said the Comte. "Neither will you. Lie back . . . what cannot be reversed must be embraced."

The Comte picked up the implement and glanced up to their balcony. He raised his voice, speaking generally to the room.

"It would be better if you descended willingly. If the *lady* brings you down, it will be by dragging you over the edge."

Miss Temple turned to Chang and Svenson, aghast.

"I *know* you are there," called the Comte. "I have obviously *waited* to speak to you for a reason . . . but I will not ask a second time."

Chang took his hand away from Svenson's mouth and looked behind for some other way out. Before either could stop him, the Doctor shot to his feet and called out over the balcony to the Comte.

"I am coming . . . damn you to hell, I am coming down . . ."

He turned to them, his eyes a fierce glare, his hand held out for their continued silence. He made a loud stomping as he reached the staircase, but as he passed thrust the pistol into Miss Temple's hands and leaned close to her ear.

"If they never marry," he whispered, "the spawn is not *legitimate*!"

Miss Temple bobbled the gun and looked up at him. Svenson was already gone. She turned to Chang, but he was stifling a vicious cough—a thin stream of blood dripping down his chin. She turned back to the balcony rail. The Doctor stepped into view, his hands away from his body and open, to show he was unarmed. He winced with disgust at this new closer view of Lydia Vandaariff, then pointed to the glass woman.

"I suppose your *creature* sniffed me out?"

The Comte laughed—a particularly objectionable sound—and shook his head. "On the contrary, Doctor—and appropriately, as we are both men of science and inquiry. My glimpse through Mrs. Dujong's mind showed no memory of an attack on Herr Flaüss. It was mere deduction to assume the true culprit was still in hiding."

"I see," said Svenson. "Yet I do not see why you waited to expose me."

"Do you not?" the Comte said, with a smug condescension. "First . . . where are your companions?"

The Doctor groped for words, his fingers flexing, then let them burst forth with scorn and rage.

"Damn you, Sir! Damn you to hell—you heard for yourself! Their throats have been cut by Colonel Aspiche!"

"But not yours?"

Svenson scoffed. "There is no virtue in it. Chang was half-dead already—his dispatch was a matter of seconds. Miss Temple"—here Svenson passed a hand across his brow—"you will not doubt how she fought him. Her struggles woke me, and I was able to break the Colonel's skull with a chair . . . but not, to my undying shame, in time to save the girl."

The Comte considered the Doctor's words.

"A moving tale."

"You're a bastard," spat Svenson. He waved a hand at Lydia without taking his eyes from the Comte. "You're the worst of the lot—for you've wasted gifts the others never had. I would put a bullet through your brain, Monsieur—send you to hell right after Aspiche—with less remorse than I would squash a flea."

* * *

His words were met with laughter, but it was not from the Comte. To Miss Temple's surprise, the Prince had roused himself from his chair and taken a step toward his one-time retainer, the snifter still cradled in his hand.

"What shall we do with him, Monsieur? I suppose the task is mine—he is my traitor, after all. What would you suggest?"

"You're an ignorant fool," hissed Svenson. "You've never seen it—even now! For God's sake, Karl, look at her—your fiancée! She is given someone else's child!"

The Prince turned to Lydia, his face as blandly bemused as ever.

"Do you know what he means, darling?"

"I do not, dearest Karl."

"Do you, Monsieur?"

"We are merely ensuring her health," said the Comte.

"The woman is half-*dead*!" roared Svenson. "Wake up, you idiot! Lydia—for heaven's sake, girl—run for your life! *It is not too late to be saved!*"

Svenson was raving, shouting, flailing his arms. Miss Temple felt Chang take hold of her arm and then—chiding herself again for being one step behind the game—she realized that the Doctor was making noise enough to cover their way down the stairs. They descended quickly to the lowest steps, just out of sight of the room. She looked down at the pistol—why in the world had the Doctor given it to *her*? Why did he not try to shoot the Prince himself? Why not give it to Chang? She saw Chang look down at the weapon as well, then up to meet her eyes.

She understood in an instant, and despite everything, despite the fact she could not even see his eyes, felt the sting of tears in her own.

"Doctor, you will calm *down*!" cried the Comte, snapping his fingers at Angelique. In an instant Svenson cried out and staggered, dropping to his knees. The Comte held up his hand again and waited just long enough for the Doctor to regain his wits before speaking.

"And I will hear no more *disparagement* of this work—"

"Work?" barked Svenson, waving his arms at the glass beakers, at Lydia. "Medieval foolery that will cost this girl's life!"

"Enough!" shouted the Comte, stepping forward ominously. "Is it foolery that has created the books? Foolery that has eternally captured the very essence of how many lives? Because the science is ancient, you—a *doctor,* with no subtlety, no sense of energy's nuance, of elemental concepts—reject it out of hand, in ignorance. You who have never sought the chemical substance of desire, of devotion, of fear, of *dreams*—never located the formulaic roots of art and religion, the power to remake in flesh myths most sacred and profane!"

The Comte stood over Svenson, his mouth a grimace, as if he were angry for having spoken so intimately to such a person. He cleared his throat and went on, his words returned to their customary coldness.

"You asked why I waited to expose you. You will have overheard certain disagreements amongst my allies—questions for which I would have answers . . . without necessarily sharing them. You may speak willingly, or with the aid of Angelique—but speak to me you will."

"I don't know anything," spat Svenson. "I was at Tarr Manor—I am outside your Harschmort intrigues—"

The Comte ignored him, idly fingering the knobs on his metal implement as it lay next to Lydia's pale leg.

"When we spoke in my greenhouse, your Prince had been taken from you. At that time neither you nor I knew how or by whom."

"It was the Contessa," said Svenson, "in the airship—"

"Yes, I *know.* I want to know *why.*"

"Surely she gave you an explanation!"

"Perhaps she did . . . perhaps not . . ."

"The falling-out of thieves," sneered the Doctor. "And the two of you seemed such *particular* friends—"

The Prince stepped forward and boxed Svenson's ear.

"You will not speak so to your betters!" he announced, as if he were making polite conversation, then snorted with satisfaction. Svenson looked up at the Prince, his face hot with scorn, but his words were still for the Comte.

"I cannot know, of course—I merely, as you say, *deduce.* The Prince was taken mere hours after I had rescued him from the Institute. You—and others—were not told. Obviously she wanted the Prince for her own ends. What is the Prince to your plans? A dupe, a pawn, a void in the seat of power—"

"Why, you damned ungrateful rogue!" cried the Prince. "The *audacity*!"

"To some this might seem obvious," said the Comte, impatiently.

"Then I should think the answer obvious as well," scoffed Svenson. "Everyone undergoing the Process is instilled with a control-phrase, are they not? Quite by accident the Prince was taken by me before any particular commands could be given to him—the Contessa, knowing that, and knowing the Prince's character would predispose everyone to think of him as an imbecile, seized the opportunity to instill within his mind commands of her own, to be invoked at the proper time against her putative allies—something unexpected, such as, let us say, pushing you out of an airship. Of course, when asked, the Prince will remember none of it."

The Comte was silent. Miss Temple was amazed at the Doctor's presence of mind.

"As I say... fairly obvious," sniffed Svenson.

"Perhaps... it is your own fabrication... yet credible enough that I must waste time scouring the memory of the Prince. But before that, Doctor—for I think you are lying—I will first scour *you.* Angelique?"

Svenson leapt to his feet with a cry, but the cry was cut to a savage choking bark as Angelique's mind penetrated his. Chang burst forth from the stairwell, running forward, Miss Temple right behind him. Svenson was on his knees holding his face, the Prince above him, raising a boot to kick the Doctor's head. To the side stood Angelique. The Prince looked up at them with a confused resentment at being interrupted. The Comte wrenched his attention from Svenson's mind with a roar. Angelique turned, a little too slowly, and Miss Temple raised the revolver. She was perhaps ten feet distant when she pulled the trigger.

The shot smashed into the glass woman's outstretched arm at the elbow, shearing through with a spray of bright shards and dropping the forearm and hand to the floor, where they shattered in a plume of indigo smoke. Miss Temple saw Angelique's mouth open wide but heard the scream within her mind, indiscriminately flaying the thoughts of every person in the room. Miss Temple fell to her knees, tears in her eyes, and fired again. The bullet pierced the cuirass of Angelique's torso, starring the surface. Miss Temple kept squeezing the trigger, each hole driving the cracks deeper, lancing into each other to form fissures—the scream redoubled and Miss Temple could not move, could barely see, flooded with random memories stabbing her mind like daggers—Angelique as a child at sea, the rank perfume of the brothel, silks and champagne, tears, beatings, bruises, distant embraces, and a piercingly tender hope, more than anything, that her desperate dreams had come true. Before Miss Temple's eyes the torso split wide below the ribs and gave, the upper body breaking against the lower in a cloud of indigo smoke and glimmering deadly dust, the pieces smashing apart as they struck the stone.

Miss Temple could not tell whether the silence was due to a shared inability to speak, or if the scream had made her deaf. Her head swam with the fumes in the air and she put a hand before her mouth, wondering if she'd already inhaled blue glass dust. The steaming ruins of Angelique lay scattered across the floor, blue shards in an indigo pool. She looked up and blinked. Chang lay with his back against the wall, staring. Svenson was on his hands and knees, groping to crawl free. Lydia was on the bed, whimpering and pulling at her ropes. The Prince lay on the ground near Svenson, hissing with pain and swatting feebly at his hand, where a splinter of glass cut open a patch of skin that had since turned blue. The Comte alone still stood, his face pale as ash.

Miss Temple turned the pistol toward him and pulled the trigger. The bullet shattered the chemical works on his table, spraying more glass and spattering his apron with steaming liquid. The sound woke the room. The Comte surged forward and swept up his metal implement from the bed, raising it up like a mace. Miss Temple aimed another shot at his head, but before she could fire felt Chang seize her arm. She grunted with surprise—his grip was painful—and saw that with his other hand he held Svenson's collar, pulling them both to the door with all his fading strength. She looked back at the Comte, who despite his rage took care to step around the sea of broken glass, and did her best to aim. Svenson got his feet beneath them as they reached the door but Chang did not let him go. Miss Temple extended her arm to fire, but Chang yanked her back and into the corridor.

"I must kill him!" she cried.

"You are out of bullets!" Chang hissed. "If you pull the trigger he will know!"

They'd not gone two more steps before the Doctor turned, struggling against Chang's grip.

"The Prince—he must die—"

"We've done enough—" Chang pulled them both forward, his voice thick, coughing with the effort.

"They will be married—"

"The Comte is formidable—we are unarmed and weak. If we fight him one of us—at least—will die." Chang could barely talk. "We have more to accomplish—and if we stop the others, we stop your idiot Prince. Remember Mrs. Dujong."

"But the Comte—" said Miss Temple, looking behind her for pursuit.

"Cannot chase us alone—he must secure the Prince and Lydia." Chang cleared his throat with a groan and spat past Svenson. "Besides . . . the Comte's vanity has been . . . *wounded* . . ."

His voice was raw. Miss Temple risked a glance, now finally running with the others on her own two feet, and saw with a piercing dismay the line of tears beneath Chang's glasses, and heard the terrible sobs within his heaving breath. She wiped at her own face and did her best to keep up.

They reached the stairwell and closed the door behind them. Chang leaned against it, his hands on his knees, and surrendered to another bout of coughing. Svenson looked at him with concern, his hand on Chang's shoulder for comfort. He looked up at Miss Temple.

"You did very well, Celeste."

"No more than anyone," she answered, a bit pointedly. She did not want to speak of herself in the presence of Chang's distress.

"That is true."

Miss Temple shivered.

"Her thoughts . . . at the end, in my mind . . ."

"She was cruelly used," said Svenson, "by the Comte . . . and by the world. No one should undergo such horror."

But Miss Temple knew the true horror for Angelique had not been transformation, but her untimely death, and her terrible silent scream was a protest as primal and as futile as the last cry of a sparrow taken by the hawk. Miss Temple had never been in the presence, been *possessed* by such fear—held tight to the very brink of death—and she wondered if she would die the same horrible way when it came to it—which it might this very night. She sniffed—or day, she had no idea what time it was. When they'd been outside watching the coaches it had still been dark, and now they were underground. Was it only a day since she'd first met Svenson in the Boniface lobby?

She swallowed and shook the dread from her mind. With a

perhaps characteristic keenness Miss Temple's thoughts shifted from death to breakfast.

"After this is settled," she said, "I should quite enjoy something to eat."

Chang looked up at her. She smiled down at him, doing her level best to withstand the hardness of his face and the black vacuum of his glasses.

"Well... it *has* been some time...," said Svenson politely, as if he were speaking of the weather.

"It will be some while more," managed Chang, hoarsely.

"I'm sure it will," said Miss Temple. "But being as I am *not* made of glass, it seemed like a reasonable topic of conversation."

"Indeed," said Svenson, awkwardly.

"Once this business is settled of course," added Miss Temple.

Chang straightened himself, his face somewhat composed. "We should go," he muttered.

Miss Temple smiled to herself as they climbed, hoping her words had served to distract Chang at least into annoyance, away from his grief. She was well aware that she did not understand what he felt, despite her loss of Roger, for she did not understand the connection between Chang and the woman. What sort of attachment could such *transacted* dealings instill? She was smart enough to see that bargains of some sort ran through most marriages—her own parents were a joining of land and the cash to work it—but for Miss Temple the objects of barter—titles, estates, money, inheritance—were always apart from the bodies involved. The idea of transacting one's own body—that this was the *extent*—involved a bluntness she could not quite comprehend. She wondered what her mother had felt when she herself had been conceived, in that physical union—was it a matter of two bodies (Miss Temple preferred not to speculate about "love" when it came to her savage father), or was each limb bound—as much as Lydia's had been in the laboratory—by a brokered arrangement between families? She looked up at Chang, climbing ahead of her. What did it feel like to be free of such burdens? The freedom of a wild animal?

"We did not see Herr Flaüss on our way out," observed Doctor Svenson. "Perhaps he went with the others."

"And where are they?" asked Miss Temple. "At the airship?"

"I think not," said Svenson. "They will be settling their own disagreements before they can go on—they will be interrogating Lord Vandaariff."

"And perhaps Roger," said Miss Temple, just to show she could say his name without difficulty.

"Which leaves us the choice of finding them or reaching the airship ourselves." Svenson called ahead to Chang. "What say you?"

Chang looked back, wiping his red-flecked mouth, out of breath. "The airship. The Dragoons."

Doctor Svenson nodded. "Smythe."

The house was disturbingly quiet when they reached the main floor.

"Can everyone be gone?" asked Svenson.

"Which way?" rasped Chang.

"It is up—the main stairs are simplest if they are free. I must also suggest, again, that we acquire weapons."

Chang sighed, then nodded with impatience.

"Where?"

"Well—" Svenson clearly had no immediate idea.

"Come with me," said Miss Temple.

Mr. Blenheim had been moved, though the stain on the carpet remained. They took a very brief time, but even then she smiled to see the curiosity and greed on the faces of her two companions as they plundered Robert Vandaariff's trophy chests. For herself, Miss Temple selected another serpentine dagger—the first had served her well—while Chang selected a matching pair of curved, wide-bladed knives with hilts nearly as long as the blade.

"A sort of *machete*," he explained, and she nodded agreeably, having no idea what he meant but happy to see him satisfied. To her amusement, Doctor Svenson pulled an African spear from the wall, and then stuck a jeweled dagger in his belt.

"I am no swordsman," he said, catching her curious expression and Chang's dry smirk. "The farther I keep them from me, the safer I'll remain. None of which makes me feel any less ridiculous—yet if it helps us survive, I will wear a cap and bells." He looked over at Chang. "To the rooftops?"

As they walked to the front stairs, the dagger's unfamiliar weight in her hand, Miss Temple felt a troubling lightness in her breath and a prickling of sweat across her back. What if Captain Smythe did not reject his orders? What if Captain Smythe was not there at all? What if instead of soldiers they were met by the Contessa and Xonck and Crabbé? What must she do? A failure of nerve while she was alone was one thing, but in the company of Chang or Svenson? With every step her breathing quickened and her heart became less sure.

They reached the main foyer, an enormous expanse of black and white marble where Miss Temple had first met the Contessa di Lacquer-Sforza so long ago, now empty and silent save for their own echoing steps. The great doors were closed. Svenson craned his neck to look up the stairs and Miss Temple followed his gaze. From what she could tell, there was not a soul between the ground floor and the top.

Behind them in the house the dead air was split by a gunshot. Miss Temple gasped with surprise. Chang pointed to the far wing.

"Vandaariff's office," he whispered. Svenson opened his mouth but Chang stopped his words with an open hand. Could they have shot Elöise? Another few seconds . . . a door slam from the same direction . . . then distant footsteps.

"They are coming," snapped Chang. "Hurry!"

They were to the third floor when their enemies reached the foyer below. Chang motioned Miss Temple closer to the wall and lowered himself into a crouch. She could hear the Contessa, but not her words. Above, the Doctor groped his way to an unobtrusive door. Miss Temple dashed to meet him, bobbing past him in the doorway and trotting up the narrower steps to where Chang waited. Chang caught her arm and leaned his face close to hers, waiting until the Doctor had caught up to whisper.

"There will be a guard on the other side of the door. It is vital we not harm any Dragoon until we reach Smythe. His men ought to outnumber our other enemies—if we can but get his attention, we have a chance to sway him."

"Then I should be the one who goes," said Miss Temple.

Chang shook his head. "I know him best—"

"Yes, but any Dragoon will take one look at either of you and start swinging. He will not do so to me—giving *me* the time to call for the Captain."

Chang sighed, but Svenson nodded immediately.

"Celeste is right."

"I know she is—but I do not like it." Chang stifled another cough. *"Go!"*

Miss Temple opened the door and stepped through, the dagger tucked into her bodice, and winced at the bitter wind blowing across the rooftop, carrying the sharp salt tang of the sea. A red-jacketed Dragoon stood to either side of the door. Some twenty yards away was the dirigible, hovering ominously, like an unearthly predatory creature, an enormous gasbag dangling a long bright metal cabin, near the size of a sea-ship but all gleaming black metal like a train car. Dragoons were loading boxes into the cabin, handing them up to several black-uniformed Macklenburgers posted at the top of the gangway. Inside the cabin, through a gas-lit window, she saw the sharp-faced Doctor Lorenz, goggles around his neck, busy flipping switches. The rooftop was a hive of activity, but nowhere could she locate Smythe.

It took perhaps another second for the two Dragoons to cry out at her presence and take insistent hold of her arms. She did her best to explain herself above the whipping wind.

"Yes—yes, excuse me—my name is Temple, I am looking—I beg your pardon—I am looking for Captain—"

Before she could finish the one to her right was bawling toward the airship.

"Sir! We've got someone, Sir!"

Miss Temple saw Doctor Lorenz look up through the window, and the shock upon his face. At once he darted from view—no doubt coming down—and she took up the trooper's cry.

"Captain Smythe! I am looking for Captain Smythe!"

Her handlers exchanged a look of confusion. She did her best to exploit it and charge from their grasp but they kept hold, despite her kicking feet. Then, at the top of the gangplank, standing next to each other, appeared the figures of Captain Smythe and Doctor Lorenz. Miss Temple's heart sank. The pair began to walk down—Smythe's face too far away in the dim light to read his expression—when the door behind her slid open and Cardinal Chang laid a blade to the throat of each Dragoon. Miss Temple turned her head—surely this was an unwanted complication—to see Doctor Svenson, spear tucked under his arm, holding the doorknob fast by force.

"They are below us," he whispered.

"Who have we here?" called Doctor Lorenz, in a mocking tone. "Such a persistent strain of vermin. Captain—if you wouldn't mind?"

"Captain Smythe!" shouted Miss Temple. "You know who we are! You know what's been done tonight—you heard them speaking! Your city—your Queen!"

Smythe had not moved, still next to Lorenz on the gangway.

"What are you waiting for?" snapped Lorenz, and he turned to the Dragoons on the rooftop—a band of perhaps a dozen men. "Kill these criminals at once!"

"Captain Smythe," cried Miss Temple, "you have helped us before!"

"What?" Lorenz rounded on Smythe and the Captain, without hesitation, shot out his arm and shoved Doctor Lorenz cleanly off the gangplank to fall with a grinding thud on the graveled rooftop, some ten feet below.

At once Chang whipped back the blades and pulled Miss Temple free. The Dragoons leapt the other way and drew their sabers, facing Chang but glancing at their officer, unsure of what to do. Smythe descended the rest of the way, one hand on his saber hilt.

"I suppose this had to happen," he said.

Doctor Svenson grunted aloud as the door was pulled, testing his grip. He held it closed, but looked anxiously at Chang, who turned to Smythe. Smythe glanced at the top of the ramp, where two confused Macklenburg troopers stood watching. Satisfied they were not going to attack, Smythe called sharply to his men.

"Arms!"

As one the rest of the 4th Dragoons drew their sabers, Svenson let go of the door and leapt to join Miss Temple and Chang.

The door shot open to reveal Francis Xonck, a dagger in his hand. He stepped onto the rooftop, took in the drawn blades and the unguarded status of his enemies.

"Why, Captain Smythe," he drawled, "is something the matter?"

Smythe stepped forward, still not drawing his own blade.

"Who else is with you?" he called. "Bring them out now."

"I would be delighted." Xonck smiled.

He stepped aside to usher through the other members of the Cabal—the Contessa, the Comte, and Crabbé—and after them the Prince, Roger Bascombe (notebooks tucked under his arm), and then, helping the unsteady Lydia Vandaariff, Caroline Stearne. After Caroline came the six functionaries in black, the first four manhandling a heavy trunk, the last two dragging Elöise Dujong between them. Miss Temple breathed a sigh of relief—for she was sure the shot they heard had meant the woman's death. As this crowd spread from the door the Dragoons withdrew, maintaining a strict cushion of space between the two groups. Xonck glanced toward Miss Temple and then stepped out into this borderland to address Smythe.

"Not to repeat myself... but is something *wrong*?"

"This can't go on," said Smythe. He nodded to Elöise and Lydia Vandaariff. "Release those women."

"I beg your pardon?" said Xonck, grinning as if he could not quite believe what he heard, yet found the possibility deeply amusing.

"Release those *women.*"

"Well," Xonck said, smiling at Lydia, "*that* woman does not wish to be released—for she would fall down. She's feeling poorly, you see. Excuse me—have you spoken to your Colonel?"

"Colonel Aspiche is a traitor," announced Smythe.

"To my eyes, the traitor here is *you.*"

"Your eyes are flawed. You are a villain."

"A villain who knows all about your family's debts, Captain," sneered Xonck, "all secured against a salary you may not live to collect—the price of disloyalty, you know, or is it idiocy?"

"If you want to die, Mr. Xonck, say one more word."

Smythe drew his saber and stepped toward Xonck, who retreated, his fixed smile now radiating malice.

Miss Temple groped for her dagger but did not pull it out—the air felt heavy and thick. Surely the Cabal would retreat in the face of Smythe and his men—how could they hope to withstand professional troops? It was clear that Captain Smythe was of the same opinion, for rather than pursuing Xonck, he pointed generally at the crowd around the doorway with his saber.

"Throw down your weapons and return to the house. We will settle this inside."

"That will not happen," answered Xonck.

"I am not looking for bloodshed, but I am not afraid of it," called Smythe, pitching his voice to the others around Xonck—the women particularly. "Throw down your weapons and—"

"It really is not possible, Captain." This was Harald Crabbé. "If we are not in Macklenburg in two days, our entire effort is undone. I do not know what this rabble has told you"—he gestured vaguely to Miss Temple, Svenson, and Chang—"but *I* can tell you they are unscrupulous killers—"

"Where is Mr. Blenheim?" Smythe interrupted Crabbé without care.

"Ah! An excellent question!" cried Crabbé. "Mr. Blenheim has been murdered—and by *that* young woman!"

He pointed an accusing finger at Miss Temple, and she turned her eyes to Smythe, wanting to explain, but before she could get the words from her mouth the Captain tipped his brass helmet toward her in salute. He looked back to the Deputy Minister, whose condemnation clearly had not had the expected result.

"Then she has saved me the trouble—for Mr. Blenheim murdered one of my men," answered Smythe, and then he bawled at them with a harshness of command that made Miss Temple jump. "Put *down* your weapons! Get *back* in the house! Your effort is *undone* as of this minute!"

The crack of the pistol echoed flatly from the roof into the open air, the sound somehow less intrusive than the impact of its bullet, which spun Captain Smythe and knocked him forward to his knees, his helmet bouncing from his head. Miss Temple spun to see Doctor Lorenz, a smoking revolver in his hand, standing underneath the gangway. Without an instant's hesitation Xonck strode forward and landed a sweeping kick on the Captain's jaw, knocking him sprawling on his back. He turned back to the men behind and screamed aloud, his eyes disturbingly bright.

"Kill them!"

The rooftop exploded into mayhem. Lorenz fired again, bringing down the nearest Dragoon. The two Macklenburg troopers clattered down the gangplank, sabers drawn, with a clotted German war cry. The men in black dashed forward after Xonck, cudgels raised, some with pistols, snapping off shots where they could. The Dragoons, stunned by the attack on their officer and taken wholly wrong-footed, finally leapt to their own ragged defense. Blades swung wickedly through the air and errant bullets whipped past Miss Temple's ears. She fumbled for the dagger at the same time Chang seized her shoulder and thrust her toward the airship. She caught her footing and turned to see Chang parry a cudgel with one of his blades and bring the other down deep into the shoulder joint of one of the black-coated men.

He turned to her and shouted, *"Cut the ropes!"*

Of course! If she could shear through the cables, the craft would rise by itself, drifting derelict across the sea—there was no way they could reach Macklenburg inside two *weeks*! She dashed to the nearest mooring and dropped to her knees, sawing away with the dagger. The cable was thick hemp, black and clotted with tar, but the blade was sharp and soon clumps were twisting away, the gap she opened straining wider as the weight of the airship exerted its pull. She looked up, tossing the curls from her eyes, and gasped aloud at the hellish bloody confusion.

Chang fought one of the Macklenburgers, trying without success to work his shorter blades past the much longer saber. Xonck's face was spattered in blood as—now with a saber—he traded vicious blows with a Dragoon. Doctor Svenson waved his spear like a madman, keeping his assailant at bay. Then Miss Temple's eye was drawn to the Comte... and the flickering flash of blue beneath his arm. The Dragoon facing Xonck stumbled and his blade arm sagged, as if it had suddenly become too heavy. In an instant Xonck's blade flashed forward. A second Dragoon abruptly dropped to his knees—only to take a bullet from Doctor Lorenz. Miss Poole stood in the door, shrouded in her cloak, overwhelming the Dragoons one at a time on the Comte's instruction. Miss Temple screamed for help and desperately sawed at the cable.

"Cardinal Chang! Cardinal Chang!"

Chang did not hear, still dueling with the German soldier and fighting for his life—his cough piercing through the din. Another man went down, dispatched by Xonck. The remaining Dragoons saw what was happening and charged the knot of figures at the door, cutting down two more of the black-coated men in their way. At once the Cabal scattered—Crabbé and Roger stumbling into Caroline and Elöise, the Contessa screaming at Xonck, the Prince and Lydia dropping to their knees, hands over their heads, and the Comte thrusting Miss Poole forward to stop the attack. The Dragoons—perhaps six men—tottered in place, like saplings in the wind. Xonck stepped forward and hacked the nearest man across the neck. There was no stopping him—she had never seen such dispassionate savagery in her life.

Miss Temple's attention caught a swirl of movement at the corner of her eye. An instant later she was facedown on the gravel, shaking her head, blinking her eyes, and feeling for the dagger. She pushed herself up to her elbows, completely dazed, realizing that the concussive impact had burst within her mind. Like an answered prayer she saw Doctor Svenson's ridiculous spear sticking out from Miss Poole's back, pinning her to the wooden door. The stricken woman—creature—struggled like a fish in the air, but each twisting movement only worsened the damage. With a snapping lurch she stumbled and the pole ripped up several inches to her shoulder. Her breaking body was still hidden beneath the cloak and Miss Temple could only see her arching neck and snapping mouth—the Comte helplessly trying to still her movement to preserve her, but she would not or could not heed him. With a final crack she fell again. The spear tore from her body altogether, splitting her collapsing torso as she fell, jumbled on the ground like a broken toy.

* * *

Across the rooftop stunned faces groped for comprehension, for Miss Poole's silent screaming had battered them all, but the lull did not last, with Xonck and one of the Macklenburg men hurling themselves at the remaining Dragoons, Chang slashing away at his own opponent, and, most strangely, Roger Bascombe running to tackle Doctor Svenson. Miss Temple leapt back to her task, gripping the dagger with both hands.

The cable gave without warning, knocking her back on her seat. She scrambled up and ran at the other cable—but the suddenly tilting airship and careening gangway had alerted the others to her effort. She saw Lorenz take aim and, before she could do a thing, fire—but his gun was empty! He swore and broke it open, knocking out the empty shells and digging for fresh bullets in his coat. A Dragoon loomed up at Lorenz from behind, but Lorenz noticed her look and spun, firing the two shots he'd loaded straight into the soldier's chest. He snarled with satisfaction and wheeled back to Miss Temple, rushing again to reload. She did not know what to do. She sawed at the cable.

Lorenz watched her as he deliberately slotted in new shells. He glanced over his shoulder. Xonck had killed another Dragoon—there were only three left on their feet—one running for Xonck, the others charging the Cabal. Svenson and Roger were a kicking knot of bodies on the ground. The cable was coming apart. She looked up at Lorenz. He inserted the final bullet and slapped the pistol closed. He pulled back the hammer and aimed, striding toward her.

She threw the dagger, end over end—she had seen this done at carnivals—directly at his face. Lorenz flinched and fired the gun harmlessly, squawking as the dagger hilt caught his ear. Miss Temple ran the other way as she threw, back to the others. Another shot cracked out behind her, but she was small and dodging to each side, fervently hoping Lorenz was less interested in shooting a woman than protecting the cable.

* * *

Chang wheezed on one knee over the fallen Macklenburg trooper, Svenson held off Roger with his jeweled dagger, Xonck stood, his boot on the neck of a struggling Dragoon, and near the door were the two Dragoons who had charged the Cabal—one with his arm around the Contessa's neck holding off the Comte and the Prince. The other stood between Elöise and Caroline Stearne, both on their knees. Neither Macklenburger nor any man in black was visible. Everyone was out of breath, panting clouds in the cold air, and all around the fallen groaned. She tried to locate Smythe in the carnage but could not—either he had moved or was covered with another body. Miss Temple felt herself near tears, for she had not accomplished her task, but then saw the relief on Chang's face—and then as he too turned, on Svenson's—simply to see her still alive.

"What do you say, Sir?" called out Doctor Lorenz. "Should I shoot the girl or the men?"

"Or should I step on this man's neck," responded Xonck, as if the Dragoons by the door did not exist. "Issues of etiquette are always so *difficult*... my dear Contessa, what would *you* suggest?"

The Contessa answered with a shrug toward the Dragoon who seemed to hold her fast. "Well, Francis, ... I agree it *is* difficult..."

"Damned shame about Elspeth."

"My thoughts exactly—I must admit to underestimating Doctor Svenson once again."

"It cannot work," called out Chang, his voice hoarse with exertion. "If you kill that man—or if Lorenz shoots us—these Dragoons will not scruple to kill the Contessa and the Comte. You must retreat."

"Retreat?" scoffed Xonck. "From you, Cardinal, this comes as a shock—or perhaps it is merely the perspective of a ruffian. I've always doubted your courage, man to man."

Chang spat painfully. "You can doubt what you like, you insufferable, worm-rotted—"

Doctor Svenson cut him off, stepping forward. "A great number of these men will die if they are not helped—your men as well as ours—"

Xonck ignored them both, calling out to the two Dragoons. "Release her, and you'll live. It is your only chance."

They did not answer, so Xonck bore down his foot on the fallen man's throat, driving out a protesting rattle like air from a balloon.

"It is your choice . . . ," he taunted them. Still they did not move. At once he wheeled and called to Lorenz. "Shoot someone—whomever you please."

"You're being stupid!" shouted Svenson. "No one need die!"

"Reason not the *need,* Doctor." Xonck chuckled, and he very deliberately crushed the man's windpipe beneath his boot.

In a blur of movement the Contessa's hand flew across the face of the Dragoon who held her, its pathway marked by a spurting line of blood—once more she wore her metal spike. Xonck hacked at the final stunned trooper, who could only parry the blow and then disappear beneath a crush of bodies as Caroline Stearne kicked his knee from behind, and the Comte himself grappled his sword arm. At once Miss Temple felt strong arms take hold of her waist and lift her off the ground. Chang flung her in the air toward the gangway, high enough to land on top of it. Lorenz's pistol cracked once, the bullet whistling past.

"Go on—go on!" shouted Chang, and Miss Temple did, realizing the airship held their only possible refuge. Again she was bundled up by stronger arms, this time it was Svenson, as she plunged into the cabin. He thrust her forward and wheeled to pull up Chang—bullets sending splinters of woodwork through the air. She raced ahead through one doorway and another, and then a third which was a dead end. She turned with a cry, the others colliding into her, and was knocked off her feet into a cabinet. With a desperate coordination Chang slammed the door and Svenson shot the bolt.

Somehow they had survived the battle, only to be imprisoned.

* * *

Miss Temple, on the floor, out of breath, face streaked with sweat and tears, gazed up at Svenson and Chang. It was hard to say which of them looked worse, for though his exertions had brought fresh blood to Chang's mouth and nose, the Doctor's glistening pallor was abetted by the utterly stricken cast of his eyes.

"We have left Elöise," he whispered. "She will be killed—"

"Is anyone injured?" asked Chang, cutting the Doctor off. "Celeste?"

Miss Temple shook her head, unable to speak, her thoughts seared by the savage acts she'd just witnessed. Could war possibly be worse? She squeezed shut her eyes as, unbidden, her mind recalled the grinding gasping crush of Francis Xonck bringing down his boot. She sobbed aloud and, ashamed, stuffed a fist in her mouth and turned away, her tears flowing openly.

"Get away from the door," muttered Chang hoarsely, shifting Svenson to the side. "They may shoot out the lock."

"We are trapped like rats," said Svenson. He looked at the dagger in his hand, useless and small. "Captain Smythe—all his men—*all* of them—"

"And Elspeth Poole," replied Chang, doing his best to speak clearly. "And their lackeys, and the two Germans—our position could be worse—"

"Worse?" barked Svenson.

"We are not yet dead, Doctor," said Chang, though his drawn, bloody face would not have seemed out of place in a graveyard.

"Neither is the Prince! Nor the Comte, nor the Contessa, nor that animal Xonck—"

"I did not cut the ropes," sniffed Miss Temple.

"Be *quiet*—the pair of you!" hissed Chang.

Miss Temple's eyes flashed—for even in these straits she did not appreciate his tone—but the Cardinal was not angry. Instead, his mouth was grim.

"You did not cut the ropes, Celeste. But you did your best. Did

I kill Xonck? No—as pathetic as it sounds, it was all I could do to bring down one Macklenburg farmboy swinging an oversized cabbage-cutter. Did the Doctor save Elöise? No—but he preserved all of our lives—and hers—by destroying Miss Poole. Our enemies on the other side of this door—and we must assume they all are here—are less in number than they would have been, less confident, and just as unhappy—for *we* are not dead either."

That he followed this speech with a wrenching, racking cough, bent with his head between his knees, did not prevent Miss Temple from wiping her nose on her sleeve and brushing the loosened curls from her eyes. She sniffed and whispered to Doctor Svenson.

"We will save her—we have done it before."

He had no answer, but wiped his own eyes with his thumb and forefinger—any lack of outright scoffing she read as agreement. She pushed herself to her feet and sighed briskly.

"Well, then—"

Miss Temple grabbed at the cabinet to avoid falling back to the floor, squeaking with surprise as the entire cabin swung to the left and then back again with a dizzying swiftness.

"We are going up . . . ," said Svenson.

Miss Temple pushed herself to the one window, round like the porthole of a ship, and peered down, but already the roof of Harschmort House receded below her. Within seconds they were in dark fog, the rooftop and the brightly lit house swallowed up in the gloom below. With a brusque sputtering series of bangs the propellers sparked into life and the craft's motion changed again, pushing forward and steadying the side to side rocking, the low hum of the motors creating a vibration Miss Temple could feel through her hands on the cabinet and the soles of her boots on the floor.

"Well," she said, "it looks as if we shall visit Macklenburg after all."

"Unless they throw us into the sea on the way," observed the Doctor.

"Ah," said Miss Temple.

"Still wanting your breakfast?" muttered Chang.

She turned to glare at him—it not being a fair thing to say at all—when they were interrupted by a gentle knock at the door. She looked at both men, but neither spoke. She sighed, and called out as casually as she could.

"Yes?"

"Miss Temple? It is Minister Crabbé. I am wondering if you might open this door and join our conversation."

"What conversation is that?" she answered.

"Why, it is the one where we decide your lives, my dear. It would be better had not through a door."

"I am afraid we find the door *convenient,*" replied Miss Temple.

"Perhaps . . . yet I am forced to point out that Mrs. Dujong does not share your *partition.* Further, while I would prefer to avoid unpleasantness, the door *is* made of wood, and its lock must be subject to the force of bullets—it is in fact an *illusory* convenience. Surely there is much to discuss between us all—need this excellent oak panel be ruined for a conclusion you cannot dispute?"

Miss Temple turned to her companions. Svenson looked past her to the cabinet she leaned against. He stepped across and forced it open with a quick prying thrust of his dagger under its lock, but inside was merely a collection of blankets, ropes, candles, woolen coats, and a box of hats and gloves. He turned back to Chang, who leaned against the doorframe and shrugged.

"We cannot go out the window," Svenson said.

"You have the only weapon," said Chang, nodding to the Doctor's dagger, for he had dropped his own to throw Miss Temple on the gangway, "perhaps it were best stowed away."

"I agree, but surely by you."

Svenson passed the blade to Chang, who stuffed it in his coat. The Doctor reached for Miss Temple's hand, squeezed it once, and nodded to Chang, who unlocked the door.

* * *

The next room was the largest of the three in the dirigible's cabin, and was ringed with cabinets and inset settees, now occupied by the various members of the Cabal, all watching their entrance quite closely. On one side sat the Prince, Harald Crabbé, and Roger Bascombe, on the other the Comte, the Contessa, and in the far doorway, a saber in his hand, blood spoiling his once-white shirt, stood Francis Xonck. Beyond him lurked other figures and movement, and Miss Temple tried to deduce who was missing. Had more of them been brought down in the final struggle? Her questions were answered a moment later by the appearance of Lydia Vandaariff, changed from her robes to a brilliant blue silk dress, bobbing under Xonck's arm and stepping—still unsteadily—toward the Prince, prompting Roger to leave his place to make room. Emerging directly after Lydia—no doubt helping with her stays—was the ever-attentive Caroline Stearne, who slipped to an empty seat next to the Comte.

"I assume Doctor Lorenz pilots our craft?" asked Chang.

"He does," answered Harald Crabbé.

"Where is Mrs. Dujong?" asked Doctor Svenson.

Xonck nodded vaguely to the room behind him. "She is quite secure... something of a return to form, I'm told."

Svenson did not reply. Aside from Xonck, no one brandished any weapon—though, given Xonck's prowess and the small size of the room, Miss Temple doubted whether anyone else *needed* one. Yet if their immediate dispatch was not their enemies' intent, Miss Temple was mystified as to what their plan then was.

At the same time, simply where they sat revealed divisions among them: on one side Crabbé and Roger, and under their arm the Prince (though the Prince would go with whoever was ascendant), and on the other the Comte and Contessa, with Caroline under their sway (though how much she counted, Miss Temple had no clue—did she, Lorenz, and Roger make up a second tier of the Cabal, or were they simply three more drones of the

Process?)—and then in the middle and unallied to either, Francis Xonck, his capacity for slaughter quite balancing, especially in these close quarters, the cunning of Crabbé, the knowledge of the Comte, and the provocative charm of the Contessa.

Crabbé looked across to the Contessa and raised his eyebrows in question. She nodded in agreement—or did she grant permission?—and Crabbé cleared his throat. He indicated a cabinet next to Mrs. Stearne.

"Before we start, would any of you care for some refreshment? You must be tired—I know *I* am tired, and the mere sight of you three—well, it amazes that you can *stand*. Caroline can get it—there is whisky, brandy, water—"

"If *you* are drinking," said Chang, "by all means."

"Excellent—of course, drinks all round—and my apologies, Caroline, for turning you into a barmaid—Roger, perhaps you will assist. Perhaps for simplicity it can be brandy for everyone."

There followed an awkward near silence where by tacit agreement all conversation paused until the business of pouring and handing out glasses was accomplished. Miss Temple watched Roger step to Chang and Svenson with a glass in each hand, his face a mask of professional diffidence that never once glanced her way. Her study was broken by Caroline's touch on her arm, as she was offered her own glass. Miss Temple shook her head, but Caroline pressed the glass hard into her hand, leaving Miss Temple the choice to hold on or let it drop. She looked down at the amber liquid and sniffed, detecting the familiar biting scent she associated with so much that was tiresome and foul.

The entire scene was strange—especially following the rooftop carnage, for she had braced herself for a second deadly struggle, yet here they stood, as sociably arrayed as any dinner party—save the men and women were drinking together—and all of it so patently false that Miss Temple narrowed her eyes. With an audible snort she set her glass on a nearby shelf and wiped her hands.

"Miss Temple?" asked Crabbé. "Would you prefer something else?"

"I would prefer you state your business. If Mr. Xonck will kill us, then let him try."

"Such *impatience.*" Crabbé smiled, unctuous and knowing. "We will do our best to satisfy. But first, I give you all the Prince of Macklenburg and his bride!"

He raised his glass and tossed off the contents, as the others followed suit amidst mutters of "the Prince!" and "Lydia!" The Prince smiled heartily and Lydia grinned, her small white teeth showing over her glass as she too drank, but then erupted into a fit of coughing to rival Cardinal Chang. The Prince patted her shoulder as she strove to breathe, her stomach now heaving unpleasantly with the stress. Roger stepped forward and offered a handkerchief, which the young lady hurriedly snatched and held before her mouth, spitting into it wetly. The fit finally subsided and, face pale and out of breath, Lydia returned the cloth to Roger with an attempt at a smile. Roger deftly refolded the handkerchief before returning it to his pocket... but not before Miss Temple noticed the fresh, brilliant blue stain.

"Are you quite well, my dear?" asked the Prince.

Before Lydia could speak, Chang threw back his glass and gargled loudly before swallowing the brandy. Doctor Svenson poured his glass on the floor. Crabbé took all this in and exhaled sadly.

"Ah well... one cannot always please. Caroline?" Mrs. Stearne collected their glasses. Crabbé cleared his throat and gestured vaguely at the room around them.

"So we begin."

"Through your determined efforts at *destruction,* we are no longer able to easily determine what you know of our plans, or in whom you might have confided. Mrs. Marchmoor is well on her way to the city, Angelique and poor Elspeth are no more." He held up his hand. "Please know that *I* am speaking to you as the one most able to control my rage—if it were any of my associates, a recitation of even these facts would result in your immediate deaths. While it is true we could subject you to the Process, or distill your memories within a book, both of these endeavors demand time we do not have, and facilities beyond this craft. It is also true we could do both these things upon arrival in Macklenburg, yet our need for your knowledge cannot wait. Upon arrival we must know where we stand, and if... within our ranks... there is a Judas."

He held out his glass to Roger for more brandy, and continued speaking as it was poured.

"This latest confrontation on the rooftop—wasteful and distressing, I trust, to *all*—only reinforces our earlier decision that we would have been best served with your talents incorporated to our cause—via the Process. Thank you, Roger." Crabbé drank. "Do not bother to protest—we no longer expect any such conversions, nor—given the grief you have inflicted—would they now be accepted. The situation could not be clearer. We hold Mrs. Dujong. You will answer our questions or she will die—and I'm sure you can imagine the sort of death I mean, the time it will take, and how distressing such prolonged screams will be in such an enclosed place as this. And if she does manage to expire, then we shall merely move on to one of you—Miss Temple, perhaps—and on and on. It is inevitable as the dawn. As you have opened that door to avoid its being needlessly broken, I offer you the chance to avoid that same breaking of your comrades' bodies—and, indeed, their souls."

Miss Temple looked at the faces opposite her—Crabbé's smug smirk, the Prince's bemused disdain, Lydia's fox-faced hunger, Roger's earnest frown, Xonck's leer, the Comte's iron glare, the Contessa's glacial smile, and Caroline's sad patience—and found nowhere a suggestion that the Minister's words were anything but true. Yet she still saw the factions between them and knew their deeper interest lay no longer in what she and the others had discovered, but only in how those discoveries spelled out betrayals within the Cabal's circle.

"It would be easier to believe you, Sir," she said, "if you did not so blatantly *lie*. You ask us to talk to prevent our torture, yet what happens when we reveal some morsel of deduction that points to one among you—do you expect that person to accept our open word? Of course not—whoever is denounced will demand that your cruelties be brought to bear in *any* case, to confirm or disprove our accusations!"

The Deputy Minister's eyes twinkled as he shook his head, chuckling, and took another sip of brandy.

"My goodness—Roger, I do believe she *is* more than you'd perceived—Miss Temple, you have caught me out. Indeed, it is the case—so much for my attempts to save the woodwork! All right then—you will, all four, be killed at length, quite badly. If any of you have something to say, all the better—if not, well, we're rid of your damned stinking disruptions at last."

Xonck stepped forward, the saber dancing menacingly in the air before him. Miss Temple retreated, but a single step brought her flat against the wall. Once more the Doctor squeezed her hand, and then cried out in as hearty a voice as he could.

"Excellent, Minister—and perhaps Mr. Xonck will kill us *before* we talk—would that suit you even better?"

Crabbé stood up, impatient and angry. "Ah—here it comes! The vain attempt to turn us against one another—Francis—"

"By all means, *Francis*—kill us quickly! Serve the Minister as you always have! Just as when you sank Trapping in the river!"

Xonck paused, the tip of his blade within lunging range of Svenson's chest. "I serve *myself*."

Svenson looked down at the saber tip and snorted—even as Miss Temple could feel the trembling of his hand. "Of course you do—just pardon my asking—what has happened to Herr Flaüss?"

For a moment, no one answered, and Crabbé was glaring at Xonck to *keep going* when the Contessa spoke aloud, picking her words carefully.

"Herr Flaüss was found to be . . . disloyal."

"The gunshot!" exclaimed Miss Temple. "You shot *him*!"

"It proved necessary," said Crabbé.

"How could he be disloyal?" croaked Chang. "He was your creature!"

"Why do you *ask*?" the Contessa pointedly demanded of the Doctor.

"Why do you *care*?" hissed Crabbé to her, behind Xonck's back. "Francis, *please*—"

"I just wonder if it had to do with Lord Vandaariff's missing *book*," said Svenson. "You know—the one where his memory was—what is the word?—*distilled*?"

There was a pause. Miss Temple's heart was in her mouth—and then she knew the momentum toward their destruction had been stalled.

"That book was broken," rasped the Comte. "By Cardinal Chang in the tower—it killed Major Blach—"

"Is that what his *ledger* says?" Svenson nodded contemptuously to Roger. "Then I think you will find *two* books missing—one with the Lady Mélantes, Mrs. Marchmoor, among others—and another—"

"What are you waiting for?" cried Crabbé. "Francis! Kill him!"

"Or you *would*," crowed Svenson, "if there was a second book at all! For to distill Robert Vandaariff's mind into a book—a mind holding the keys to a continent—to the future itself!—would have opened those riches to any one of you who owned it, who possessed a *key*! Instead, the man given the task to do just that did *not* create a book—so yes, there is one book broken, and another never made *at all*!"

The Contessa called out firmly to Xonck—"Francis, keep watching them!"—before turning to Crabbé. "Harald, can you answer this?"

"*Answer?* Answer *what*? Answer the—the desperate—the—"

Before the Minister could stop sputtering Chang called out again, a challenge to Roger. "I saw it myself, in Vandaariff's study—he wrote it all down on parchment! If I hadn't smashed a book they would have had to do it themselves—convincing you all that Vandaariff's memories were gone, when *they* held the only copy!"

"A copy I took from the Minister himself," cried Svenson, "in a leather satchel—and which Bascombe took from me in the ballroom. I'm sure he still has it with him—or is that what Flaüss noticed when he joined you at Lord Vandaariff's study . . . and why he had to die?"

In the silence Miss Temple realized she had been holding her breath. The words had flown so quickly back and forth, while in between stood Francis Xonck, eyes shifting warily, his blade an easy thrust from them all. She could feel the fearful state of Svenson's nerves, and knew Chang was tensed to futilely spring at Xonck—but she could also sense the changing tension in the room, as the Minister and Roger groped to refute their own prisoners.

"Aspiche took the satchel from Svenson in the ballroom," announced Xonck, not turning to the others. "And Bascombe took it from him . . . but I did not see it when we met up in the study."

"It was packed away," said Caroline Stearne, speaking quietly from her place. "When all was being readied for the journey—"

"Is the satchel here or isn't it?" snapped Xonck.

"I have its contents with me," said Roger smoothly. "As Caroline says, safely stowed. Doctor Svenson is wrong. They are Lord Vandaariff's planning papers—notes to himself for each stage of this enterprise. I do not know where this idea of Lady Mélantes's book comes from—*two* books—*no* books—"

"Doctor Lorenz identified the missing book as Lady Mélantes's," spat Svenson.

"Doctor Lorenz is *wrong*. Lady Mélantes's book—also containing Mrs. Marchmoor and Lord Acton—is safely stowed. The only book missing—the one broken in the tower—is that of Lord

Vandaariff. You can check my ledger, but anyone is more than welcome to look in the books themselves."

It was an effective speech, with just the right amount of protest at being accused and an equally moving touch of professional superciliousness—a Bascombe specialty. And it seemed as if his upset superiors, perhaps persuaded by his own subservience via the Process, were convinced. But Miss Temple knew, from the way Roger's thumb restlessly rubbed against his leg, that it was a lie.

She laughed at him.

He glared at her, furiously willing her to silence.

"O *Roger*..." She chuckled and shook her head.

"Be quiet, Celeste!" he hissed. "You have no place here!"

"And you have surely convinced everyone," she said. "But you forget how well I know your ways. Even then you might have convinced me—for it *was* a fine speech—if it wasn't you who actually shot Herr Flaüss, after *convincing* everyone of his disloyalty, I am sure... or was it to keep him quiet? But it *was* you who shot him, Roger, ... wasn't it?"

At her words the cabin went silent, save for the low buzz of the rotors outside. Xonck's saber did not waver, but his mouth tightened and his eyes flicked more quickly back and forth between them. The Contessa stood.

"Rosamonde," began Crabbé, "this is ridiculous—they are coming between us—it is their only hope—"

But the Contessa ignored him and crossed the cabin slowly toward Roger. He shrank away from her, first striking the wall and then seeming to retreat within his own body, meeting her gaze but flinching, for her eyes were empty of affection.

"Rosamonde," rasped the Comte. "If we question him together—"

But then the Contessa darted forward, sharp as a striking cobra, to whisper in Roger's ear. Miss Temple could only catch the odd word, but when she heard the first—"blue"—she knew the

Contessa was whispering Roger's own control phrase, and that by speaking it before any of the others, the woman had made sure Roger must answer her questions alone. The Contessa stepped away and Roger sank down to sit on the floor, his expression empty and his eyes dulled.

"Rosamonde—" Crabbé tried again, but again the Contessa ignored him, speaking crisply down to Roger, his head at the level of her thighs.

"Roger . . . is what Doctor Svenson tells us true?"

"Yes."

Before Crabbé could speak the Contessa pressed Roger again.

"Were Lord Robert's memories distilled into a book?"

"No."

"They were written down."

"Yes."

"And those papers are on board?"

"Yes. I transferred them to the Prince's bag to hide them. Flaüss insisted on managing the Prince's bag and realized what they were."

"So you shot him."

"Yes."

"And in all of this, Roger, . . . whom did you serve? Who gave the orders?"

"Deputy Minister Crabbé."

Crabbé said nothing, his mouth open in shock, his face drained of any color. He looked helplessly to the Comte, to Xonck, but could not speak. Still facing Roger, the Contessa called behind her.

"Caroline, would you be kind enough to ask Doctor Lorenz exactly where we are on our route?"

Caroline, whose gaze had been fixed on Roger Bascombe's slumped form, looked up with surprise, stood at once, and left the cabin.

"I say," muttered the Prince, aggrieved. "He put those papers in *my* bag? And shot my man because of it? Damn you, Crabbé!

Damn your damned insolence!" Lydia Vandaariff patted her fiancé's knee.

"Your Highness," hissed Crabbé urgently, "Bascombe is not telling the truth—I do not know how—it could be any of you! Anyone with his control phrase! Anyone could order him to answer these questions—to implicate me—"

"And how would that person know what these questions were to be?" snarled the Contessa, and then pointed toward the captives. "At least one of them has been provided by Doctor Svenson!"

"For all any of us know, whoever has tampered with Bascombe's mind could be in league with these three!" cried Crabbé. "It would certainly explain their persistent survival!"

The Contessa's eyes went wide at the Deputy Minister's words. "Bascombe's mind! Of course—of course, you sneaking little man! You did not halt the examinations in the ballroom for Lord Robert or the Duke—you did it because Roger was suddenly forced to accompany Vandaariff! Because otherwise the Comte would have seen inside his mind—and seen all of your plotting against us plain as day!" She wheeled to the Comte, and gestured to Bascombe on the floor. "Do not believe *me,* Oskar—ask your own questions, by all means—some questions I will not have *anticipated*! Or you, Francis—help yourself! For myself I am satisfied, but do go on! Roger—you will answer all questions put to you!"

The Comte's face betrayed no particular expression, but Miss Temple knew he was already suspicious of the Contessa and so perhaps was genuinely curious, unsure which—or was it both? Or all?—of his confederates had betrayed him.

"Francis?" he rasped.

"Be my guest." Xonck smiled, not even moving his eyes as he spoke.

The Comte d'Orkancz leaned forward. "Mr. Bascombe, . . . to your knowledge, did Deputy Minister Crabbé have anything to do with the murder of Colonel Arthur Trapping?"

The Contessa spun to the Comte, her expression wary and her violet eyes dauntingly sharp.

"Oskar, why—"

"No," said Roger.

The Comte's next question was interrupted by Caroline Stearne, whose return had brought Doctor Lorenz into the doorway.

"Contessa," she whispered.

"Thank you, Caroline—would you be so good as to fetch the Prince's bag?" Caroline took in the tension of the room, her face pale, bobbed her head once and darted from the cabin. The Contessa turned to Lorenz. "Doctor, how good of you to come—though I do trust *someone* remains at the wheel?"

"Do not trouble yourself, Madame—I have two good men *aloft,*" he answered, smiling at his nautical reference. The Doctor's smile faded as he took in that it was Bascombe on the floor being questioned, and not the prisoners.

"Our position?" the Contessa asked him crisply.

"We are just over the sea," Lorenz replied. "From here, as you know, there are different routes available—remaining over water, where there is less chance of being seen, or crossing straight to shadow the coast. In this fog it may not matter—"

"And how long until we reach Macklenburg proper?" asked the Comte.

"With either route it will be ten hours at the least. More if the wind is against us . . . as it presently is . . ." Lorenz licked his thin lips. "May I ask what is going on?"

"Merely a disagreement between partners," called Xonck, over his shoulder.

"Ah. And may I ask why *they* are still alive?"

The Contessa turned to look at them, her eyes settling at last upon Miss Temple. Her expression was not kind.

"We were waiting for *you,* Doctor. I would not have any bodies found on land. The sea will take them—and if one does happen to wash up on a beach, it will only be after days in the water. By that time even the lovely Miss Temple will be as grey and shapeless as a spoiled milk pudding."

Caroline appeared again, the bag in one hand and a sheaf of papers in the other.

"Madame—"

"Excellent as always, Caroline," said the Contessa. "I am so glad you retain your flesh. Can you read them?"

"Yes, Madame. They are Lord Vandaariff's writings. I recognize his hand."

"And what does he write *about*?"

"I cannot begin—the account is *exhaustive*—"

"I suppose it would be."

"Madame—would it not be better—"

"Thank you, Caroline."

Caroline bobbed her head and remained in the doorway with Lorenz, both of them watching the room with nervous fascination. The Comte frowned darkly, beads of sweat had broken out on Xonck's forehead, and Crabbé's face had gone so pale as to seem bloodless. Only the Contessa smiled, but it was a smile that frightened Miss Temple more than all the others rolled to one, for above her scarlet lips and sharp white teeth the woman's eyes glittered like violet knife-points. She realized that the Contessa was *pleased*, that she looked forward to what would come with the bodily hunger of a mother embracing her child.

The Contessa drifted to Xonck, placing her face next to his.

"What do you think, Francis?" she whispered.

"I think I should like to put down this sword." He laughed. "Or put it *in* someone." His eyes settled on Chang. The Contessa leaned her head against Xonck's, somewhat girlishly.

"That's a very good idea. But I wonder if you have ample room to swing."

"I might like more, it's true."

"Let me see what I can do, Francis."

In a turn as elegant as if she were dancing, the Contessa spun toward Deputy Minister Crabbé, the razor-sharp spike in place across her hand, and drove it like a hammer into the side of his skull, just in front of his ear. Crabbé's eyes popped open and his body jerked at the impact... then went still for the four long seconds it took for his life to fade. He collapsed onto Prince Karl-Horst's lap. The Prince hopped up with a cry and the Deputy Minister bounced forward and onto the cabin floor with a thud.

"And no blood to mop." The Contessa smiled. "Doctor Lorenz, if you would open the forward hatchway? Your Highness? If you might assist Caroline with the Minister's remains?"

She stood, beaming down as they bent over the fallen diplomat, his eyes wide with the shock of his dispatch, doing their awkward best to drag him to where Lorenz knelt in the cabin beyond. On the sofa, Lydia watched the corpse's progress with a groan, her stomach once more heaving. She erupted wetly into her hands and with a disgusted sigh the Contessa shoved a small silk handkerchief at the girl. Lydia snatched it gratefully, a smeared pearl of blue at each corner of her mouth.

"Contessa—" she began, her voice a fearful quaver.

But the Contessa's attention turned at the clicking of a bolt, as Lorenz raised an iron hatchway from the floor. A burst of freezing air shot through the cabin, the grasping paw of winter. Miss Temple looked through at the open hatch and realized that something seemed wrong... the clouds outside... their pallid veneer of light. The round windows in the cabin were covered by green curtains... she had not noticed the dawn.

"It seems we divide the future in ever expanding portions," observed the Contessa. "Equal thirds, gentlemen?"

"Equal thirds," whispered the Comte.

"I am agreeable," said Xonck, a bit tightly.

"Then it's settled," she announced. The Contessa reached out to Xonck's shoulder and gave it a gentle squeeze.

"Finish them."

* * *

The dagger was in Chang's hand and he slashed toward Xonck, catching the saber on the dagger hilt and pushing Xonck's weapon aside as he rushed forward. But Xonck spun on his heels and chopped his bandaged arm across Chang's throat, knocking him backwards to the ground, both men crying with pain at the impact. Doctor Svenson darted for Xonck, a half-step too late, and Xonck whipped the saber hilt up and into Svenson's stomach, dropping the Doctor choking to his knees. Xonck retreated a step and wheeled to Miss Temple, his blade once more extended toward her face. Miss Temple could not move. She looked at Xonck, his chest heaving, wincing at the pain in his arm . . . hesitating.

"Francis?" said the Contessa, her voice glazed with amusement.

"What?" he hissed.

"Are you *waiting* for something?"

Xonck swallowed. "I was wondering if you'd prefer to do *this* one yourself."

"That's very sweet of you . . . but I am quite content to watch."

"I was merely asking."

"And I assure you, I appreciate the thought, as I appreciate that you might also wish to retain Miss Temple for intimate scrutiny . . . but I would appreciate it even more if you would get *on* with it and *stick* her like the vicious little pig she is."

Xonck's fingers flexed around the saber hilt, shifting his grip. Miss Temple saw its merciless tip not two feet from her chest, light rippling along the silver blade as it rose and fell with Xonck's breathing. Then Xonck leered at her. She was going to die.

"First it was the Minister wanting people to get on with it . . . now it's the Contessa," she said. "Of course, *he* had his reasons—"

"Must I do this myself?" asked the Contessa.

"Do not *hound* me, Rosamonde," snapped Xonck.

"But the Comte never finished his questions!" cried Miss Temple.

Xonck did not lunge. She shouted again, her voice rising up to a shriek.

"He asked if the Minister killed Colonel Trapping! He did not ask who *else* might have killed him! If *Roger* killed him! Or if he was killed by the *Contessa*!"

"What?" asked Xonck.

"Francis!" cried the Contessa. She snorted with rage and strode past Xonck to silence Miss Temple herself, the spike raised high. Miss Temple flinched, trembling at whether her throat would be cut or her skull perforated, unable to otherwise move.

Before any of these could occur, Xonck wheeled and hooked the Contessa about the waist with his bandaged arm and swept the woman off her feet and with a shriek of protest onto the nearest settee—exactly the spot where Harald Crabbé had just died.

The Contessa glared with an outrage Miss Temple had never seen in life—a ferocity to peel paint or buckle steel.

"Rosamonde—" began Xonck, and—too late again—Miss Temple darted for Chang's fallen dagger. Xonck slapped the flat of the saber blade hard across her head, sprawling her atop Doctor Svenson, who groaned.

She shook her head, the whole right side stinging. The Contessa still sat on the settee, next to the Prince and Lydia, miserable as children marooned in the midst of their parents' row.

"Rosamonde," said Xonck again, "what does she mean?"

"She means nothing!" the Contessa spat. "Colonel Trapping is no longer important—the Judas was Crabbé!"

"The Comte knows all about it," managed Miss Temple, her voice thick.

"All about what?" asked Xonck, for the first time allowing the saber to drift toward the Comte d'Orkancz, who sat opposite the Contessa.

"He won't say," whispered Miss Temple, "because he no longer knows who to trust. You have to ask *Roger*."

The Comte stood up.

"Sit down, Oskar," said Xonck.

"This has gone far enough," the Comte replied.

"Sit down or I will have your God damned head!" shouted Xonck. The Comte deigned to show actual surprise, and sat, his face now quite as grave as the Contessa's was livid.

"I will not be made a fool," hissed Xonck. "Trapping was my man—mine to discard! Whoever killed him—even if I would prefer not to believe—it follows they are my enemy—"

"Roger Bascombe!" shouted Miss Temple. "Do you know who killed Colonel Trapping?"

With a snarl and three iron-hard fingers of his sword hand Xonck took hold of Miss Temple's robes behind her neck, yanked her to her knees and then, with a roar of frustration, tossed her down the length of the cabin through the doorway to land with a cry at the feet of Caroline Stearne. The breath was driven from her body and she lay there blinking with pain, dimly aware that she was somehow even colder. She looked back to see her shredded robes hanging from Xonck's hand. He met her gaze, still furious, and Miss Temple whimpered aloud, convinced he was about to march over and step on her throat just like he'd done to the Dragoon . . . but then in the panting silence, Roger Bascombe answered her question.

"Yes," he said simply. "I know."

Xonck stopped where he stood, staring at Roger. "Was it the Contessa?"

"No."

"Wait—before that," broke in the Comte, "*why* was he killed?"

"He was serving Vandaariff instead of us?" asked Xonck.

"He was," said Roger. "But that is not why he was killed. The Contessa already knew Colonel Trapping's true allegiance."

Xonck and the Comte turned to her. The Contessa scoffed at their naïve credulity.

"Of course I knew," she sneered, looking up at Xonck. "You are arrogant, Francis, so you assume that everyone wants what you do—your brother's power—and Trapping especially. You hide your cunning behind the mask of a libertine, but Trapping had no such depth—he was happy to deliver every secret of your brother's—and yours—to whoever best indulged his appetite!"

"Then why?" asked Xonck. "To preserve the Comte's *Annunciation* project?"

"No," said Roger. "Trapping hadn't yet agreed on a price to save Lydia—he'd only given Vandaariff hints."

"Then it *was* Crabbé—Trapping must have learned his plans for distilling Vandaariff—"

"No," repeated Roger. "The Deputy Minister would have killed him, to be sure...just as the Comte would have...given time and opportunity."

Xonck turned to the Contessa. "So you *did* kill him!"

The Contessa huffed again with impatience.

"Have you paid any attention at all, Francis? Do you not remember what Elspeth Poole—stupid, insolent, and barely regretted—displayed for us all in the ballroom? Her *vision*?"

"It was Elspeth and Mrs. Stearne," said Xonck, looking through the doorway to Caroline.

"With Trapping," said the Comte. "The night of the engagement."

"We were sent to him," protested Caroline. "The Contessa ordered us—to—to—"

"Exactly," said the Contessa. "I was doing my best to *indulge* him where the other guests would not intrude!"

"Because you knew he could not be trusted," said the Comte.

"Though he could be *distracted*—until we had time to deal with Vandaariff ourselves," observed the Contessa, "which we then did!"

"If Colonel Trapping alerted Vandaariff then our entire enterprise could have been compromised!" cried Caroline.

"We are all aware of it!" snapped the Contessa.

"Then I don't understand," said Xonck. "Who killed Trapping? Vandaariff?"

"Vandaariff would not kill his own agent," said a hoarse voice behind Xonck, which Miss Temple recognized as Doctor Svenson's, pushing himself up to his knees.

"But Blenheim had Trapping's key!"

"Blenheim moved the body," said Svenson, "on Vandaariff's orders. At the time he still controlled his own house."

"Then who?" growled the Comte. "And why? And if it was not for Lydia's fate, or Vandaariff's legacy, or even control of the Xonck fortunes, how has the murder of this insignificant fool torn our entire alliance asunder?"

The Contessa shifted herself on the settee, and looked fiercely at Roger, whose lip betrayed the slightest quiver at his fruitless attempts to remain silent.

"Tell us, Roger," said the Contessa. "Tell us *now*."

As Miss Temple watched the face of her former love, it seemed she looked at a puppet—remarkably life-like to be sure, but the falseness was readily, achingly, apparent. It was not his passive state, nor the even tone of his voice, nor the dullness of his eye, for these were explained by their strange circumstances—just as if he had screamed or gnashed his teeth. Instead, it was simply the content of his words, all the more strange, for Miss Temple had always attended instead to the way he said them—the way he took her arm or leaned across a table as he spoke, or even the stirring those words (whatever they might be) might spark in her own body. But now, *what* he said made clear the extent to which Roger's life had become separate from hers. She had assumed through their engagement—no matter where their own discrete days took them—they remained symbolically twinned, but now, spreading through her heart like the rising dawn outside the hatch, she saw that their wholeness—an idea beyond facts, however vain and foolish and doomed—lived only in her memory. She truly did not know who he was anymore, and never would again. And had she ever? It was a question she could not answer. The sadness she felt was no longer for him—for he was a fool, nor for herself—for she was rid of one. But somehow, listening to Roger speak in the freezing air, in Miss Temple's closely bound heart she mourned for the world, or as much of it as her sturdy chest could hold. She saw for the first time that it was truly made of dust... of invisible palaces that without her care—care that could never last—would disappear.

"The night before I underwent the Process," Roger began, "I met a woman at the St. Royale Hotel whose passion met my own in an exquisite union. In truth I had not decided to undergo the Process at all, and even then contemplated exposing everything to the highest authorities. But then I met this woman... we were both masked, I did not know her name, but she hovered hesitant on the same cusp of destiny, just as I did. As I strove to choose between the certain advancement brought by betraying the Deputy Minister and the utter risk of following him, I saw how she had given over the whole of her life to this new chance—that all before had been released, all attachment and all hope. And even though I knew that in giving myself to the Process I would give up my former aspirations to romance and marriage, this woman somehow in one night stirred me to my soul—a sadness matched with such tender care for our one lost instant together. But the next day I was changed and any thoughts I ever had of love were changed as well, directed and more reasoned, in service to... larger goals that could not contain her... and yet three days after that I met her again, once more masked, in the robes of an initiate to the Process... I knew her by her scent... by her hair—I had even been sent to collect her for the theatre, where she would undergo her own irrevocable change. I found her with another woman, and with a man I knew to be a traitor. Instead of collecting them I sent her friend ahead and the man away, and revealed myself... for I believed our temperaments were such that an understanding might survive, undetected by all... that we might ally... to share information about you, Contessa, about Minister Crabbé, Mr. Xonck, the Comte,

Lord Robert—to serve both the goals we had sworn to and our own mutual ambition. And make an alliance we did, rooted no longer in anything called love... but in sensible expedience. And together we have served you all, our masters, and watched patiently as one after another those above us have been enslaved or slain, rising ourselves to the very edge of power until we are positioned to inherit everything, as each one of you turns on the other—as you are doing even in this instant. For we are without your greed, your lusts, your appetites, but have stood silently to the side of every plan, every secret, for the Process has made us stronger than you can know. All this we saw together, a dream when we both thought we would never dream again. It was later I found the man had not gone away as I'd thought. He'd seen us together... overheard everything... and wanted payment—of many kinds. That was impossible."

"*You* killed him?" whispered Xonck. *"You?"*

"Not me," said Roger. "Her. Caroline."

Every eye in the room turned to Caroline Stearne.

"Hold her!" shouted Xonck, and Doctor Lorenz reached past Miss Temple to seize Caroline around the waist. Caroline lashed out with her elbow, driving it into the Doctor's throat. In an instant she turned on the choking man and pushed him with both hands. Doctor Lorenz vanished through the open hatch, his fading howl swallowed by the wind.

No one moved, and then Caroline herself broke the spell, kicking the Prince's leg and swinging a fist at Lydia's face, clearing a path to the iron staircase that rose to the wheelhouse. A moment later the cabin echoed with an ear-splitting scream and down the stairs bounced the body of one of Doctor Lorenz's sailors, blood pouring from a pulsing puncture on his back.

Miss Temple kicked herself away both from the bloody man and the open hatch, as chaos erupted around her. The Contessa was on her feet and after Caroline, lifting her dress with one hand to step over the sailor, the other hand holding her spike. The Comte and Xonck were close behind, but Xonck had not taken a step before he was tackled by Svenson and Chang. The Comte turned, looking back and then forward, hesitated, and then ripped open a cabinet near his head, revealing a rack of bright cutlasses. As Chang wrestled with Xonck for the saber, Svenson took a handful of Xonck's red curls and pulled his head away from the floor—Xonck snarling his protest—and then slammed it down as hard as he could. Xonck's grip on the saber wavered and Svenson smacked his head again on the planking, opening a seam of blood above his eye. The Comte ripped free a cutlass, the massive weapon looking in his hand like a particularly long kitchen cleaver. Miss Temple screamed.

"Doctor—look out!"

Svenson scuttled back as Chang finally scooped up the saber, forcing the Comte to pause. Miss Temple could not see the Comte's face, but she doubted his alchemical knowledge included swordplay—not when he faced a bitter opponent like Chang, even if Chang was weaving on his feet.

But her scream had another effect, which was to remind the Prince and Lydia of her presence. Karl-Horst dropped into a cunning crouch and leered at her, yet to her greater distress she saw Lydia weave the other way, behind the open hatch, where Elöise hung gagged and bound to the wall. Lydia clawed at the ropes with a determined grimace, watching Miss Temple across the whistling open hatchway.

Too much was happening at once. Chang was coughing horribly, Miss Temple could not see Svenson or Chang for the Comte's broad back and his enormous fur. Lydia pulled apart one knot, attacked another. Coming at her, his hands clutching wickedly, was the Prince, pausing to stare at Miss Temple's body. Miss Temple realized how exposed she was without her robes, but that the Prince could find the time—at this pitch of a crisis, to *ogle* a woman he was hoping to *kill*—was but another spur to her courage, for she had already seen what she must do.

She feinted to the stairs and then dashed the other way, leaping the hatch straight at Lydia, forcing the girl to drop the ropes. But Miss Temple dodged again, over Elöise's legs, just avoided the Prince's flailing arms, and then hurled herself at the Comte, digging at his fur with both hands, finding the pocket even as he turned and swatted her into the far settee with his mighty arm. Miss Temple landed in a sprawl, mid-way between the Comte and Chang, but in her hands, plucked from the pocket where the Comte himself had stowed it so many hours ago at the St. Royale, was her green clutch bag. She thrust her hand inside and did not bother to pull her revolver out, but fired through the fabric, the bullet shattering the cabinet near the Comte's head. He turned with a roar of alarm, and Miss Temple fired again, the bullet swallowed by his coat. She fired a third time. The Comte coughed sharply once, as if a bit of dinner had stuck in his throat, lost his balance and cracked his forehead hard against the corner of the cabinet. He straightened himself and stared at her, blood beading down above his eye. He turned to leave, almost casually, and caught his feet together. His knees locked, and the great man fell face down like a tree.

Xonck grunted, trying to crawl away. Chang sank to his knees and drove a brutal punch with the saber hilt across Xonck's jaw, stilling him like a pole-axed steer. Through the open doorway Miss Temple saw the Prince and Lydia watching in terror, but it was a terror mixed with defiance, for between them they had untied Elöise and held her precariously over the hatch, where with the gentlest push she would plummet to her death.

Miss Temple extracted the revolver from her bag and stood, taking a moment to yank what was left of her petticoats into position over her revealing silk pants, relieved that no one was looking at whatever parts she had exposed sprawling on the settee. Chang and Svenson advanced past her to the far doorway, Chang with Xonck's saber and Svenson availing himself of a cutlass from the cabinet. She stepped up between them, giving her petticoats just one more tug. The Prince and Lydia had not moved, rendered mute and still by the sudden fates of the Comte and Xonck, and by the truly vicious screaming that now reached them all from the wheelhouse.

The heated words passing back and forth between Caroline and the Contessa could not be made out over the roar of the open hatchway, but they were punctuated by the Contessa's snarls of rage and Caroline's shouts—tenacious, but terrified—the mix further complicated by the cries of the remaining crewman, who seemed by his pleading oaths to be German.

"Do not worry, Elöise," Miss Temple called out. "We shall collect you directly."

Still gagged, Elöise did not answer, for her gaze was fixed—indeed, it was held—on the freezing abyss beneath her, suspended by Lydia's tight handful of her hair, while, a step behind, the Prince had wrapped his arms around Elöise's legs. Wrists and ankles tied, Elöise could do nothing to prevent them dropping her through.

"Let her go!" cried Chang. "Your masters are down! You are alone!"

"Drop your weapons or the woman dies!" replied the Prince, shrilly.

"If you kill that woman," said Chang, "I will kill *you*. I will kill you *both*. If you release her, I will not. That is the extent of our negotiation."

The Prince and Lydia exchanged a nervous glance.

"Lydia," called Doctor Svenson. "It is not too late—we can reverse what has been done! Karl—listen to me!"

"If we *do* release her—" began the Prince, but Lydia had begun speaking at the same time and overrode his words.

"Do not treat us like children! You have no idea what we know or what we are worth! You do not know—*do* you?—that all the land in Macklenburg purchased by my father was settled in *my* name!"

"Lydia—" attempted the Prince, but she swatted at him angrily and kept on.

"I am the next Princess of Macklenburg whether I marry or no—whether my father is alive or no—no matter if I am the only person alive on this craft! I insist you drop your weapons! I have done nothing to any of you—to anyone!"

She stared at them wildly, panting.

"Lydia—" The Prince had finally noticed the smear of blue across her lips, and glanced to Svenson, suddenly confused.

"Be quiet! Do not talk to them! Hold her legs!" Lydia's stomach heaved again and she groaned painfully, spitting onto the front of her dress. "You should be fighting them yourself!" she complained. "You should have killed all three of them! Why is everyone so useless!"

The crewman above them screamed, and at once the entire airship careened to the left. Chang went into the wall, Miss Temple into Chang, and Doctor Svenson to his knees, the cutlass sliding from his hand. The Prince fell toward the open hatch, keeping his hold on Elöise so he drove her like a ram into Lydia, knocking both women into the opening. Lydia screamed and hit the lip of the hatch with her thighs and began to slide through. Elöise disappeared up to her waist—only the Prince's grip on her legs preventing her fall, a grip that was visibly slipping as he tried to decide whether to drop Elöise in order to save his bride.

"Hold her!" shouted Svenson, throwing himself forward to catch Lydia's feverishly clawing hands.

The airship careened again in the other direction, just as suddenly. Miss Temple lost her balance as she tried to reach Svenson. Chang leapt past them both toward the Prince. The Prince retreated in terror, releasing his hold on Elöise, but Chang caught her legs, digging his fingers in her ropes, and braced his foot on the hatch plate. He shouted to Miss Temple and gestured to the wheelhouse.

"Stop them—they'll kill us all!"

Miss Temple opened her mouth to protest, but as she watched—the Prince hunched in the corner beyond them—she saw Chang pull Elöise out to her hips, and Svenson do the same to Lydia.

She tightened her grip on the revolver and rushed to the stairs.

The second crewman lay draped over the topmost steps, blood bubbling on his lips. Lining either side of the wheelhouse were metal panels of levers and knobs, and at the far end, in front of the windows—where Miss Temple had first seen Doctor Lorenz from the roof—stood the wheel itself, made of brass and polished steel. Several levers had been broken off, with others jammed into positions that set the metal gears to grinding horribly. From the tilting floor it seemed certain the craft had swooned into a curve, spinning gently downwards.

In front of her lay Caroline Stearne, on her back, arms outstretched, an empty hand some inches from a bloody stiletto. Crouched on top of Caroline, her hair disheveled and her spike-hand smeared with blood like a glove, perched the Contessa di Lacquer-Sforza. A crimson pool drained to the side with the angle of the floor. The Contessa looked up at Miss Temple and sneered.

"Why, look who it is, Caroline—your little charge."

Her fist flashed forward, driving the spike into Caroline's throat with a meaty smack, causing Miss Temple to flinch and Mrs. Stearne's still body to react not at all.

"Where is everyone else?" she asked with a smirk. "Do not tell me you alone are left? Or if you're here, I suppose it is more accurate to say *I* am the only one left. How *typical*."

She rose to her feet, her dress dripping blood, and gestured with her free hand to the whining machinery.

"Not that it mattered—I could have cared less who killed Trapping—if this romantic idiot hadn't killed Lorenz and our crewmen—much less set off my own *anger*—we could be sharing *tea*. All of this for nothing! *Nothing!* I merely want people I can control! But *now*—just listen!" She gestured at the grinding machinery and scoffed. "We're all finished! It makes me so very... *savage*..."

She stepped closer, and Miss Temple raised her pistol—she was still looking into the wheelhouse from the stairs. The Contessa saw the revolver and laughed. Her hand shot out to a lever and wrenched it down. With a shudder that shook the airship to its very frame—and threw Miss Temple all the way to the bottom of the staircase, her stinging fall broken only by the distressing cushion of the first crewman's body—the spinning momentum reversed direction. A broken chopping sound erupted from one of the propellers. The grinding from the wheelhouse rose nastily in pitch and volume, and as she shook her head Miss Temple heard the Contessa's footsteps coming down the iron steps.

She clawed her way free of the body—she was moving too slowly, she had dropped her revolver—and looked ahead of her, hair hanging in her eyes. The hatch was closed, but the sudden jolt had knocked everyone off their feet. Chang sat on the floor with Elöise, cutting her bonds. Svenson was on his knees, facing Lydia and the Prince, skulking in a corner just beyond his reach. Miss Temple pulled herself toward them, feeling stiff as a tortoise.

"Cardinal!" Miss Temple gasped. "Doctor!"

Ignoring Miss Temple utterly, the Contessa's voice shot out from above.

"Roger Bascombe! Wake *up*!"

Chang and Svenson turned as Roger did just that, returning to awareness in an instant. Roger leapt to his feet, took in Xonck and the Comte on the floor, and threw himself at the open cabinet of weapons. Chang raised the saber—Miss Temple was dismayed to see still more blood around Chang's mouth—and struggled to stand. Doctor Svenson collected his own cutlass and reached his feet with the help of a brass wall bracket. He shouted to the Contessa.

"It is finished, Madame! The airship is falling!"

Miss Temple looked back, relieved she was not dead, but having no idea why it was so. The Contessa had paused on the little landing mid-way down the stairs, where in a small alcove—emblematic of the cunning use of space so necessary aboard vessels of all kinds—her minions had lashed into place an enormous steamer trunk.

Miss Temple heaved herself to her knees. She saw her revolver, slid half-way across the floor, and screamed at the Doctor as she flung herself toward it.

"She has the books! She has the books!"

The Contessa had both hands in the trunk and when she pulled them out each held a book—in her bare fingers! Miss Temple did not know how the woman did it—indeed the Contessa's expression was ecstatic—how was she not swallowed up?

"Roger!" called the Contessa. "Are you alive?"

"I am, Madame," he replied, having retreated at Chang's approach to the other side of the unmoving Francis Xonck.

"Contessa," began Svenson, "Rosamonde—"

"If I throw this book," the Contessa called, "it will surely shatter on that floor, and some of you—particularly those underdressed and sitting—will be killed. I have many of them. I can throw one after another—and since the alternative means the end of *every* book, I will sacrifice as many as I need. Miss Temple, *do not touch that gun*!"

Miss Temple stopped her hand, hovering above her revolver.

"Every one of you," cried the Contessa. "Drop your weapons! Doctor! Cardinal! Do it now or this book goes *right... at... her*!"

She glared at Miss Temple with a wicked smile. Svenson dropped his cutlass with a clang, and it slid with the tipping of the craft toward the Prince, who snatched it up. Chang did not move.

"Cardinal?"

Chang wiped his mouth and spat, his blood-smeared jaw like the painted half-mask of a red Indian or a Borneo pirate, and his bone-weary voice from another world altogether.

"We are finished anyway, Rosamonde. I'll be dead by the end of the day no matter what, but we're all doomed. Look out the windows... we're going down. The sea will smother your dreams along with mine."

The Contessa weighed a book in her hand. "You've no care for your Miss Temple's painful death?"

"It would be quicker than drowning," answered Chang.

"I do not believe you. Drop your weapon, Cardinal!"

"If you answer a question."

"Don't be ridiculous—"

Chang shifted his grip on the saber and pulled back his arm, as if to throw it like a spear.

"Do you think your book will kill me before I put this through your heart? Do you want to take that chance?"

The Contessa narrowed her eyes and weighed her options.

"What question then? Quickly!"

"To be honest, it is *two* questions." Cardinal Chang smiled. "*First,* what was Mr. Gray doing when I killed him? And *second,* why did you take the Prince from his compound?"

"Cardinal Chang—*why*?" asked the Contessa, with a sigh of unfeigned frustration. "Why *possibly* do you want to know this *now*?"

Chang smiled, his sharp teeth pink with blood.

"Because one way or another, I shan't be able to ask you tomorrow."

* * *

The Contessa laughed outright and took two steps down the stairs, nodding Svenson and Miss Temple toward Chang, her expression darkening at Miss Temple's quite brazen snatch of her pistol before she went.

"Join your comrade," the Contessa hissed at them, then looked at Elöise with disdain. "*And* you, Mrs. Dujong—one wonders if you are professionally helpless for a living—*hurry*!" She turned to the Prince, her tone sweetening. "Highness . . . if you would climb to the wheelhouse and do what you can to slow our descent—I believe most of the panels have helpful *words* on them . . . Lydia, stay where you are."

Karl-Horst darted up the stairs as the Contessa continued down, stepping over the crewman, to face all four of them in the doorway. The Doctor had pulled Elöise to him and held her hand, while Miss Temple stood—feeling rather alone, actually—between the Doctor and Chang. She glanced once over her shoulder at Roger in the far doorway, his face pale and determined, another expression she had never seen.

"What a gang of unlikely rebels," said the Contessa. "As I am a rational woman I must recognize your success—however inadvertent—just as I can find myself truthfully wishing that our circumstances were other than they are. But the Cardinal is right. We will most likely perish—all of *you* will, certainly—just as I have lost my partners. Very well, Mr. *Gray* . . . it is no secret now—not even to the Comte, were he still alive. The mixture of indigo clay was altered to decrease the *pliability* of the new flesh of his *creations*. As a defense, you see, if they became too strong—they would be more brittle. As it happened, perhaps *too* brittle . . . ah, well . . . it seems I was rash." She laughed again—even at this extremity a lovely sound—and sighed, going on in a whisper. "As for the *Prince*—well, I do not like him to overhear. In addition to taking the opportunity of implementing my own control phrase for His Highness, he has also been introduced with a poison for which I alone have the antidote. It is a simple precaution. I have secretly made an adherent of his young cousin's mother—the cousin who must inherit if the Prince dies without issue. With Karl-Horst so dead, Lydia's child—and the Comte's dire plan for their offspring—is swallowed in a battle for the succession that I shall control. Or perhaps the Prince shall live, continuing to consume the antidote in ignorance—it is all preparation."

"And all of it rendered academic," muttered Svenson.

Above them the Prince had found a helpful switch, for one chopping propeller switched off, followed a moment later by the other. Miss Temple looked to the windows, but they were still covered with curtains—were they still losing altitude? The cabin righted itself, and grew silent save for the whistling outside wind. They were adrift.

"We shall see," said the Contessa. "Roger?"

Miss Temple turned at a noise behind her, but it did not come from Roger Bascombe. Francis Xonck had somehow regained his feet, steadying himself with his injured hand on a settee, the other holding his jaw, his lips pulled back in a wince of pain that revealed two broken teeth. He looked at Miss Temple with cold eyes and reached his good hand toward Roger, who immediately passed Xonck his cutlass.

"Why, hello, Francis," called the Contessa.

"We'll talk later," said Xonck. "Get up, Oskar. This isn't finished."

Before Miss Temple's eyes the enormous man on the floor, like a bear rousing itself from hibernation, began to stir, rearing up to his knees—the fur coat flashing briefly open to reveal a shirtfront drenched in blood, but she could see it had all seeped from one superficial line scored across his ribs—the crack on the head had brought him down, not her shooting. The Comte heaved himself onto a settee and glared at her with open hatred. They were trapped again, caught between the books and Xonck's cutlass. Miss

Temple could not bear it an instant longer. She spun back to the Contessa and stamped her foot, extending the gun. The Contessa gasped with pleasure at the notion of being *challenged.*

"What is this, Celeste?"

"It is the finish," said Miss Temple. "You will throw the book if you are able. But I will do my best to put a bullet through the book in your other hand. It will shatter and you will lose your arm—and who knows, perhaps your face, perhaps your leg—perhaps it is you who will prove most *brittle* of all."

The Contessa laughed, but Miss Temple knew she laughed precisely because what Miss Temple said was true, and this was just the sort of thing the Contessa *enjoyed.*

"That was an interesting plan you described, Rosamonde," called Xonck. "The Prince, and Mr. Gray."

"Wasn't it?" she answered gaily. "And you would have been so surprised to see it unveiled in Macklenburg! It is such a pity I never got to see the finish of *your* secret plans—with Trapping or your brother's munitions—or *yours,* Oskar, the hidden instructions to your glass ladies, the triumphant birth of your creation within Lydia! Who can say what monstrosity you have truly implanted within her? How I should have been amazed and outflanked!" The Contessa laughed again and shook her head girlishly.

"You destroyed Elspeth and Angelique," rumbled the Comte.

"Oh, I did no such thing! Do not be temperamental—it is not becoming. Besides, who were they? Creatures of need—there are thousands more to take their place! There are more right before your eyes! Celeste Temple and Elöise Dujong and Lydia Vandaariff—another triumvirate for your great unholy sacrament!"

She sneered a bit too openly with this last word, caught herself, and then snickered. A certain lightness of mind was one thing, but to Miss Temple's wary eye the Contessa was becoming positively giddy.

"Karl-Horst von Maasmärck!" she bellowed. "Come down here

and bring me two more books! I am told we must finish this—so finish it we shall!"

"There is no need," said Xonck. "We have them trapped."

"Quite right," laughed the Contessa. "If I did throw this book the glass might spray past them and hit you! That would be *tragic*!"

The Prince clomped down the stairs into view, with two books bundled in his coat under one arm, in the other carrying a bottle of orange liquid identical to the one Elöise had taken from the Comte's stores in the tower. Xonck turned to the Comte, who muttered, just loud enough for Miss Temple to hear.

"She does not wear gloves..."

"Rosamonde—" began Xonck. "No matter what has been done—our plans remain in place—"

"I can make him do anything, you know," laughed the Contessa. She turned to the Prince and shouted out, "A nice waltz, I think!"

As under her command as he'd been in the secret room, the Prince, his face betraying no understanding of what his body was doing, undertook a stumbling dance step on the slippery metal landing, all the time juggling his fragile burdens. The Comte and Xonck both took an urgent step forward.

"The books, Rosamonde—he will drop them!" cried Xonck.

"Perhaps I should just start throwing them anyway, and Celeste can try to shoot me if she can..."

"Rosamonde!" cried Xonck again, his face pale.

"Are you *afraid*?" she laughed. She motioned to the Prince to stop—which he did, panting, confused—and then raised her arm as if to make him continue.

"Rosamonde," called the Comte. "You are not yourself—the glass against your skin—it is affecting your mind! Put down the books—their contents are irreplaceable! We are still in alliance—Francis has them in hand with his blade—"

"But Francis does not trust me," she replied. "Nor I Francis. Nor I *you,* Oskar. How are you not dead when you've been shot? More of your *alchemy*? And here I had grown quite used to the idea—"

"Contessa, you must stop—you are frightening us all!"

* * *

This was from Lydia Vandaariff, who had taken several steps toward the Contessa, and reached out one hand, the other still clutching her belly. She tottered, and her chin was streaked with blue-tinged drool—yet however hesitant her carriage, as always for Lydia, her tone was both restive and demanding.

"You are ruining everything! I want to be Princess of Macklenburg as you promised!"

"Lydia," rasped the Comte, "you must rest—take care—"

The girl ignored him, raising her voice, piercingly plaintive and peevish, to the Contessa. "I do not want to be one of the glass women! I do not want to have the Comte's child! I want to be a Princess! You must put down the book and tell us what to do!"

Lydia gasped at another spasm.

"Miss Vandaariff," whispered Svenson. "Step away—"

Another gout of blue, much thicker than before, heaved into Lydia's mouth. She gagged and swallowed, groaned and whined again at the Contessa, now in a tearful fury. "We can kill *these* others any time, but the books are precious! Give them to me! You promised me *everything*—my dreams! I insist you give them to me at once!"

The Contessa stared at her with wild eyes, but to Miss Temple it did seem the woman was genuinely attempting to consider Lydia's request—even as if the words came from a great distance and were only partly heard—when Lydia huffed with impatience and made the mistake of trying to snatch the nearest book. Showing the same speed she had used to overcome Crabbé, the Contessa, all sympathy vanished, whipped the one book from Lydia's reach and slashed the other book forward, chopping it with a cracking snap some two inches into Miss Vandaariff's throat.

The Contessa let go of the book and Lydia fell backwards, the flesh of her neck already turning blue, the blood in the back of her mouth and in her lungs hardening to crystal, popping like gravel beneath a wheel. The girl was dead before she hit the floor, her solidified throat breaking open and separating her head from her shoulders as neatly as an executioner's axe.

From the stairway the Prince let out a bellow of shock, roaring at the spectacle of Lydia dead, jaw quivering, mere words beyond him. Whether it was grief for the woman or outrage at an attack on one of his own, for the first time Miss Temple saw within the Prince a capacity for regret, for sentiment beyond mere appetite. But what to Miss Temple might have rendered the Prince infinitesimally admirable, for the Contessa changed him to a danger, and before he could take another step she hurled her second book into his knees. The glass shattered above his boots and with a piercing scream the Prince toppled back, legs buckling, juggling the books, landing heavily on the stairs, his boots still upright where he'd left them. His upper body slid down to rest against the fallen crewman and did not move.

The Contessa stood alone, flexing her fingers. The delirious gleam in her eyes grew dim and she looked around her, realizing what she'd done.

"Rosamonde . . ." whispered Xonck.

"Be quiet," she hissed, the back of her hand before her mouth. "I beg you—"

"You have destroyed my *Annunciation*!" The Comte's rasping voice betrayed an unbecoming whine, and he stood up, weaving, groping another cutlass from the cabinet.

"Oskar—stop!" This was Xonck, his face pale and drawn. "Wait!"

"You have ruined the work of my *life*!" the Comte shouted again, pulling free the cutlass and surging toward Miss Temple.

"Oskar!" the Contessa shouted. "Oskar—wait—"

Elöise took hold of Miss Temple's shoulders and yanked her from the Comte's path as the large man shouldered through, eyes fixed on the Contessa, who dug hurriedly to restore her metal spike. Miss Temple held her pistol, but it did not seem possible that she should shoot—for all this was the final confrontation with their enemies, she felt more a witness to their self-destruction than a combatant.

Cardinal Chang felt no such distance. As the Comte d'Orkancz passed by, Chang took hold of his massive shoulder and spun the man with all his strength. The Comte turned at this distraction, eyes wild, and raised the cutlass in an awkward, nearly petulant manner.

"You *dare*!" he cried at Chang.

"Angelique," spat Cardinal Chang in return. He drove the saber into the Comte's belly and up under his ribs, cutting deep into the great man's vitals. The Comte gasped and went rigid, and after one hanging moment Chang gave the blade another push, grinding it in halfway to the hilt. The Comte's legs gave way and he took the blade from Chang with his fall, his dark blood pooling into the fur.

His cough trailing into a thick rattle, Chang dropped to his knees and then slumped back against the doorframe. Miss Temple cried out and sank to his side, feeling the Doctor's nimble fingers snatch the revolver from her hand as she did. She looked up from Chang's haggard face to see Svenson extend the gun at Francis Xonck—caught flat-footed by the Comte's death. Xonck stared into Svenson's hard eyes, his broken mouth desperately working for words.

"Doctor—too much hangs unfinished—your own nation—"

Svenson pulled the trigger. Xonck flew back as if he'd been kicked by a horse. The Doctor now stood face-to-face with Roger Bascombe.

He extended his arm, and then thought better of it and wheeled to the Contessa at the far end of the airship's cabin. He fired, but not before Roger had leapt forward and shoved the

Doctor's arm. The bullet went wide and the Contessa ran for the stairs with a cry.

Svenson grappled with Roger for the gun, but Roger—younger, stronger—wrenched it away as the Doctor tripped over Xonck's leg. With an ugly grimace he aimed the gun at Svenson. Miss Temple cried out.

"Roger—do not!"

He looked up at her, his face disfigured by hatred and bitter rage.

"It is over, Roger. It has failed."

She knew there was one bullet left in the gun, and that Roger was too close to miss.

"It is *not,*" snarled Roger Bascombe.

"Roger, your masters are dead. Where is the Contessa? She has abandoned you. We are adrift. Both the Prince and the Duke of Stäelmaere are dead."

"The Duke?"

"He will be killed by Colonel Aspiche."

Roger stared at her. "Why would the Colonel do that?"

"Because I ordered him to. You see, I learned the Colonel's control phrase."

"His what?"

"Just as I know yours, Roger."

"I have no control phrase—"

"O Roger, . . . you really do not know after all, do you?"

Roger narrowed his eyes and raised the revolver to Doctor Svenson. Miss Temple spoke quickly and clearly, looking him straight in the eye.

"Blue Apostle blue Ministry ice consumption."

Roger's face went slack.

"Sit down," Miss Temple told him. "We will talk when there's time."

"Where is the Contessa?" asked Elöise.

"I do not know," said Miss Temple, "how is Chang?"

Doctor Svenson crawled to the Cardinal. "Elöise, help me move him. Celeste—" He pointed to the iron steps, to the Prince. "The orange bottle, if it is not broken, fetch it at once!"

She ran to it, stepping carefully around the glass—grateful for her boots—doing her best to avoid eye contact with the disfigured corpses.

"What is in it?" she called.

"I do not know—it is a chance for the Cardinal. I believe it is what saved Angelique—in the greenhouse, the mattress was stained orange—"

"But everyone we met was terrified of it," said Elöise. "If I made to break it they ran the other way!"

"I am sure they did—it must be deadly indeed, and yet—fire to fight fire, or in this case, ice."

Miss Temple found the bottle, nestled in the crook of the Prince's arm. She pulled it free, glancing just once at his horrible face, the open mouth with its stained teeth and blood-red gums, the lips and tongue now tinged with blue, and then looked up the stairs. The trunk of books was where it had been, and she heard no sound from the wheelhouse save the wind. She ran back to Chang. Elöise knelt behind him, propping up his head and wiping blood from his face. Svenson doused a handkerchief in the orange fluid and then, with a determined sigh, clamped it over Chang's nose and mouth. Chang did not react.

"Is it working?" asked Miss Temple.

"I do not *know,*" replied the Doctor. "I know he is dead without it."

"It does not *appear* to be working," said Miss Temple.

"Where is the Contessa?" asked Elöise.

Miss Temple looked down at Cardinal Chang. The Doctor's cloth had partially dislodged his spectacles, and she could see his scars, wounds of a piece with the blood that dripped down his face and neck. And yet beneath this history of violence—though she did not doubt it was integral to his soul—Miss Temple also saw a softness, an impression of what his eyes had been like before, of that underpinning and those margins where Chang located care and comfort and peace—if he ever did at all, of course. Miss Temple was no expert on the peace of others. What would it mean if Chang was to die? What would it have meant to him if their positions were reversed? She imagined he would disappear into an opium den. What would she do, lacking even that avenue into depravity? She looked down at Elöise and the Doctor working together, and walked back to Roger. She took the pistol from his hand and made her way to the iron steps.

"Celeste?" asked Svenson.

"Francis Xonck has your silver cigarette case—do not forget to collect it."

"What are you doing?" asked Elöise.

"Collecting the Contessa," said Miss Temple.

The wheelhouse was silent, and Miss Temple climbed past the dead crewman and onto the bloody deck, looking down at Caroline's body. The woman's eyes were open in dismay, her beautiful pale throat torn open as if a wolf had been at it. The Contessa was nowhere to be seen, but in the ceiling above another metal hatch had been pushed open. Before she climbed up, Miss Temple stepped to the windows. The cloud and fog had finally broken apart. Whatever its course had once been, the dirigible's path had become hopelessly skewed. She could see only grey cold water below them—not far below either, they were perhaps at the height of Harschmort's roof—and the pale flickers of white on top of the dark waves. Would they drown in the icy sea after all? After all of this? Chang was perhaps already dead. She'd left the room in part so as not to watch, preferring even at this extremity to avoid what she knew she would find painful. She sighed. Like a persistent little ape, Miss Temple clambered onto the shelf of levers and reached up to the hatch, pulling herself into the cold.

The Contessa stood on the roof of the cabin, holding on to a metal strut beneath the gasbag, wind whipping at her dress and her hair, which had become undone and flowed behind her head like the black pennant of a pirate. Miss Temple looked around her at the clouds, head and shoulders out of the hatch, her elbows splayed on the freezing metal roof. She wondered if she could just shoot the Contessa from here. Or should she simply take hold of the hatch and close it, marooning the woman outside? But this was the end, and Miss Temple found she could do neither of these things. She was transfixed, as perhaps she'd always been.

"Contessa!" she called above the wind, and then, the word feeling strangely intimate in her mouth, "Rosamonde!"

The Contessa turned, and upon seeing Miss Temple smiled with a grace and weariness that took Miss Temple by surprise.

"Go back inside, Celeste."

Miss Temple did not move. She gripped the gun tightly. The Contessa saw the gun and waited.

"You are an evil woman," shouted Miss Temple. "You have done wicked things!"

The Contessa merely nodded, her hair blowing for a moment across her face until with a toss of her head it flowed once more behind her. Miss Temple did not know what to do. More than anything she realized that her inability to speak and her inability to act were exactly how she felt when faced with her father—but also that this woman—this terrible, *terrible* woman—had been the birth of her new life, and somehow had *known* it, or at least appreciated the possibility, that finally she alone had been able to look into Miss Temple's eyes and see the desire, the pain, the determination, and see it—see her—for what she was. There was too much to say—she wanted an answer to the woman's brutality but would not get it, she wanted to prove her independence but knew the Contessa would not care, she wanted revenge but knew the Contessa would never admit her defeat. Nor could Miss Temple prove herself—overcome the one enemy who had always bested her effortlessly—by shooting her in the back, any more than she could have made her father care for her by burning his fields.

"Mr. Xonck and the Comte are dead," she shouted. "I have sent Colonel Aspiche to kill the Duke. Your plan has been ruined."

"I can see that. You've done very well."

"You have done things to me—changed me—"

"Why regret pleasure, Celeste?" said the Contessa. "There's little enough of it in life. And was it not exquisite? I enjoyed myself immensely."

"But I did not!"

The Contessa reached above her, the spike on her hand, and slashed a two-foot hole across the canvas gasbag. Immediately the blue-colored gas inside began to spew out.

"Go back inside, Celeste," called the Contessa. She reached in the other direction and opened another seam, out of which gushed air as blue as the summer sky. The Contessa held on to the strut within this cerulean cloud, in her windblown hair and bloody dress a perilous dark angel.

"I am not like your adherents!" Miss Temple shouted. "I have learned for myself! I have seen you!"

The Contessa ripped a third hole in the slackening gasbag, the plume of smoke roiling directly at Miss Temple. She choked and shook her head, eyes stinging, and groped for the hatch. With one last look at the glacial face of the Contessa di Lacquer-Sforza, Miss Temple pulled the hatch shut and dropped with a cry to the slippery wheelhouse floor.

"We are sinking to the sea!" she shouted, and with an aplomb she scarcely noticed stepped past and over mangled bodies all the way down to the others, never once slipping on blood or nicking herself on the scattered broken glass. To her utter delight, Chang was on his hands and knees, coughing onto the floor. The spray around his lips was no longer red but blue.

"It is working . . . ," said Svenson.

Miss Temple could not speak, just glimpsing in the prospect of Chang alive the true depths of her grief at Chang being dead. She looked up to see the Doctor watching her face, his expression both marking her pleasure and vaguely wan.

"The Contessa?" he asked.

"She is bringing us down. We will hit the water at any moment!"

"We shall help Chang—Elöise, if you could take the bottle—while you attend to *him*." Svenson looked over his shoulder at Roger Bascombe, sitting patiently on a settee.

"Attend to him how?" asked Miss Temple.

"However you like," replied the Doctor. "Wake him or put a bullet through his brain. No one will protest. Or leave him—but I suggest *choosing*, my dear. I have learned it is best to be haunted by one's actions rather than one's lack of them." He re-opened the hatch in the floor and sucked his teeth with concern. Miss Temple could smell the sea. Svenson slammed the hatch shut. "There is no time—we must get to the roof at once—Elöise!"

Between them they caught Chang's arms and helped him up the stairs. Miss Temple turned to Roger. The dirigible shuddered, a gentle kick as the cabin struck a wave.

"Celeste—forget him!" shouted Elöise. "Come *now*!"

The airship shuddered again, settling fully onto the water.

"Wake up, Roger," Miss Temple called, her voice hoarse.

He blinked and his expression sharpened, looking around him, taking in the empty room without comprehension.

"We are sinking in the sea," she said.

"Celeste!" Svenson's shout echoed down the stairs.

Roger's eyes went to the pistol in her hand. She stood between him and the only exit. He licked his lips. The airship was rocking with the motion of the water.

"Celeste—" he whispered.

"So much has happened, Roger," Miss Temple began. "I find . . . I cannot contain it . . ." She sniffed, and looked into his eyes—fearful, wary, pleading—and felt the tears begin in her own. "The Contessa advised me, just now, against regret—"

"Please—Celeste, the water—"

"—but I am not like her. I am not even like myself, perhaps my character has changed . . . for I am awash in regret for everything, it seems—for what has stained my heart, for how I am no longer a child . . ." She gestured helplessly at the carnage around them. "For so many dead . . . for Lydia . . . even poor Caroline—"

"Caroline?" asked Roger, a bit too suddenly, the words followed by an immediate awareness that perhaps this wasn't the proper subject, given the circumstances, and the pistol. Miss Temple read the hesitation on his face, still grappling in her heart with the fact she had been found wanting twice in Roger's rejection—first as a matter of course to his ambition, and then as a companion—and a lover!—to Caroline Stearne. This was not what she intended to talk about. She met his eyes with hesitations of her own.

"She is dead, Roger. She is as dead as you and I."

Miss Temple watched Roger Bascombe take in this news, and understood that his next words were spoken not out of cruelty or revenge, but merely because she now stood for everything in his life that had thwarted him.

"She is the only one I ever loved," said Roger.

"Then it is good that you found her," said Miss Temple, biting her lip.

"You have no idea. You cannot *understand*," he said, his voice bitter and hollow with grief.

"But I believe I do—" she began softly.

"How could you?" he shouted. "You never could understand—not me, nor any other, not in your pride—your very insufferable pride—"

She desperately wished Roger would stop speaking, but he went on, his emotions surging like the waves that slapped against the cabin walls.

"The wonders I have seen—the heights of sensation—of *possibility*!" He scoffed at her savagely, even as she saw tears in his eyes, tears rolling down his cheeks. "She *pledged* herself to me, Celeste—without even knowing who I was—without a care that we must die! That all is dust! That our love would lead to *this*! She knew even then!"

His hands shot out and shoved her hard, knocking her back into the cabinet. He stepped after her, arms flailing as he continued to yell.

"Roger, please—"

"And who are *you,* Celeste? How are you alive—so cold, so small of heart, so absent of feeling, without *surrender*!"

He caught her hard by the arm and shook her.

"Roger—"

"Caroline gave herself—gave everything! You have murdered her—murdered me—murdered the entire world—"

His groping hand found her hair and yanked her close—she felt his breath—and then his other hand was on her throat. He was sobbing. They stared into each other's eyes. She could not breathe.

Miss Temple pulled the trigger and Roger Bascombe reared back. His face was confused, and instead of snapping forward again he merely faded, like a dissipating curl of smoke, a shapeless figure in a black coat, falling onto the settee and then slipping with an easy movement to the floor. Miss Temple dropped the gun and sobbed aloud, no longer knowing who she was.

"Celeste!"

This was Chang, roaring out from the rooftop despite his pain. She looked up. Miss Temple felt an icy stab at her feet and saw that water was seeping through the floor. She stumbled to the iron staircase, blind with tears, and groped her way, gasping with unspent grief. Doctor Svenson crouched in the wheelhouse and hauled her up. She wanted to curl into a corner and drown. He lifted her high and more hands—Elöise and Chang—helped her onto the roof. What did it matter? They would die in the cabin or die above—either way they would sink. Why had she done it? What did it change? The Doctor followed her out, pushing her legs from below.

"Take her," Svenson said, and she felt Chang's arm around her shaking shoulders. The gasbag above was slackening, carried to the side with the wind, still enormous but sagging into the water—as opposed to collapsing on top of them—and tipping the roof at an angle. The spray slopped over the cabin, spattering Miss Temple's face, as waves rocked their precarious platform. Chang's other hand held on to a metal strut, as did the Doctor and Elöise. Miss Temple looked around her.

"Where is the Contessa?" She sniffed.

"She was not here," called Svenson.

"Perhaps she jumped," said Elöise.

"Then she is dead," said Svenson. "The water is too cold—her dress too heavy, it would pull her down—even if she survived the fall . . ."

Chang coughed, his lungs audibly clearer.

"I am in debt to you, Doctor, and your orange *elixir*. I feel quite well enough to drown."

"I am honored to have been useful," answered Svenson, smiling tightly.

Miss Temple shivered. What clothes she wore did nothing to cut the wind or the chilling water that splashed onto her trembling body. She could not bear it, no matter how the others tried to joke, she did not want to die, not after all this, and more than anything she did not care to drown. She knew it for an awful death—slow and mournful. She was mournful enough. She looked at her green boots and bare legs, wondering how long it would take. She had traveled so far in such a small amount of time. It was as if her rooms at the Boniface were as far away, and as much a part of the past, as her island home. She sniffed. At least she was back to the sea.

* * *

Miss Temple felt her flesh going numb, and yet when she looked down again the water had not climbed. She craned her head toward the open hatch to find the wheelhouse awash with rising water, with the sodden dress of Caroline Stearne swirling just under the surface. Yet why were they not sinking? She turned to the others.

"Is it possible we are *aground*?" she asked, through chattering teeth.

As one the other three echoed her look into the wheelhouse, and then all four searched around them for some clue. The water was too dark to reveal its depth. Ahead and to either side they could only find the open sea, while the view behind was blocked by the dirigible's billowing, sagging gasbag. With a sudden burst of energy Cardinal Chang hoisted himself over the metal strut and clambered onto the canvas bag itself, each step across it pushing out gouts of trapped blue smoke. He dropped from Miss Temple's view at the trough of each wave that passed beneath, and then she lost him altogether.

"We could be *anywhere,*" said Doctor Svenson, adding after a silence where neither woman spoke, "speaking cartographically . . ."

A moment later they heard Chang's whooping cry. He was bounding back toward them, soaked to his waist, the canvas significantly flattened by his efforts.

"There is land!" he shouted. "God help us, it's land!"

Doctor Svenson averted his eyes as he lifted Miss Temple over the metal struts, and then did the same for Elöise, Miss Temple taking the other woman's hands. They helped each other over the dying gasbag, not halfway across before they were wet to their knees, but by then they could see it—a scumbled line of white breaking waves and a darker stripe of trees beyond.

Chang was waiting for her in the water and Miss Temple jumped into his arms. The sea was freezing, but she laughed aloud as it splashed against her face. She could not touch the sand with her toes and so she pushed herself away from Chang, took one look at the shore for a target, and then ducked herself under, the cold tingling the roots of her hair. Miss Temple swam, kicking her legs, unable to see in the dark water, the tears and sweat on her body dissolving in the sea, knowing she must hurry, that the cold would take her otherwise, that she would be even colder once outside the water, soaked and in the wind, and that from all of these things she still might perish.

She did not care about any of it. She smiled again, certain for the first time in so long exactly where she was, and where she was going to be. She felt like she was swimming home.

About the Author

Playwright Gordon Dahlquist was born in the Pacific Northwest and lives in New York City. His second novel, *The Dark Volume,* will be available from Bantam Books in spring 2009.